Resounding praise for the remarkable
RITA Award winning author
JUDITH IVORY

"An excellent author."
Dallas Morning News

"An extremely talented writer with a distinct voice."
Susan Elizabeth Phillips

"One of the most talented fiction writers working in historical romance . . . One of those writers who not only delights readers but also inspires awe and envy in fellow writers."
Albany Times-Union

"Judith Ivory writes lush, lyrical romance that seethes with passionate intensity."
Amanda Quick

"She's fresh. I love her books. There's no one else writing like her in the genre."
Patricia Gaffney

"Judith Ivory understands sexual tension the way Neil Simon understands comedy."
LaVyrle Spencer

"Ivory's writing is exceptional."
Minneapolis Star-Tribune

Other Avon Romances by
Judith Ivory

BEAST
BLACK SILK
THE INDISCRETION
THE PROPOSITION
SLEEPING BEAUTY

JUDITH IVORY

Untie My Heart

AVON BOOKS
An Imprint of HarperCollins*Publishers*

AVON BOOKS
An Imprint of HarperCollins*Publishers*
10 East 53rd Street
New York, New York 10022-5299

ISBN: 0-380-81297-5
www.avonromance.com

First Avon Books paperback printing: November 2002

Printed in the U.S.A.

10 9 8 7 6 5 4 3 2 1

This book is for my parents,
whom I would pick as dear friends
if nature hadn't already done it for me.
I love you.

ACKNOWLEDGMENTS

A big hug and thank-you to my brother, Gary, and his wife, Mary, who let me live with them in Yorkshire while researching this book, took off time from their own work, carted me around, and especially to Mary who, even after I'd gone home, would research things for me via e-mail about her beloved England. A special thank-you to both of you for "suffering" through all the rock and roll, teasing, laughter, and champagne as we trekked together from one end of the Yorkshire countryside to the other.

Also I wish to thank author pal Jennifer Crusie, who graciously shared with me her research of confidence artists (not to mention discussions of scams, literature, politics, kids, house-building, Walking Ware, Pat's dreams, Finney, Wolfie, Mose, the rest of the pack, parakeets, and toasters, etc.). Several of the research titles I used to produce my book came from Jenny's hard work in gathering appropriate material as she herself wrote her own version of a confidence game story, *Faking It*. Is it coincidence or something cosmic that good friends would suddenly begin books on the same topic without mentioning it or realizing it for weeks?

There is no excellent beauty
that hath not some strangeness in the proportion.

—Francis Bacon
Essays, "Of Beauty," 1625

Prologue

STUART Aysgarth returned home from a month-long hunting trip in the Caucasus Mountains to find the following two letters awaiting his attention. They were postmarked three months previously, having traveled from London across the seas to his home in St. Petersburg, then over land to Tsarskoe—just missing him as he had been gathering up companions for his hunting trip—then forwarded south to his country home in Odessa. There, they had lain upon his library table for nearly the whole of his hunting-trip absence.

26 March 1892
London, England

To Stuart Winston Aysgarth, the sixth Viscount Mount Villiars:

I regret to inform you that your father Donovan Alister Francis Aysgarth, the fifth Viscount Mount Villiars, has at age fifty-seven passed on. Your being his only son, it is imperative that I locate you. Alas, all I have is this Russian address, found among your father's papers. Indeed, no one in England is certain of your where-

abouts, how to contact you, or if you live. Please contact me at your earliest convenience, then make arrangements, if you will, to come personally to London. You are the immediate heir to the former viscount's entailment as well as a large and complicated estate—which, you must know, comprise not only a title but also a sizable fortune, future incomes, and many properties.

I condole in your hour of suffering.

Yours most humbly,
Daniel P. Babbage, Esquire

3 April 1892
London, England

Mount Villiars,

My last letter to you cannot possibly have found you yet, but I felt I must advise immediately that your uncle, Leonard Xavier Francis Aysgarth, has come forth as the heir to your father's title and estates. He believes you dead. Moreover, he has convinced several others, men of importance, that such might be entirely the case. Indeed, it might. This letter may go unanswered. If you receive these words, however, please telegraph me immediately, so I might halt the process of your uncle's assuming the title and assets of the viscountcy into his own use.

Yours most humbly,
Daniel P. Babbage, Esquire

That Monday at seven in the morning Stuart was at the telegraph office in Odessa, from where he sent a wire to Daniel P. Babbage. It read:

TELL LEO TO PUT A PUNTING POLE IN IT STOP I AM ON MY WAY STOP MUCH TO DO TO SETTLE MATTERS HERE BUT I AM ALIVE AND VERY VERY WELL STOP WELL ENOUGH TO MAKE LEO REGRET ANY IMPRUDENT DECISIONS STOP MOUNT VILLIARS

It took Stuart eight days to gather monies, put his estate in Odessa up for sale, and travel to Tsarskoe, where he made his formal good-bye to the tzar and court, put his new and elegant home there up for sale also, and gathered more money. When he finally arrived at his apartment in Petersburg, however, a further telegram was waiting for him.

MANY INTERDEPENDENT ON MOUNT VILLIARS MONIES STOP YOUR WIRE ARRIVED AFTER HOME SECRETARY MOVED QUICKLY STOP HAD COLLEGE OF ARMS CLOSE ALL ENTAILMENT'S ACCOUNTS STOP YOUR PRESENCE GREATLY NEEDED STOP CAN'T PREVENT UNCLE FINDING SECONDARY CREDITORS WHO BELIEVE YOU DEAD STOP MUCH CONFUSION MORE PROBLEMS BUT COMPLICATED STOP HURRY STOP BABBAGE

Highly alarmed, Stuart left three households of retainers in the hands of his butler, all to follow, then took off on his own with only his manservant. On his way to Paris he sent the following:

SEND SOMEONE TO GUARD CASTLE DUNORD STOP UNCLE MAY RANSACK LIKE AN ARMY OF HUNS STOP MOUNT VILLIARS

In Paris, the response read:

DUNORD LOOKS LIKE HUNS ATTACKED STOP UNCLE SAYS HE TOOK NOTHING STOP HAVE HIRED SMALL STAFF TO GUARD BELATEDLY STOP BABBAGE

From Cherbourg, Stuart wired:

UNCLE WOULD TAKE ANYTHING VALUABLE AND PORTABLE STOP WORRIED ESPECIALLY ABOUT A STATUE IN NICHE OF STAIRWELL STOP PRESS UNCLE FOR STATUE STOP ARRIVING TONIGHT STOP MOUNT VILLIARS

In Southampton, when Stuart stepped down onto English soil—for the first time in twelve years—he regretted his last two telegrams. A statue? One he hadn't thought of in years? It must have been a belated reaction to the information that his father was dead, his own life once more changed dramatically by his detestable sire. Foolish. Stuart traveled to London by train, clattering along to the rhythm of self-reproach.

All could be put aright. Leonard was easily enough subdued. A small statue didn't matter so much one way or the other.

There was nothing for it. And Leonard would get away with little of his attempt to usurp a peerage. For one thing, anyone only had to look at Stuart to know who was the heir to all connected to Donovan Aysgarth. He was the spitting image of his handsome father.

A fact that, at times, could tie Stuart's stomach in knots.

No matter, though, he liked the idea of assuming one of England's most powerful, wealthy titles. The statue, however, appeared lost for good. For Leonard simply denied and denied and denied that he had it. He argued that the castle in Yorkshire had lain dormant, uninhabited, for more than a decade. That things were missing didn't immediately say that he had them. Anyone could have taken anything from the old place at any time by simply walking in and tucking it under his arm. Why was Stuart making such a row over something he'd left more than a decade ago and upon which he'd never looked back?

Why, indeed. Why did Stuart's heart sink when he finally confronted the empty niche with his own eyes?

"Lost," he muttered. Lost.

Yet he could envision it suddenly. Green, glittering, vaguely frightening, fascinating. An old, Byzantine animal creature, as he recalled. And in that moment the little lost statue felt, for the life of him, like the only thing he had had to come home to: something he remembered fondly from a time before memory was affixed—mapped and landmarked—with words.

PART ONE

The Lamb

Lamb Stuffed with Crottin, Spinach, Rosemary, and Toasted Walnuts

Bone a leg of spring lamb and put the removed bone into a hot oven to roast. Meanwhile, in a bowl, with knife and fork, cut and mash together two giant handfuls of fresh, washed spinach, the goat cheese, and the leaves from several sprigs of rosemary. Crack and clean a small apronful of walnuts; chop the nutmeats till crumbly. On a separate pan, toast the nutmeats briefly (about a minute) in the oven beside the roasting bone. Add half the toasted nutmeats to the stuffing mixture; reserve the rest. Fill the opening in the roast left by the bone with the stuffing, tie securely, then remove bone from the oven, reduce oven heat, and roast stuffed leg 30 minutes per kilo. While the lamb roasts, boil the roasted bone in four cups water with an onion, several carrots, salt, pepper, and the stalks from the rosemary. Reduce to a cup; strain and discard solids. (A feast for your favorite dog.) Remove cooked roast from oven and drain off the heaviest fat, being careful not to disturb the sticky bits on the bottom. Deglaze the pan with the reduced stock plus one cup brandy, letting the liquid boil till it is rich, brown, and slightly thickened. Pour reduction over roast and sprinkle with remaining walnuts. Accompany with potatoes roasted with carrots and fennel bulb.

—EMMA DARLINGTON HOTCHKISS
Yorkshire Ways and Recipes
Pease Press, London, 1896

Chapter 1

Rams are the most difficult to shear. There is nothing like trying to move around three hundred pounds of indignation and hard-horned obstinance.

—Emma Darlington Hotchkiss
Yorkshire Ways and Recipes

THE events that would drop Emma Hotchkiss—verily sink, she might have said—into a quagmire of sin and crime began on the first sunny day she'd seen in a week as she galumphed gracelessly across a green Yorkshire field in the vicar's unbuckled muck boots. His boots, with her in them, clopped along, as big as buckets on her feet, making a nice rhythm: a hollow *plock* on the lumpy ground, then a *clap* as her foot knocked forward, her ankle catching at the gum rubber instep. She held her skirts high as she made good progress, collecting nary a mishap. That is to say, out of habit and despite the protective boots, she stayed clear of sheep droppings while making a fairly direct path for the far road, which she had to cross to get to her neighbors', the Tuckers', farm. She was headed there to collect their mending, which was how she brought in the extra shilling or two.

Emma was about fifty yards from the road, when she heard the unusual noise: a rising clatter that halted her, making her twist at the waist to look sideways down the road.

There, on the other side of the hedgerow, from around the far bend, a huge coach appeared, one of the largest she had ever seen. The driver atop it, hunched forward, *heeyahed* the horses as he energetically cast and recast his whip, calling to his team of eight. The whole thing, vehicle, team, and driver, shook and rolled hell for leather up the lane toward Emma, an unbelievable sight.

And not just because of the size and noise and lightning haste of the vehicle. The horse team comprised, shoulder to shoulder, eight of the shiniest black coaching stallions she'd ever laid eyes on—like black glass—with glimpses above the hedgerow of galloping white socks to their knees and hocks. Any more perfectly matched horses could not have existed, nor galloped better in time. Their braided manes jarred along in perfect synchronicity to a jangle of tack and the clatter of wheels, the brass fittings sparkling in glints from the sun. The coach itself shone: As it came closer, its black and green and gold filigree paint all but leaped into relief, bright, crisp, and clean in the way of new things.

It was a new brougham, in its seat a coachman in new livery, while, peering over the back, two footmen held on for all they were worth—each with one arm through a metal rail, the other gloved hand clamped to the crown of his top hat. Such rolling magnificence did not often frequent the country roads this far north of London. There was only one reason such an event should happen today, and, as the vehicle sped by, the family crest on the side of the carriage confirmed her suspicion: The new Viscount Mount Villiars was taking up residence. At jolly high speed.

Not that he would like what he saw when he got there. If he took the time to see it—the old place, Castle Dunord, had fallen into disrepair. Though what did it matter? He wouldn't stay long. The Viscounts Mount Villiars never did.

She shook her head, thinking how dangerous it was for a carriage to race through narrow, crooked roads bordered by hedgerow and stone boundaries as old as the Roman invasion. The new viscount was going to kill himself (which was, come to think of it, what the last viscount did).

But, no, in the next moment, her silent rebuke heralded a different disaster, one more her own: For, up the road, from within a huge cloud of dust, the careening coach barely visible within it, came an exclamation, the coach driver yelling something. This quickly blurred into the scrape of carriage wheels, the creak of springs, a din of metal and stone. After which Emma distinctly heard a small thud and a tiny outcry.

Not human. Animal. Thank God, she thought at first, though her heart sank. For she knew the cry instantly—as it came again—to be the loud, plaintive bleat of a sheep.

The bleating pierced the air with distress, louder, clearer as the clatter of the carriage dimmed—the vehicle swerved in the lane, then trundled off again with nary more than a pause. While the bleating continued, high-pitched, desperate, hurt. No, not a sheep. A lamb. A baby. The sound was thin-voiced, forlorn: The wee animal bayed.

Emma was running. She wasn't sure when she'd begun, only that she moved her legs as fast as they would go, her skirts hiked in her fists, her heart thudding loud in her chest. The air she breathed felt hot in her lungs as her feet beat against the ground up into her shins. Or clomp-hopped—somewhere, she'd lost a boot in the bargain, so her gallop had become lopsided. As she came up on the hedgerow, she saw the carriage disappear completely in a puff of dust at the next bend, its rumble fading to a distant drone. Gone. She clambered up and over the thick bushes, her clothes and hair tangling in them. The hedgerow held her for a minute, with Emma struggling, shoving at it, branches snapping, scratching. Then it released her, and she was out onto the road.

Silence, all but for the rasp of her own breathing and the *thump-thump* of her heart that echoed in her ears. On the road though, no sound. Quiet reigned as she spotted the lamb. It was only a few yards up, midway in the short straightaway. She hurried over, then squatted beside it, a pathetic thing at the edge of the roadbed. The animal lay on its side at an awkward angle, a tangle of thin black legs, the rear ones bright with blood. Its hips and abdomen oozed, the red spreading into the woolly white coat so quickly, it was as if the creature lay on some sort of gluey red fountain. It didn't look real.

"Oh, poor dear," she said as she stroked its woolly, oily white shoulder. Its dark eyes shone, focused on her. It bleated again, a puny sound, a lamb whimper. "It won't hurt for long now," she murmured. Oh, dear, oh, dear, what a mess that coach made of you.

Somewhere off, a sheep called. Emma could hear its *baa* growing closer. The lamb's mother's response to her offspring's unique voice, to its call for her. Before the ewe could locate her lamb though, her son—the injured lamb was an uncastrated male—had stopped calling for help: beyond it. He moved his soft black mouth once, showing his pink tongue, then, openmouthed, grew perfectly still, his eyes staring straight.

"Oh!" Emma breathed out, covering her mouth with her palm. Oh. Her eyes welled for a second.

Stop, she told herself. It's just a sheep. There were thousands in Yorkshire.

Precisely. And no one who lived here doubted the value of every single one of them. Especially the spring lambs. They were the future. A sheep farmer counted his or her rise and fall by the number of new lambs produced each year—and a male, uncastrated, by late August, was breeding stock. A fine herd of sheep meant milk, wool, food on the table, a sheep farmer's livelihood. Emma wasn't a sheep farmer herself. Her flock was too small to be said a living came from it. But one day—

That was when she saw the purple splotch of paint on the animal's back—her mark. She looked at its dead face, took in its limbs, proportions, and *still* couldn't believe it. *Her* lamb?

Worse: *her* male! She only had one. She looked at it again. Oh, bollocks it all! She wanted to weep, scream, bellow! What was he doing *here*?

Uselessly, she continued to stroke the lamb, a male who would have been old enough by winter to see it through its first raddling. What was it doing off the fell, where it was supposed to be grazing with its mother?

What was it doing here lying dead in the road?

Emma made herself straighten her legs, but could only get up as far as a stoop: bent over, her hands between her knees. She squeezed her eyes, fighting tears; she used her anger to do it. *Blast!* Here she stood alone over her hope of a future, a hope lying dead in the road, with her standing in one boot and a sock of a husband who was not a year gone himself. *Blast!* she thought again, then stood all the way up, and shouted.

"Blast it!" she said toward her ewe, waving her hands to shoo the animal back toward the meadow. "It was that west border again, wasn't it?" she asked. Her west pasture was marked off by an old stone wall, built by the Romans, upright chiefly from its wide-base design and the glue of time. Periodically, a sheep jostled a stone loose, though usually nothing more came of it than Emma cemented the stone back. "Where? Where is the hole this time?" she yelled.

The ewe skittered away at a lope. Good riddance, Emma thought and wiped her hands on her apron—they were wet with a clamminess that had come over her. "Ah, life, drat you anyway," she muttered as, with her forearm, she pushed her hair off her forehead. *Ah, life.*

And blooming, bleeding death, curse it all.

And reckless viscounts, may the devil take them, who ran over helpless lambs in the road and kept on going.

The next morning, at the crack of dawn, Emma, in her best frock and bonnet, pulled herself up onto Hannah the mule—the community property of herself and several of her neighbors—and made the eleven-mile trek uphill to Castle Dunord, the residence of the new viscount and seat of the viscountcy.

She would speak to her new neighbor, who had undoubtedly done her damage only by accident. He'd been inside the coach after all; he might not even realize it had struck a lamb. She would tell him. He was a gentleman, wasn't he? He would act honorably and take responsibility.

Indeed, when she turned down the castle's lane of trees, her heart lifted. A quick resolution seemed to lie upon the horizon, for the new viscount obviously had money enough to right a thousand dead lambs and hardly notice. Emma took in the sight of the old castle for the first time in years and was astonished. Its old stones, ghostly and dingy for decades, were clean, while the grounds were alive with activity: a regular beehive of journeymen, gardeners, and what-have-you in the way of servants and workmen. The regal old building was being refaced, its garden replanted, its roof mended.

She tied Hannah up in the midst of pots of new plants, some tall, some bushy, their foliage shushing in the breeze, then walked past where the old fountain had been, with two men staring down its plumbing, another hammering, *kong, kong, kong*, on new copper tubing.

Despite the noise—and there was more inside, of large things clapping, moving about—a neat butler in tails greeted Emma at the front door very formally.

No, the viscount wasn't "receiving visitors." When she explained it was more than a visit, that she had business with him, the butler a little irritably then told her, no, he wasn't "doing business yet either, not without prior arrangement."

"The viscount killed my lamb."

The man in uniform blinked, then said, "The answer is still no." The opening of the doorway narrowed. "I am not to allow anyone to disturb his lordship. He is busy. Good day."

She leaned forward. "Then may I please make an appointment to see him, when he is free?"

"Do you have a calling card?"

A calling card. Now wouldn't that be a la-di-da luxury. "I have a name: Emma Hotchkiss."

The man raised a smug eyebrow. The door would have closed all the way, but a sound, someone's voice, stopped the butler, making him twist at the torso and pause, rigid. As if something strange and remarkable, as alien as a dragon, had come up behind him.

A low voice addressed the man, a passing shadow. Whoever it was was tall. The butler, looking upward and behind, replied instantly with all but fearful deference, "A local woman, sir."

In the servant's distraction, Emma pushed the door open slightly and leaned closer, shifting an inch this way, then that, trying to see to whom the butler spoke. All she could be certain of was dark: dark coloring, dark clothes, long limbs. Or perhaps she was only looking at elongated shadows; hard to say. Though she heard distinctly the hushed reserve of a quiet, deep voice, a masculine register.

This voice rolled out another unintelligbly low tune of words, the speech having almost a musical rhythm, slow, measured, considered—then the tall shadow moved away, gone.

The butler turned back to Emma, more smug than ever. "His lordship has no time for local squabbling—"

Local squabbling? Emma risked her hand by putting her gloved palm flat on the door's surface—did she dare push her way in? She wanted to. By jings, she wanted to latch hold of that shadow and give him a piece of her mind. *Local squabbling? That's* what that low voice had been saying? For most assuredly the voice had belonged to the viscount himself. Within two feet of her, yet he would not deign to discuss her grievance. Gentleman, indeed.

In the garden behind her, construction, commotion grated.

Hammers clapped, rather like her heart, mirroring a rage that grew louder, banging in her ears. Such anger!

The butler eyed her hand on the outside of the carved wood door, as if he eyed the hand of a beggar, a strumpet's—certainly a lady didn't soil her white glove with such temerity. Then the doorway narrowed anyway, pushing at her arm as his face became a strip of whiteness in the dark, noisy interior.

Emma lifted her chin and spoke quickly, with the kind of youthful folly—the conviction that right would win—she could both berate herself for yet not stop herself from feeling. "What am I supposed to do," she asked, "if his lordship won't make good on this injury? I haven't the money myself. So am I simply to be set back a year of breeding because the viscount likes to travel fast? He *must* see me. I am the widow of the former vicar of the parish, a woman of some respect in the village—"

"Indeed," came a murmur over the last of her words. It was spoken almost with amusement: as the door quietly shut in her face.

Emma stood there stunned, then rode home fuming. She passed her own cottage and continued on to John Tucker's, who, besides being her neighbor, was a local magistrate.

A lamb lost in the road could be worse, she decided: She could have not known the culprit. Too often, all a farmer had was an animal carcass, a casualty of fast conveyances on a winding country road. When the guilty party was known, however, Yorkshire courts were blissfully biased, nearly everyone being sheep owners themselves. Local laws did not tolerate running down one of the region's chief resources. When a person was caught killing one, he paid dearly because hardly anyone was ever caught. A known offender, on the law books, paid for all the future sheep the dead lamb might have produced—a progenitor rule—though, in fact, he paid truly for all the sheep who had been killed with no culprit to hand. It was a jurisprudence of balance. And thank God for it.

She intended to snag the shadowy Mount Villiars with it and hang him by his local squabbles.

The sun slanted low through the west window of John's parlor, making the faded curtains brighter than otherwise—they showed how ill his wife, Margot, was and for how long. Everything, once bright, was dull in the house these days. It was one of the reasons Emma couldn't arrive here without washing things up a bit and dusting things out, since Margot couldn't, and John didn't seem to know how. Emma had spent the afternoon helping out, then had tea with them.

Only then did she finally trust herself to broach the subject of her dead lamb and her wanting to string up the villain who'd killed it.

"A villain. Straightaway he be a villain, Em," John said. He'd been calling her by her given name, or a part of it, since she was a minute old.

He scratched his head as he sat in his overstuffed chair by his freshly lit hearth—which made her pull her mouth sideways. The long, pausing gesture meant he was looking for a way to express deep disagreement with someone he liked.

"Now make no mistake," he said. "I be right sorry aboot your lamb. No one sorrier, dearie. But bullying Mount Villiars, jings! Ye got no logic to ye, woman. He be our neeb'r, now. Not to mention a bloody vee-count. Vee-counts ain't villains. And *this* vee-count be the new one of the district, our *only* one. They say he may even take his seat"—his seat in the House of Lords, John meant, which added up to possible political power for the district. "So ye wanna that his first contact with us in, oh, the thearty years or so since he be gone, be with some hen a-harping at him? Ye don' know what ye'r aboot, girl."

"His coach didn't even stop, John, then he wouldn't see me—"

"Shush. Ye went to Doon'r?"—how the locals pronounced the name of the castle that overlooked their village.

"I did. He wouldn't even promise to see me later." She made a face, then made her point. "Too fine for locals, you see."

"Write to him."

"Write to him!" She burst out laughing. Oh, fine. Write the viscount who wouldn't give her the time of day a letter. *Dear sir. You killed my lamb. Please pay up.*

John explained, "These city fellas hold a lot of truck with paper. Send him some. Tell him what happened in writing. Ye know how. And be humble aboot it, ye hear me? A polite letter, respectfully addressed to the lord of the district." He shook his head at her, knowing her too well. "Ye get too uppity, Em, when ye think ye been crossed. I say this fer yer own good. Be humble."

She sighed, taking to heart what he said as she rose and picked up her hat along with the tall pile of sewing—his and Margot's mending would fetch her one shilling three pence, a special price she made for them since Margot shook too badly ever again to wield a needle.

As Emma headed toward their front door, she felt deflated. Even a little defeated. Though she couldn't say why; she shouldn't. A letter was perhaps reasonable enough. The viscount didn't drive his own coach or answer his own door, and though he might shrug past someone standing on his stoop, surely he read his own mail. A letter. A polite one. She'd write one; she'd rein herself in. John was right. A sheep farmer, a female one at that, didn't take on a viscount. No, she'd been living long enough with her own wayward temper to know better than to let it carry her off, half-cocked.

At the door, though, she realized something else. The melancholy she felt had another aspect: loneliness. What John was saying was, if she couldn't get Mount Villiars voluntarily to do what was right, no one in the district wanted to cross him just yet. She'd be on her own against the new "lord of the district," as John called him.

From behind, her neighbor called to her, "Ye want that I

get the cart, Em, and run ye home? Hannah can board here till next someone needs her."

It was growing dark. It had been a miserable twenty-four hours. Emma nodded. John called to Margot, in bed already, almost always in bed, that he'd be right back.

They rode in silence. John, seventy or more, was spry as a young man. A little stooped, a lot wrinkled, but as energetic as a man of twenty. Emma liked him more than a little. He was a favorite among her friends in the village. In fact, he was a favorite of nearly everyone she knew. Hardly a soul in Malzeard-near-Prunty-Bridge didn't like the man, respect him.

Which was why her heart sank a little lower still when at her own gate he reminded her, "Don't go daft on us, a' right?"

Daft. Once, she'd gone "daft," as they liked to say. When her parents had wanted her to marry, at age thirteen, randy Randall Fitz. She'd up and taken herself to London, stayed there, too. She hadn't come back for four years, and, when she did, she was married already, this time to a man more of her own liking: Zachary Hotchkiss.

She made a little nod as she scooted off the wagon bench. She had no intention of going "daft." She'd learned her lesson. Even Zach hadn't been as much her own choice as she might have liked, though she'd loved him and missed him now he was gone. It was just London was no place for a girl to keep herself on her own; it was as simple as that. She'd needed Zach, and he'd been a darn sight better than a sheep farmer's lecherous, dull-witted son. Zach had been interesting; no one could say otherwise.

At her porch, she turned and waved through the semidark toward John's silhouette sitting hunched atop the farm cart.

He called to her. "Ye'r a good girl, Emma Hotchkiss, all'll be fine. Ye'll see."

Right, she thought. She let herself and Giovanni, Zach's tomcat, into an empty house: no fire lit till she lit it, into a cold front room that served as parlor and scullery both. There, in a drawer, she found a small piece of candle, which she lit and carried into the rear, the house's only other room. It was a bedroom fit for a monastery: bare wood walls, a neatly made bed, a washstand with a basin. On the far wall, a wood cross hung over the empty cot where Zach had spent his last days. At one time, that same wall had been lined with his books, rows of uneven colorful spines. He'd sold them several years back, which had all but broken Emma's heart—she'd only gotten through half of them, most of the novels and poetry, almost none of his readings from university and seminary. Being the hardest to read, she'd been saving those for last, for when she was smarter, she hoped, after reading the rest.

When Emma envisioned Zach now, what she usually saw was his lying here, the sight of this bare wall with its martyr's cross, and the back of his head where he lay on the cot. Or, if she struggled, reaching down into sad memory, she could see his head's slow rotation at the sound of her cheerful steps—a rhythm she intentionally put into the clink of his teacup, *clickety-clickety, clickety-clickety*, as she carried in his supper tray. His dark head would linger in that turned-away direction, such a fascinating wall, till the last accountable moment, when finally he'd turn his bleary gaze toward her, toward the room's interior—toward life, she used to think—with rheumy, weary interest.

The dearly departed. She'd thought of him that way for weeks before he'd actually gone. She'd missed him for longer still, perhaps years.

How long had she been alone? It was hard to say. Longer than the five months of her widowhood.

As Emma set the Tucker's sewing into her basket in the shadows beside her big feather bed, the cat rubbed against her legs, then against something else that clopped over. Ah, one of Zach's ill-fitting boots, her favorites for working in the pasture or mucking out the barn. Her favorites, period. She preferred them to the shin-high lace-ups she was wearing. To no one, or to the cat perhaps, she muttered, "My lamb

is dead. And there may be little or nothing I can do about it."
God knew, there was nothing she could do about Zach; there never had been.

Some days, it was hard to believe that anything would ever be fine again.

Emma did write. She even said "please" and signed it "yours most respectfully" and used her best handwriting, which she'd learned, thanks to the Public Education Act, then refined beyond imagining in her dealings with Zach and his friends in London.

Her response came in the form of a letter from the viscount's "London friends": his lawyers. Emma was surprised by the little stab of wonder as she read the postmark. London. Then, when she opened the letter, the solicitors' business card fell out. *A calling card.* And she was bemused for a second.

She used to own a little silver box of calling cards herself, more than a dozen years ago now. She hadn't thought much about London in the interim, yet seeing the embossed card from the London firm made her suddenly remember odd things: a line of half a dozen beautifully scripted calling cards on the mantel . . . a first-rate meal at a fancy restaurant . . . a play seen from a velvet-cushioned seat, a well-written play with good actors on a bright, footlit stage. London had been such a marvel to a young girl.

Before, of course, Zach's games there, which had sustained them, had ended up scaring the Sweet Jesus out of both of them and sending Zach into the arms of God. From marvel to mayhem in one easy lesson. No, she wasn't unhappy to have fled London. Even wearing a fine dress while receiving and leaving a trail of ornate calling cards in one's wake, the city was dirty and hard going: It became downright dangerous.

She shoved the dratted business card into her apron pocket and unfolded her formal response from the viscount's attorneys—at which point a cheque fell out as well.

Emma was overjoyed one moment, then chagrined the

next. The draft was on a French bank for the sum of fifteen francs. She read the explanation:

The viscount's lawyers informed her that his lordship was "egregiously sorry" for her loss, though the viscount himself knew nothing of his part in such matter. Still, since she was a neighbor—and his lordship being such a generous fellow, his lawyers implied—he wished to offer her the enclosed cheque toward a new sheep, which was the rough equivalent of two pounds sterling. The letter went on to assure her that the draft could be converted straightaway to cash at the Bank of England in London, and that in due time the draft would also be honored somewhere in York, at a bank there and its provincial branches; if she could simply wait, they would tell her which one as soon as they knew. His lordship, they claimed, newly arrived in England, was still in the process of setting up his accounts here. In due time, her fifteen francs might actually turn into two pounds.

Emma was livid. Mount Villiars, a viscount, for goodness sake, probably carried a dozen times two pounds in loose change.

She returned the preposterous check, this time scribbling her response as fast as she could get the words down, never mind fine handwriting or the hemming and hawing of undue respect:

Dear sirs,

What the blazes am I to do with a draft on a French bank? Go to London with it? It costs two quid to get to London, stay the night, then turn around and come home. Go to York "in due time"? What for? I couldn't buy a new lamb, chop at a time, for two quid, let alone breeding stock. Meanwhile, my own lamb, had he lived, would have fathered hundreds of lambs in only several years, a fact that a Yorkshire court would be more than happy to take into account—dead sheep in the road here, though not frequent, are ongoing, the bane of local sheepmen since the Roman chariot, and local courts are sensitive to the matter. That is to say, my dead tup is worth much more than two pounds sterling, and I would have his lordship please attend to the matter with the attention and respect it deserves. He will please contact me directly at his earliest convenience.

She crossed out the last four words. No, too mild now.

He will please contact me directly.

Never mind his convenience. She considered eliminating the last *please* as well, but left it in.

The viscount's response to this missive made Emma believe for a brief moment that she was at least coming face-to-face with the man himself. A knock at her door brought her to her window, made her lift her curtain, and she saw a tall, formal man standing on her front doorstep.

When she opened the door, she believed for an instant the thin, sallow man in a hamburg was the viscount. But, no, he introduced himself as Edward Blainey, "assistant secretary" to the Viscount Mount Villiars—he presented a card. She laughed as she accepted it, which took him aback. (Assistant? Typical. Given the viscount's penchant for indirect contact, an army of secretaries seemed almost reasonable.)

She glanced over yet another printed card, this one in embossed, raised black ink on ivory—she began to think the viscount kept all of London printing alive on cards alone for his minions.

Handing the card back, she asked, "Does Mount Villiars exist or is he simply a fiction invented by a hundred people who print cards, write letters, contact attorneys—and kill sheep—then arrive on my doorstep? Or, no, perhaps he is such a sorry case he needs a hundred scurrying people about him to prove how utterly and hopelessly important he is." She leaned forward, a small woman with a large grudge at this point. "Where *is* he? I ask you."

The man blinked, cleared his throat, and tipped his hat, a tall, thin, older man, tidy in appearance, with the faint, sweet odor and thick, veiny nose of a gin-lover. "Elsewhere, madam. I've been sent to settle your complaint on my way into town."

Indeed. An incidental inconvenience on a list. *Buy champagne, order caviar, settle complaining widow.* All right, good. Finally. She wouldn't grouse.

In the next five minutes, the man offered her ten quid. An improvement. She refused. She volunteered to settle for thirty, which was still too little, though at least it would mean something to her. The man smirked. He shook his head. He made fun of the smell of a sheep who—happily—nudged him at the back of his trousers, momentarily scaring the devil out of him, a sheep who smelled of sulphur as it should, having been carefully dosed and dipped with Coopers. Which brought Emma and Mr. Blainey, and indirectly the viscount, once more to a stalemate.

The assistant personal secretary stood with the bank draft in his fingers, dangling between himself and Emma—signed by Mr. Blainey himself, she noticed, a power with which she herself would not have trusted him. Though less smug than the butler, more weathered in the face, for all his conservative polish—his spotless gloves, small-brimmed hat, and white, starched collar—Mr. Blainey didn't come off quite the dignified Englishman he seemed to want to portray so much as unctuous, almost wily. It was something in his posture, his expression.

Emma kept her back to her own front door, not allowing him to see inside her home, while she finished dusting flour from her fingers—she'd been making bread, something she did for the entire village on Saturdays to bring in extra money. She eyed the viscount's man, waiting to see if he was authorized to offer any further suggestion.

He must have thought she was cleaning her hands in preface to examining the draft at least. When she finished, she tucked the rag into her apron, then said *no* more firmly by folding her arms over her chest and asking—it occurred more out of curiosity than anything else—"Why is it this rich man keeps offering me money in forms that are actually rather difficult to turn to cash?"

This draft, while at least in English currency, was still on the Bank of England, which had no rural branches. It would take a goodly time to make its way through a clearinghouse, unless she wanted once again to board a train for London.

"Not that I would take it," she continued, "but why not simply offer a ten-pound note? A viscount must surely be floating in those."

Interestingly, Mr. Blainey's expression faltered. He even looked a little unsettled then, a nervous mannerism, once more cleared his throat. There was a reason! Though he wasn't going to tell her. He said instead, "Take the draft. It will be good a week from Monday."

She laughed, involuntary. "It isn't even good?"

"It will be." He looked a little sheepish, then volunteered, "And any amount larger, of course, wouldn't be honored for a while longer, till his lordship finalizes the larger transactions of the account—"

"Is the viscount in financial trouble?"

"Yes." He blinked. "Well, no." He shook his head and shrugged as if a straight *yes* were a foolish answer. "He's rich as a tzar. It's just that all his money is coming from foreign banks. And then there was the business with his uncle—"

"His uncle?"

Mr. Blainey was nonplussed for a moment. He'd put his foot in it somewhere, which fascinated Emma. The small man stood straighter and for the third time in two minutes cleared his throat once more. "*Ahem,* his lordship's finances are complicated . . ." He mumbled something more, but his voice trailed off.

Emma put on her most sympathetic face and shook her head. "It's that uncle," she said. "How awful." What uncle?

Mr. Blainey waved his hand, as if he could wave away any mention of an uncle-bunkum-any-relative. "Oh, no, that problem's over." He added quickly, "Not that it was ever a *true* problem. There was never any question of the title the moment his lordship set foot on English soil again, no, no." He denied something—though she wasn't sure exactly what—vehemently.

"Of course not," she agreed and puzzled over all that was left out.

"In any regard, that's the reason for the formality of a particular and peculiar signature for large amounts." He indicated the cheque. "And why the accounts are so difficult to set up. His uncle opened so many. Money went the wrong places. And now there are these debts and questions as to whom they belong to, with creditors trying to levy against accounts before they are even open. It's a mess."

"Oh, dear, yes. I can see that." Not clearly, but she was getting the drift. An uncle had laid claim to the title with his nephew out of country. There were double accounts.

The secretary sighed, grateful for the understanding, then shrugged again, completely without remedy for Emma herself: a situation quite beyond his control. "So you see, it's impossible for me to offer a draft for a larger amount, since anything over ten pounds will require the viscount's particular signature"—he left a small, rather awestruck pause—"that only his lordship can produce."

Really? Emma, when she'd been "daft," had briefly gotten by on an odd little gift she had for reproducing almost any signature. She had in fact, in her youth, fallen in with some men and women, Zach among them, who "prospered on the fundamentally dishonest nature of their fellow men": that is, a group who earned their living through various bits of quasi knavery in London. At fourteen, she'd discovered that a girl on her own there had three choices besides outright crime: the gray life of factories, out-and-out selling herself on the street, or the borderline fringe of legality called confidence games. The choice of how to support herself had not required a lot of thought—and resulted in acquaintances in London who would have loved Mr. Blainey.

Men like Mr. Blainey, who thought themselves right-minded, always made the best marks. They never questioned themselves when, faced with the "deal of a lifetime," they sold off any scruple they might have possessed.

All the more reason not to deal with him. Emma said good day firmly. He fussed a moment more, woe-faced, declaring her to be making a grievous error. "His lordship does not *have* to do anything. That is what I am saying. I take care of small matters."

"I would like to become a larger matter then," she told him and took childish pleasure in stepping back, ready to close the door in his face. Then couldn't. More civilly, she said, "It appears this matter cannot be settled between us. Tell his lordship I shall file a legal complaint and let English justice determine what is right. Good day again."

She watched him go—with his displaying such sad, head-shaking reluctance it bordered on the histrionic. What malarkey. She had the keenest feeling that, if faced with, say, a person who confided a sad story, a widow with her life's savings, for instance, buried in a ditch, money she was willing to split with anyone who'd simply help her dig it up: the man would grab a shovel, run, beat her to it, and take it all.

Not that it was any of her business, but she hoped the viscount was aware of the man's character. It sounded as though "his lordship" had a bit of a sticky situation to sort out, and this Blainey fellow would take advantage if advantage came his way.

Then she realized she was worrying over a man who could run over a lamb and leave it to die in the road, not blinking: fight about it, in fact. At which point, she went back to her bread and stopped fretting for the Viscount Mount Villiars altogether.

John reluctantly explained to Emma how and where to file. In mid-December, the case came up before him and Henry Gaines, the other sitting magistrate, in the Petty Session of the borough court held quarterly in the church vestry. A little alarming, a London barrister showed up on the viscount's behalf, explaining he was staying up at the castle and present "merely as a courtesy" to the viscount.

Overall, the proceeding was more tense than Emma had expected. No one, not even John Tucker, very willingly ruled against an English "lard and gen'leman," as John kept calling him, who had "no rec'lection of hitting nought." She had to fight them all, but she did it and was proud of herself for it.

She simply insisted at every turn, "It was *his* carriage, the crest plain, shiny, and new. I saw it with my own eyes. The Viscount Mount Villiars's coach struck and killed my lamb in its wild hurry."

The barrister's chief argument was, of course, that the only witness was a woman who would turn a handsome profit from her version of the facts. John and Henry listened, unflappable, while Emma sat there, feeling the lonely bearer of truth in a roomful of doubters. When the barrister grew bold enough, however, to use the word *opportunistic,* John pulled his mouth sideways and held up his hand. "Sir," he said, "Emma Hotchkiss's honesty in this riding be unquestioned. She'd not mek anything up." He let out a long sigh, looked face-to-face around the vestry, then said, "If the veecount's coach hit the animal, even if he weren't in it, there be the matter of responsibility."

He then explained to the lawyer the Yorkshire codes and legal precedents regarding the killing of another man's, or woman's, sheep—something with which the Londoner was not well acquainted. John and Henry conferred briefly in murmurs.

And awarded fifty pounds to the plaintiff—her! Emma realized—explaining they hoped the viscount understood that under the circumstance this was a modest sum. Via his barrister, they sent an admonishment to drive more slowly. The area was a patchwork of meadows stitched together with hedgerows and ancient walls. "It might be worse than a lamb kilt next time," John said.

Fifty pounds! Emma walked out of the side room of the small church (the room where Zach had once put on all the raiments and robes they had both liked so well) and into the sunshine. *Ah*, she thought, *over at last. I have satisfaction*. Fifty pounds would go a long way in making up for the lost income, the lost productivity. Good then.

Four days later, however, she received a letter. It read:

Dear Mrs. Hotchkiss,

Enclosed is a draft for ten pounds sterling, the funds available onward from Thursday at any branch of the York Joint-Stock Banking Company. For your information, and for anyone else's who cares to interfere in the matter, I do not believe I killed your lamb to begin with. And even if I had, a lamb is not worth fifty pounds, a fact upon which I shall stand and die before I pay you the sum. You may cash this draft, eat it with mung beans, or stuff it up your very nervy bum. The sheriff may arrest me, if he dare, while my lawyers and I refile for an unbiased hearing of the case.

Most sincerely,
On behalf of the Viscount Mount Villiars,
Mr. Edward Blainey, Assistant Personal Secretary

The viscount could speak! Or dictate at least! He had a mouth, though not a very nice one. Her nervy bum, indeed!

Still, a personal response thrilled her for some reason. Her nemesis had acknowledged her. Though only in dictation. He hadn't signed the letter. But still. . . .

Her pleasure was short-lived. The same day that brought the letter the sheriff served Emma with a rolled, ribboned sheaf of legal pages. When she opened them out, she found that her Yorkshire verdict had been referred to a Quarter Court for revision in appeal. This higher court could not hear the case for another month and a half. Until then all fines and recompense were withheld.

Then, worse, a day later more legal documents arrived, the gist of which was that the Quarter Court had referred the case to a new jurisdiction. It would be heard in London at the Old Bailey. The viscount's barrister had been busy.

"What does this mean, John?" Emma asked as she accepted the papers back into her gloved hands, then gave the stupid packet of pages a little shake. She and John stood outside on a cold day, having met halfway across his field, him on his way to town, herself on her way to show him her latest outrage.

John scratched his head with a crooked knuckle that protruded from his knit, open-fingered gloves. Winter was bearing down on them, near full force with Christmas—the bleakest, it seemed, she would know in years—only days away now. "It means ye' lost, Em."

Emma, in her heaviest coat, stomped the ground to keep warm, clomping up and down in Zach's boots, well padded with thick-knit stockings. "I won. At the very least"—she shook one of the pages, wrestling the wind for it—"this letter puts him in contempt." She tugged at the shawl she wore up over her head and tied about her shoulders, pulling it up against the blast of wind.

"It ain't contempt to take a case further, though I give ye that: The letter be rude. Still, his secret'ry's words be hearsay; he dint write 'em; he dint sign it. Ye'd hafta find a magistrate willing to hold him in contempt, and ye no' be looking at one, Em."

She sighed and let her hands, the legal documents with them, fall against her coat. "Why would he go to so much bother?"

"No bother to him. Ye be a gnat in the big soup of his bringing hi'self back to England. I hear he been to all sarts of fareign places. He picks ye oot and keeps going." Her neighbor paused, his crinkled old eyes wrinkling further for having to squint into an icy draft of air. "Em, he's offered ye money, off the coort record, when in all likelihood he won' hafta give ye a farthing."

"I won't take the draft to the bank. It's short of what I won."

"Then ye'll hafta find yerself a solicitor and barrister and go to London to make yer case."

She frowned. "You know I can't afford—" She broke off, staring hard at the horizon at the far end of the pasture. The chestnuts and oaks that dotted the meadow were leafless. Beneath them and around, the grass was sparse but mostly green; it gave way only occasionally here and there now into the remains of white drifts, the first heavy snow of winter half-melted, half-hardened to ice.

"Em."

She looked at her neighbor's stooped form as he scratched the back of his neck again with a gnarled finger. He said, "Several of us feel right sympathetic with ye. We wanna pitch in. Margot says ye kin take o'er the books at church. Ye be good at it, an' ye can take the assistant's Saturday tithe fer yer bother. Ross says ye kin do his and his missuss' sewing. We all got t'gether a promise: You kin borra' anyone's ram for nought—"

"You all knew this would—"

"Naw, but I suspected. We talked aboot it, 'case it turned bad, ye know? Ye'r oot a' yer class, tha's all. Enoof. Don' nettle Mount Villiars any moor. We mus' live beside him—"

"Precisely." She lifted her chin. "How are we to live beside such a tyrant?"

"Gently," he said. "Till we know moor aboot him. Till we've all taken our hats off and nodded to itch other under more conginnial circ'nstance. We should see that he knaws he's welcome a' church, include him with high honors a' the New Year's Day Fair—"

"Oh, there's a fine idea. We'll honor a—a—a man who thinks himself above the law, who thinks he can murder innocent sheep in the road and get away with it—"

"He dunna want t' 'git away' with it exackly. He's offered ta—"

"Or name his own terms. No. If you invite him to the New Year's Fair, then don't bother looking for me there."

"Oh, Em. Don' get yer dander up. Or his any further."

"Don't 'oh, Em' me. I'm right."

"Being right ain't ev'rything."

She pressed her mouth, looked away, folding her arms, the legal papers flapping in the wind at her armpit. Then she glanced back, momentarily brighter. "Mabelle's son studies law. He's working with some barristers in London. He could—"

"*Ach*, for God's grace, give oop." John folded his bottom lip over his top one, like an envelope, then the lip flapped once, a *pah*, from the force of his letting out a long breath. He said, "Even if you could git yerself to the Ol' Bailey and hold the case, he'd only take it the next higher. Ye could end in the House of Lards."

Emma laughed—she loved that he occasionally called them *lards* without cracking a smile.

John continued. "The man's making his point. He's a blewdy vee-count. He ain't having nuthin' to do with a hen making him dance o'er a lost lamb."

Emma snorted, but she had "nuthin' " more to say.

And nuthin' more to do: A legal battle in London was impossible. She hated the place anyway, even worse than she hated arrogant *lards*—or *yahs* as her Scottish mother had called them: rich, public-school boys who thought they ran the world. For a moment she knew a drop of pure, glistening hatred for the stupid, bloody "vee-count" on the hill, for his arrogance, his money, and all the power at the beck and call of his entire class.

Then she let the feeling go. Ah, never mind. London was too far. She had a farm to work—her neighbors were offering their rams for raddling, and she should take them up on the offer, see her ewes set for next spring. Her life was busy. She was getting by. She hardly had the time, let alone the money, to do anything more over the matter.

It was done. She'd lost. By default. Outmonied, overpowered.

She glimpsed over her shoulder at the papers that ruffled and chattered in her fist. "Thank you, John. I suppose you're right. I hate it, but you're right."

She turned with him, stuffing her gloved hands with the wad of documents into her pockets, heading back toward home. At the road, they parted, him for the village, her for her house across the meadow.

About halfway home, she found herself stopped though, reading the crumpled papers again.

York. Her mind fixed on the word. The bank draft was on the York Joint-Stock Banking Company and would be "available onward from Thursday."

York. The town was three hours away—an hour into Harrogate, then a two-hour train ride.

Don't be daft, she thought.

Still, her gaze held, unbroken, on the bank cheque signed by the wrong name. The wrong name at least for a "large amount."

She bent over, turning against the wind and smoothing the papers out against her coat, her skirts and legs beneath. The winter sun struck the cheque, bright, shadowless, as she stared, scanning it from corner to corner. This one was printed with the viscount's family name. Stuart Winston Aysgarth. Stuart. She claimed the name there and then, her tribute to a man who didn't deserve any respectful titles.

"Well, Stuart," she said to the papers at her knees and thrilled to the irreverent sound of it. Stuart.

Under the bank's name was, again, the city: York.

It wasn't daft to go to York. York wasn't London. And she could be there and back in a day.

Stuart, Stuart, Stuart. She wanted more; there was more. She raised up, shuffling through papers until she was looking at the last page of one of the legal documents. It was filed on behalf of "Stuart Winston Aysgarth, The Right Honourable the Viscount Mount Villiars, Viscount Aysgarth, Baron Darcaster of Kilnwick, Baron Aysgarth of Dare, and baronet, serving Her Royal Majesty Queen Victoria." The string of titles startled a laugh out of her. He sounded like a bloody army of men—all of whom relished laws and rules and regulations, being as he was a member of the class, race, and sex who'd invented them all and how to use them.

What a shame for him they didn't play by them any longer she thought.

Chapter 2

The trick to shearing a sheep is to give it no cause for alarm—while you dump it over onto its rump and roll it where you want it. You leave it helpless, all four legs out and waggling, that is the key. But gently, always gently. Handle one roughly and you have an edgy sheep, kicking and flailing, which can lead to more wrestling, more chance of nicking the skin, more fear, a crazed animal. You never muscle a sheep into it. You dance him into it.

—Emma Darlington Hotchkiss
Yorkshire Ways and Recipes

IN the hands of an expert, separating a sheep from its wool was a kind of ballet. A real artist could shear the fleece off a big, surly ram in a piece, slipping it off like a discarded vest down onto the floor: able to divest, as it were, the same ram who might, under different circumstances, be able, horns down, to chase a woman off his field. Rams could be so imperious, Emma knew, so self-important, downright dangerous. If a body were going to shear one, all the more reason to wield the clippers with a great deal of finesse.

Emma's father, gone ten years now, had been the local shearer, sustaining his small family—himself, his wife, and daughter—on a few sheep of his own and the annual removal of the fleeces of everyone else's. He was a taciturn man, who, on the rare occasions when he did have something to say, almost always related it to his profession. *You never muscle a sheep into it. You dance him into it.* Emma had grown up full of awe of his skill and wishing she could do this dance herself, without the size or reach for it. She always thought that was where the idea of shearing people with Zach had taken root, what had helped to make it all right in London. Till that fateful afternoon when it had become decidedly otherwise, it had seemed a gentle game, where the one being sheared ended up a little frightened, but no true harm done, with a byproduct that was nothing but useful: money, gently removed from those whose own greed fairly well predicted they'd grow more soon enough.

Shearing. It was what she sat thinking of as she gazed out the tall, double-glazed—velvet-draped, gold-tasseled—windows of the York Joint-Stock Banking Company. Shearing a headstrong ram.

From this side of the glass, now that her cheeks and nose had thawed, she felt a pleasant sense of anticipation. In a warm bank—a virtual monument to English adaption, with its forced-air fireplaces and vast oriental carpet, holding winter at bay—she waited along with everyone else for their first sight of an elusive viscount whom no one had seen yet, despite his having arrived in the country more than four months ago. Mount Villiars. He was late. But he most assuredly would show up, since his signatures were required on papers he himself had initiated. Everyone—from the bank's governor to the various officers all the way down the row of windows to the tellers—was alive with the knowledge, with expectation and curiosity that wafted in the air as tangibly as heat crackling in the several hearths, rippling in waves all the way to the high, coffered ceiling.

Emma herself suppressed her excitement, afraid to give it full rein. Patiently, she watched the snow she'd just trudged through outside. It whirled peacefully, white-flecked air currents, leaving deposits, near-blinding white, on rooftops, in windowsills, collecting in wedges at the windowpanes. All in all, a fairly gentle Thursday morning for the end of December (three days past Christmas), a time of year when it could sleet sideways with the wind blasting so forcefully it could knock one off one's feet.

There was much to be thankful for. She sat, for instance, at one corner of a long table as the designated amanuensis to take down all notes necessary—having been sent over by the Mason Krimple Temporary Record Keeping, Accounting, and Amanuensis Service, since, alas, the viscount's personal secretaries, both of them, had taken leave abruptly. (With luck, no gentleman would think it seemly to discuss who exactly was paying her. No one was. She'd invented the agency after sending Mr. Blainey and his associate, a Mr. Harlow, into London on a wonderfully silly wild-goose chase.) The table was empty but for her and the governor to her left at the table's head, the deputy governor at her right, Mr. Hemple and Mr. Fogmoth, respectively. A dozen empty chairs other than this, all in ready.

More for something to do, she shifted on her chair's leather cushion, lifting her stenography pad, kicking up her skirts just enough to recross her legs in the other direction, then settled the notepad back onto her knee with the *shushy* noise of moving taffeta. Her movement drew the attention of both men at the table. She'd worn a rather risqué petticoat for the occasion, one that announced itself at every turn.

She caught the men's gazes, one then the other, and smiled. After a brief hesitation, they each smiled back. She blinked, fluttering her eyelashes, and blushed shyly, deceptively, looking down as demurely as she knew how. She wore a rather fusty frock, wool and striped silk faded to pale blue, with a high collar and skirts that looped up at the sides and back. She liked it well enough, though it was hard to say how out-of-date it was, since it had been secondhand already when she'd bought it in London a dozen years ago. Still, it suited the purpose. It fit snugly, barely containing her generous bosom. It was tight enough around her ribs and waist that she didn't like to breathe too deeply for fear the buttons would give. As an extra precaution, she wore a steel watch (that had ceased to work, alas) pinned low on her right breast, on the off chance that anyone here might miss how wholly—that is to say, frivolously—female she was.

Even frivolously, it was surprisingly nice to feel female again. She hadn't bothered to for so long, she realized.

Emma liked her voluptuous little body. It was generous at every curve, too full and short to be considered elegant, yet as feminine as the female form came. The snug dress and noisy petticoat worked with that notion rather than against it. Since she would be the only woman at the table, the only way not to stand out—to invisibility—was to become what men generally expected in a woman, a sweet piece of confection, all heart, no head: born to serve.

Alas, she wasn't going to serve them as well as they thought. She didn't know a stroke of shorthand nor how to type. She thought she had rather a nice knack, though, for scribbling as if she took shorthand. And she didn't intend to stay around long enough to type anything. She was here strictly to see, firsthand, the viscount's "particular" signature—and, all right, satisfy her curiosity for what the hard-driving, smart-mouth recluse was like in the flesh—then the "viscount" would write out a countercheque to cover the rightful cost of her lamb, and she would be off to submit the draft to a distant branch. Their amanuensis would disappear after tea, she imagined.

At the very moment, the room stirred, and Emma's heartbeat picked up as not one but two large carriages rolled past the window: one of them familiar. How strange to see the exact same shiny, black-lacquered coach that had struck her lamb. How perfect! The viscount's big, gorgeous carriage from months ago—with liveried servants hanging off it from all directions—rolled to a stop directly in front of the window behind the second vehicle. Carriage doors opened. She could only see the backs of men as they poured from the carriage and the one ahead of it, the snowfall making of them a speckled blur of dark coats, canes, capes, and a lot of bobbing black hats. Oh, men were so amusing, weren't they? she thought. Such a self-important sex.

A moment later, the bank's double doors swung open. A gust of cold blew in that she could feel all the way across the lobby. It preceded two footmen in umber wool with greenish gold braid, the colors of the Viscounts Mount Villiars for centuries. These servants battled the heavy doors, holding them open as through the entranceway passed a parade of men: the first two in bowler hats, the next in a top hat, the three of them stomping their somber shoes, yet unable to stomp off the mien of solicitors; it was all over them. Two more men entered behind them, both sporting hamburgs, one with a foreign-looking mustache; they carried the sort of leather folders that accountants liked to cart about, or have someone cart for them. Two younger men came in behind them, then another young man, hurrying.

There followed a small space of time, a few heartbeats, before a presence—there was no other word for him—walked into the doorway: He took over the doorway, in fact, in his tall top hat and billowing greatcoat.

After months of trying to see him, there was no doubt: Stuart Winston Aysgarth, the Right Honourable the Viscount Mount Villiars, la la, she thought, *and all those other titles*. Yet, despite herself, Emma could not hold down a certain amount of awe. And surprise. What was she expecting? Not this.

The viscount stopped in the doorway, head bent, the round oval of his top hat gleaming, as he wiped his feet. No somber shoes for him: He wore high-polished black boots reminiscent of Hessians, as shiny as black mirrors, fitted, foreign-looking. Then he looked up, pausing to stare out from the shadows of the brim of his top hat, leisurely—one might have said *lordly*—perusing the bank's vast gallery, as if to decide whether the place were worthy of entering.

He stood there a long moment: *Stuart,* she reminded herself, trying to recapture—ground herself in—her own disrespect. Yet he wasn't at all what she'd imagined: tall, slender, broad-shouldered, and younger somehow than she'd concocted in her imagination. She realized the boy who lived on the hill, taken away by his father at six, had been near her age at the time, which would make him presently one-and-thirty. His tailored form now, backlit against a sunny white afternoon, made the colors of the street behind him seem flat. Two half-timbered storefronts with swinging signs, a fading, out-of-season Christmas wreath under a doorway, all of it obscured by flurries: unreal. He looked for a moment as if he inhabited one of those children's globes, the updrafts and downdrafts of rotating flakes as chaotic about him as though someone had shaken the town of York with his being the only fixed piece.

He stepped forward. Behind him, his footmen won over the heavy doors that closed with the *swooshing* finality of an airtight vault. And the Viscount Mount Villiars—the recluse who raced along country roads, the expatriate come home, the surly correspondent and careful, private, quarrelsome man Emma had not been able to get near till now—began toward them across the long lobby at a kind of march.

Within half a dozen steps, smartly clicking till his footfalls struck the carpet, he reduced the whole place to utter silence. Customers turned at the teller windows, gape-jawed. Employees tiptoed from the back only to stop dead in their tracks.

He strode beneath a long dark greatcoat that flapped close to the ground about his legs, trimmed at the hem, cuffs, and lapels in silver-gray fur as thick and dense as batting. Amazing fur; she'd never seen anything quite like it. It lay, silvery and smooth, against vast amounts of dark wool. A simple style, yet . . . more somehow than most Englishmen would wear. Likewise, the coat was longer, more tailored across his broad chest and wide shoulders, narrower to his waist than English tastes allowed, while being oceans more voluminous about his long-striding legs.

Clothes. He was all clothes, she realized. She couldn't honestly see him. Still. She found herself turned in her chair, craning.

The chair down one from her scraped. She glanced and realized one of the solicitors had claimed the chair next to the deputy governor; two other men were sitting down opposite them. The long table was filling in, and—oh, jings, double jings, he was almost surely going to sit somewhere down from her, out of sight: After all this time, she was not going to get a good look at anything but his hat and coat! No. It was simply too much. She had to make a closer inspection—get his scent as the old Zach would have said.

She pushed her chair back, setting her notepad on the corner of the dark wood table. "Excuse me." She looked at the men on either side of her, holding her pen up. "My nib. I left the new one in my coat. I should replace it before we begin. I'll only be a moment." With that, she was up and off.

She walked briskly across the bank gallery, setting a trajectory for her coat by the door as she wove her way through the last of the viscount's advancing phalanx: stepping sideways to maneuver her skirts and shoulders between the two young men who weren't paying attention, the third giving way to her, the two footmen separating off to the sides. All the while she watched the viscount in her peripheral vision—then dropped her pen, looked down and to the right, presumably searching for it as she stepped back, turning. She backed up directly into Mount Villiars's path.

The collision was a bit more successful than she intended: He walked smack into the back of her, mostly her buttocks, then had to catch her or she would have been knocked off her feet. He weighed more—more solid, more mass in motion somehow—than she'd expected. Then more amazing still: As he caught her round the waist, with her twisting to grab his shoulder, his dark eyes did a kind of classic double glance. He looked once, then looked quickly back again, the second time down at her with what could have been called awareness, even approval.

Emma was nonplussed. As she turned, trying to get her balance, his hand went flat against the small of her back. The two of them did a kind of dance for a few steps that would have been risqué under any other circumstance. And still she couldn't see him; he was a tangle of coat, a play of shadows under the brim of a hat. Though she could smell him, a warm, suede-soft odor so distinct it was like walking into a subtle, spicy cocoon of it, exotic: foreign. Meanwhile, she could have sworn he leaned, keeping them off-kilter a moment more than necessary, putting them both at risk of falling simply to extend their little pas de deux. Then, just as suddenly, he righted her and let go.

Which left her breathless, unable to speak. For one thing, she'd had the wind knocked out of her. For another—

Well, not that she considered herself unattractive. Far from it. It was just that she thought of herself as good, solid country stock (if a bit on the runty side when it came to height). She'd learned in London that men liked women, period. A girl didn't have to be a variety hall showgirl to have a trail of fellows sniffing about. On the other hand, she carried a stone or two more weight than, oh, say, a Russian ballerina. It was a curvaceous two stones. Many men responded to her, appreciated her femininity. It was just that she wouldn't predict a wealthy, handsome viscount—and, in a glance, Mount Villiars was handsome without any immediate accounting for how or why—fresh from the Continent and beyond to succumb within the near instant of meeting her. Yet he kept staring at her, there was no doubt.

She made her best sweet-fluttering smile up into the shadows of his face—dark coloring, that was all she could be sure of—her fluster entirely concocted. Then he spoke, and her mouth came open.

"Are you al-l-l right?" The sentence—in a smooth, deep voice, rich—had the slowest, most rhythmic melody she'd ever heard out a man's mouth.

She blinked. What? She'd lost her train of thought. "I—um—" Oh, yes. "I'm fine." She tried to gather herself, while patting the back of her dress, brushing her skirts down over her rump. There was an odd little place at her low back where his gloved palm had pressed, the pressure having left a lingering sensation—the way, if one stared at a light, then looked off, for a few seconds one saw a luminous halo over everything else.

She said honestly, "Goodness, if you hadn't caught me, I'd have gone sprawling—"

"Yes. I'm so sorry I—"

"No, no, my fault—"

"Mine," he insisted.

"No, I wasn't watching—"

He made a nod, a kind of gracious bow of acquiescence that immediately contradicted itself: "My fault en*tire*ly." Again the slight protraction. "I hope I didn't hurt you"—there followed a kind of measured pause before he said—"unintentionally."

She giggled. The delay gave his apology a possible second meaning—indeed would he truly not mind hurting her, so long as he meant to? "My fault. I backed into you," she insisted, then found herself laughing. Nervously.

He stared. She took in what she could of his features beneath the hat brim, and for a moment all but wanted to take back the word *handsome*. His face was more . . . magnetic. Striking. Or perhaps *handsome* was the word, since there was not a pretty feature anywhere, his visage starkly masculine: strong, angular planes, an aquiline nose like the beak of an eagle though as thin as the blade of a knife, with a break at the bridge, a tiny deviation that drew one's gaze to deep-set eyes, with irises, she suspected, that even in full light would be as black as night.

She had the complete attention of these eyes: the eerie impression that he was aware of the smallest shift in her skirts, the tiniest lift of her shoulder. Yet he answered with calm, near stoic, detachment, "We neither one were watching. But you're all right?"

His voice. It was so low and fluid: mellifluous. Utterly mesmerizing. His slow vowels and syllables rang neat, controlled—it seemed almost incidental that they were so perfectly public-school British upper class he could have been a textbook example of the Queen's English well-spoken. While Emma found herself waiting for another example of . . . what? The odd hesitations in his speech? He paused, didn't he? Was it an esthetic? A compensation for a mild speech problem? For unease? Shyness? What? Where was the curious rhythm she'd heard at first? Or thought she'd heard?

And why were they still standing here?

Oh. "My, um—my pen," she said, holding out her hand. Only, of course, her hand was empty; she'd dropped the item in question. She glared down at the carpet. "It's on the floor somewhere, I think. I was looking for it when—"

He bent immediately—they bent together—but the pen was nowhere. Emma knelt, more and more discombobulated, half-wishing she'd stayed in her chair. The blooming pen had to be here somewhere. It was probably under the folds of his coat, which pooled so copiously it took over the carpet's center medallion.

What a coat. Its charcoal gray wool—no, as she lifted an edge by his boot, its fabric wasn't wool exactly. It was lighter, more supple somehow. Cashmere perhaps, though even that didn't seem quite right, not silky enough in texture. Ooh, la, his coat was fine. And, in point of fact, its hem, cuffs, and lapel—silvery white fur mottled with light and dark gray—weren't trim exactly. They were overflow. The coat was *lined* with the stuff: lined through and through with the softest, thickest, silvery, speckled fur she'd ever set eyes or fingertips upon. She couldn't get over the extravagance.

At least the money for the lamb, she could safely assume, would not be missed.

While, Oh, my lord, she thought, and, What animal? she wondered. She couldn't name the fur, so seldom did she see it. She couldn't stop brushing a finger, a knuckle into the hem or up underneath, ostensibly looking for her pen. All she found though—

She straightened up onto her knees immediately. "Oh, no." Ink. She lifted the bottom of the coat, the mark of her pen having been there: a black ink splotch the size of her fist on the fur.

"It will"—he said, as she hung on the low-voiced word while it seemed to take an eternity to leave his mouth—"come out," he finished.

"It won't. It's India ink." How on God's earth was she to fix his coat?

And why try? another voice asked inside her. The stupid sheep-murdering scoundrel didn't deserve a perfect coat: He'd certainly made a mess of her lamb's.

How annoying to find his stature, his speech, his face, his blessed clothes interesting, beautiful. When they should only serve to remind her of how difficult he was to contact, how hard it was to discuss with him any disagreement, how many times she had been turned away by others, his minions: how many people stood between him and anything he didn't wish to deal with.

Your nervy bum, she reminded herself. *Mung beans. Local squabbling.*

Then found herself being drawn upward by her elbows, his thumbs resting in the bends of her arms—and she knew it felt wonderful, despite herself. A capable, powerful man pulling her up to her feet, paying her so much attention. She was aware she liked it, and so was he. That was what he was watching; he was gauging her interest in him—

No, no, she told herself. The idea made her giddy to contemplate. The irony overwhelmed. The man she was going to take for fifty pounds by the end of the day seemed struck enough by her she could have worked him over for a hundred fifty. A thousand fifty. If she could have kept her own head long enough. If she had wanted to do it.

If the whole notion of taking him for anything at all didn't—for no explicable reason—suddenly, mildly unsettle her all at once.

They stood up, and his coat dropped back down around him with a waft of that warm, faintly Eastern scent. The fabric held a rich, spicy fragrance; frankincense, myrrh. While Emma was left to stare bewilderedly at the floor, a "stenographer" without a pen.

She murmured, "I—I'm the, um"—she actually stammered—"the, um, temporary amanuensis—"

He said nothing. For one uncanny second, she thought, He has difficulty with English. It's not his first language. Yet that would make little sense. Wherever else he'd been, he'd been raised up the road from her till the age of six.

She continued, "Provided by the bank, of course," she said boldly. "Since we understand your amanuensis was delayed." Now everyone thought the other had hired her, and gentlemen didn't dirty themselves, bless them, with discussions of filthy money when the matter had already been settled. She pointed toward her coat. "I, ah—I was just getting a new nib for my pen, when—well—" She couldn't think where to go with the rest of the sentence.

Behind her somewhere, someone cleared his throat, while before her the viscount's gaze remained steady. In the shadows of the brim of his top hat, he had the eyes of an Arab, large, heavy-lidded eyes, sad somehow, the whites glowing in his dark face: the eyes of a snake charmer or rug salesman who hawked his wares in the streets of Baghdad. Unfathomable.

As if to further the illusion, like a magician, with a turn of his wrist at the end of his black-gloved fingers, he produced her pen, worn nib up. "Yours?" he said. The question was rhetorical—a bass-deep assertion spoken so softly the word wouldn't have carried two feet: just for her.

"Aah." She blinked, opened her mouth, then could only answer, "Well." Still nodding her head, "Thank you." She took the pen, then attempted to smile sweetly, though her efforts faltered.

His face remained stoic, contemplating hers: keen interest without a hint of returned friendliness, not a speck. Though finally he said more than one sentence, a huge outpouring for him, and his speech demonstrated once and for all its odd cadence. "You are *all* right then, I take it? For a moment, I thought I had *mowed* you down. You seem perfect though, after all, no harm done *I* can see." He lingered over certain words, a rhythm that was almost predictable, like a kind of poetry. It was indeed some sort of speech impairment, yet it sounded beautiful to Emma. So beautiful she was half-afraid she might inadvertently imitate it.

She had to be careful as she answered, "I'm fine." Then she coached herself to a cheerfulness she didn't quite feel. "And I'll be right there." She indicated the table. "As soon as I fetch my new nib."

With that, she left him behind, walking at a good pace to her coat on the wall across the room, then digging into its pocket with a kind relief. Oh, she felt glad to be free of him, happy in fact she wasn't sitting near the man—

Then she was.

When she returned to the long table, she found the viscount—Stuart, she staunchly told herself—putting the finishing touches to his own arrangement: *You sit here. You sit there. Here, you take that chair.* He moved everyone down, including her, so he could seat himself between the bank's governor to his left and her to his right.

When he pulled out her new chair for her, Emma hesitated. Then sat, smoothing her skirts under her, feeling all the while that somewhere she'd completely lost control.

By way of explanation, he raised his shoulder, a small shrug. "I may as well"—he paused in that odd way he had—"sit beside the prettiest one here." He spoke his flattery less like a compliment, more like a conclusion he'd reached of unquestionable logic.

She couldn't figure him out, except that the word *unhappy* came to mind. When he sat—in her corner chair, as if he would remain at the sidelines of all that was about to take place—his movement seemed weary. He shed his coat onto the chair behind him, then crossed his legs as gentlemen could do, and as anyone less than a gentleman couldn't without appearing effeminate. He had quite the air about him, educated, cultured. And power. *Lord Mount Villiars*. And *your lordship.* She realized, in the near-reverent introductions—everyone was so ridiculously pleased to meet him—he himself never returned a smile, though it seemed more through preoccupation, melancholy, than from rudeness exactly.

In a casual remark from the deputy governor, she was surprised to learn that the viscount's power extended beyond money and position. He was "on loan" from London, having to return the next day "to vote." Emma was nonplussed to realize he'd taken his seat in the upper house—on the very opening day of the new session, as it turned out, full regalia, processions, the queen in crown and parliamentary robe, speeches, state coaches, the whole business. How unpredicted. No Mount Villiars had sat his seat in generations, let alone taken it seriously this time of year, when most members of parliament were still in the country, galloping with their dog packs, wreaking havoc on the local wildlife.

The newest sitting member of the House of Lords sighed lightly as dossiers and documents and papers came out.

Then never paid another moment's attention to her as a woman through the entirety of his business; flirtation over.

She realized, ten minutes into the transactions of the day, she was miffed. *Prettiest one here, indeed.* The only female was more like it. Perhaps that was it. He simply enjoyed possessing, like a sultan, every female within view. His lordship here certainly had the looks, money, and mien for it, odd, interesting stammer or not.

Meanwhile, she pieced together his story through the business proceedings. The viscount, whose father had died six months before, had returned from his travels to claim his inheritance, only to find his father's brother already had. The returning son and the College of Arms had brought the uncle into check, but not until there were double accounts and plenty of avuncular debt, all run up to the viscountcy, backed by the title's property and good name.

The genuine heir, beside her, was presently transferring a great deal of foreign currencies, converting other assets to cash, selling land, keeping them carefully separate from the mess of the estate.

All of which, theoretically, Emma wrote down in small, tidy unreadable symbols that she fancied looked a great deal like shorthand. If only these symbols had meant something, for she herself might have liked to think this story through again sometime.

It took half an hour for them to get down to the specifics, wherein Mr. Hemple, the bank's governor, cleared his throat and untied a big leather-bound folder. There was a stack of papers within it: loan notes to be signed. Mount Villiars was taking out personal loans, wary of enmeshing himself in the viscountcy's monies till his uncle's damage was sorted out and covered. The governor read out the content of a promissory note for fifteen thousand pounds sterling, no less, unguaranteed, extended simply in view of the returning Englishman's new title. Thus began a trail of papers, passed to the viscount's solicitors, who each read a sheaf as it came by them, then passed it round the table toward her, then the viscount himself.

As she handed him the first sheet, Mount Villiars turned toward her, tilting his hat up slightly to where she could see his dark eyes again (they had circles under them as if he didn't sleep well), and stared at her a long moment.

"Did you"—his pause—"get that?"

"What?"

"What Mr. Hemple said. About the loan being due."

"Yes." No. She looked down at her several pages now of gibberish. Happily, she was fairly sure no one around her knew shorthand either. She certainly hoped the viscount had a good memory—

Then she prayed he didn't.

He asked, "Could you please read me the *las-s-st*"—the esses stretched out, unhurried—"paragraph? I've lost my train of thought."

She wet her lips, stared at him, then down at the tablet. Her eyes grew hot. She could see nothing, not even her own scribbles. Think, think, she told herself. What had they been saying? She said what first came to mind: *"That the undersigned, Stuart Winston Aysgarth, the sixth Viscount Mount—"*

"That's not it. The date and details."

"Oh." She turned a page of scribbles and tried to remember. "On the seventh of April will hereby—"

"It was the tenth."

Emma let her dismay show, exaggerating it in fact. "Did I get it wrong?" she asked meekly. She scratched out a line, then jotted furiously. "I have it then. Go on. I have it now."

The viscount looked at her a long minute as he unbuttoned his frock coat—it was warm in the room—and leaned back against the rich greatcoat behind him draped over his chair. He said, "My secretaries have always used Pitman."

"I don't," she said quickly. The vest beneath his dark frock coat was surprising: bright blue silk. She stared at it.

He said, "I presently have two, who both had to leave unexpectedly." The information held no judgment, no accusation, yet Emma felt a little tingle of heat.

She forced a smile. "Good thing, then, I could be here."

He continued to stare, unnerving her with his silent gaze. Then he nodded once, looked back at the stack of papers accumulating before him, and let out a sigh strong enough to flutter the next page passed to him as it settled on top of the others.

The stack grew. The Viscount Mount Villiars, soon to be one of the richest men in England, was bridging the gap between the present and when the bulk of his personal investments, mostly in French francs and in properties being sold abroad, could be converted to English currency and his use. And ultimately, of course, till the viscountcy would be his alone, unhindered by questionable debt. He needed two accounts to do it, a personal one with the signature of Stuart Winston Aysgarth and one for his entailment with the signature of Mount Villiars.

Emma's eyes boggled at the numbers as she mentally tallied the flow of both across her portion of the table. The fifteen thousand pounds was the tip of it, a pittance compared to the whole. He was borrowing almost nine hundred thousand pounds, some of it just on his name, the rest backed by various properties, stocks, and assets.

Good, she thought. He wouldn't even notice fifty pounds gone missing in all these transactions. My goodness, were his finances complicated!

Better still, when he sat forward to sign the first of the documents, she watched very stylized writing flow from his hand, lots of loops, florid. Ha, she might have known! It would be easy to imitate; the fanciest always were. If this was it, she couldn't imagine what all the fuss was about.

After signing, however, he brought forth from the inside pocket of his frock coat a flat gold case, opened it, and took out a seal and stick of red wax. Well, of course, she thought. Two men jumped up to offer a flame for melting the wax onto the document. The bank governor won, offering an official-looking lighter of some sort, a bird with a flame out its bill. The viscount's gloved hand held the wax stick in the flame, his eyelids lowered as he stared down at it. The small light made a faint, rather satanic waver up over his severe face, offsetting the shadows of a deep brow and a hat brim.

For a moment, light played up into his face with its wide, clean-shaven jaw and high cheekbones. And Emma thought, oh dear, there was a certain type of woman, more the pity for her, who would not stand a chance against such a man.

Mount Villiars was romantically handsome, his face severe in its Anglo-Saxon proportion, if dark from coloring of peoples farther south. A sharply angled face, underlined by hollow and bone and coloring. Not to mention a bearing, an air about his tall, slender body. It made one wonder at the logic of nature that a man who already had so much should have this too—a stunning physical presence.

His dark eyes—even in good light as dark as Turkish coffee—blinked when wax splashed down: two small red splotches onto the white page. More drips quickly pooled into a bright bloodred puddle of wax. He covered this with his seal and pressed, rocking the instrument once.

Emma caught herself: Turkish coffee. When was the last time she'd drunk that? Ah, never mind; in London. But didn't old Stuart here embody every last rare thing, come to think of it, that was available in the wicked, old cosmopolitan place?

Done, she thought with satisfaction, as she stared at red wax hardening into an embossed salamander, the emblem of French kings, if she remembered correctly. (*Ah, Zach, where are you when I need you?* It was the sort of useless information he could have confirmed in his sleep—in a stupor, dead drunk.) In any case, she could easily do a reverse impression of the seal, and the viscount's neat, ornate handwriting was going to be a breeze to duplicate. She could already feel the triumph: the flow of his signature in her mind, its curve and stoke within her fingers. Aah, the old, talented fingers—

That was when he produced another thin box, this time silver. It was smaller, looking like an antique patch box, the sort carried two hundred years ago by the aristocracy when "beauty marks" were all the vogue as a way to cover facial flaws. He opened it, *click*, and there was what looked like . . . an ink pad. She frowned as he set this down and took the finger of one glove in his teeth, pulling. He removed the glove, revealing long, slender fingers on a large palm, fingers that turned up slightly at the tips, smooth, round, trimmed nails. He folded his graceful hand into a loose fist, extending his thumb, and pressed it onto the ink pad, then onto the document.

His thumb print in blue ink. Emma stared down at the first loan paper, blinking at how colorful it looked despite all the black writing, the colors of the Union Jack: white paper, red seal, blue thumbprint.

When she discovered herself to be glaring over it at the viscount himself, she made her eyes return to her lap. She jotted a few lines of nonsense, wanting to write, *Idiot, jackanapes, scoundrel, purely difficult, overcareful ridiculous man!* She stared at the tablet, while she tried to compose her own features. She kept glancing up though, more and more irritated.

He did the same thing, a thumbprint, on each page as it came before him, on both accounts, she herself having to pass most of the papers over to him from the string of solicitors and accountants who judged them as they came by: He signed, then sealed, then pressed a dark blue, impossible-to-counterfeit mark just below each signature. As he put his last thumb's impression on the last page, the sight of it made her so angry her vision blurred.

Could he *be* more troublesome? Could he make this any harder? She sat there fuming. How many obstacles had she come over? How many ways had she tried to get him to pay his debt? And now this. A thumbprint, which she couldn't possibly fabricate.

Think, think, she told herself again. How might she be able to? Whom might she know who could help her? First, though, she'd have to have an impression, the thumbprint. She could lay her white cuff over it, hope to take a likeness in wet ink. No, what a mess that would be, and it would bleed and lose detail. She could hand him something while his glove was off—

Right-o! Her cousin worked in Scotland Yard now. They did all sorts of things with fingerprints. She dropped her pen, then watched it roll as she realized, No, it was too round; she wasn't sure a fingerprint would lift easily from it.

Think, think, think!

She crossed her legs and shoved her tablet off her lap with her knee. But, no, that would be too soft. When she bent to get her dropped tablet, she found her cloth purse. Beneath everyone's line of view, ostensibly as she felt around for her tablet, she opened the drawstring, then rose up, noisily clattering out all the contents, dumping them. There must be something in there. "Oh, dear," she said and dived under the table to look.

Upside down over her skirts in the dimness under the table, she watched her own mirrored compact skid. Yes, that would do it! Hard and smooth.

The compact came to a stop in front of the far leg of the viscount's chair, a bit difficult to reach.

"I have it," he said above her.

Or she thought he was above her. They were suddenly both under the table. Together. He'd removed his hat. He hair was dark, much longer than was stylish, and curled slightly. Her heart leaped into happy rhythm. Oh, yes, your lordship, you get it for me, she told herself. But the dark under the table became interesting in ways beyond obtaining his thumbprint. It had something to do with the way his round, shadowed eyes fixed on her, looking at her till she felt the blood rise in her face.

She pulled back, sitting up in her chair abruptly, feeling

fidgety as she stared down at his wide back where it curved toward his shoulders. He was down on one knee—he had a true gallant streak, if nothing else. Or else a marked inclination to earn indebtedness from the hired help. Did he sleep with his housemaids? His laundresses? He was interested in her sexually, she would have bet money on it now. While she was only a secretary, for goodness sake. What was he doing, with all these long, heated looks?

Then she smiled to herself. *He was interested in her sexually*. When was the last time *that* had happened? Or, no, when was the last time it had happened, and she'd felt anything at all in return? There was the difference. Years! Though he was hardly her usual type. She usually went for the bad boys, the misfits and make-dos, the rebelliously wicked ones. Goodness, perhaps she'd grown up.

Then, no. As he rose back up into his chair, she remembered his mean letters, his refusal to obey the court decision, his dark, unsmiling glances—and she sighed inwardly at herself. No, thank you.

He offered her compact that contained sifted face powder out to her. In his gloved hand, his right hand. Along with it, he also deposited on the table in front of her: her pen, her tablet, a comb with a missing tooth, and yesterday's to-do list, which read neatly and boldly:

—feed Giovanni leftover lamb liver
—take old bread to church
—make ripped towel into monthlies rags

She blushed again, all the more annoyed because she could not remember blushing this much in her lifetime, let alone in a single afternoon.

Mount Villiars said, "I hope I didn't get ink on anything." He held his bare hand with the inked thumb up, out of the way.

Emma's tongue felt thick, her face hotter by the minute.

She muttered, "I'm so clumsy today." Ugh. Oh. She certainly was. She had botched this. All her trouble, all her risk, for naught. She couldn't make anything work. She hadn't been able to for four months now, and she was so frustrated by it—by *him*, this *man*—she wanted to wail, to stand up and overturn their blasted table, screaming. *Do you know what this miserable no-account has done? This* wicked *man, whom I am not the least bit interested in because I am done with wicked men and even reformed wicked men? Do you have any idea what a powerful one can get away with? And, the scoundrel, he doesn't even care! That's the point. They never do. Someone truly ought to teach Lord La-di-da here a lesson. . . .*

Oh, what a rant she had inside herself.

The stupid meeting went quickly from there. No wonder lawyers were willing to do him the odd favor. His financial life was producing enough work to retire the entire population of the Inns of Court. The last of the papers circulated, being verified and reverified; one of them was re-signed, resealed, and reimprinted. She crossed her legs irritably and actually kicked old Stuart once.

"Sorry," she said.

He looked at her again.

Which forced her to smile and say much more sweetly, "I'm so sorry. I didn't mean to kick you, your lordship." No, she'd prefer to throw up on him.

The next moment, he was standing, pulling on his glove. As he looked over at the bank's governor, he said, "I would like the matter tidied up by tomorrow?" His smooth voice rattled the words out perfectly, no hesitation. And though intoned as a polite question, neither his syntax nor his manner left it one.

"Tomorrow?" The governor, half-risen, all but choked. "We can't possibly—"

The viscount paused in pushing his glove down between two fingers, so as to focus all his desire to make a quick business of this into one furrowed look of deep, imperious displeasure.

At this unlikely moment, the word *vicuna* came to Emma. It was the name of the wool of his coat. While the fur inside it, which invisibly composed most of the garment, was *chinchilla*. Old words. Words she hadn't thought in a long time. Which meant, dear God, his coat cost more than the average piece of English real estate. And was so thick and double-bunny-smooth, where it brushed against her hand—Mount Villiars swung it up off the chair and down onto his arms in a single movement—she wouldn't have minded building a wee cottage on it, moving in, living there. If only she could have gotten him out of it first.

She must have murmured the word. "Vicuna." Because they all looked at her.

Then—as if a brilliant idea—the bank's governor said, "Your excellent references, Miss Muffin—"

"Miss Muffin?" the viscount repeated, looking at her.

"Molly Muffin," she said. Her idea of humor. She always used absurd names when she didn't use her own real, not entirely dignified one.

The bank's governor cleared his throat and began again. "Your excellent references said you also know how to do double entry bookkeeping."

Indeed. She had sterling references—some of them even real.

Years ago, Molly Muffin had done the bookkeeping for the bishop. And made him tea and hopped across the street for hot cross buns to go with it. She was actually better at bookkeeping than typing or taking shorthand, though that wasn't saying much. Her strong suit had been fetching the hot cross buns.

She sighed. She didn't want to stay up all night doing their bookkeeping for them. Let them get their bookkeeper to do it.

"You see, our bookkeeper is out ill till tomorrow. We

thought, *um*—" Mr. Hemple paused, then smiled. "If you could help us, Miss Muffin, we'd make it worth your time."

No, no. What could possibly be worth staying up all night—what it would take to get all they had done here today entered into their books—with a lot of numbers and papers? Emma said sweetly, "I have to get home to my aging father—"

"Surely, he could wait a few—"

"He has to have help: He's lame."

"But a few hours more, one way or the other—"

"And deaf."

"We'd pay handsomely." He hesitated, looking for an enticing amount that yet wasn't too much that he'd regret offering it. He settled on, "Four shillings an hour for your time."

Emma pressed her lips and looked up, not pleased. But the idea began to rattle around inside her head, *the books, the books*. She might be able to do something with them, alter them. Such a thing was more complicated than forging a withdrawal—though *not* more complicated than forging Stuart Aysgarth's ridiculous signature. No, unlike *that,* it was actually possible. Plus four shillings was a fine wage for a female, though they'd pay a male bookkeeper more.

She might have bartered. She was sure, under the circumstance, she could have bilked them for eight or ten shillings an hour; they were desperate. But such outright thinking for herself might have made her suspect. She bowed her head, looking at her hands, and nodded, murmuring, "How generous. I'm sure my father would appreciate"—she glanced up pitifully, almost tearful with gratitude—"new spectacles. You see, he's nearly blind as well."

From above her, the viscount asked in his slow, even voice, "How old is he?"—his tone so low, so soft, like the rumble of distant, harmless thunder.

She glanced toward him to see his arms folded, his hat brim low again on his head, his arms once more in his marvelous coat. It hung open. She was struck again by how interesting he was, how unexpected somehow. He stood squarely, erect. Though no older than she, it occurred to her, he was yet so much more world-weary somewhere.

There was something about him, something that said he was less gullible than the others, though neither did she think he was on to her. Just suspicious, less susceptible to sentimental ploys.

"Ninety-two," she answered, which was near the truth. Had her sheep-shearing father been alive, bless his soul, he would have been exactly that many years.

"Then it's settled," the bank's governor was quick to say. He stood. "We'll take care of everything and have your accounts functional by tomorrow afternoon. The larger cheques should clear by the end of the week." He smiled as the viscount nodded and turned.

And turned and turned. There was so much to him. It was not just his entourage and their shuffling of chairs. It was the man himself. His greatcoat had all the excess and drama of a Russian novel: As he buttoned it about him, tight and fitted, it showed the line of his shoulders, narrowing down his broad chest to a slim waist, after which it billowed to the floor. Then he tugged on a silvery cuff, ran a hand down a wide lapel. A coat Karenin would have worn in St. Petersburg. Emma had never been there, but she had read of the book. A coat out of a Tolstoy novel.

Which was from where, come to think of it, some of the funds were coming. Stuart Aysgarth, never mind the viscountcy, had land in Russia, among other places. He had lived there. It was the origin of his clothes, she realized, some of his tastes. A Continental flair with a whiff of the East.

The new English viscount adjusted his soft black kid glove down over a knobby ring underneath, then folded a gray scarf down into his coat. His silk cravat bloused more generously than anything an Englishman would wear and tucked down into a vest, she remembered, of blue silk, silk as bright as if cut from a nomad's tent. He was a piece of work, Mount Villiars.

She watched him pull himself together, preparing to embark out into a cold winter afternoon. Their separate ways, she thought and felt a little sad, his life so different from her own. Still, she felt an unnameable kinship, too. Or perhaps it was just sympathy. The new viscount wasn't a dandy so much as that he had become a foreigner. A stylishly sophisticated one, yet as separate from all the English understatement around him as might be, oh, a sultan. Or Tzar. A stranger in his own country, having claimed an estate in a shire where he didn't fit in with his neighbors for dozens of reasons, his un-Englishness only one of them. He had power here, but he would not immediately have friends.

And, given how often he smiled—he had not cracked one the entire afternoon—under the best of circumstances, she suspected, he had few enough of those. Minions, she thought again. He was a man to have minions, not friends.

She knew a moment of pity for him, compassion. There he was, so seemingly full of himself. The bigger they are, et cetera, she thought. Distant, unreachable.

Then, in a kind of whirl of manly shuffling and doffing of hats, he and his entourage made their hasty way out into the cold. Poor fellow, she thought.

The bank governor and deputy governor waited till the viscount had left before they brought out the bank's books, then laid them on the table in front of Emma.

She wasn't sure what she was supposed to do with them, but she opened them up. And—Jesus, Mary, and Joseph—it was like opening up a gift, an answer to a prayer. It was the ledger of all transactions of the York Joint-Stock Banking Company for the month of December. She glanced down the columns of numbers and format. Quite standard. She smiled, took up her pen. As the fill-in bookkeeper, they expected her to record the day's transactions, and in particular the viscount's, from a stack of slips and documents. The entries would be in her own hand!

She grew more excited. Of course she would have to write it in correctly on the present pages. Others might check. But it was a sewn binding, and she was a lovely seamstress. Her mind raced. The binding thread could be lifted in a piece; she could reuse the cord. As she wrote down the transactions, her own creativity on the spot amazed her.

She could undo the seam and lift out any old pages she chose—they were the variety that ran in sixteen-page sheaves to a quarto with plenty of unwritten bundles. And she would only need to replace one. Given time, she could alter anything in the bank's bookkeeper's hand, readjusting her own entries to suit. And here was the real beauty: She didn't need to take the money today. She found a cheque among the viscount's documents, one made out to Stuart Aysgarth for fifty-six pounds eight shillings. Close enough. She would invent a third account at a branch bank, one under a very similar name to Aysgarth, then simply sign the cheque for deposit into that account, put it into the bank's system, then pick the money up later. There would be nothing new, nothing in addition. Just a tiny, redirected amount, every ha'penny neatly accounted for in the bank's books and in Mount Villiars's accounts themselves.

Perfect, she thought. Then—again for no reason she could name—that little needle of guilt or regret or something visited her. This time, though, she admitted to herself part of it at least had to do with the unexpected attraction she felt. She would like to have seen him again, watched him—all right, talked to him again, as dangerous as that would be. The impulse was no more than a dim-witted womanly esthetic: the way, when entering a room of, say, a hundred men, she would have been inclined to ignore them all, then seen one, only one, so specific she could have pointed to him. That one. I would like that one to see me, to come over and talk to me, because of something in the way he slouches and the angle of his hat and the way his jaw muscle flexes when he chews his cheek.

The misfits and scoundrels. Yes, they were her sort—she'd taken up with two of them, married one, and had silent, biding crushes on another half dozen. Though *misfit* and *scoundrel* didn't truly describe a sitting member of the House of Lords. Not really. Not one who raced back to London to vote. Which left only Mount Villiars's dark demeanor. Was that what attracted her?

Dark. The word made her remember a bit of his history, then, she thought, no small wonder this man seemed to walk around under a pall of grief: His mother, when alive, had been an object of pity, her husband abandoning her the day after their wedding night. Quite the scandal, if Emma recalled correctly. What she did remember was that Stuart's mother had been unattractive, and that was a kind way to put it. Ugly Ana, they'd called her down in the village. Stuart's father, the eldest son of an impoverished viscountcy, had been pressured by his family to marry her; she'd been filthy rich. All the money over which Stuart and his uncle were arguing undoubtedly came from her side.

Village stories, rumors. It was hard to know what was true. Still, it seemed likely, given the evidence of his absence, that Stuart's father had stood in open opposition to the match, that he truly might have called himself "sold, a lamb to the slaughter," as rumor said. Though "lamb" wasn't how Emma had heard it later. *Horror* was more like it. Once he had money, the life he led in London made people pale; it made him notorious. When the infamous father had made one more trip to Dunord—to claim his offspring—the village had been glad to hear that the young man had been palmed off onto some public school: glad he'd escaped a father too busy leading a dissolute life to deal with his own son, only wanting him for the pleasure of taking him away from the wife he hated.

Emma tried for a moment more to remember how the old viscount had recently died. It was tragic, too, though such a minor event in her life, she couldn't recall the details. Still, there was tragedy enough here to make the little boy on the hill a quiet man, a circumspect man.

Pity. That was the reason she remembered. Conscience. If Stuart was arrogant and difficult, insensitive—whatever adjectives for him her anger wished to drum up—he was almost surely a ruddy sight better than his father. Not that that forgave him anything. His father was dead. He himself was an adult. He was responsible for his actions.

She looked down at the entries, blinked. Yes, there were many transfers to branch accounts into the nether regions in the English countryside. One more would disappear among them. Realizing how straightforward it all ultimately was brought release. Not quite the joyous sort she had hoped for, but nonetheless a sense of justice. For six weeks she'd been waiting for it. And here it lay in neat columns, entirely within her ability.

She looked up at Mr. Hemple sweetly. "I shall need a pot of tea and another nib if you have it." And while you're at it, get the shears.

She bent over the books, thinking, *Roll over, dear heart. I like to do the belly first. There you go. You'll feel lighter, perhaps even freer for it later. We both will. Let Emma lead you through the dance.*

Chapter 3

I have outlasted want and desire,
My dreams and I are grown apart;
My grief is all that's left entire,
The chaff and cull of a vacant heart.

—Pushkin, 1821, DuJauc translation, 1881

STUART waited at the front of the bank, inside his coach, himself wedged back into the far corner of the vehicle, the leather covering of the window beside him closed tightly to keep the wind from cutting through—the far carriage door hung open. He sat in his corner, his hat angled down, his fur collar and lapels snugged up about his neck and cheeks, his chin tucked into a cashmere scarf. He was cold, but somehow comfortable—another reason simply to sit here: He rested in the mild inertia of a man having found a cozy nook, a man who'd been in flight for months finally at rest, if only for the moment.

His coachman, as the fellow had climbed atop the carriage, had expressed grave concern that they should "tarry in this weather." "Five minutes," Stuart had told him. They'd waited twenty already, though of course the man was right. The Viscount Mount Villiars needed to be a dozen places, none of them here. (*Viscount Mount Villiars*. There. He'd thought the name without wincing. When he'd first arrived, when people had first addressed him as such, he would startle, then find himself warily looking about for his father. Good, he was getting over that.) The new viscount had a hundred worries, a thousand things he could do to avert half of them.

Still, Stuart sat in his corner, his eyes peacefully closed, waiting, vaguely mindful of inconveniencing everyone and everything else. He could feel the jostle of the footmen behind and overhead shifting on their perches, the carriage responding a degree this way, then that on its springs; he could hear the stomp of the horses, restless, rocking the wheels an inch forward, then back as the whip leaned on his brake: the tug of animals, human and otherwise, that knew all was ready, yet here they stood in the snow. Because their employer withheld the signal to leave on hardly more than a whim.

The snow was falling faster. Whenever Stuart cracked his eyelids, he could see its furious descent through the white-bright rectangle that was the open carriage doorway. He remained unimpressed. Yorkshire snow fell like tiny feathers, crystalline bits of nothing; it lay in mounds one could kick with one's feet. As if the clouds overhead were *duvets* ripped open, a continuing, downy earthward drift. The English knew nothing of cold—cold so blasting it could freeze the sea to a foamy frazil of churned ice and free-floating plates. Russia was cold. Finland was cold. Yorkshire was merely seasonal. It was winter, the perfect time to enjoy a fire, a shot of brandy, and the comforts of another body alongside one's own down under a mountain of covers, sweating and panting beneath them.

That was the goal here. A warm body alongside his own tonight. Warm and easy. *Easy* was very high on his list. He didn't have time for anything else. One night. Thank you, my dear. Good-bye.

Meanwhile, he considered it a very encouraging sign that his mind would aspire to such an end for even a night. After four months in England, he'd begun to think he might never again fret over anything beyond money and the complicated thievery of his uncle Leonard—every day revealing a new twist to it, every new kink removing Stuart, who should have been an extremely rich man by now, another degree from full use of his own money, except in dribs and drabs. Today should have helped, though it by no means solved the whole of his problems. Nonetheless, it solved enough that this afternoon Stuart did indeed aspire to fulfilling more human needs than those of mere coin.

Even as his body gave a faint shiver, he felt also a wonderful flow of blood elsewhere, low in his belly. It was faint, but thank God he could still feel it; it was full of promise. And all due to the woman inside the bank. He couldn't even remember why she took his fancy, but few enough Englishwomen did that he was willing to sit in the cold and wait till she came out. He'd reasoned that she had to eat, and there was no food in the bank—and that she had enough spunk in her and meat on her bones that he was fairly certain no one could starve her.

Meat on her bones. Yes, he liked that. He sat there, warmed by the glow of anticipation, trying to remember what else he'd liked. It was all rather vague. She was—

What? He had to think, then decided upon *cute*. All blond ringlets and Wedgwood blue eyes, sitting there in a dress that looked both in fadedness and fit as though she'd bought it at fourteen. Ah, a fourteen-year-old country innocent. Perhaps that was it; perhaps he was becoming more perverse than even he'd realized. This one was older than fourteen, of course, though he couldn't tell by how much. She was still youngish. And so helpful and self-effacing: so feminine. So impressed with him.

Aah. Stuart smiled inwardly and snugged down further into his coat. He loved to be impressive, especially to women. He closed his eyes again and waited, promising himself: *easy.* He didn't expect a rich, handsome fellow such as he to have a moment's trouble with a little amanuensis, especially if even half the nonsense about her ailing father were true.

In fact, though, his wooing did begin with the small trouble of having to wait almost forty-five minutes (his servants ready for mutiny), before the bank doors opened and spilled her out: a little trundling bundle in a hurry. Before she got very far, his footman waylaid her, directing her to the open coach door. She came right up and stopped before it, blinking, puzzled, her lovely pale face shining out from layers of wraps as snow filtered down onto her shawl-covered head. Her face, a little moon shining out, was round with creamy skin, more flawlessly smooth in the white afternoon light than memory had allowed. A blue-eyed, English pink face. This face scanned the interior of the coach, seemingly unable to find Stuart inside—it must have been too dark, he decided, with the window up and no lamp lit.

She jumped when he said, "Would you like lunch?" and he was sure he'd taken her by surprise completely. She hadn't been certain there was anyone in the coach at all.

Her answer was to stare, eyes widening, directly into the coach, searching, yet unable to locate him. He enjoyed her bewilderment a moment: his being able to see her completely, her knowing he was there but unable to identify his presence—though he was aware of the moment when she located the toe of his boot. It gleamed from the floor's shadows where his legs were stretched out. Her gaze tried to follow the boot up, but couldn't apparently, for she leaned, daring to peer closer, her expression a wonder of contradiction: startled, cautious, interested, utterly taken aback. Like a blinking deer staring down the barrel of something unknown, unthinkable.

"Lunch?" Stuart repeated, then remembered the English didn't eat lunch. Ah, he tried to keep the tedium from his voice as he corrected, "Tea?"

"No!" she said swiftly, straightening.

In the darkness, he raised his eyebrow. No? Why would a poor young woman refuse a meal with a rich man? A mistake; it could be corrected. With a rap of his gloved knuckle, he indicated the interior, tapping the drawn leather window curtain as he said, "Step inside."

"Goodness, no!" She stepped back. She looked of two minds: about to run, yet so amazed she was unable to move her feet.

Good. Amazement was good. "Then I'll come out."

He lifted his long body, bending down and forward, having to doff his hat to get under the doorframe. Bareheaded, he leaned out into daylight: And the girl took another step back, banging her rather generous, bundled bottom on the leather armrest of the open door. This startled her further, catapulting her forward just as he stepped down onto crunching snow. He caught her in his arms. She was light for all her layers—her worn gray coat, a plaid shawl inside it up over her head, another woolly navy scarf sticking out at the neck. Alas, as he held her, inside all her wintry clothes she squirmed like a bagged rabbit, scrambling to get free with nothing short of panic.

He let go rather than alarm her further, and she stepped backward fully three feet, as far as the edge of the door would let her, looking faintly horror-struck. He could see the rate of her rapid breathing in puffs of air before her mouth.

Now, Stuart was used to frightening women just a little. First of all, his presence—his height or the dark severity of his looks or perhaps a . . . a dourness, he wasn't sure, his glumness—took them universally aback. Secondly, his social position, especially when much higher as here, often did little to improve matters. Most importantly, though, he rather enjoyed frightening them: a little cat and mouse before putting them at ease. It gave him the upper hand, which he relished. But with this young thing it was slightly ridiculous. She'd seemed feisty enough inside the bank. Presently, though, she looked appalled enough as to expect he might murder her here on the street.

He told her, "I'm not actually that dangerous," then with a dry laugh added, "not to you at least."

She blinked, not at all reassured. She was shorter than he'd remembered. A plump, pretty little bumpkin. That was it. *That* was what he so liked: sweet, naive. Simple. Deeply impressed with wealth. Hardly a brain in her head. Yes, his favorite. Why, he hadn't had a country girl in—

He'd never had one, he realized. They didn't live in Paris, or else in Paris they quickly became something else. The variety who visited Petersburg didn't smell right to him. But this one, in the bank's lobby as they'd looked for her pen, had smelled of . . . he remembered: clover, English clover. How did she do that in the dead of winter? Oh, yes, this one was ideal. He felt such a pleasant response to her right here as they stood in the street, he wished he could simply drag her into the coach—

Not that he had to be primitive about it (though *primitive* had its appeal at the moment). Returning his hat to his head, he nodded once in deference to a woman almost a foot shorter than he, a woman with startlingly blue eyes as big as saucers. Gorgeous eyes. After her creamy skin, her best feature: the eyes of an angel. And—aha!—for all their fright, these eyes were curious. Another mark in her favor. Stuart mated best with women who possessed a high degree of curiosity, being an adventurer in that realm, to say the least.

"So where do you live, Miss Muffet?" he asked. On a tuffet? he wondered.

"Muffin."

"Muffin. Yes." Perfect. Delicious, edible. "So, Miss Muffin, where in York do you live?"

For all the politeness in his voice—and he did try to seem gallant, cordial—the enormity of what he asked became apparent to her. He liked that. He took back the brainless part. She was sharp enough, just unsophisticated. Her face realized immediately that he was asking not for conversation's sake but for himself, for the possibility—since lunch was apparently out—of arriving at her address.

Stuart wouldn't have dared ask a female of his own class such a forward question. Which allowed him to enjoy the astounded confusion that spread onto the girl's face, for he shouldn't have asked her either. But what could she do? Nothing. A man who was completely out of reach in terms of courtship or marriage had just declared his interest in calling on her. A man who was important to her employer, a man she didn't wish to offend. Easy, he told himself. Like picking off ducks from a pond with swan shot.

Her reaction fascinated him. She blinked for a second, then frowned, smiled hesitantly—a flicker—then winced. He enjoyed the wince, the little flicker of conflict, of virtue compromised. Her wince became a scowl, which in turn pressed her lips together. Her compressed mouth, almost despite itself, then turned up a tiny bit at the edges, a smile in spite of the unseemly context as she at last relaxed a little. She even seemed . . . almost relieved. (Relieved? Why? What on God's earth *else* could he have possibly wanted of her?) She bowed her head, hiding whatever expression might have come afterward on that remarkably open, responsive face of hers.

Stuart himself felt removed from his own emotions, while this woman clearly lived in the thick of hers: They flitted, one following the other so fast across her features, they changed too quickly to catch them all.

Then a surprise. A strong emotion made itself aware in *him:* He utterly loved the commotion he produced in her. He adored it. He found himself watching the air she breathed, the movement of her chest beneath her heavy coat, its rise, the little pause, then the letting-go of warm air in little clouds out her slightly chapped mouth. Her cheeks, where her shawl met her face, were turning bright pink. A lock of silver-blond hair escaped at one side, just one piece. She had a hole in her coat, a place worn through at the side where her arm rubbed against her full breast.

She was poor. Yet, despite the obvious advantages of

obliging him, she shrugged shyly almost in apology, as if she would very much like to accommodate such a fine lord but couldn't see how. Her fright had evaporated though. He had no idea what had become of it. Clearly, he'd been more reassuring than he'd realized.

Or intended, which made him laugh somewhere inside: at himself.

He watched snow gather lightly on her eyelashes before dissolving, making her lashes spiky as she smiled rather boldly up now.

No doubt about it, she was delightful: She went to speak and, instead, little clouds of condensing giggles came out. "Oh," she said and looked down, uttering more visibly nervous—literally—laughter; it came out in puffs. "Oh, I can't believe—my goodness—" Now that she understood what he wanted, she was flattered.

Good.

"I couldn't possibly—"

Bad. "Why not? Of course, you could." Could what? What specifically were they discussing? His heart gave a little leap.

Then she said, very kindly—and the kindness was the killer: the intended discouragement. "No. Though thank you. But really, no." When she laughed again, he wasn't misled by her laughter; she meant what she said. Yet somehow she found their exchange—perhaps even something larger, life itself—funny.

My Lord, he thought, she was like champagne. He wanted to drown in her minute movements, in all the ticks of emotion that came off her: tickle her, do things to her till she laughed herself into tears, till she screamed. "Why?" he asked. "What's the harm in saying where you live? I was only curious."

She looked up then, fully into his face. Her damp, pointy eyelashes were darker than her fair hair, though like her hair they were thick and curling. They lined her blue eyes, a pewter-dark emphasis. She had fine, arching eyebrows, a small turned-up nose, a little ball of a chin, with the hint of a second one under it, small, rounded cheeks as pink as roses.

She was round everywhere, he realized, soft-looking, yet very pretty. Pudgy-pretty. Like a little muffin, indeed. Not fat. Padded. She had just enough extra flesh to eliminate angles, to be all curves. Even in a few places where one might expect an angle on a female—her jaw, the knuckles of her round, little hands, her elbows—she had none.

For one split second, he felt a pang, such an urge . . . He wanted her, hang the cost or consequence. It was a marvelous feeling. Extravagant. Vivid. He wanted to drop his long, angular body—skeletal, hard-muscled—down onto her yielding flesh, press himself into her softness, drown there. All her easy curves seemed an answer somehow. As if by sinking into her, the pain and pinch of living could be eased away.

She watched behind her this time as she stepped more carefully back and around the carriage door. Then she slowly walked backward, giddily raising one hand. Stuart sidestepped to see her better and was rewarded with a little goodbye wave from a small, round woman with bright blue eyes. A cherub. A grown-up, female cherub.

"Thank you again," she called from ten feet down the street. She shook her sweet head, the ringlet at the edge of her shawl jiggling at her cheek. Oh, she was really too much.

"My pleasure," he answered and felt his mouth draw up, a faint smile, a rare sensation, his one eyebrow raising in surprise more at himself. He smiled. He couldn't think of anything that had made him smile in months.

At which point, she cocked her head, paused, then turned and bolted down the street.

Her hips rocked, loose-jointed, when she ran, a voluptuous little wobble that kicked up her legs and frothed her petticoats. Oh, he loved that. He stood there in the snow, staring, marveling, as she disappeared into a flurry—as if a white curtain whipped up, wrapped around her, then whisked itself out again, empty: gone.

He was left standing there, tapping his hat on the side of his knee, thinking, What the blazes had happened to *easy*?

"Your lordship?" It was his cheeky whip, the reins in his hand, leaning toward him from the driver's box. "Shall we go then?"

Stuart shot him a glare, then a pull of his mouth. "Right. As soon as you hop inside and get the woman's address. Don't come out till you have it." He narrowed his eyes as the man clambered down. "And don't lollygag. The horses need to move." It was a fact.

But it wasn't the reason the fellow hightailed it into the building. Though the man could be surly enough, he, along with the rest of the servants, feared any context that might engage their employer's wrath; they fairly much thought they worked for a monster, a tyrant. Alas, though Stuart was not proud of it, neither did he hold any illusions: There were times when they did.

His servants were not alone in worrying that the new viscount had sometimes near-terrifying similarities with the old.

The upshot of what Emma did by the end of that night was open an account on paper at the Hayward-on-Ames branch of the York Joint-Stock Banking Company. Hayward-on-Ames was a market town thirty or so miles from her own village, where she could travel with reason. John Tucker's sister, Maud Stunnel, had a tup that she and her husband just might possibly be willing to sell at a good price. Emma could go have a look and pass through the town without anyone paying much notice. Thus, she opened on paper, near the Stunnel farm, an account under the name of one Stuart Agsyarth, closed Y, open G, where she then sent through the bank draft for fifty-six pounds and change made out to Stuart

Aysgarth from some company, "Ltd," though signed with the slight difference. It was an old fraud, but a good one.

In a few days, once the paperwork had cleared, she'd collect her money on the way to the Stunnels' farm, a withdrawal, then close the account, ending the trail: a tiny pip in the financial fruit of Yorkshire banking that no one should even notice. And if they did, it would be too late. Though inking in the account took work—it took her all night—the rest should be clean and simple.

Less simple was the way, in the wee hours, she hummed as she sewed the binding of the bank's records back together where she sat alone (or almost, since Mr. Hemple was in the far office, waiting—snoozing actually—for her to finish) at the ailing, absent bookkeeper's desk. To accomplish her bit of chicanery, she'd had to replace a quarto of pages from the back. She'd opened the branch account "a week ago" in the bookkeeper's handwriting, adjusting dates up till today, after which the transactions were in her own hand, as expected. La la, she hummed to herself. This is all going so well, the binding going back in with nary a wrinkle, on top of which the viscount, irrefutably, finds me attractive.

The afternoon's small flirtation had been just what she'd needed, that extra bit she'd wanted. It had made her happy—even though good sense said it should make her cower: If the viscount ever laid eyes on her again, he'd recognize her. If he ever met Emma Hotchkiss, he could put her together with Molly Muffin. She might have worried, if any viscount in the past fifty years had come down into the village from Castle Dunord. But none had, and she doubted seriously this one would be the exception.

They all stayed in London. And even if this one did venture from the city, there was about him the family's tradition of pomposity that fairly well assured he would not mingle with the riffraff. Up to this point, the tiny village of Malzeard-near-Prunty-Bridge had never had anything to offer its English lords on the hill, and she was fairly certain it never would.

Which allowed her the luxury of fantasy: Emma Hotchkiss, a handsome viscount's mad obsession. Never mind that the real man was an arrogant fellow— who fully deserved what she and her nervy bum were in the process of doing. All that power, she thought, and here she sat, circumventing it. La-di-da, wasn't she something? While he was so sure he was . . . *dangerous*, wasn't that the word he'd chosen? So sure he was more in charge of those around him than any one man could be. Oh, what a mark he would make, so full of himself.

And what a delight he'd been to look at, speak to, smile at.

Emma laughed, closing the book. She patted it once, then scooped it up in her arms and hopped off the bench: on her way to take it to Mr. Hemple.

The bank, as it turned out, had for Miss Molly Muffin only the address of some temporary amanuensis service. Stuart cursed himself, for he had had the address for five days before he actually found the time to travel to it. By then, the service seemed to have gone under. Or that was his best guess, because its York address was that of an empty storefront, its window scraped of lettering and covered in brown paper so one couldn't see inside. He was flummoxed and none too happy about the dead end. But what could one do? Some things weren't meant to be. He'd find another pretty little country dumpling.

Though he dreamed of this one. Twice. Vivid dreams of how meltingly warm she'd be, a warm little muffin lifted from the snow. But, no, how foolish. He barely knew her—not at all, in fact—so it was something else . . . some yearning in himself he dreamed of. Another woman would eventually fit the bill.

Meanwhile, a pitiful fifty-six pounds disappeared from the final accounting at the York banking company, and no one could explain it. They told him *he* was mistaken, though he knew for a fact his investments in a South African mine had paid a dividend. He'd seen the statement, though could not now be sure he'd seen the bank draft; he'd sent what he had to his accountants weeks before. He had no idea what had become of it; he hadn't signed it.

He tried to let the matter go, but he couldn't shake the suspicion his uncle had intercepted one last cheque. By God, Leonard, if I can pin this on you, I'll see your thieving backside in jail. Fifty-six pounds. Honest to God, he thought. If his uncle was going to continue to rob him, he should at least make it worth the time in the gaol. And Leonard had promised. He'd said they were square. Even though they still argued over a few things he'd taken from the castle in Malzeard. He'd said the money was done. Now this? On top of everything else? For so little?

The puny amount niggled at him. It felt especially annoying in light of the fact that Stuart himself was having the bloody-damnedest time getting any sizable amount of money, unquestioned, from his own inheritance, free and clear of creditors, Uncle Leonard, and the law: his key financial problem since entering England. It was a slap in his face that Leonard would so breezily remove so little, and Stuart found himself wanting the stupid fellow's balls for it.

He called the sheriff, who offered his "complete cooperation," though that meant nothing since there was nothing to cooperate over yet: a cheque that only Stuart remembered. He wired the Boes South African Mining Consortium, Limited, asking them please to verify, to the bank and his accountants, they had sent him a cheque (which could take weeks, they wired back) and please to send notice if and when and where it was cashed (which could take months or forever). Dead ends, dead ends, dead ends. Stuart felt buried under all he'd begun that he couldn't bring to completion.

Then a stroke of marvelous luck that dropped his uncle, or so Stuart thought, directly into his hands.

While at a rural inn near a northerly village (where Stuart was dallying with the local baker's wife—he found himself lately with an unholy attraction for short, sweet-faced Yorkshirewomen, the baker's wife being the second woman in six days, though both were missing something which he hesitated to call *refinement*, yet that appeared to be what it was, for lack of a better word), he chanced to meet a fellow in the common room over ale who thought he knew Stuart. Or knew his name. Only it turned out *not* to be his name exactly. Agsyarth. The fellow was a teller at the local branch of a bank used by most of the farmers of the district. And then the branch turned out to be a branch of the York Joint-Stock Banking Company, and Stuart grew terribly interested.

It turned out, this small branch office had had a remarkable cheque come through—from a diamond mine company. Farmers didn't see such a thing very often.

"Diamonds! Can ye fathom that? Some bloke with a name similar to yours gets big fat cheques off his mines in Africa." The fellow shook his head.

Fifty-six pounds was a long way from fat, but Stuart talked to the man for half an hour about it, paid for all his drinks and dinner, then was at the bank the next day, laying a trap for Leonard, shoulder to shoulder with the local constabulary. He filed a complaint of criminal misconduct, intending to have the damned relative out of his hair for thirty years. Forgery. Fraud. Theft.

As it turned out, the cheque had been deposited, but the monies hadn't cleared the clearinghouse in Leeds—the London bank of the African consortium, he suspected, was dragging its heels, having been alerted to a possible problem. Stuart wired them to let the cheque go through in hope of catching the culprit when he picked up the cash.

At which point, it became a simple matter of waiting. The sheriff's office was across the street and down one block from the bank. A messenger was set up to watch and fetch the sheriff at the appropriate moment. When Leonard arrived, Stuart and Sheriff Bligh (the perfect name!) would be ready. Stuart himself, very quietly without so much as a valet, took up residence in the only hotel—of five rooms, three of which he rented just so he could have peace and quiet on either side of him—on the only high street in Hayward-on-Ames, the town where the branch bank held the account.

Then, bliss of pure blinding bliss—a sure sign he was in God's grace—the third day of Stuart's stay at the hotel, while sitting in the lobby, who should walk in but the lovely Miss Molly Muffin, full of smiling good humor, replete with bouncing blond curls—more of them than last time dangling out from the same plaid shawl she used to protect her head.

At first Stuart thought, no, it was wishful thinking. Because she somehow didn't look herself. Her clothes were newer, coarser. And she had about her—the way she walked, nodded, chatted cheerfully, inquiring after a room—a kind of indomitable . . . confidence, yes, that was the word. Molly Muffin here wasn't self-effacing for a moment, but rather was all bustle and aplomb in a way that simply hadn't been there the last time he'd seen her.

Still, beneath that familiar gray coat with a sturdy navy wool skirt rippling out, was the unmistakable swish and swing of a most singular bottom.

As Molly Muffin, no other, registered there for the night, Stuart nearly dropped his newspaper. But didn't. Instead, he watched, holding his Monday *Times* up just enough to stare around its edge. He watched her shed her coat in the warm lobby, then bend over the registry book, her glorious backside outlined in a navy skirt that ended upward in a striped blouse. Beneath the skirt, even more out of character, she was wearing boots. Large, gum rubber boots so oversized for her proportions they suggested they belong to someone else: a man. Which made Stuart all but rock in his seat, until he told himself *her father's*. They belonged to her blind, lame, deaf father.

When her perfect backside swiveled around and made its way toward the stairs—he would be galled later to remember—he actually had to still the impulse to rush after her. Or at least rush up to the concierge and find out if there were a place, anywhere, that had flowers this time of year in the country, a hothouse. Send that woman six dozen something-or-others that smell . . . that smell at least as good as clover.

Even as a frown descended deeply into his brow, as the print blurred before his eyes, one part of his imagination could still see huge, surprising bouquets of hothouse roses or forced tulips or lilies or fragrant narcissus or all of them. A card with his name. An invitation to dinner, since—what a coincidence!—they were staying at the very same hotel. He would approach her again, this time with more flourish. *Your humble servant*, bowing his head, removing his hat. *Yes, you're welcome for the whatever-they-turned-out-to-be flowers. Yes, yes, so beautiful, so unusual in winter, lovely gesture. So perhaps dinner—*

Stuart's daydream stopped here, because his frown had deepened to the point of crimping his face till the blood beat in his cheeks. Anger, such anger rose up as he considered the possibility:

Why was the woman who had been taking dictation at the bank in York—where his fifty-six pounds had disappeared, where she had done the double entry bookkeeping for the day—why was she suddenly here exactly in the strange little village where the cheque had turned up? What kind of a coincidence was this?

He remembered the baffling, papered-over window of her reputed employer.

He remembered, before that, standing in the street, while wondering what on God's earth else she might have thought he'd wanted from her. Then her relief when she'd realized: only sexual favors.

Though, alas, now another possibility for her befuddlement materialized: guilt. Fear.

And for good reason. She was right to worry.

Stuart tried to squelch his fury, tried to imagine a rational explanation: Why would a total stranger, a woman—if she had, though he kept telling himself, surely it was a mistake, but still, if she had—why take him for such a paltry amount? He could think of nothing, no reason. All that would come to mind were the many punitive measures with regard to this woman that would make him feel much better about the whole situation. My God, he thought, if she had manipulated him and his already terribly tangled finances . . .

He sent a note to his own messenger stationed at the bank. It read:

If a woman comes to draw on the account, tell her the money will be ready the following morning. Delay her, then report to me. Tell the bank they may give her the money when she returns for it tomorrow. I emphasize: In the instance that a female arrives to make the withdrawal, do not go to the sheriff without speaking to me first.

Chapter 4

There is in human nature, generally, more of the fool than of the wise, and therefore those faculties, by which the foolish part of men's minds is taken, are most potent. Wonderful like is the case of boldness . . . a child of ignorance and baseness . . . [which] nevertheless doth fascinate, and bind hand and foot, those shallow in judgment, or weak in courage . . . and wise men, at weak times.

—Francis Bacon
Essays, "Of Boldness," 1625

EMMA arrived on the first Monday in January in Hayward-on-Ames, where she registered at the hotel down the street from the bank so she'd have a place to change. There, she went directly to her hotel room, where she padded herself out in a pillow, dropped a huge dress over herself that she'd borrowed from the church collection for the needy, tucked her light-colored hair up under a gray wig, then slipped out the hotel's service entrance: off to the bank on behalf of Mr. Stuart Agsyarth, her employer, who had sent her along with all the proper paperwork to withdraw what was to be her retirement benefit—fifty-six pounds eight shillings—then close out his account for him. For fun, she even signed a jolly good facsimile of the viscount's own signature, except for the G and Y, as a kind of joke.

The whole thing didn't go quite as smoothly as expected, however. At the bank, first the teller on the other side of the grid told her, Fine, thank you, come back tomorrow. He'd have the money ready then.

What? she asked. No, no, this wasn't the way a bank worked.

He claimed she was missing a paper.

No, she wasn't. Which one? she demanded.

Oh. Well. Yes. He reconsidered. It was simply that the withdrawal had to be put on a list of transactions to be run, by telegraph, through the parent bank in York. Some sort of preliminary approval. Again, he said, come back in the morning.

What a lot of bumfodder. No, sir, she told him, she wasn't waiting till any morning beyond this one, thank you. She was having the money today.

Looking a little uneasy, he said, Well, in that case. He could put in a request of urgency. He could perhaps have it within a few hours.

No, she wasn't waiting any "few hours" either. It was her money. Emma knew for a fact, from having reviewed dozens of such transactions in the books in York, that she had all the right paperwork, and that it entitled her to her money immediately. What, for goodness sake, was the world coming to? she thought. How did anyone of less resolve than herself battle a simple bank teller these days?

He hemmed. He hawed. He consulted. She did the same, loudly asking the tall, long-faced fellow at the window next to hers if he put up with such shenanigans. When Emma turned to ask a similar question of the nosy, balding young man who stood behind her, looking over her shoulder, the teller interrupted, actually threatening to have her removed.

"I beg your pardon?" she said, leaning into his grid. "If you lay one hand on me, I'll call the sheriff myself."

"Sheriff?" he said, his enlarged eyes—he wore thick spectacles—blinking behind their glass lenses. He frowned deeply, in at least two magnifications, then said, "No one is supposed to call the sheriff."

Well, good, she decided. Come to think of it, she didn't want the sheriff either. Bring on the bank's governor.

Local branches didn't have a governor, it turned out. Then bring on whoever was in charge, she insisted. Oh, dear, this popped up both heads from behind the two narrow wooden cubicles on the far side of the customer counter. Two more men, both tall, one with a thin face that bore a droopy mustache, the other with heavy-boned features on which hung pouchy cheeks, came around their cubicles toward her.

It took another half an hour, but in the end Emma battled three moronic men at the little country branch of the York bank, all of whom for some reason thought they could brush off a gray-wigged old lady until they were in the mood to give her her money; and won. She rode to victory on the coattails of the morning postman who arrived with a handful of business for them—the pouchy-cheeked man immediately started going through the bank's mail, as if to emphasize how unimportant was the present discussion. Happily, though, the postman took over on her behalf. He himself, he said, wagging the next patron's morning post at them, was always able to withdraw his own money the same day—the same minute—he asked for it, provided there was enough in his account to cover the withdrawal. Why else would someone use a bank at all? To tie up one's money from oneself?

My point exactly, she said. Thank you very much. I will take my money now please.

The fellows on the other side of the window grate all exchanged the exact same worried look, passing it from one to the other across their very different faces—from the small, thick-eyeglassed teller to mustachioed Mr. Thin-Face on to Mr. Pouchy-Cheeks, who even stopped tearing open letters long enough to make a fretful grimace. Then the morning's post distracted him and Mr. Thin-Face, leaving the large-eyed, bespectacled teller alone to deal with her. He hemmed and hawed some more, looked plaintively over his shoulder.

Then gave her the money.

The whole business took more than forty minutes. Men, Emma thought to herself. Always thinking they were in charge, being their usual batch of idiots.

Still, as the teller counted out the money and passed it under the grate, she had to restrain herself from doing a little jig.

There was some further mix-up. The account wouldn't close, theoretically from some sort of paperwork problem again. Only God knew what was wrong. She doubted seriously it had to do with anything on her end in York, especially given what a mess these folks had made of a simple withdrawal. It didn't take two seconds, though, to realize that all she had to do was abandon the idea of closing the account. It wasn't as neat, but who cared? With men like these crossing all the wires, no one would ever trace anything to her anyway. She received her fifty-six-plus pounds in cash, in fivers and change, as requested. She felt jubilant as she left the bank!

It was more money than she'd seen at one time in twelve years.

As she sashayed back to the hotel, pink-nosed from the cold, she grew more and more cheerful: her hands deep inside warm pockets full of money. The victor. A woman on her own who could handle herself, the world, and any man in it; she didn't need one.

For the first time in her life, she felt sure of that. And glad. She needed no Zach to protect her. No John Tucker to offer help. No father to support her or insist she marry the wrong fellow. No no one. Just Emma herself. What a wonderful zing the idea put in her step.

At the door to her room, she had trouble with her key, but then it gave. She was relieved to step inside and yank off the itchy wig. She caught a blast of heat—someone must have been in to stoke the fire. What a nice hotel, she thought. Perhaps she should stay for a nap. In a hurry to be more comfortable still, she immediately hiked up her skirts to uncinch the belt that strapped her old-lady-pillow belly to her.

She was standing there, leaning more or less backward against the door for balance, two wads of skirt tucked into her armpits, her petticoats above her bosom, while she attempted to see over her blasted breasts that were so large they got in the way of pretty much everything, trying to undo the belt buckle—

The buckle gave just as a sarcastic voice from nowhere said, "Oh, *most* attractive."

Emma leaped an inch straight into the air, falling back to clonk her head on the door. "Sw-swee'Jesus—" she breathed and scrambled around. *Out of here!* It was all she could think of. *Le' me out!*

The voice though—soothing, low, with a familiar rhythm to it—mollified her. First it laughed, a deep, slow chuckle, then said, "You are truly something, do you know that?"

Well, yes, she did. Carefully, she turned around, her hand still on the doorknob.

The voice cautioned, "That's a good girl. Don't run." There was a pause, possibly a snort. "I'd only catch you: You run like a three-legged rabbit. I'd have you before you were down the hall."

She jerked, blinked. A three-legged rabbit? Was that an insult? It wasn't a compliment. And have her? She very seriously doubted that. She had a ten-foot start, and he—for it was *a he* up there under the shadowed canopy of her high hotel bed—looked very settled in. She could see the sole of one boot, his foot on her bed.

Nonetheless, it gave her a start, her heart unwillingly swelling up into her throat, to realize she was staring at a person here in a room that was supposed to have been empty, no one in it but her.

The shadowy shape made no aggressive move, while she tried to comprehend, heart pounding, what someone might be doing here, threatening to chase her: a man, a long man with one leg extended, one knee in the air, his other boot sole on the counterpane. Or, no, his tall, black boot—glassy smooth leather oiled to a high gloss—was on his own coat. And that was when her heart sank back down so suddenly and so low it made her stomach flip over.

The Viscount Mount Villiars's coat lay on her bed, the viscount himself on it, she was fairly certain. The coat lay discarded carelessly under him, shrugged off, crumpled under one leg. Stuart Aysgarth sat with his back on her pillows on his coat's fur lining, a silver white run so dense it crowded in on itself there in the shadows, fur so thick it wrinkled in places.

Emma quietly turned the doorknob behind her.

He reiterated, "Truly. Don't run. I'd have you so quickly, it would knock the breath out of you, and I'd rather your breath were in you at the moment. We must talk."

She pulled a face. *Ran like a rabbit* indeed. *Knock the breath out of her.* Not likely. Then she remembered, *her nervy bum.* She hated this man. No, she wouldn't run; she'd have him thrown out. What was he doing in her hotel room? Where was the concierge? Whom did she call to have him ousted?

From under the canopy, as if they were having a nice chat, he said, "And I'm quite struck by the bounce and swing of you, if you took offense."

Which she did. Bounce indeed. She didn't bounce. She ran in a very ladylike manner, with a slight, unavoidable wiggle of hips having to do with her being a girl.

"I'm struck by *you,* your movement, your demeanor, what appear to be your *ha*bits." That interesting low-voiced pausing again, that left her waiting for each stupid, deep-voiced public-school syllable as it came out his mouth. "Most attractive. In truth." As if she might not believe him, he pressed his backhanded compliment further. "Sincerely. You are quite attractive. Even in that tentlike frock."

He sat forward to rest an arm over his knee, which put him into better light. It was he, hatless, handsome, dark, with those round, sad eyes and his mesmerizingly quiet voice. Dear God. Emma squirmed, fingering the smooth-carved glass doorknob behind, in turmoil as to what to do, while he looked her over, up, then down.

"It's simply," he explained, "that, as a means of locomotion, your running isn't very effective. Please don't do it. Just stand there and tell me why you would want to rob me of more than five hundred pounds."

Hundred? She almost blurted "fifty-six," but didn't. No, she wasn't falling for that one. Yet he looked earnest. Hundred. Five *hundred* pounds. She shook her head, as if to make sense of the number. She flushed. She blushed. She couldn't account for all that was going on inside her. The remarkable thing was, when she finally found words, they were so perfect. She said with utterly heartfelt innocence, "I didn't."

"Ah, you did, you see." He leaned further forward, reaching across himself—he was left-handed, the only part of his signature that was a challenge at all to duplicate—to unfold the edge of his coat.

In a dip of fur lay a wad of banknotes. A lot of them.

He continued, "You sent several cheques through in the morning's post, all drawn on the York Joint-Stock Banking Company itself, no clearinghouse, so they had to cash them. Rent, you see, from my local tenants. The only cheques I happened to have with me. Lord, but you were difficult. If you had only given me a day, I should have run much more money through. But there's no hurry, I suppose. This is a nice beginning. Anyway, *you* sent the cheques, as it turns out, sneaked them somehow from my accountants, so far as I can tell, then ran them through the bank, which delivered all this to your room just now, as *you* instructed. Lovely little account you set up for us, Miss—"

He paused and consulted something. Gad, he appeared to have the hotel registry book on the bed at his hip. He ran his finger down a page, then continued. " 'Peep,' is it, this time?" He laughed. "Not enough courage, I would presume, to make your first name 'Bo'? Alas." He shook his head with genuine remorse. "No, only Mildred. Lovely. Mildred Peep, distant relative to Molly Muffin. What is your real name?"

Emma couldn't open her mouth, even if she had wanted to.

"All right, don't say. But thank you. I honestly never would have thought to run my money through this new account, if you hadn't. In fact, I wouldn't have known how to set it up. I owe you so much. In a blink, you have solved a problem I have been working on for months without half your success. Thank you, abundantly, whoever you are."

He shifted to his side, swiveled, and came to the end of the bed, dropping his legs over the edge, putting him and her within four feet of each other, in good, clear daylight.

Lord, he was better-looking than she remembered. It had something to do with leaving behind all his furs and gloves and hats. Just himself, slim, muscular. He wore no frock coat, no vest, just a generous, starchy-white shirt, his dark cravat loosened, buff-colored trousers. His stiff collar was unbuttoned, open at the neck. He'd certainly made himself at home. The heel of his black boot kicked the bedframe as he studied her. *Clack. Clack-clack.* Even his long, loose-looking legs hadn't length enough to reach the floor from the high bed top.

She licked her lips once and mumbled, "You're welcome." Then realized, frowned swiftly, and said, "What? No, you're not. You can't—You'll—"

He shook his head, holding up his hand. "Tut-tut, no complaining. I only ran half what I need through. You didn't give me time for more." He laughed. "My goodness, but you were tough at the bank today. You had them running in circles. Me, too, once my messenger came back with the news. You are fierce, do you know that? A tiger."

The bald young man, she thought, the nosy fellow behind her. He'd disappeared at some point. Oh, criminy.

"Anyway," said the viscount, "I must put through a few more cheques, because five hundred isn't quite enough, even though"—he clicked his tongue in mock sympathy—"it's going to make you look like a bigger thief still. A shame, but I need the money. *C'est la vie*." He shrugged, then shook his head in honest appreciation. "It's so much simpler to cash them this way, isn't it? As this other fellow? And no one says a thing. It's even my signature."

Emma blinked. Oh, fine. She put her hand to her mouth. She felt dizzy, faintly nauseated.

He made a gracious nod. "I simply can't thank you enough. I've had a devil of a time with the flow of my monies up till now. I think you've f—" Did he start one word, then in a blink change to another? If so, he did it so quickly she couldn't be sure.

"—solved the problem."

The small shifts. The protracted vowels. Emma would think she heard them, then not. They remained missing long enough that, each time one came up, it seemed new, unexpected. His speech flowed over them.

With perfect lack of logic, or care for personal safety, she stood there, hand to mouth, heart in throat, hanging on the possibility of more words out this peculiar human being's mouth, wanting the cadence of them: The strange poetry—the personal song—of an adept, quick-witted adult in control of a stutter.

There was no awkwardness; it was fluid, in fact. He didn't even think about it, she suspected, so perfectly in harmony he was with it, like riding a bicycle. It was why it was so hard to discern, why it was so hard to pinpoint the "country": It was his own personal "foreign" accent.

When he crossed his arms and grew quiet, just staring at

her, she took matters into her own hands. "Listen, Stuart—" she began.

He cut her off with a snort—it could have been humor or not; it was certainly startlement. "Stuart?" He brought his boot to his knee and gave it a light slap. He flexed the ankle and stretched his calf. "Yes, of course, you'd know my given name. You've signed it often enough."

"What do you want from me?" she asked.

He thought a moment. "Well, for one thing, that you stop using the account. I'm going to be very busy with it."

She closed her eyes. Oh, God. She let out a long airy breath, resignation. "All right. I already had. But you truly shouldn't—"

"Stop complaining. How did you know how to do it?"

"Do what?"

"Make it work? Fix the books?"

"I used to do it in London. Years ago." When she saw the look on his face—he was interested!—she said, "Oh, no, don't imagine you can extend it in any way. In fact, you must close that account. It's a nightmare waiting to happen. They'll catch you."

"Actually, it is probably you they'll catch."

"Perhaps. Though only if you're careful and quick. Look here," she said and let out a breath. "The only reason what I did worked was because it was small. If you bilk your account for large amounts, it will become an embarrassment to the bank, and they'll put private people, private money behind finding the culprit. What I did can't bear that kind of inspection."

He tilted his head at her and said, "You know a lot about 'bilking banks,' as you call it, don't you?"

She only rolled her lips together, making a line of her mouth. She wanted to say no, but the answer was obviously, sadly yes. She said nothing.

He likewise simply contemplated her for a moment. Only

God knew what was going on behind his large, dark eyes. He had thick, high-arching eyebrows, black slants that began at the brow bone to rise over deep sockets to an outward angle, before a quick downward bend. These gave his face, even at peace, she suspected, the perpetual air of frowning. They went with his thick, kohl black eyelashes, which outlined the roundness of his eyes, eyes set deep to further the impression in his face of dissatisfaction, if not outright anger, and sadness, melancholy: Though all of it could be an illusion of facial structure, the mere set of his features, as could also be the look of keen intelligence in his peculiarly attentive manner of speculation. His eyes looked sharp, savvy, emphatic, dramatic—their whites snowy white, their irises Moorish black.

These eyes seemed to come to a decision. They blinked, as he tilted his head, and said, "I want your help."

"Help?" She laughed nervously. "With what?" Thinking he meant the account, she answered her own question. "Bamboozling the British banking system? I wouldn't know how. I'm small-time."

"No, I know how to do what I need there, thank you. And I'll finish up quickly, as you suggest. Very kind of you to point that out. But, no, I need help with something a little more delicate. Were you always?"

"Was I always what?"

"Small-time."

She looked at him, blinked. "No. I was in on the Big Game half a dozen times, played small parts in it." To hear it out her mouth was shocking. The admission of it. But also—more so—the small, old note of pride was still, inappropriately, there. Few had ever played the Big Game. It was the cream of confidence games; it took capital, experience, and skill. Zach had known it, run it—and nearly gotten them all killed the last round, seen most of them arrested, people shot, Emma one of them, and his own sister had died in jail.

"The Big Game?"

Why was she saying this? It was his blessed eyes. The eyes of a priest, she decided. They just concentrated on you, implying the patience of Job, the understanding of a saint. They held no judgment, while they implied they could see right through you, so you may as well tell the truth.

The truth. Well, there you had it, Emma thought: Confidence games were stupid. Pride indeed. There was no glamour to them. Talking about them to anyone who thought there might be was like talking to a tourist at the Tower of London, showing him where queens and archbishops and earls had knelt while having their heads cut off.

"The Big Store," she explained. "The Wire. It has a dozen names. It's complicated, and you run it with a lot people, usually, for a lot of money, which inevitably makes it extremely dangerous. People get upset over losing small fortunes and downright murderous over large ones." She shook her head. "I'm out of it now and glad. It was an unnerving way to live. I haven't done it for a dozen years."

His expression, though, had changed. He'd sat up straight, not properly put off at all. "London," he repeated. "How exciting for you."

"Not exciting enough," she said and rolled her eyes.

This won another rare enough laugh out of him, a dry, short burst. "And started up again: on me." He shook his head. "My dear," he began, "my uncle, whom you are aware of, took some things from my house that I—"

Ah, the uncle. This time, though, Emma was already shaking her head so vigorously, Mount Villiars knew enough to shut up. There was no point in continuing to describe what he wanted from her: She was having no part of it. Just in case though, if her unspoken refusal wasn't enough, she put it emphatically. "I won't do it. I can't. Never again. Not ever. Not for a million pounds sterling."

She met his gaze levelly, letting him see she couldn't be manipulated. She'd said as she meant it: a million ways, no.

"Fine," he said.

She let out a sigh of relief. She'd stood up to him, and it had paid off.

He hopped off the bed and came forward, grabbing hold of her arm. She was startled, then puzzled as he took her sideways so fast she could barely keep her balance. And there was that smell again—of the Orient, faintly citrusy, lemony, perhaps bergamot—so slight, she couldn't pinpoint it, yet very pleasant, masculine. Clean. Him. As suave and civilized as his coat. And in direct counterpoint to the fact that he lifted her by the arm so high, she was on tiptoe to stay in touch with the floor.

"What the—" She tried to twist away.

He had quite the grip, this smooth, loose-limbed Londoner. Cool as you please, while turning her, walking her backward, he reached to his neck and unknotted his cravat. It slipped easily against itself, then a little *zizz* of foulard silk as he yanked, pulling it through the fold of his white, starchy collar. It jerked free, loose in his hand.

"Oh, no!" Emma understood and started to fight.

She bucked. She jerked. She bent over, folded, tried to back out of his grasp, all to no avail: His grip on her was vaguely akin to that which she put on a sheep when she wanted to mark it with hot pitch after clipping. They wrestled earnestly, strength for strength. What she lacked in power she made up for in wiggle and squirm.

Inarticulate to the end, Emma managed the identical phrase again, when he scraped a chair out, a small one that had been pushed under a corner writing table. "What the—" Which in no way expressed her confusion and fear as he thrust her into it.

What the, indeed. It was obvious the next second what he was doing. And that she was losing their battle on every front.

"I'll scream," she threatened as he took her wrists behind her.

"Do. I'm sure the sheriff, or whoever comes to help, will

understand that I had to subdue the larcenous Miss Muffin or Peep or whoever you are"—that dry laugh again, which she definitely didn't like—"in order to detain her for arrest." He tsked. "With all that money sitting there, why, I'm appalled."

"You can't—*oofm-mm-m*—" She fought, more for air than anything else, as a whole noseful of that smell came up against her face: He lashed her hands to the chair's lattice back, bending over her from the front with her cheek and nose smashed up against his chest. He literally lifted her and the chair, teetering them both back onto two legs, her own legs off the ground, holding her against him as he applied the cravat in back.

Round and round, he wrapped her wrists to the chair with silk. It happened so quickly that it was over and done, then he turned her, letting the chair's legs come forward with a sharp enough clap that her jaw snapped shut.

He stepped out of sight.

"This is not going to help your cravat, you know," she told the near wall. Where was he?

He laughed from somewhere off to her right, just out of her line of vision. "What happened to the sweet, yet now somehow insipid, Miss Muffin?" he asked, then snorted. Approvingly. Perfect. A miscreant who liked to tie "tigers" to chairs.

"Your neckcloth will never tie properly again," she insisted.

"Not at my neck. We'll save it for your wrists. Our extra little plaything."

She twisted her mouth. He was only trying to scare her. She turned this way, then that, trying to find him over alternating shoulders. Nonetheless, a shiver ran through her that couldn't quite shed the word *plaything*. "This is *so* unnecessary," she said. "I *told* you I won't use the account. I'm done. It's yours. I can't help you with the rest. I've lost my nerve, among other things. And gained my head, my good sense." It sounded so reasonable. Why wasn't he listening?

She could feel him behind her, busy, as she caught a glimpse of the toe of one boot. It put him down on one knee.

Pressure and tugs meant he was threading the neckcloth through the lattice better, wrapping it, affixing her to the chair as securely as a goose being trussed up for Christmas dinner. Then—oh, fine—she felt his hand grab her foot, the ankle of her muck book.

"Ugh!" he said suddenly as if he'd grabbed a snake. "These are terrible!" And, like that, he yanked both off. She was suddenly in her stocking feet. Worse and worse.

He took her foot, then the other. He'd found something—a ruffle off her own petticoat, because she recognized the quick pop of stitches releasing in a path around her, when he ripped off the second piece—with which he bound her ankles to the chair legs. Lovely.

She was trying to take it in stride. Yet her voice sounded strange, small, even to herself when she said, "Stop." She pleaded, no doubt about it, "Oh, please, stop."

Right at her ear she heard an exhalation, a light breath—he could move suddenly, appear from nowhere in a new place: and sound cynical without so much as uttering a word. *Ha,* she heard him breathe, then whisper, "Oh, that is pretty. Taking me for fifty quid, then begging sweetly as if it shouldn't count." He let out another of his aggravating snorts. "I am feeling, oh, let's simply sum it up as *violated*."

Violated. The word made her stiffen, a fine time to hear it with her legs spraddled to the chair's.

He continued. "My uncle has taken me, and now you have been into my private account. I am up to my chin, my eyeballs with a sense of invasion, my privacy shattered, my life in shambles because other people have taken liberties—"

Liberties. Other people taking liberties. No, she didn't like the sound of this any better.

Emma opened her mouth, deciding to take her chances on screaming, then her voice caught in her throat as the whole chair with her in it suddenly went over backward. She had just enough time to brace herself for hitting hard, when, with a jerk, reality altered: Her descent stopped. The ceiling was overhead one moment, then the next—*flop*—there was nothing at all: The hem of her dress fell up over her face.

Upside down and blinded by her own skirts, she lay breathing hard, frightened, helpless. Her body hovered on the chair seemingly in midair. Then gently, it sank backward till, behind and overhead, she felt the *clop-clop* of the chair's upright posts, their slightly uneven meeting with the floor.

Then nothing. No sound except her own: kicking, squirming, blowing, trying to spit her own skirts off her face.

Chapter 5

Whilst it is the nature of most sheep to freeze under stress, some—especially those who've been shorn before and know what it's all about—will kick and attempt to get to their feet.

—Emma Darlington Hotchkiss
Yorkshire Ways and Recipes

EMMA lay in the dark of her own skirts upside down, tied to a chair, her legs bare but for knickers and her old gray wool stockings with a hole at each toe. She'd kill him, she thought. If Mr. Take-Liberties here was ever unwise enough to let her off this chair, she'd tie *him* to it and set it on fire.

So much anger. Though the main purpose of it seemed to be to hold her fear at bay. She lay there dumbstruck, terror-struck, fuming. Who would have thought a bloody member of Parliament could be so surprisingly agile and ruthless: not a gentlemanly reservation in him? Willing to turn her upside down, leave her helpless, breathing like a bellows and frightened out of her blooming mind?

After a lot of kicking and struggling, all to no avail, the fabric of her skirt slid down on its own, revealing Stuart Aysgarth's face three feet above: directly, squarely above—which put the man who had just discussed *violation* between the chair's legs and thus coincidentally between hers. He stood bent over her, bracing his weight on the seat edge with one hand, his other long arm extended—it was his finger, she discovered, that moved her skirt down her cheek as delicately as if dusting dirt from the face of a child.

There was nothing childish at all, however, in how his finger continued over the curve of her jawbone to her neck, taking the hem of her dress down her tendon all the way to her collarbone. His eyes followed his finger to the hollow of her throat, where at last he hesitated, paused, then—thank goodness—stopped. She shivered, involuntary, tried to speak, but ended up only wetting her lips, dry-mouthed.

The path his finger had traveled left a tiny, traceable impression down her neck to her clavicle, a trail so warm and particular it seemed traced by sun through a magnifying glass.

"You"—he said finally, then paused in that soft, slow way he had that was mildly terrifying now under the circumstance—"are a very hard woman to frighten, do you know that?"

She blinked up at him. "I can assure you, you're doing a good job. You can stop, if that was the goal."

He laughed. A rare sound, genuine, deep, though she definitely didn't like his sense of humor, now that she heard it. For a second more—with him leaning on both arms, his shoulders bunching, pulling at his shirt where they held his weight—he hovered over her, surveying her in that very disarming way again. Then stood up completely.

Good God, was he tall. From her angle, his head seemed to all but touch the ceiling.

He stared about them, perplexed for a moment, as if he'd lost track of what he was doing, then seemed to remember. And backed up.

To take a gander at his handiwork, it seemed. Over her knee, she watched him back two feet to the windowsill and sit his buttocks into it, his back flattening lace curtains. There, he crossed his arms over his chest, tilted his head, and viewed her incapacitation from this new angle.

He then said, "Do you know, I think I could do anything to

you, absolutely anything, and there would be nothing you could do about it."

"What a cheerful piece of speculation," she said, a little incensed.

"Save complain. Which you do very well."

She shut her mouth, advising herself to take John's advice and be humble. Or at least quiet.

Mount Villiars laughed again, entertained by his own iniquitous turns of mind. "And whatever I did, afterward, I could hand you over to the sheriff, and, even complaining, he'd just haul you away." The sarcastic jackanapes shook his head as if in earnest sympathy. "Such is our legal system and the power behind the title of viscount. I love being a viscount. Have I mentioned that? Despite all the trouble that arrived with my particular title, I find it's worth fighting for. By the way," he added, "I like those knickers."

Oh, fine, she thought. On top of everything else, he was making fun of her underwear—they were old and faded, flannel. Humble, Emma. Humble. She glared, biting her tongue.

"They're threadbare," he said. "What is it about the mystery of a woman, where a hint is almost better than knowing? You can almost see through them in places, which purely tickles the imagination, doesn't it?"

She blinked. "N-na-no," she got out. No one was tickling anything here. Then, before she knew her mouth was even moving, she found every expletive in her head suddenly out in broad daylight, a stream, as if she were the village idiot unable to stem the flow. "You no-good, ratbag, bad-penny, humbug bastard—"

"Now, now." He laughed out loud this time—it turned out he wasn't all that melancholy, but only needed the right reason to laugh his asinine head off. "What a vocabulary, Miss Muffin! Does Mother Goose know about this?" He couldn't contain himself enough to continue. All he could do was laugh, raucous, his head back, moving the curtains. His laughter rumbled in his chest, a low sound interspersed with a kind of bass staccato in breaks where he'd catch his breath. A villain's laugh, she decided. *The arsehole, devil's own, son of a—*

Was she muttering?

She must have been, because her chair came up an inch—he seemed to have hooked the toe of his boot under the top rung and lifted, making her stop short. He said with a smirk, "Son of a viscount, and don't forget it. From whom you stole. And make no mistake: Having you arrested for it has its appeal. Once I get a bit more money through that account, of course—"

She shook her head. "Oh, you mustn't. You really can't—"

"Why? You know what the best part is? I'm not even certain I'm doing anything wrong." He chuckled some more. "If they 'caught' me, what would it be for exactly? Signing my own checks with my own signature? Depositing them at a branch of my own bank?" He lifted his hands, helpless. And amused by it. After a pause, though, he repeated very seriously for what had to be the third time at least, "Of course, if they catch anyone, it won't be me, will it?"

Emma closed her eyes, pressed her lips between her teeth, then wet them. "I—I'll fix it," she offered. "I'll give you back what I took. The lamb doesn't matter this much." An understatement.

Like some sort of joke, he asked, "What lamb?"

Their eyes met. Hers widened, as from jolting down into a rabbit hole one didn't know was there.

His also, with dawning knowledge. He jerked back, a man repelled. His arms unfolded and dropped to his sides at the same moment her chair clonked down again. He stood up straight onto both legs. While full realization spread into his countenance the way light could preternaturally wash across dark countryside from overhead thunderclouds suddenly illuminated by lightning.

"You're the sheep woman!" he said. "Fifty-six pounds! I should have known!"

A kind of fury brought him forward with a clap of bootheels, till he towered over her head.

Looking down from six or more feet above, he said, "Why wouldn't you take the bloody ten pounds? I couldn't afford fifty, you ninny—"

"You most certainly could. Why, that carriage alone—" she pointed out.

"My uncle's. I took it from him. He'd bought it with my money, painted my coat of arms on it. And left every ha'penny tied up in lawsuits."

"You could have sold it."

"I could have. And walked. And fired all the people who maintained it."

Emma, so Emma to the bone, she would think later—insane—argued from the floor. "And—and—there's all that rebuilding going on at your house—"

"On credit." He turned away and paced. "All of it on credit. I kept trying to think of ways to maintain appearances enough so I could sign loans on the strength, the promise, of my name. A name that, if I was to have it, I had to win with an army of lawyers. We were in two courts plus the College of Arms at one point."

"How could you afford the lawyers?"

"They take their fees at the end. They're all sure I'm good for it."

He was, wasn't he? Oh, blast, English lords didn't deal in shillings and tuppence. He was lying. Yes, yes, she thought (though it was perhaps a tiny bit stupid to keep confronting him, with his being loose and now pacing within inches of her, while she was rather affixed at the vertex of his steps). The devil take him, he could still have paid what he owed. Look at his coat over there on the bed, for one thing. "You could have spared fifty pounds," she insisted.

"My de-e-ear," he said and stopped cold; she wished she'd been quiet. He bent down to her, again talking into her face, though upside down this time and much, much closer, bent over. "What do you think it costs to pack up three households into trunks, then trek them from Russia these days? And I expected to have money once I arrived here. What I did *not* expect was a near-million-pound inheritance I couldn't touch—still can't, even today, not easily or in any large measure, not till you, thank you—not without a week of correspondence with the College of Arms or so they tell me; I've yet to have that work. Nor did I expect, while the money was sealed off from me, I'd be handed huge apologies, then eighteen properties and fifty-seven servants, with not a shilling to run any of it. It is a nightmare. I keep thinking I've solved everything, when a new twist appears—the bank in York has, as of this week, an injunction now which does not allow me more than a hundred pounds in any one transaction until my lawyers can settle with a tailor, no less. A bloody tailor to whom my uncle—don't ask—owes one thousand seven hundred twenty-two pounds six shillings. And for *that*, I can't pay the French chef that came with Dunord the amount he deserves."

Pay the chef? His cook? He couldn't pay his cook?

Stuart continued, "And that doesn't count the twenty people I brought over myself. What was I supposed to do with *them*, I ask you? Leave them? Most of them have been with me from England, halfway round the world, then back again.

"And, foolish me, I felt rather secure, since I brought with me what I thought were fifty thousand pounds in rubles. But, no, no one likes rubles at the moment. The exchange rate is in the gutter, because England is a little unnerved by some new group calling themselves Marxists who are marching in Petersburg, wanting not the tzar but someone else, themselves presumably, to rule Russia. Nonetheless, I changed the rubles anyway, taking a beating, just to keep things going."

He stopped long enough to take a breath, then said, "My dear, I can't help these things. I'm just caught in them—a very rich man forced to move three households across two seas into eighteen properties, all with my hands tied behind my back, so to speak, by politics, exchange rates, and an uncle who took my English monies and properties precipitously, running up debts for which we still can't get a full tally." He threw up his hands. "Untie you? You're lucky I don't pick the chair up and throw you and it out the window. A sheep!" he said and pivoted, pacing off, presumably to cool down.

Good. He needed to. Emma let out a long exhalation herself. Goodness!

But he wasn't quite finished. He merely circled once and came back, pointing one of his long, slightly crooked fingers—that strangely attractive upward-arching tip—down into her face. "And you! I was down to a hundred twenty-seven pounds they would actually let me have in my pocket, when you—*you!*—came after me: I was flat out broke with more properties than any one human can use that came with seventy-seven people, you idiot woman, all of whom look to me for support, while I was trying to convince all of jolly old England that I was financially sound enough to loan thousands to!" His voice had risen loud enough that she had some hope of people hearing, of help rushing over from the next room. Oh, please, she thought.

She didn't like to see it: He grew more agitated—she had an excellent view of his boots as they clicked on the floor past her head. Snug, black, taut, butter-soft leather, laughably severe, now that she thought about it. He was going to kill her. Indeed, throw her out the window. Or, no, maybe he'd kick her to death with these strange boots that came up higher in front, covering an inch of his knee, with a tassel at the top, cut away at the calf so the back of his leg bent freely. Yes, he could get a good momentous kick going here with his Russian boots.

"Nothing I did shook you." He spun himself around at the bedpost. "Nothing satisfied you. I couldn't lose you. You are relentless! Why didn't you take the ten bloody pounds!" he asked again.

"I—I—" Why didn't she? "I don't know." She blinked. "It would be fine now. If you'd like to untie me, give it to me, I swear, I'd leave, your lordship." Dotty. The man was certifiable.

He continued to rant. "I can't believe you wouldn't! God. I should drop you out the window and tell the sheriff you jumped."

"No, no." She shook her head vehemently against the back slat of the chair. "No, I'm quite happy here on the floor, very comfortable."

A lunatic. An evil, wild, stuttering lunatic with a penchant for overspending. Dishonest to his bone, possibly violent. God save her, she thought as she stared up at him—or at his boots actually as he strode by again. Old Stuart—long-legged, well dressed, handsome as blazes, clever, cultured, and possibly trying to save the world or at least seventy-seven servants in it—old Stuart here was a madman.

And she was, as the saying went, in his clutches. Up to her eyeballs. Up to her threadbare flannel knickers.

Stuart stayed by the window, his back to her, presumably staring through the curtains, his back widely filling out his generous shirt for the fact that his arms appeared to bc folded in front again. Silence. While he gathered himself, Emma hoped.

Finally, though, it was she for whom the silence dragged on too long, and an admission found its way her mouth. "I suppose," she offered tentatively, "you might be having a wee bit more of a hard-go than I'd imagined."

Without turning, he said, "Thank you." It took another full minute before he twisted to look over his shoulder—down between the tops of her knees at her face. He asked, "Why would a lamb be worth fifty quid?" It was an honest question.

And his eyes, their sad angle: she felt a twinge of sympathy for him. "Do you suppose we could discuss this with the chair at least upright?" she asked. "My hands are going to sleep."

For one cheerful moment, she thought that was what he

intended, because he turned around and came over. But he only walked smack between the chair legs again, her legs, and bent over her, leaning his palms once more on the wood seat at either side of her hips. He frowned down into her face as if she were a complicated conundrum. Then told her from straight overhead, "Your hands are tied at the small of your back. Arch your lumbar. You're in the most comfortable position possible."

Emma made a twist of her mouth. "Tied up a lot of women, have you?"

He raised one eyebrow, whatever that meant.

"A bit odd, are you?" She was being sarcastic, trying to taunt him into a sense of guilt. While perhaps bursting any bubble in herself of misguided, soft-hearted concern for a man with sad eyes and complicated wealth.

Though his sexual inclinations were perhaps not the wisest of barbs to do either. He looked down at her, speculative. "Difficult to say." He actually answered the question seriously. "Legally? Decidedly. But then British laws on the subject are so guilt-ridden I'm surprised we've propagated as a race." He made a small, grim smile. "How delightful we're having this conversation. And what is it *you* like?"

Emma's tongue grew fat. It wouldn't move in her mouth.

He continued, "Me, I have no limiting fetishes—though neither do I have apparently the usual boundaries. Mostly, my appetites seem to be rather like those of someone who can eat and enjoy anything, provided it's eaten in excellent company." This amused him. He lifted an eyebrow again. "So to speak." He added, "The pleasure, I would gauge, has more to do with the woman, the intimacy between us, than any particular act per se." He made a small shrug of one shoulder, barely a movement. "Though I'm rather fond of the main event." He left an intentional pause. "So? How do we match up?"

Emma stared wide-eyed, openmouthed, unable to hide how perfectly scandalized she was by his dissertation. And changed the subject. "Do you really have seventy-seven servants?"

"More or less." He made a shake of his head. "It's a mistake. I don't want them. My uncle had too many. My father had more still, while I had quite a few of my own. They accumulated. I seem to have all of them now, and I can't sack people who have been in my family's employ, some for years, just because—" He broke off, his brow lifting as his round, dark eyes widened for a dismayed second: He didn't know why. It annoyed him that he couldn't fire them, but he couldn't.

Well, Emma thought, what a surprising little soft spot in this otherwise blackguard of a human being.

"What do you *want* from me?" she asked.

He hesitated. From overhead—staring down, leaning, while he stood between the legs of a woman he'd personally trussed up—the man eyed her now as if *she* were the one not to trust. Then he said, "I told you: my uncle. You said no." He chewed his lip a moment, then offered, "Of course, the idea here was to influence your decision, encourage you to reconsider. You have?"

She said nothing, a mild horror dawning over her. She hadn't. And if she never did, what did he mean to do with her? Could she lie here and simply wait him out?

He took her silence for encouragement and smiled ruefully down into her face. "Exactly *how* you'd help," he continued with a small shrug, "I must say, remains a little vague at this point—"

He broke off, as if losing track in a quick glance. His eyes skimmed her bosom, her lapful of skirts, her threadbare thighs, spread, as it were, enough that he could stand comfortably between them. This survey took less than two seconds, but it put her unmistakably in mind of his offer in front of the bank: Some of his ideas weren't too vague.

She fidgeted, trying to settle herself with what latitude left her.

He continued, "My uncle Leonard took some things." He

made again that quick distracted scan of her, as if he were trying not to, but it kept coming back—his suggestive interest without doubt included her incapacitation: He liked it. "So I was thinking"—he raised his gaze slowly, reluctantly, all the way to her face, that ironic eyebrow of his rising simultaneously, till she was staring up again into that pure upper-class snottiness he could convey in the proverbial flick of an eye—"given your tenacity and abilities for exacting justice by circuitous means, that we might—"

Might what? How curious. He balked, stopped.

He gave a pat to the chair seat and stood up, towering once more up into the room. Absently, he remarked, "It could be a little illegal, I'd venture."

"So is tying women to chairs," she pointed out. No, there was some other reason he hesitated, one he didn't want to pronounce.

He jerked his gaze down to her. "Tying thieves to chairs isn't." He spoke with such earnest indignity that, blast him, Emma herself was momentarily struck by his point. She'd been thinking of *innocent* women, she supposed.

Finally, in a rush he made the leap. "I want us to take back two of the things my uncle took from my house in Yorkshire."

Robbery? He wanted her help in robbing his uncle? Yet she couldn't get past the word *house*. She murmured, "Your 'house' has, I think, almost four hundred rooms."

He nodded, unfazed, even agreeing. "Indeed. Dunord is the largest house I own or ever have. In any event, my uncle took many things. I don't care about most of them. Just two: one is extremely valuable, the other merely puzzling, a trinket of personal significance to me. He denies it, but I know he has them. I want both back. Without sending my only living relative to jail, if possible, while not incurring his wrath either—if I simply took them, he'd only come after me. For something this complicated, I need help, and I'm fairly sure you'd know how to give it. We could—what did you call it? We could run that store or wire or whatever it is—"

Emma let out a short, surprised burst of giddy laughter, unstoppable.

"I thought you were frightened," he said drolly, staring down at her.

"Hys-hysteria, I th-think now," she got out. Then, "We can't."

"Why?" He shifted his weight, his upper calf coming against one chair leg, brushing against her ankle. "You can do it. You sent my secretaries away, didn't you? One could have recognized you, while you didn't want the other filling in. You wanted the job of secretary that day at the bank. You arranged it."

She nodded, still laughing. "I did. But, honestly, we couldn't possibly run the Wire or Big Store. My heavens, that takes dozens of people and hundreds of pounds to set up."

He made a disconcerted face. "Then something else. You're full of invention. I know. I've been the victim of it."

She shook her head. No. He couldn't be asking her to go back into confidence swindles. She'd already said she wouldn't and meant it. They were wrong. They were dangerous. She wasn't even sure she'd remember how, when it came to the bigger, more complicated setups. "I—I won't—"

He tilted his head, giving her his full, intent consideration. "If it's money, I'll just run whatever more required through that account you've set up for us. How much—"

"None! No! God, no! You've taken out too much already—"

"If you don't help, you realize, I will hand you over to the sheriff. Given the amount we've run through to date, and the fact that it all points to you, I'd say you could end up doing ten years."

"I—I—" She frowned up. "This is serious," she said. "Don't joke." Why wasn't he listening?

He bent low over the chair again, hands braced once more on the seat edge. "Will you look at how and where you're lying at present, Miss Muffin or whatever your name is?" He leaned a little closer, elbows bending, as he descended toward her, down further over her. She looked directly into large, dark eyes that narrowed. "Do I seem to be joking? What part of this do you find funny?"

"I—I—I don't want to go to jail." She would have faked a sob, except a real one came out too suddenly, taking her by surprise. She caught her breath, hiccupped. Emma honestly didn't want to go to jail. Honestly, absolutely, truly.

Jail was where Joanna, Zach's sister, died. Jail was why they stopped their games in London. Confidence games operating on the edge of the law were hard to catch and more difficult still to prosecute, since the victims were often embroiled in the dishonesty as deeply as those laying the game. But once caught and convicted, jail sentences—rather like sheep sentences in Yorkshire—tended to be steeper than the crime because authorities were so blooming happy to have hold finally of a slippery culprit. Joanna had been dragged kicking and screaming to what had amounted to a life sentence—in her short instance, turning out to be exactly a year and three months.

There were many excellent reasons to lead an honest life, but here Emma was up against one of the more convincing, one she'd been sure once she'd never look in the eye again: punishment.

"I—I suppose, I would do pretty much anything to avoid jail." Dear Father in Heaven, she was going to rob his uncle with him, unless she could think of a way out.

He blinked, looked perplexed, then distracted again. He asked, "Truly?"

"Oh, yes." She had to convince him. "Positively."

He glanced at the bed. He didn't mean to, and he caught himself. But for one instant it was there: clear. He shook his head, a little jerk, as if he could shake the idea out.

"Except that," Emma said quickly, the back of her head pressed to the chair slat, full alarm.

He was going to pretend she had it all wrong, that that flicker of his eyes hadn't happened: that he wouldn't consider for an instant making her female body, her sovereignty over it, a part of their bargain for her getting up off this chair and staying out of jail.

She wouldn't humor him. "You should know," she explained, patiently, explicitly, "I—I don't sleep with men for money or any other reason, except that *I* might choose to." It was a lifelong decision she was proud of, and it wasn't as if she hadn't had opportunity or as if rationalizing wouldn't have made matters easier at various points in her life. As now.

"Slept with a lot, have you?" He looked curious, not disappointed.

"No." In fact, one, when it came down to it. Her husband, when he was able, and, years and years ago, *almost* with a boy of seventeen. She pressed her mouth closed, a taut line, and stared up, vigilant.

"You're going to jail," he pronounced and stood again, dusting his hands on his thighs. He pointed at her—"You wait here"—and snorted.

A joke. Told to a woman bound hand and foot to a chair upside down on the floor. "Very funny." When he walked out of her line of vision, though, anxiety got the better of her. "Where-wh-where are you going? Don't! Oh, don't—"

"Don't find the bloody sheriff? Don't have you hauled away as you deserve?"

"Yes. No. Right, don't—" Quickly, defensively, "I'll tell. I'll tell them you took the larger amount."

"I'll show them the wig. They saw you today. They know this room number. There's nothing to link me. I'm just here trying to stop you. It's all yours, Miss Muffin—what *is* your name, by the way?"

"Emma."

"Emma?" He came back into view, looking again at her upside from his tall height overhead. "How lovely." He studied her, really studied her.

Till she looked away. She had to fight another odd little

moment of humanity, connection, something . . . something she didn't want to feel for him.

He added, "It suits you better."

How would he know? she told herself. Then, aloud, suggested, "I—I, ah—I have an idea for your uncle." Oh, anything to get out of this mess.

He frowned. After several long seconds of silence, he said, "I'm listening."

"Wha—" She couldn't say it at first. Oh, she hated what she was about to offer. "Wha—what did he take? How much?"

"There's no recouping the money. I told you, that's not the issue." He shrugged. "Besides, my father was a cruel man; his younger brother no doubt took the brunt at times. Leonard is entitled to something. Just not the viscountcy nor, willy-nilly, whatever his greedy mind might happen to land upon." The pause he left said that the two things—yes, that's what he'd said, "things"—would be much more difficult to recoup than money. He told her, "Though he denies it, Leonard took a statue. I know he has it; I want it back. He went to Dunord before I could get there and took a lot, but the statue is dear to me, not to mention worth a fortune. And he also took"—he laughed—"the damnedest thing: He took a pair of my mother's earrings, the only pair I ever remember her wearing. I want both returned to me, the jewelry and the statue." He raised that eyebrow. "Can you get them?"

"Yes." No. Who knew? She'd promise anything at this point. Time to make it sound real. "We could do, I suppose, a poke with a send."

The authority of the two words, *poke* and *send*, made him grow still—cautiously regardful. She had him. From upside down, his shadowed eyes focused on her with new interest.

A poke with a send. Could she do it? Did she want to? That was the real point. There were a dozen very good reasons not even to begin. For one, the last time she'd done a poke with a send, four people had ended up shot, herself one of them. "Th-though I can't just—I mean, I have responsibilities. My sheep—"

"Who's taking care of them now?"

"My neighbor. Though I did everything this morning before I left. And I bake bread—"

"We'll have one of my chefs do it."

"For half the village—"

"They have a lot of new ovens."

"And a cat—"

"Whoever looks after the sheep—"

"I do other things—"

"Make a list."

"Some only I can do," she insisted, frowning, resistant, plaintive.

It won her only a sideways pull of his mouth. "No one is irreplaceable, Emma."

Emma. They were even. They'd each appropriated—inappropriately—the other's given name.

"Make a list," he repeated. "How long will it take to do this—what did you call it? A poke"—he paused, amused; he liked poking—"and a what?"

"A send. A poke with a send that involves the statue." Ah, well, she supposed, there were worse things than being shot. Staying on this chair for one minute longer, for instance. She told him, "We'll get the earrings another way, separately. With me running—oh— What does your uncle like? Art? The stock market? Gambling?"

"Oh, definitely gambling. And art, damn his hide. That's what the statue is about, I think. Both." He laughed with satisfaction. "So how long will it take?"

The question brought a flash of unwanted memory. Forever, she thought. It is forever . . . people shot, friends going to jail, yourself going home, not a favorite place, in a foggy, angry, guilty muddle, with a new husband and faltering marriage, both mortally though invisibly wounded in a way that would take twelve years to kill them completely. While, silently, she had grave reservations, aloud, she listed, "To plan the game, snare your uncle, run him through it, have him bring the statue." She added up the time it would take to get truly free of this chair, this room, this mistake, to get free of Stuart: "Two weeks."

"Two weeks!" He was delighted. "Excellent! In the meanwhile, perhaps once in between you can visit your sheep. I'll pay the train fare."

She blinked, taken aback by his fit of generosity, no doubt brought on by optimism. Or despotism. His offer reflected his power to give it, though it was a benign despotic gesture, she supposed. "That probably won't be possible, but thank you. So will you please untie me now? I'm awfully tired of this."

"And I make all decisions," he said. "I'm in charge."

At first, she didn't know what he meant. Who else was in charge, given there were only the two of them here, and one of them was lying on the floor tied down? Then she realized: He was worried about her running the ruse on his uncle. Stuart's hesitations all came together in that instant.

Indeed, his lordship here *would* be partial to legality, wouldn't he? When a man manipulated his position and the law as well as this one, it must be jolly unnerving to step outside them. More importantly, though, the viscount who loved being a viscount had recognized, once he and she began, there would be times when only one person would know how to get them through safely, and it wasn't the one standing here talking about being in charge. Emma wanted to laugh.

Ah, Stuart, what a very smart fellow you are.

If he allowed her to direct the play of his uncle, their positions would shift. For all his authority and wealth, Stuart Aysgarth was an innocent, when it came to small-time swindles: more like a mark than a big-time confidence man. He'd been having a devil of a time keeping a straight face, while only setting up perfectly legal loans he probably could make good on down the road anyway—while she, gussied up and with a veneer of city sophistication, had lured richer, sharper, more powerful men than he to their undoing. Or at least she had as a participant, when she was younger. And all it had taken was a little unscrupulousness on the mark's part, which Stuart had by the chairload, didn't he?

She could take him, she thought. She could let the power between herself and her "partner" here do its natural shift as she showed him how to set up his uncle. Then take them both. Not that she would. It sounded as if the man didn't need any more betrayal in his life. But she could. If she wanted to. Rather like the threats he was making with his eyes and innuendos. He wasn't going to do anything. Nor was she. But the opportunity was built into the situation. She could have him, and for a bundle. With only a little more work than it would take to set up his uncle.

Oh, Emma, she cautioned herself as she lay there, *what are you doing?* Disintegrating. Going to hell.

Still, in for a penny, in for pound. What else was there to do?

She nodded. Yes. *Dear Lord, let me get myself out of this, and I'll be good. I'll be so, so good, You'll see.*

Stuart tilted his head at her, his very handsome head. His long body stood up, slightly more attentive, his wide, angular shoulders back. "Truly?" he asked. He eyed her up, then down again. Disbelief. Or else a man reluctant to untie a woman he had designs on.

But then the chair swung upward in an arc—he lifted it by the slat at the back of her head. Oh, yes!

On her way up, she asked, "What will you tell the bank? What about the money you took out?"

The chair halted, just shy of upright. Her feet remained in the air. He spoke down into her face across his own chest. "I'll let it ride for now, let them look for it."

"Will you take out more?"

"I have to. I'm sorry, I need it."

She drew in her breath. They'd be looking for her.

"Also, Emma, you realize," he added: "It's what I have over you."

She frowned. The chair rocked, suspended, not up, not down, balanced on its rear legs.

"I'll fix it though," he continued, "once we're through. Plus my lawyers can keep you out of jail for two weeks easily, even if the bank does discover you."

No, no, this wasn't how she imagined it. She frowned, frustrated, and threw her weight forward, trying to make the chair right itself. "Put me down. Fix the chair. Untie me."

The more she heaved, though, the more the whole thing seemed unstable. She teetered, tipping backward on the chair legs in a kind of midair seesaw. For a few seconds, she wasn't sure if he had safe hold or not.

He kept her there, balanced, looking at her. "You know," he said finally, "you truly believe you'll be able to control me, don't you? You think you can do as you will?" He huffed air down his nose with a *hmmph.* "What on God's earth can we do to pry you from this highly unprofitable notion? Because we're going to butt heads over it for two weeks otherwise, and I simply don't care to, Emma." When she did nothing but glare, he laughed, incredulous.

"You're a bully," she said into his laughter.

"Yes. Good." He nodded as if she'd understood something important, something they agreed on. "A highly successful one," he said. "I've probably bullied more people simply to have the breakfast I want—without even speaking their language—than you've bullied your whole life."

With his free hand, he brushed a piece of her hair that had flopped onto her cheek, just the tips of his fingers, yet touching her at all, while she tottered helplessly, felt strange, eerie. It made her belly lift.

He continued very softly, almost kindly, "Emma, I *have*

power, so throwing it around makes a certain amount of sense: You don't. We'll get through this so much easier if you simply own up to it, concede, let it go."

The backs of his fingers grazed her cheek again—no lock of hair for excuse this time. Then he dragged his index finger, just its knuckle, lightly across her lips. His hand was dry and warm, his touch sure. Emma grew perfectly still, motionless at the bizarre sensation, so foreign: both interesting and repellent. Arousing, off-putting. Confusing. Held in midair, her face caressed while the rest of her was confined.

He dropped his hand away, the chair seesawing for a second more. She was trying to sort out what she felt: lips dry, cheeks on fire, her body arched in the chair, taut, her emotions a mess—embarrassed, aroused, angry, antagonized. The list went on, while she tried to hide that he'd struck a chord at all. Yet such was her turmoil that, the more she tried to pretend innocence, insouciance, the hotter her whole face became. She couldn't meet his eyes.

"Oh, you *are* delightful," he murmured, whatever that meant.

And the chair came up with a sudden swoop. Her stomach flipped over, then jolted as the last two chair legs in front struck the floor with an uneven *clack.* And Stuart Aysgarth disappeared, going behind her, out of sight.

She felt a tug on the cravat. Hallelujah! Then at her neck a silky tickle: sending a shot of pure, blind panic through her.

She understood the extremity of her alarm by her disproportionate relief. An ocean of it released in her veins, letting her breathe again, as she realized that what tickled was only his hair at the crook of her neck, at the side of her cheek. His head was bent over. He was untying her! Oh, yes! At the back of her chair, his fingers worked on the cravat where it was woven through the slats. Sweet Jesus, thank you!

The first part of the knots gave, and her bound wrists came free of the chair. Emma slid forward immediately, arching her back, stretching. As she felt Stuart lean between her shoulders and the chair to work at the ties holding her wrists together, she felt all but lighthearted. Free of the chair slats, soon to be free entirely, free, free, free, without having paid any of the steep prices she'd feared. She'd held his sexual interest at bay (though she was covered in goose bumps, she realized). She wasn't going to jail (thank goodness). She even grew a little miffed (come to think of it) that he'd made such serious threats.

It was *he*, after all, who had turned what she'd done into something ten times worse, then threatened her with it. How fair was that?

Over her shoulder, she told him, "You were only scaring me. You wouldn't really give me to the sheriff. I mean, I only took fifty-six pounds. It wouldn't be right to send me to prison for taking five hundred." Quite happily, she announced, "You were just being mean, getting even, admit it."

Why did she say this? Why would she want him to admit anything?

Of course, he didn't. He stopped.

She sat there, her arms free of the chair, while—she gave a useless, thwarted yank—her wrists remained caught in a loose-wrapped snarl of cravat, her feet yet lashed to the chair legs. The devil's own throne, she thought, where a dolt such as she might stay forever . . . *dolt, idiot, fool*—

She would have gone on berating herself. But Stuart, with fewer words and less effort, took over much more effectively. He stepped around into view, squatted directly in front of her, and stared up into her face. "Mrs."—a pause—"Hotch. Kiss." He separated her name as if putting it together for the first time, remembering. "That's your name. Do I recall it correctly from all the documents and letters?"

She blinked, bit her lip. "Yes."

"No," he said, as if contradicting, but then repeated, "No, you did not have a right to go into my private account. No, I am not joking. Yes, I'll haul your bum over to the sheriff's office if you displease me in any way or fall short of that on which we've just agreed. What you did is serious. You robbed me."

"I only took what was mine." She lifted her chin.

"Excuse me, but not legally, it wasn't. Legally, the money in your pockets over there belongs to me."

"I won it in court."

"No, you didn't. The matter is back in court, a new court, with due process proceeding."

She frowned, exasperated. "That's wrong. It shouldn't be. I can't afford to fight you there."

"Then you can't afford to win."

She jerked on the chair, kicking, trying to pull her legs free. "You swine, you—"

"Quiet. I'm making a point here. You are an adult. I'll give you, that in your circumstance, I might well have tried something similar. I understand your frustration. But still, as an adult, you can face the consequences of your actions, and the consequences of lifting money from an account that isn't yours, which by the way is larceny and a felony, since you've been caught, could result in—since you had the misfortune to be caught by someone who upped your ante—ten years' penal servitude in a British prison."

Emma sat back into the chair with a jerk, as if she'd been struck: deservedly. It was as if time itself had come forward, traveling through him to stare her in the face as he squatted there, retelling her a lesson she apparently hadn't absorbed very well at seventeen. Even though she'd been sure she had. Leave it to life to shovel out a lesson twice, when the first time wasn't enough.

Humble. For once she didn't have to reach for humility. It swamped her. He was right.

He continued. "But, see here, there's no reason to be so depressed about it. You are fortunate after all. You're going to get away with it this time."

As she had last time, she thought, which actually hadn't

made her feel too good. She'd "gotten away" bleeding, shot at her temple and ear, sure she was the walking dead—who would have thought a person could bleed so much and not die from it? But that hadn't even been the worst: Others hadn't gotten away, three others shot *and* arrested, ten in all hauled off, with herself and Zach certain, simply certain, that Joanna was right behind them, when she wasn't. "Getting away with it" had been a blithering, blooming, literally bloody mess.

He continued, "If you help me, I'll protect you, and you'll be fine. Exactly as you hoped. Or *rather* as you'd hoped. I suppose you'd hoped not to have to satisfy me. But, honestly, will that be so difficult? You seem to be quite up to it."

Emma's gaze dropped to the floorboards between his boots. She felt so downhearted all she could do was mutter, "If we're caught, we'll *both* get ten years. I can't see how that's an improvement."

"It's a huge improvement, since we haven't been caught yet: and you have. Plus, there is another big difference: I *didn't* legally owe you the money you took. My uncle *does*. He *stole* what we are going to trick him into giving back. Huge improvement. Huge difference. Don't you see it?"

She saw a vague difference. A difference she would hate to have to argue from the dock of the accused. She shook her head, dismal, dispirited.

A hand lifted her chin. Stuart rolled forward onto one knee in his squat. He didn't have to lift her chin very far till their eyes met. "You know how to set it up, yes? There's no need for us to get caught, correct?"

"Maybe." She shrugged. "I think so."

"Good. Then we're set." A pause. They stared at each other. He seemed to be thinking on something. Then came to a conclusion. "I'm going to drive my point home though. I think I should."

Her eyes locked on his: His were level, serious—and slightly dilated. Involuntarily, she glanced down and saw, where his trousers pulled in his squat, the beginning outline of partial male sexual excitation. She hadn't been bold enough to look before, but she suspected it had been there off and on for the last forty minutes or so. From the start. She looked back up at him, her mouth dropping open a little, undone. He met her eyes steadily, openly, undenying. Her stomach twisted again. A point? He was going to drive home a point? What point? Not the one in his trousers, she hoped.

He said, "You don't seem fully to appreciate what you did to me. You take it lightly. And now you're going to get away with it. But not before I demonstrate how wrong going into places that don't belong to you, uninvited, is—"

"No," she shook her head. No!

"Be quiet. If you were fragile, I wouldn't do it. But you aren't, and it will only take two minutes. For two minutes you can live with what it's like to have surprising places of your privacy transgressed. As I have for four months now, I might add, thanks to my uncle, the Crown, the College of Arms, the courts, lawyers—and now you." He let out a complaining snort. "Nothing I have seems inviolable anymore, financially speaking at least, but you'd be surprised how invasive that is. They've been through how I pay people, what I buy, where I go, how much it costs, whom I see, whom I pay for what. And some of it is not entirely pleasant to explain, though I accept that I must—the consequences of my making myself so remote from my father that he didn't even know I was alive: for arriving so late to lay claim to my titles and their entailment that I gave my uncle his day in the sun. So. For two minutes, you now get this privilege as well. Welcome to the world of consequences, retribution, and personal trespass."

Trespass? No, no, no, she kept shaking her head. He wouldn't. Surely, he didn't mean *that*. Two minutes? A man couldn't force a woman to—well, not in two minutes, he couldn't, could he? No, that would take longer. Or, for her, it certainly would: She would see to it. So what did he mean?

What were her options? Could she throw herself and the chair on him? Would that do any good? She scooted back, deeply into it, retreating as far as possible. While anxiety came up through her like a clacking bell. *What did he mean? What did he mean?* The question echoed as her heart began to thud so hard her chest wall vibrated in rhythm. *What did he mean? What did he mean? Whadittymean?*

He did nothing except reach out, though that was enough. Emma grew rigid, holding her breath. But he only laid his fingers against her cheek, then ran his thumb across her lower lip, back, then forth.

Involuntarily, a reflex, she wet her lips, her tongue coming in brief contact with his dry thumb, leaving a bitter spot at the tip, an acrid taste, like ink or pennies. He left his thumb there against her mouth, wet, studying her as if she were an interesting development. Or dilemma. Then with the light weight of his thumb he rolled her lip down, open. She let it roll, did nothing to take her mouth back, already appalled by herself that she'd tasted his thumb, made it slippery—and that, for God's sake, she had to hold herself in check or she would have done it again.

She wanted to lick his thumb. How bizarre was that?

It was going to be the longest two minutes of her life, because all he did was watch her for the first minute and simply that much frightened her, thrilled her: that whatever he planned—and there was something behind his eyes—he had the nerve for it. Something sexual . . . there was something sexual here, the whole notion unfamiliar, riveting. She couldn't assess it, though she was virtually certain he could: that he had her at a supreme disadvantage by virtue of far greater experience. So what was he doing? Gauging the likelihood of her biting him?

She felt his thumb trace the bottom ridge of her lower lip, then down the undercurve to the indentation above her chin. In a way, she wanted to sink her teeth into him. Then did. Of sorts. When he slid his thumb back up, her teeth found the flesh at the edge, and she took hold, firmly though not hard, gently, and tasted his thumb again. She ran her tongue along the edge of it, her eyes closing.

Immediately, his fingers curled, and his warm hand cupped the side of her cheek, her chin. She sighed as a momentary wave of pleasure came over her so strong she couldn't see for a moment, blinding.

Then in the next, no, it felt wrong. She pushed his hand away the only way she could—by closing her wet lips and pushing his thumb forward. It rested there, balanced on the end of her wet, puckered mouth, as if on a kiss, and their eyes met. He and she stared at each other.

Then—quite surprising, almost disappointing—*he* broke the tension by letting out a breath, then a light laugh. He took back his thumb with a contradictory, half-smiling shake of his head, looking down.

He remained there like that, on a knee and a foot, an expression of rue or self-rebuke or both on his averted face. Then, as if he could turn everything he'd just said and done on its ear, he bent forward, rising, straightening at the knees as his face came toward her, and said, "The truth is, I want to kiss you like this. Let me."

Let him? He was asking permission?

If so, he didn't wait for it. His hand guided her face as he brought his mouth squarely against hers—against the mouth of a befuddled woman, rattled to the point of shaking: While under the rather outlandish circumstance of her being utterly helpless to prevent it, the Viscount Mount Villiars placed his full mouth onto hers.

And it was no light peck or buss he wanted. His thumb returned to roll her lower lip down again, gently opening her mouth as he took a full, deep kiss, his thumb remaining a part of it, moving in the wetness of their mouths across her lower lip, then into her mouth itself, out again. Her face became surrounded by him. Horrible. Delicious. The fingers of his other hand, their tips, dug into her hair at the base of her skull, spanning nape, neck, and jaw as he took her face in both hands to kiss. Oh, good heaven, it felt so abominably, breathlessly wonderful—and odd, like nothing she was familiar with—she hardly knew what to do.

His mouth and thumb and tongue did. Sweet heaven, such a burning kiss, so full of unabashed want. He kissed her full-passioned, openly, flagrantly carnal, unhampered by shame or self-censure. His mouth on hers was purely flabbergasting. Something Emma couldn't match, though simply to feel its melting languor on the other side of her mouth was marvel enough. She let him kiss her like this—did she kiss him back? She must have; she certainly opened her mouth, too amazed, dazed, drawn in to do otherwise, while Stuart's sexuality communicated itself: dark, blossoming, florid like his other tastes, varied, complex. It seemed almost wholesome for its lack of self-consciousness, unapologetically passionate, individual—what Stuart Aysgarth wanted in particular, singularly and exactly, the only limit being his own appetite under his own limber, fluid exploration . . . willing to kiss a woman lavishly, handle her face, penetrate her mouth, while she was tied to a chair. . . .

Then what he wanted was her thigh, because the backs of his fingers drifted there, to the inside at her knee, gliding upward, which made something light up inside her and also made her all but pant into his mouth with a kind of panic. He caught, literally, her little, terror-struck breaths into his mouth, and his hand dropped away in seeming response. Good.

He turned his head, standing up slightly onto his knee, his renewed deep kiss a relief after that little scare. Sweet. She let its sensations wash over her. How long had it been since a man had kissed her? She couldn't remember. Like this? Never. Stuart's kiss was so utterly warm and soft and strong: as delicious as a lump of sugar melting on her tongue. His tongue moved in her mouth in a curious new way, not a thrust, not a mimic of coitus. More like an exploring, as if the inside of her mouth were something interesting he wanted to know in taste, shape, and texture. She could smell him again, the citrusy spiciness, so faint she decided it might have come merely from soap. Yet so distinctive, it could only be he.

Stuart Aysgarth was the most sensuous, sensual man she'd ever met, she realized. The way he felt, smelled, looked, sounded, and, alas, tasted—it was as though he'd set out single-mindedly to engage every sense in her like some extravagant intruder who barges in and lights every candle in the house.

Somewhere along the way, his hand returned to her knee, light, dry, warm, possessive. Just his hand on her knee. For balance. Still, for a second, she knew a tiny panic. He stroked it away. His thumb rubbed the inside of her knee, two soft, short strokes along the bend, the first reassuring, the second bringing such a shocking physical rush of blood to the core of Emma, she nearly lost her breath. Her legs . . . dear heaven, her legs. She felt all at once exposed . . . aware how close he was to . . . well, he could have put his hands, that thumb, those fingers anywhere.

Almost gentlemanly, sweetly, as if he read her mind, he broke away long enough to lean over sideways. With one hand, he yanked at the ties at her legs, ripping them in part, setting her right leg free first—oh, lovely!—coming back to kiss her again briefly—then stopping long enough to lean in the other direction. She lifted her free foot out, straightening her leg to stretch, as he undid her other one. Not that he was letting her free or up exactly, because as soon as her legs were freed, he came back to that astonishing kiss, having her rather trapped against the chair.

Then, the next thing she knew, his hands hooked under her knees, and he lifted her legs up as he moved forward and straddled the chair himself, sitting, while in the same movement lifting, running his hands under her legs down her calves to her ankles. He sat, taking her legs up over his. He still had to bend forward slightly, he was so much taller, but he was less awkward, more comfortable, she thought, sitting on the chair—until he moved forward and brought their bodies close, up against each other. She would have slapped him perhaps. Maybe. Difficult to say, since her hands were still held behind her. In any event, it was a shock at first to feel him—his male body up against her spraddled female one.

He bent forward, kissing her harder. One moment, his hands were at the sides of her, gripping the chair posts over her head. He curved his hips, hard against her, and she knew the heady thickness of him. All so oddly familiar, yet not. The next moment, one of his hands was between them, at her waist, then the back of his hand glided down her belly, almost protective. Then he took his hand away—and nothing. Absolutely, positively nothing whatsoever was between them. Unless one counted something else she hadn't felt in a very long time: a very capable, fully naked, and perfectly beautiful male erection.

He either knew or was inventing on the spot how to have sexual congress on a chair . . . they were about to . . . she was letting him . . . no, she jerked on her hands, they weren't free in back . . . she was his prisoner . . . wasn't she? Was she letting him? She wet her lips to say *stop*. The word didn't come out. Did she want him to? Now was certainly the moment to say so. Decisions seemed to hang, demanding her attention, yet her brain couldn't seem to keep up with her body.

She felt herself swollen, lit, as the head of his penis dropped against her. It slid down the length of her in an instant acknowledgment of how ready she was. The warm movement of his hand was there, adjusting himself into position—here was certainly the moment to protest. *Did she want to?*

Then it was too late to protest anything. With a swift, sure movement of hips, he thrust himself deeply, thickly inside her. Her body all but pulled him into her, swallowing him up.

His arms were at either side of her again, enfolding her against the chair, against him, his chest, the spicy-warm smell of him . . . his strong, muscular shoulders hunched toward her, one hovering at her face till the starchiness of his shirt rose into her nostrils like steam, till she tasted it in her mouth . . . his hips under her, his presence inside her, hot and substantial, driving . . . intrusive, amazing . . . he lifted into her with a kind of rhythmic spasm that was so satisfying she bit down on his shirt, clenching her teeth. Seconds. It lasted seconds—perhaps three deep, solid stokes of Stuart's body into hers. While her own contracted around his the moment of entry and simply kept contracting . . . tighter and tighter and tighter . . . until an explosion . . . or implosion, things collapsing and shoving and moving inside as she couldn't remember in years, maybe ever . . . with both herself and Stuart making such noises, mutters, animal sounds, groans.

She came to her senses again like this, her heart pounding with him right there in her face, his body up against her, still inside her.

Two minutes. Had it taken two minutes? Feasible. It was entirely feasible.

Chapter 6

Semper praesumitur pro negante.

—The ancient rule in the House of Lords whereby, in the event there are an equal number of votes on both sides of an issue, the negative holds

WHAT had happened here? Emma's mind couldn't absorb it. Had she just . . . accidentally . . . had sexual union with the Viscount Mount Villiars? On a chair? With her hands tied behind her?

Was that possible?

Judging by the way the man's shirttails hung out and how he was fixing himself under them: yes.

Stuart had risen from the chair. He stood, giving his full, long-tailed shirt one tuck, before he thought to reach around her and completely free her hands. The moment Emma owned them again, she drew her arm back and hit him as hard as she could. She meant to catch him in the face with her palm, but because he stood up too fast, she caught him across the shoulder with the side of her hand.

"Hey. Ow!" He flinched. "It wasn't *that* bad." He rubbed his arm. "A little brief, but, second for second, rather near paradise. For me at least." He frowned and asked, "I've never done a chair before, have you?"

Done a chair? She hadn't *done* anything in eight years. "No," she said. She would have hit him again, but he looked as confused as she felt. She let it go, instead rolling her shoulders, then stretching her arms. Lord, it felt good to be able to move again.

Then it felt awkward: It registered that her underclothes were back together. She had to think a moment to remember his being bent over her, his hand on her: The man before her had slid off the chair, then fixed and retied her drawers, while she had sat there like a lump. He'd settled everything back exactly as it should be—she touched her belly to be sure, finding the smoothness of a well-arranged corset, corset cover, chemise, drawers, petticoats, everything more or less in order. He'd undone them; he'd fixed them. Stuart Aysgarth understood the complexity of an Englishwoman's undergarments, something Zachary Hotchkiss after twelve years of marriage never had gotten right.

She blinked, trying to take that information in.

While Stuart asked, one arm behind him, "How did we do that?" He continued to tuck his shirt as he threw a bewildered glance just over her head, at the chair posts: as though the inanimate object could tell him.

Emma snorted. "Can we leave?"

He looked up from his trousers abruptly, stopping in mid-motion, his long fingers pausing over the first button and buttonhole of his open fly: apparently only now putting together that she'd tried to slap him and wasn't happy. "Oh, wait," he said as if *he* were the wounded party. "You aren't going to claim you didn't let me do that."

She stopped rubbing and flexing her wrists to fix him with a glare. "Let you? My hands were tied."

"I know." He actually laughed, shaking his head. "I'd have never guessed: Aren't you the perverse little thing?"

"N-no, I'm not. You made me—"

"Oh, please. I didn't. I wouldn't. You chose to, exactly as you said. I'd hardly rape you." Then he blinked, laughed, and recanted. "Unless you wanted me to." He raised that eyebrow. "Aren't *you* the dark one? I simply can't get over it."

"I most certainly am not!"

"You liked it. For godssake, you all but bit my shoulder at the end. You—"

Bit his shoulder. Had she? No, surely not. At which point, she bit her lip, her face heating, because she did remember something else. She'd done that thing, she realized that she could do sometimes. She grew warmer still as she let it fully register. Oh, dear, that convulsing, quivering—oh, blast, that really good feeling, only it had never been quite so quick to arrive, and, worse, the sensation hadn't wholly departed yet. She had no name for it, for what her body had just done, yet there its aftermath was, an echo of "it," that feeling, that lingered as a warmth in her belly as a kind of liquidy, pourable languor, only better and everywhere, but particularly in her pelvis and right between her legs.

"I did *not* bite your shoulder," she muttered.

"Here," he said, that eyebrow coming up in an expression of both amusement, the jackass, and mild annoyance. "Look," he said as if *he* were put out! Oh, the cheek of the man! He pulled at his shirt. He was going to untuck it again, unbutton it, show her his shoulder—

"Keep your shirt on," she told him sarcastically. "All right. I let you. Just don't imagine I ever will again. I won't." She could barely believe she had this one time. Within the first forty minutes of their being alone together. With—this really upset her now—her hands tied behind her. What kind of a depraved woman did such a thing?

It was his fault.

And, all right, her own, she thought with disgust: Dear God, didn't she love the good-looking ones, though? And wasn't old Stuart here one of *those*? Good-looking ones with renegade casts of mind, the rogues and rascals and black sheep. And wasn't this member of the upper house, who returned his attention to the buttons of his fly here, a surprising, though fully initiated, member of *that* club? He could outscoundrel the darkest blackguard she knew.

She stood up ever so slowly, yet recognized she was fine. Better than fine. That odd, warm feeling in her pelvis persisted. She felt relaxed in her belly in a way she hadn't in years. Relieved somehow. Probably from all the fright, she thought. Not that she wanted to think about it. "We won't be doing it again," she repeated.

He looked at her with such deep scrutiny, she had to look away. She heard him say, "A shame. You don't want to talk about it?"

"No."

Out the corner of her eye, she caught a glimpse—he was frowning at her as he ran his hand down his buttoned fly, shifting on his feet a moment as he also shifted his privates to a comfortable place in his trousers, then dismissed the whole business. "Whatever you want," he said. "Here." He tossed her a boot. "So what is the plan?" he asked.

"What plan?"

"The poke. Whatever you call it. If that was the poking part, then we're up to the send." He let out a syllable of laughter, just full of jokes.

"Very funny."

Emma took her boot and sat down on the floor, unable to face putting her bottom back on the only chair in the room. She drew on one boot, then the other in utter silence, so unnerved—or unused to the exercise she'd just had—her muscles trembled a little as she shoved her foot into the sloppy boot.

"Are you ready?"

She cranked her head around. Stuart stood by the door. He had her coat and clothes, the little sack in which she'd brought what she was wearing, her stupid wig, his own coat, and presumably the five hundred pounds—the money wasn't on the bed any longer. "Where are we going?"

"To my room to pack, then to my house, where you're going to explain in great detail everything we need to do in order to outsmart my uncle."

"I can't." She suddenly thought of a host of unarguable

reasons not to do what they'd just agreed to. "There's a tup I made an appointment to see. At the Stunnel farm. I have to go there. They're expecting me." She pulled a sarcastic face. "I was going to buy a new ram with your fifty quid, since you killed my other."

He nodded thoughtfully. "Is the Stunnel farm far?"

"Six miles from here."

"We'll go together. I'll send for my carriage."

Delightfully, this brought forth another reason they couldn't proceed. "I have a mule at the livery—"

"We'll have my footman fetch it. Where would you like it taken?" He hitched his things and hers up under one arm, letting his shoulder drop against the door: a tall, long-legged man in a white shirt resigned, as far as could be told, to further delay.

It must have been the fit of his clothes or the way he carried himself. The quality of the fabric. Something. Because, in a shirt, no neckcloth, and country breeches tucked into black boots, in these simple clothes, as he leaned there, he was so genuinely upper-class, so elegantly handsome, he all but hurt the eyes.

Emma stared at him. They were really going through with this. She and Mount Villiars, the viscount. Whom she'd just—no, she wouldn't think about what she'd done. That was past now. *Live in the present*, her mother used to tell her. Or words to that effect. *You are such a dreamer, Emma*, she had said when Emma was young. *Stop dreaming. Stop making things up*, and so Emma had. *Become practical*, she reminded herself now. *Concentrate on the man before you.* Who was actually, practically proceeding to drag her into swindling his uncle.

She had to gather her wits a moment to answer old Stuart's question—*Stuart, Stuart, Stuart*, she told herself. No false respect, just what is due him. Let him have her respect the old-fashioned way: Let him earn it, if he could. "Um, John Tucker's, I suppose," she answered with a degree now of equanimity. "Do you know where that is?"

"Will someone in the village? If so, my footman can ask and find the place. Anything else?"

He knew she was stalling. Then—yes!—she thought of another potentially immovable obstacle they hadn't explored yet. "Are you serious about your seat in the House of Lords? If you aspire to success there, you can't set up your uncle. You can't afford scandal."

"We aren't talking about a scandal. Are we?"

"There's a risk." What a surprise. He didn't deny political ambition. This unorthodox peer actually had some interest in the seat he'd assumed in the upper house. She felt a shot of glee. For a moment, she was sure she had something over him—she could make quite a stink merely over what he'd done so far.

Then he said, "For your information, I'm quite serious about sitting my seat. Though none of the important debates will begin till after Easter session break. As to scandal, I don't want it, but politics is not clean, Mrs. Hotchkiss. I presume, having navigated my way through the whims of Turkish caliphs, Persian protocol, and the court in Petersburg, I'm one up on most Englishmen when it comes to political intrigue. I'll manage." He added, "Though thank you for your concern."

Ha, she thought. "I could tell people what you're doing."

"You could. I'd say otherwise."

"It wouldn't matter what you said. It would all make interesting reading in the newspapers."

"Without doubt."

She pivoted on her skirts, slowly spinning to face him fully as she encircled her knees with her arms. "People would think badly of you."

He laughed. "Those who don't know me, and some who do, already think badly of me. What concern is that to me? If anything, people love to imagine their leaders have steel bollocks. Getting back at both my uncle and you in one blow, once all the facts were out, might even make me popular. The way I'm going about it would certainly make me a household name."

What an amazing view for a politician—more amazing still: He was one. "Aren't you frightened what they might do to you?"

"They? Who?"

"People. The newspapers. If not the law."

He shrugged. "I can take care of myself, if I have to. You've just seen an example. I'm formidable: not by nature a cruel man, but, if you'll notice, when someone is unfair to me, I can protect myself in a very large way."

She snorted again, shaking her head as she stood, dusting her skirt, onto legs that were still faintly shaky from all this, the monster. "You enjoyed frightening me," she accused.

"Yes," he agreed as if she were a promising student who'd just caught on. "That's why," he said. "If I must frighten someone, I do it with gusto. Coming?" He put his hand on the doorknob again.

She remained where she was, standing fully, staring at him, feeling unsettled again.

"Emma." The man at the door answered her discomposed look almost patiently. "It's a dark, nasty world, and you are looking at a well-adapted piece of it. There's no point in causing someone discomfort, then hating yourself for it. If it's appropriate, I go after people in a way that thrills me. Enjoy every moment of life is my motto, even the mean ones. Come on," he said and turned, taking the doorknob into his hand.

Just for her own "enjoyment," she didn't move.

He did. He opened the door wide this time and waited, expecting her to precede him. When she didn't, he looked back over his shoulder, seeming perplexed. Good.

"Are you coming?" he asked.

"No."

His eyebrows shot up, his whole face clouding over. He certainly had a quick temper, when a person flouted him.

"Yes, yes, yes." She laughed. "I'm coming. I was just teasing you, Mr. Democracy. 'Enjoying' myself, as you call it."

As she passed through the doorway, she shot him a look that said, *Lordy, are you ever impressed with yourself.*

By then, though, he was smiling faintly again, unfazed, the level look of a man who *was* impressive and knew it. Once more Emma felt the unfamiliar swing—like a boom cutting across her prow—of humility. Watch yourself, dear. Don't underestimate the reach of this man's power.

Old Stuart, on a number of levels, wasn't run-of-the-mill.

That feeling, that quivery feeling. Emma couldn't forget it for its traces lingering inside her. It left her limbs weak. As she and Stuart traipsed down the hallway, her belly still felt melty from it. Such a strange feeling, so familiar, yet distant. One moment, her mind wanted to remember it; the next, she wanted to hide from any recall of it, never face where the feeling came from or what it was exactly ever again. She was in Stuart's room, her buttocks leaning back on his door, her hands behind her, watching her new confidence game partner collect his possessions, before she pinpointed the last time she'd known this feeling: with Zach in London. Jesus God save me, she thought. She closed her eyes a moment.

When she opened them again, Stuart had dragged a suede satchel up onto his bed, spreading its hinge wide. He dropped her own things he'd carried into his leather bag, then shook the money into it from his coat as well, then laid the coat down. He threw in a book by his bed, then another from his pillow. Books. God, she'd loved Zach's books. She stared at Stuart and felt something inside her chest move, as if her heart had literally slid down six inches in her chest. He was too many things she liked. He was everything she liked. It frightened her silly, just looking at him.

No, sir, she told herself. Not in a million years. *Don't let him near you*, she told herself.

Yes, she would help as she'd promised, because she had to in order to keep herself out of jail, but he wouldn't touch her again, not for love nor money. She wouldn't let him within three feet of her. Not for any reason. One Zachary Hotchkiss per lifetime was enough for any woman. She'd cried herself sick over Zachary; she didn't plan on starting again.

"So what is the plan?" Stuart asked for at least the third time, as he looked at her across the bed and his filling satchel: He threw in a nightshirt—made of generous amounts of heavy white silk, rolled hems—very masculine, very luxurious. He slept apparently with all the ostentation of a white peacock.

No, Emma thought, the plan could wait. She needed to get this one point across. "Your lordship," she said with enough exaggerated respect that it came out rather disrespectfully, "I want you to understand that I did not like what we just did in the other room. For other reasons, besides the sexual. I do *not* want to do it again. If you attempt it, I'll do far worse than bite you." Not that she'd bit him the last time, but since that seemed to be a concern of his, she'd use his fear for all it was worth.

"Fine," he said. "I won't force you: I didn't last time."

"I did not like my hands tied."

"You could have fooled me. But all right. I won't tie them again. How's that?"

"Better."

"So you like your hands free?"

"Yes. At all times."

He laughed that deep, dirty chuckle he had, unfazed, as he bent to retrieve a pair of navy velvet-and-leather slippers, which he then tossed into the satchel.

You are sick, tying women to chairs, she wanted to say. While *I* am not. Best, however, she drop the subject. The man was hopeless.

He tossed in a sheaf of papers from the bed, legal documents of some sort, then braced his hands on the brass-hinged edge of the bag and contemplated her for a moment, as if he couldn't figure out how to say something. He said finally, "You know, Emma, you were married. Surely your husband had his moments—"

"His moments?" she broke in. Why did he make her so furious? She wanted to slap him again. She held her hands behind her back, literally gripping them: tying herself.

"His own idiosyncracies to lovemaking," said the nervy viscount before her.

Stuart, she reminded herself, then answered, "My husband made love to a bottle of gin most of the time. And to his sorrow and guilt over all the mistakes he'd made that he thought we're so unique and original and entirely his own doing, as if he were God—" She stopped.

They both stood there blinking at her admission: her tirade.

After London, Emma could count on one hand the times she'd made love with her husband, and not once had it been without incident or embarrassment—after London, Zach perpetually lost his erection at just the wrong moment. It had been the despair of both of them that the good Reverend Hotchkiss had never been able to perform as well as had the bad Reverend Hotchkiss—though in the end she'd stood by her husband, for better or worse.

She was no stranger to the pleasure between a man and woman, though, now that she remembered it. It was fine; it was normal. Yet neither did she know much about the sort of thing that had happened here just minutes earlier, which was *not* normal, she decided. Nor did she want to know. She had always assumed that variety of pleasure was confined to the bedroom, to being under the man, to wordless movements in the dark.

Dark indeed. Stuart's darkness was open, brazen.

She bowed her head. Silence. When she looked up again,

Stuart was taking out a handful of fresh cravats from a drawer of the nightstand, all of dark, dark blue silk, almost black. There was more fabric to Stuart's cravats than to the usual English one; they were more voluminous, almost French, if she remembered correctly. He drew one around his shirt collar, then slid a handful of others through his fingers like slithering snakes as he more or less poured them into the satchel. Perfect, she thought. The devil here wore snakes around his neck.

He began to tie his new cravat. She couldn't think what had become of the other one, didn't know where it was.

She looked away, surveying his room, trying to get her bearings, make herself feel better. The room looked exactly like hers, except for one less window. She'd been surprised to walk down the hall and realize his rooms were right next door. He'd rented three, for goodness sake, "for privacy." He slept in this one, the middle. As her gaze came back to him—he could tie a cravat without looking in the mirror, simply knot it, and it came out neat, splendid, dapper—she stared across his mussed sheets, no maid yet. Their mess seemed strangely provocative. He didn't sleep peacefully, she thought. He kicked his sheets.

Oblivious, Stuart found more possessions to toss through the hinged opening of the bag: a pressed, unworn shirt, a neatly folded vest, a spare collar. He rethought something, digging through the satchel suddenly, and pulled the sheaf of papers out. He rolled them, tied their ribbon, then set them on his coat by the satchel, apparently planning to carry them.

Then he turned his back on her, the bed, the satchel, and walked over to the sink. No undergarments, she realized. He'd picked up everything from the bed, the floor, and nightstand, but there were no undergarments whatsoever. Nor nightcap. Zach wore a nightcap to bed. Didn't all men? Seemingly not.

At the washstand, he picked up a hairbrush, its silver handle scrolling with fanciful engravings, initials, she'd guess, the handle mildly tarnished around the grip of finger impressions. He stuck a tortoiseshell comb into the brush's bristles, then gathered up a shaving cup with a fairly fresh bar of dry soap at the bottom, since she could hear it rattling around. He stuck a folded razor and damp lather brush into the cup as well, wrapped it all in a small towel, then dropped the whole bundle into a smaller case beside the water pitcher, as well as a toothbrush and tooth powder, then closed the case by means of a little trick of the leather, *pop*, that cleverly folded it in on itself.

When he turned completely it was to toss the case the short distance into the suede satchel. Then just Stuart himself. He stood in the middle of the room, apparently packed, pulling on his frock coat.

She was suddenly struck by how mortal he looked. Just a man. A handsome one, but ordinary. She said, "Where is everyone?"

He glanced up from buttoning his vest. "Everyone?"

"Your—" She hesitated. He didn't seem insulted, so she went ahead. "Your crew, my captain. Your acolytes. I didn't think you went anywhere without at least a half a dozen people."

He answered her question with a question. "How does a countrywoman know words like *acolytes*?"

"Married to a learned man for twelve years." When he wasn't foxed, Zach was brilliant. Half the time he was brilliant even when he was. "Four years in London with a lot of quasi-learned ne'er-do-wells."

Stuart pondered the information, frowning, as he smoothed his coat, then said, "I'll ring downstairs. My 'acolytes,' as you call them, will bring my carriage. What is the name of the farm we're going to again?"

"The Stunnels."

"After the Stunnels, shall we stop by your house? Do you have any clothes you'd like to pick up?"

Clothes. That was a laugh. "I have a better skirt and

blouse in that bundle you just threw into your satchel. Other than that, I have the one dress you saw at the bank and all the clothes I want"—she indicated the big, baggy dress she wore—"from the church charity bazaar." A bright thought occurred to her. "You're going to have to buy me better clothes, if you intend for me to play your uncle."

"Of course. What do you sleep in?"

Of course? He was buying her clothes? Then she glared at him. What did he mean, what did she sleep in? "None of your business."

He sniffed a breath of amusement down his nose, picking up his papers, then his coat. "For your *com-m*fort," he insisted with one of his pauses. "I notice you have no nightgown. Do you want to stop by your house and get one?" He laughed more leisurely, fully at ease, as he added, "I love how dirty-minded you are. It's one of my favorite things. Everything with you is about sexuality."

"I am *not* dirty-minded! It's you! You asked about my nightclothes."

He only smiled. "Fine," he said. "Don't sleep in a nightgown. Sleep naked for all I care. In fact, I rather prefer you do, though it's going to be damned cold in the winter."

"I—" Where had she gone wrong here? "I—I sleep in Zach's nightshirt. I don't have one of my own."

"He didn't buy you one?"

"H-he liked that I liked his."

"Then you can sleep in mine."

"No!" She thought of all that heavy, sliding silk on her body and . . . well, it would . . . oh, God. She didn't know. She couldn't wear Mount Villiars's nightshirt. Could she? "Zach's is flannel. It—"

"It's a poor man's nightshirt," he finished. "Emma, do we have to bring your husband along with us on this? I take it he wasn't always an asset. Let's not bring his nightshirt. Mine will be fine. It won't devour you." He let out a light laugh. "Only I want to do that. The nightshirt is harmless. It will be far too big, but warm and comfortable for the time being. Then we'll buy you some very pretty things in London."

Yes. She frowned. No. He was going to buy her very pretty nightgowns? No, he meant he was going to buy her very pretty clothes, and she would need them to convince his uncle of her authenticity as an underground art dealer. Very pretty clothes. This was good, wasn't it? Stuart here would pay for them. This was all harmless. She was being foolish. She liked pretty clothes.

So why was she uncomfortable? And angry again?

It occurred to her, "Don't expect it to get you anywhere."

"Oh, I don't," he said immediately and smiled, shaking his head. Then smugly, "I don't need help. I'm very capable of getting where I want to on my own, without buying you anything."

Right. She blinked. Here was why she was angry, not the other: He'd already gotten where he wanted once without so much as a sweet word. Just a chair and his neckcloth. What was wrong with her? There was something here he understood better than she did. And the damn man intended to use it. While she had the eeriest feeling that if she didn't figure out what it was soon, she was going to end up in bed with him again.

He picked up her coat, the satchel, carrying everything. Emma's hands felt empty, bare. With Zach, she carried everything and, half the time, him.

She took one last look at Stuart and said, "I don't want to go. I don't want to go to London and swindle your uncle."

"We've already been through this. Why are you hedging?"

"Besides the fact that it's a stupid idea?"

"What's stupid about it?"

"It's dangerous."

"So was robbing me."

"I didn't see that."

"Ah. So swindling my uncle is more dangerous than swindling me?"

"I don't know. What are your uncle's limits? Will he shoot us if we make a mistake and he realizes the truth? Is he violent?"

Stuart frowned. "I can't say for sure. If he's like my father, yes. But you've done this in London. So then you've dealt with all sorts: You know how to deal with potentially violent people."

She turned away. She did. "A cackle-bladder," she murmured.

"A what?"

"It's a way to deal with the violent ones. You make them party to the consequences of violence, make them believe they've murdered someone."

"Well, there you go then. We'll make Leonard think he's killed someone? Who?"

"You or me. One of us shoots the other before Leonard thinks to. We use a gun with no powder in the bullets, blanks, and a little bladder of turkey blood that one of us puts in his or her mouth just before the shot. Then you break the bladder with your teeth and bleed all over him."

Stuart laughed, startled. "My goodness. Oh, let me bleed on Leonard. Then how does he not find out? I mean, I'm a member of the Legislative Council. I'll have to be there the next vote."

"Leonard won't be. If all goes well, if he's scared enough, we send him to some far corner of the world to hide out forever. Timbuktu."

"Goodness, this sounds rather like a lot of fun." Stuart was delighted. "Not *only* do I get my possessions back, I never have to lay eyes on Leonard again. I can *hardly* wait to bleed on him." His odd-appealing pauses again—*only*, then *hardly*—provided a kind of emphasis and rhythm. The more she talked to him, the less she noticed the pattern. She made a special note to herself to listen, to see if she was simply getting used to it or if he was doing it less.

"Just pray it isn't your own blood," she told him. "It's not a joke, Stuart, what you're planning. I wish I could talk you out of it. You simply can't account for every possibility." She hesitated, because she hated to remember: "We had a mark once who had a real gun. No one knew. He shot four people, myself one of them."

Stuart's expression grew grave. He furrowed his brow. "I'm glad you lived. Where were you shot? You look perfectly fine."

"Here." She touched her temple and ear, running her fingers into her hair, holding them there a moment. "And I am perfectly fine, but of the ten people involved, I am the only one who is."

As she said the words, something inside her quaked, something she held down by tightening the muscles of her chest till the feeling subsided. Steel. Zach used to say she was made out of steel. *You are so strong, Emma. As if your flexible, sturdy spine, each disk, were made of Excalibur-hard metal: mettle. I love your sturdy mettle.*

While she'd loved how he loved her and that he could express it while playing with words. A long cry from any sheep farmer's son.

Confidence. She'd been so full of confidence in herself once. Confidence games. Arrogance games. She didn't trust herself anymore. Not as she once had, and perhaps that wasn't so bad.

Nor did she trust the man standing before her. Stuart watched her, waiting, loaded down with a satchel, papers, his fine coat, her own raggedy one, his hat, gloves: the man from the bank. "Shall we?" asked her most recent lover.

"Certainly," she said, lifting her big, baggy skirt as if it were one of the ball gowns she'd once worn, while inwardly shaking her head. She'd mated with him. Like a ewe in estrus. She still couldn't grasp it. Why? How?

Then worse: As he reached for the doorknob with the arm loaded down with his satchel, he winced, then gripped his shoulder, pushing his thumb into the muscle, massaging. He stood a moment, then actually set the satchel down.

"What's wrong?" she asked, when she should have remained quiet.

"My shoulder," he said. "I think you really did bite it."

"Oh, I did not! You have the gout."

"All right. Wait." He let go of their coats as well and began yanking at his coat.

"Stop," she cautioned. "I don't want to see your chest."

"My shoulder. *I* want to see what you did."

He shrugged partway out of his coat to undo again the top of his shirt and cravat.

Emma looked away.

Out the side of her eye, though, she saw he'd pulled his shirt open nonetheless. She caught a glimpse of his neck and upper chest—a remarkably muscular chest with a hint of fine black hair down the center—then he shrugged a thick, sculptured shoulder forward, and Emma found herself staring: at faint teeth marks sunk into the top round head of muscle, deep indentations even if they didn't break the skin.

"Look at that!" he said, laughing.

Emma bit the edge of her lip. "It's not from something else?" A tattoo, for instance, to make women feel bad.

"No."

"Um. My, ah"—she tried to piece it together, now that she saw the reality—"my, ah, hands weren't free—" Yes, that part was right. "And I, um—wanted to feel your, ah—" She kept staring at the marks she'd left, asking herself how they could have gotten there. "Well, your shoulder— Because. Um. It seemed to be very hand"—she couldn't admit the whole word at once—"some. So I wanted to. Feel. It."

"Why, thank you."

She looked to his face.

He was smiling as he straightened his shirt, buttoning, self-satisfied. "To tell you the truth, I barely noticed at the time. I was"—he laughed—"preoccupied elsewhere. It's all right. I can take it. You don't bite hard, though to tell you the truth I'd rather you didn't do it."

"I'm sorry." She'd be more careful. Or, no, there wouldn't be opportunity to be more careful. But, still, one shouldn't hurt people unnecessarily.

He said to her bowed head, "I'm not. No regrets or apologies here. It was damned exciting. You have a little vicious streak. A little one, not a bad one; it's delightful."

"Oh, I don't. I'm a nice woman."

He was smiling, his dark eyes dancing, riveted to her. "Who bites." He laughed, then repeated, "A dark, nasty world, Emma. Welcome to the human race."

She allowed herself a sheepish, befuddled smile. There was something funny here, if embarrassing. If he was laughing over it, teasing her with it, then how bad could it be that she had—

Dear goodness, that she had bit the man? A little. Lightly. On the shoulder.

She'd bit him. And licked his thumb. Not since she was seventeen had she thought *this* dangerous thought: Men were delicious. Or the right one could be.

Tightening his cravat back in place again, he asked once more, "Shall we?"

She nodded, a little subdued, though she'd regained a measure of her poise by the time he held the door wide. "Yes," she said, "we shall," and wheeled around two handfuls of frumpy skirt, as regal as a queen. She knew the walk, the talk, how to handle herself. She remembered. It was with mixed pleasure, though, that she waltzed past Mount Villiars through the doorway.

PART TWO

The Poke

Yorkshire Pudding

Sift three-quarters cups flour and a half teaspoon salt into a bowl. Measure out a cup of milk, but then only add enough of it to the flour mixture to make the thickness of heavy cream. Beat two eggs in a separate bowl until slightly thick, then combine with the remaining milk. Combine two mixtures and beat until large bubbles appear on the top. Let this stand one hour (the last hour of roasting meat, from which you will use some of the fat). Take roast from oven and drain off fat, pouring enough of these drippings into each cup of a popover pan to cover the bottom. Put popover pan into oven at 425 degrees and heat until fat is spitting. Remove from oven and fill each little cup half full of flour, egg, and milk mixture. Return to oven and bake twenty-five to thirty minutes. The puddings will rise up over and brown. Serve immediately from hot oven with gravy.

—EMMA DARLINGTON HOTCHKISS
Yorkshire Ways and Recipes

Chapter 7

What's meant for ye will not get by ye.

—Scottish saying

EMMA and Stuart waited less than a minute on the hotel steps before his black-lacquered coach and eight rolled around the corner. The temperature was falling. The wind was icy as it cut through her coat. As the vehicle pulled to a halt, it seemed so much larger than she remembered—or perhaps simply more huge as one proceeded toward it. Walking out to the big, black thing made her heart thud.

Impressive wasn't quite the word for the carriage anymore. *Daunting* seemed more appropriate. The coach to Hell. Its interior seemed larger than the back room of her house. It took more horses to pull it than she and her neighbors owned in total. The shiny, black carriage gleamed against the white winter afternoon, by contrast fit for the devil himself, the devil's own footman awaiting her, his hand on a filagree brass door handle. The clean lines stood out vividly. And the windows. She had never noticed how many windows it had—perhaps because over each dangled the gold tassel and fringe of a window shade, her guess being that most of the time these shades were down, obliterating the windows.

Presently though, the windows were wide, high, and unshaded, their clean glass reflecting a picture-perfect elongation of the yellow stone hotel with its black door and blue awning, then herself, bareheaded, coming down the walk with a dark, neatly dressed gentleman at her elbow. Stuart looked every inch the viscount coming toward his carriage: a tall man in a long greatcoat and high top hat, his clothes making him seem taller still. He towered over her and his footman.

The vehicle's door latch *clicked,* then swung open, the gold fringe of its window's privacy shade shimmying in a little dance of heavy, twisted silk. Inside the lining of the door matched the carriage seats: dark red, button-tufted leather. The servant bent to set the step, then offered his hand. Emma was about to ascend into a cavernous interior of dark leather, polished wood, brass, crystal, velvet . . . so much luxury, it was hard to take it all in. Then a horse whinnied, several stomped, adjusting, and the carriage shifted an inch—and the two footmen, the driver, and the viscount himself all responded by turning their attention sharply toward the team of eight in front.

"Are they giving you trouble today?" the viscount called up to his driver.

"No more than usual, sir."

Stuart veered, turning away from the carriage entrance to walk down his line of skittish horses.

The closest lead animal snorted again, yanking its head up.

"Easy," Stuart murmured, though he approached the horse cautiously. It stomped and gave a kick, sharp enough that the animal behind it grew worried. The whole team was unstable for a moment. Stuart grabbed the tack of the near lead and pulled the animal's head down by the bit. "Easy," he said again, then stroked him as he slowly eased up. "Easy."

He let go. The animal seemed better, calmer. It knew him. Stuart stayed there a moment, then backed up, speaking to the driver overhead in a conversation she couldn't quite hear. The viscount nodded, then looked at the horses again as he folded his arms over his chest.

Emma waited, thinking any moment he would return,

they would get going. But he seemed inclined to pose there by his horses—alas, as fine a sight as they in his slightly foreign-looking clothes: black top hat, black gloves, his long, fur-lapeled greatcoat. His coat blew, unbuttoned, in the wind, showing its rich inside by furls and billows. Likewise, about his shoulders, his gray scarf fluttered loose, animated by the wind—floating up one moment on a ghostly breeze, then darting the next on a wintry blast.

The second footman, having finished putting their things in the boot, approached the driver and viscount, offering something more, presumably to do with the horses. Stuart listened, questioned him. The driver called down further comments from his overhead box. The three of them, driver, footman, and employer spoke together, with Stuart erect, direct, all business. She was reminded of the man from the bank again, the man who did not smile easily. Hardly at all, in fact.

The man with the ironic humor and dark smiles seemed to have been left upstairs. It was as if, when his servants lined up behind him, when he put on his hat and frock coat, his scarf and gloves—the regalia of a viscount—they weighed him down.

He should get away, take all these clothes off more often, she thought.

Oh, dear. Her eyes widened as she abruptly looked down at her own feet. No, no, perhaps not, she thought. Best he keep all his clothes on, come to think of it, the more the better as a matter of fact.

Damned, rich, snotty, handsome. . . . She glanced up to where he stood, so straight and tall, dallying over his fancy horses. She called suddenly to him, "If everything is all right, can we go? I don't have the leisure you do."

He stopped in midsentence and turned toward her. They all did: staring at the woman in the tattered coat who would interrupt a viscount in the business of his favorite horses.

"Can we go?" she asked no less emphatically. She was purely peeved to have so little control over her own life.

He lifted his chin. She could see beneath the brim of his hat for a moment—he had that one eyebrow cocked at her.

She wasn't sure if his look was some sort of command or prompt, but she decided it did no harm to say, if a little sarcastically, "Please?" Then decided to add, "Sir?" then more elaborately, "Your lordship?"

He let out a kind of gasp of humor, surprise. "Gadzooks," he pronounced, an old-fashioned expression, which he perhaps knew was such; said to amuse. Still, it made him sound out of touch with what she knew of the clubs and smoking rooms of London, when he added a word he seemed to know better, one of those foreign mouthfuls that wanted to be ten syllables that his tongue compressed into three. It began with *nyaow*, like the yowl of a cat, and ended in *chnyee*. Russian, she judged. It didn't matter; she liked the sound of his speech. She could listen to it appreciatively, even when it meant nothing at all to her.

Then he said in English, "Yes. We can go. How lovely that you can be so respectful. It's a nice step, Emma." He pivoted. "Let's." He began to walk toward her. Halfway there, he called to her, "When?" He seemed to realize the question wasn't enough and clarified, "When was your lamb hit?"

"Um—" She had to think a moment. "Um, August."

"I took the coach in August. When in August?"

He hadn't had the coach the whole month? Emma frowned, mentally sliding around on the implications of his question. "You're saying your uncle may have killed my lamb?"

He came up to her, lifting his head slightly to make eye contact. In the shadow of his hat brim his eyes frowned, then he shook his head and let out a large sigh as he dropped his hands into the pockets of his coat. "It doesn't matter." He let out a little snort of self-rebuke, letting his inquiry go. "You had me right the first time. I am capable of having killed your lamb, then given you a hard time about it." He looked down at the snow, then squinted up again to ask her, "Though is that so terrible?"

The look on his face seemed to be asking no less than if he were a terrible person.

"It was fairly terrible for the lamb."

"The horses," he jerked his head toward them. "They're fast. I've grown fond of them." He pulled a face. "They are also the most crazed animals I have ever tried to manage. I keep attempting to soothe them. My father"—he raised that sarcastic eyebrow—"what a surprise: He beat them, denied them food—" He broke off in revulsion for a moment, couldn't speak, then met her eyes again. "In any event, I keep thinking gentleness will bring them back to some semblance of normalcy. Do you think that's possible?"

She felt less qualified than most to answer, but she offered, "For some it is; for some it isn't." She didn't know horses, but that's how it was with people.

"They are gorgeous, don't you think?" He turned to enjoy again the view of them with her. "And even more remarkable for being so well matched."

"Yes."

"And their speed and heart—" He broke off.

She waited.

"Two or three of them," he continued, "are coming around, I'm quite sure. The lead on the left, though—" The left lead was bobbing his head, impatient. Stuart, in profile, shook his head. "But even the one who bites and kicks, even he gallops with the team. That's a good sign, isn't it? They, all eight, put their souls into hauling the coach as if their lives depended on getting to the next place as quickly as the road can take them. My driver says they drive him, that that is the only way to manage them: a loose rein."

He loved his horses. His bad horses. He was trying to save them. Along with seventy-seven servants. What was going on here? She frowned up at him, feeling the cold on her face as she tried to comprehend this man and why he would speak so earnestly to her, of all people, about his concerns.

She asked, "It's dangerous, isn't it? I mean to you, not just to lambs."

He looked directly at her. "It doesn't feel unduly dangerous. They stay to the road." He shrugged and looked down. Then admitted, "I can't tell. Normally, they gallop around things. I think the road must have been bent, too little space to shift, once they saw your lamb."

"They shouldn't have been going that fast."

He disliked this unpleasant, unwanted answer. With a quick frown, he said, "They are the only living connection to my father who doesn't take advantage of me, who bears me no ill will." He sighed. "And now you're saying they aren't innocent either."

"They're animals. All animals are innocent."

He looked at her. "We're animals."

"Other than man. Horses, dogs, cats, they are guilty of nothing. They are just following their nature."

He contemplated her narrowly a moment. "Perhaps that's all we do, too."

She considered his words, then modified her own thinking. "Responsible then. We aren't guilty, just responsible in a way that they aren't."

He nodded, took one gloved hand from his coat, offering his hand. She took it and quickly stepped herself up into the coach. She settled herself into a well-padded seat of leather so dark a red it was almost black. The appointments of the interior were gleaming—polished wood that showed the grain, side lamps of cut crystal, brass fittings and handles, velvet-rope hand straps. The highlight, though, was indeed the windows with their shades up. They offered a panorama to the passengers, a view in almost all directions.

And the smell—settling back into Stuart's coach was like sitting into a rich little corner of Marrakesh. As if someone had rubbed the leather and wood with sandalwood, bay, and clove . . . or, no. These were smells she knew. Lotus? What did lotus smell like? Frankincense? She knew no name for the smell that permeated the interior, only the sweetness of it. And the recognition of it: It was the odor that faintly lingered on his clothes, in the fur of his coat.

Indeed, the smell had a name: Stuart Winston Aysgarth, the Viscount Mount Villiars.

From her seat, she watched him climb in after her. In one movement—a smooth lift, bow, and pivot—he slid into the seat facing her, his footman shutting the door. Stuart *was* what Zach could only imitate: part of the worldly, creamy upper class.

"Have you eaten lately?" he asked as he settled himself into the seat.

She startled. "This morning."

He furrowed his brow, then leaned to put his arm out the window. He made a motion with his gloved fingers.

A moment later, his footman appeared again just outside at the window. "Yes, sir?"

"Is there anything special you want?" he asked her. "I don't remember much of Yorkshire cuisine."

She was hungry. She'd eat anything. "Not lamb," she couldn't resist saying, however. "I've had my fill of that lately."

"Be specific. I don't know what to ask for at the shops here."

She named some favorites. "Yorkshire pudding, pork pie, and mushy peas."

To his man, he said, "Ask the concierge where to find Yorkshire pudding, pork pie, and"—he glanced at her askance—"mushy peas. We're going to the Stunnel Farm. Have Freeman meet us there with these delicacies. Meanwhile, you go to the livery stable and pick up a mule left by Emma Hotchkiss. Sign my name for it." To Emma again, he asked, "John Tucker's, correct?"

She had to think a moment, not quite able to keep up with him. "Um, yes."

"Can you give easy directions to his farm?"

"Across the meadow and road from my house."

"Which is where?"

"Down the hill about eleven miles from yours."

He frowned, then turned to the footman. "Find John Tucker's farm. Do you have the rest?"

"The rest?" The fellow looked worried.

"The food, the livery."

Concern crossed the footman's face. "Ah— Not precisely perhaps."

With a kind of humorless patience and the specificity of someone used to giving orders to those who could misunderstand, Stuart said, "Have Freeman bring Yorkshire pudding, pork pies, and mushy peas to the Stunnel Farm. You are to pick up Mrs. Hotchkiss's mule at the only livery in town and take it to Malzeard-Near-Prunty-Bridge. Ask around for someone named John Tucker. Take the mule to him. Then get yourself home."

The man nodded this time, said, "Right-e-o," and disappeared.

"There you go," Stuart told her.

Emma twisted her mouth. "Well. Snap your fingers, and someone fixes everything. That must be nice." Her words came out with a little more hostility than she'd meant to allow.

He faced her, the brim of his silk top hat lifting till he was looking at her squarely, then he said absolutely straight-faced, "Actually, it's not. I find it rather an onerous responsibility. It would be easier to do many things myself." He shrugged, as if none of it could be helped, tilted his head, his face dropping back into shadow, and grew silent.

Then more unexpected still: Instead of signaling to go, he added, "You can keep the fifty-odd pounds. And when we're finished, provided you deal straight with me, I'll explain the whole situation, tell the bank, the authorities that I want you to have the money. I'll explain my part in it. It's my own account. I shouldn't get into too much trouble for taking money from myself, even though it violates some court orders. I'll get a slap on the hand." He shrugged. "Whatever I get, I'll face it. The fact that I come forward will help."

She stared at him. He was offering her a clean slate. And the fifty-six pounds she'd stolen. Provided she helped him. "All right." What else could she say? "Thank you."

Yes. Of course, she wanted this. She sat there staring into his dark eyes under the brim of his hat, trying to fathom what Mount Villiars was about, what made him tick.

While Stuart met her eyes, thinking, Yes. At last. His first inroad on what he called to himself their Hotel Accident. *I seem to have accidentally shagged her*, was how he phrased it silently. It just happened. He couldn't explain it. Other than to say that a once-in-a-lifetime, unbelievably erotic moment had arrived before him, and its odd tenderness had simply not been something he'd wanted to throw away. So he'd given in to it—though now he was fairly certain that doing so had somehow been a mistake.

She bit her lip, then said, "You may be proving some of my darker suspicions about you wrong."

"Excellent," he said and laughed. "Not all, though, I trust." His laughter became rueful—and, for the life of him, he could not contain a dirty edge to it. It was too delicious to tease her. A wicked part of him loved her doubt of him; it loved her off-balance.

He sat there smiling at her. *Your lordship* indeed. She had not a whit of respect for his title. Which was why, perhaps, she amused him so. It gave them a secret, unspoken point of agreement. He thought it ludicrous, too, that an accident of birth, having nothing to do with his own actions, should mean anything at all to people around him. But mean something it did. And he wasn't willing to give up the privileges his birth bestowed simply because Mrs. Hotchkiss saw through it. She would toe the line like everyone else—it would be his pleasure to see to it.

After a moment, he caught himself, remembering what they were about—he might have sat there staring at her all day—and raised his hand. He struck the ceiling with his gloved knuckles, and the coach took off. Like that: He tapped and the wheels dug into the gravel in almost the same instant, as if the horses had been pulling, raring to go, just waiting for him to let them out the gate.

As they took off up the street, he called to her over the gathering noise, "Are these not the fastest, most responsive horses you have ever known?"

She only eyed him, perhaps too afraid to open her mouth. Or too contrary.

It didn't matter; he loved his coach and eight. They were the one extravagance of his uncle's he agreed with. The coach leaned and darted through the village lanes, as fast as it dared. It was when they pulled out onto country roads, however, that the horses truly seemed to take to the air.

Stuart closed his eyes, strangely at peace. For a moment, he was gliding on the blades of his sleigh, outside Petersburg, cutting across the open snow, moving fast, no impediment in sight. Just white, white snow as far as the eye could see. His English carriage had in common with his Russian troika the small miracle of grace and speed and movement, the power of strong, beautiful animals that pulled wonderfully, galloping in unison. He jostled gently, lulled by the rhythmic ring of a single bell that made time to the jingling tack. His bell. He had in fact taken it off his troika, the sleigh left behind. He'd cut it from the high center harness an hour before he'd departed, thinking to bring with him the sound of something familiar.

He didn't think anything could ruin his pleasure in the horses. Until he opened his eyes and happened to glimpse Emma's face, contorted with worry. She held on to the hand strap for dear life. He frowned at her caution, wishing he could convince her otherwise. He watched her heed, then sat up straighter himself. It became an effort to relax while witnessing her tension.

Indeed, it was only when the horses' clatter *whoa'd* to a halt, to silence, that Emma could let out breath—she would never have dreamed eight horses could gallop so fast for a mile, let alone the six miles to the Stunnels' farm.

She sat there a moment in Stuart's coach, staring at their destination: a little brick house at the top of a snowy rise of land, more snow on its roof, icicles dangling from it, melting in the sunny afternoon. She felt all but stunned by the normalness of the sounds outside. A sheep calling. A bird somewhere. They were here—the fact that they had arrived seemed a miracle. They'd covered the distance between town and the farm in a quarter hour.

As he helped her down, Stuart frowned, and said, "It was an accident."

The lamb. He was uneasy, too, now. Uneasy and annoyed, apparently, that she'd introduced doubt in him regarding his beloved horses.

But she wouldn't feel sorry for it. It seemed all right to have a degree of doubt, when a misstep could land you in a ditch or worse. Good. A little doubt seemed good in this instance. Have a little care, Stuart.

Chapter 8

THE Stunnels were an older couple. Maud, John Tucker's elder sister, was tall, spare, and in both posture and topography absolutely as straight as a plank. Longevity apparently ran in the family, because she looked ancient, though solid and in no way ready to leave this earth: a long, thin slab of a woman, a gray rock, with a lot of cracks and grooves. Her husband, Pete, if slightly taller, looked agelessly similar, as if they had grown to resemble each other over the course of the longest marriage Emma had ever heard of. Tomorrow, their children would arrive to celebrate their sixty-seventh wedding anniversary.

Which was why, on January 7, Maud told Emma, "After ye look at the tup, we was hoping ye'd help us cut doon a tree." A Christmas tree. Maud, Pete, and Emma discussed the tree on their walk toward the ram's pasture. "To spruce oop the place"—she passed a look to her husband, as if they shared a joke—"for the wee lads and lasses. All the grandchildren and two great-grand-'uns," she announced proudly, "be coming here, ye see." She had exactly John's northerly accent.

It turned out they wanted a spruce tree cut down in order to stand it up in their front parlor. They claimed there were several such trees in their far west meadow, which was just "a hop away" from their northwest pasture where they kept the ram they wanted to sell. They'd been waiting all day in hope that, after they settled the sale of the ram, Emma would be able to help with the tree.

They most surely needed help, she thought. Between the two of them, there was not a finger that didn't zigzag from arthritis. Neither Maud nor Pete could have gripped a saw well enough to pull it back and forth through a tree trunk. Emma could, she supposed. Her hands were strong. She was sturdy. She was willing. Willing, that is, if Stuart would wait.

He remained down the lane by the coach, blowing visible breath in the air as he murmured to his horses.

"Fine," Emma said, as they arrived at the fence over which she could see a ram. Let Stuart come up and get her, if he wanted her.

As she put her forearms across the top of the fence, Maud, then her husband, one on each side, looked slightly askance down at Emma: about six inches down. She was considerably shorter than either of them; her arms, where she rested them on the fence, came to her chest.

All right, it had to be a small, squatty tree. What other choice did they have? They had been hoping for a bigger human being to arrive, she supposed.

From the fence, they talked over their business transaction: what the ram's habits were, what the scar on his back leg was from. At some point, the Stunnels began to throw glances at the tall man in the distance. Oh, yes, by all means. Emma laughed inwardly. Fat lot of good it would do them to want the viscount to cut down their tree. Though, come to think of it, perhaps his wiry coachman could do a better job than she could.

Meanwhile, the ram was a full-grown and rather rowdy fellow. Emma hadn't realized: She wanted a quieter animal or, better still, a younger one that she could work with a little. When she told the Stunnels their tup wasn't what she was looking for—a little embarrassed not to have known her own mind better—they barely paid attention. They had both stopped to stare fully at the man at the end of the lane by the prancing team of horses. He'd left his coat in the carriage, taken it off ten minutes ago for being too warm. Coatless, in clear view, he stood, contemplating his animals: a man tall enough to lean an elbow on the coach's high wheel as he casually bit at the side of his fingernail.

His driver was hunched overhead in the seat, a man who, come to think of it, when he stood, was only an inch taller than Emma. Stuart's two footmen were at the rear, both of them thin, under twenty, neither within six inches of Stuart's tall height, none of them with his robust build.

It was true. For sawing down trees, Stuart would seem to be the pick of the lot. Emma was rather amused to see that the Stunnels intended to have him. How to tell them that the only large, truly strong person here had fifteen snotty titles and seventy-seven servants, so he didn't have to drive his own coach or even open its door or so much as sign his own name?

Maud Stunnel waved at him.

Stuart saw her and froze. He glanced up at his driver. Emma was certain he would send the man. Then he didn't. He realized they wanted something of him specifically. And, blast, if he didn't start toward them, cooperative the one time Emma would have liked his usual standoffishness. She didn't want to introduce him. She couldn't think how to explain their association. And whatever was said would travel back to John and thus the entire village. Oh, fine.

Stuart actually had to leap a fence to get to them, or else walk around the house the back way, which he didn't know to do. He took his hat off as he approached the fence, then, one hand on the wood rail, he took it—a sideways lift of his whole body in a single motion that brought him over. He didn't even break stride, coming over a fence as high as his chest with the jauntiness of a dressage curvet: as if he were a great big shiny Thoroughbred, who could kick his heels over fences twice that high. Something in Emma sighed—he was so blessed graceful she could have watched him do that particular maneuver a dozen times. Go back, Stuart. Go back and vault the fence again.

As he came up, she saw him as the Stunnels must. The sort of tall, slender, broad-shouldered man made to wear layers of fine clothes and look nothing but elegant, healthy. His broad-shouldered frock coat looked well filled out. His vest, in lustrous stripes of dark blue satin, buttoned snugly across a wide chest. His light gray trousers tucked into his outrageously festive—foreign—riding boots strode on long, strong strides. Ah, yes, a lumberjack, if ever she saw one. A lumberjack with a silk hat in hand. Indeed, he was a picture, the effect perfectly set off by his dark good looks and slightly too-long hair. A lock in fact fell forward, long enough to flop at the bridge of his nose as he walked. He looked like a foreign prince, the Russian tzar come to join them.

Emma asked of the Stunnels, "Where's the saw?" Since she knew where all this was going, best to get them there without explanations.

They looked at one another, flummoxed. They were hoping for great big, fancy explanations, no doubt about it.

Too bad. "The saw," Emma reminded them. She was finished with the tup. Now she wanted to be finished with the whole business.

They had a saw actually hanging out a tree they'd started down the meadow, having wrestled the tool as far as they could.

With a grunt, Pete Stunnel tugged a wood-handled, three-foot, jag-toothed saw from the inch cut that held it in an eight-foot-tall Norway spruce. When he handed the saw to Stuart, Emma giggled; she couldn't help it.

Stuart stared at it, holding it by the handle backward. She took it from him, turned it, and put it correctly into his long, uncallused fingers. "Drag the teeth back and forth till the tree falls over," she said.

"Fancy that." He lifted his haughty eyebrow at her, then pulled his mouth. "It's not a difficult concept."

She laughed. Right, he cut down trees every day. No problem.

Surprise of surprises, he attempted it. It was a struggle for a full minute, with the Stunnels looking back and forth at each, part-perplexed, part-amused. He had the strength, just not the experience. Emma herself was greatly entertained: the local viscount trying to hack down an evergreen two weeks after Christmas for some dotty old couple she barely knew.

Then all at once Stuart got the rhythm. He drew a few efficient strokes, back then forth, realized he had it, then for some reason stopped. He took off his frock coat, folded it neatly, unbuttoned his collar in forty-degree weather, then his vest. After which the man blitzed through an eight-inch-diameter pine tree in under two minutes. Not only did he saw it down, afterward, much to Emma's amazement, he picked it up by the trunk and dragged the heavy thing behind them all the way to the fence, where he pitched it over, did that lovely leap on his one arm again, then helped each of the other three of them over: She herself, he grabbed by her bum as she came to the top of the fence, then smiled as he set her down beside him. The Stunnels were already on their way to the house by then, oblivious, too busy exclaiming over how much quicker it was this way than dragging the tree around the back of the house.

Maud Stunnel was thrilled that their "new neighbor"—how she and her husband began to refer to Stuart—stood their Christmas tree in the stand for them in the middle of their small parlor. She said chattily, "The place looked so dreary," waving a gnarly hand that resembled a crab. "The children'll never guess we dint havvit oop all along." Other than, of course, it was a bright, soft, dewy fresh green.

To Emma, their front parlor looked cluttered, if not exactly deary. Its furniture seemed as old as its owners, with now a big, sappy tree crowding in on an assortment of chairs, unmatched, seemingly borrowed from everywhere; they were expecting a houseful. Nonetheless, the tree smelled lovely. Maud's smile was beaming: all but toothless, but bright and good-humored with merry, milky blue eyes. Pete, quietly puffing a pipe he got going, nodded and nodded at the sight of the tree, looking well pleased himself. Emma liked the couple's enthusiasm. And their cheerful agreement on such a belated piece of home decoration, not to mention the fun of fooling their own progeny.

At which point, daunting boxes of candles, garlands, and ornaments came out, along with broad hints that they'd like some help. Stuart wished them well as he put on his coat again. In the end, though, he put up a few ornaments on the tallest branches, the ones they couldn't reach as easily or safely. It was as if their bodies were made of matchsticks, Emma thought, delicately glued at the joints. One wrong move and they'd crumble into a heap. Yet something in them also flourished. Inwardly. She envied them their good-natured maturity.

And Stuart. He surprised her. She didn't know what to make of the fact that he could be so pleasant and biddable, when he chose.

"Last thing, last thing," Maud promised as she handed him a tin star with holes in it for a candle to twinkle out. Emma was happy to hear the woman call it a star, because it looked to her more like a child's top; she wouldn't have guessed.

It was when he stretched his long arm out to place the star on the top of the tree that Maud finally gave in to curiosity. She said to Emma, "So your escort here would be?"

Maud Tucker Stunnel, old though she might be, was not going to let anything get past her. She'd figured it out and wanted confirmation: their new neighbor. Or a neighbor if one counted that they lived forty miles from Castle Dunord, but when it came to something as rare and interesting as a viscount, people counted forty miles close, especially when on a clear day as today, from their front window, one could dimly see the castle itself on its hilltop.

Emma sighed and said, "Ah, this is the Viscount—" Blankness. Her brain stranded her in one of those moments wherein she could pull no name at all from her resistant, preoccupied mind.

"Mount Villiars," Stuart supplied.

The Stunnels' eyebrows in unison went up. Delight. There followed a long, pregnant silence as their heads, together, turned in Emma's direction.

She struggled to make a logical connection between a viscount and herself, why they were here together. "Yes, we're—"

"In love," Stuart interrupted. "Off to London, you see, to celebrate."

She gawked.

With a mild smile, he expanded further. "Two folks born in Yorkshire, you see. We have so much in common." He shrugged. "Nothing we can do for the fact that we can't marry. I mean, my being a viscount and having responsibilities that go beyond my sweet Emma. But that's no reason not to have our two weeks in London."

"One week. We're coming back, remember?" Emma added poisonously, "Dear." In love, indeed. She'd give him *in love.*

"Yes, to check on things, then going right back to the city afterward. After which, if we like our sojourn together, she'll probably move into Castle Dunord. Until we tire of each other, I suppose." He looked at her, then added, daring her to contradict him, "Sheriff Bligh's daughter lives around here, doesn't she?"

Maud Stunnel answered. Stuart could actually keep up a conversation with them. While the Stunnels stared from him to Emma, wide-eyed. Stuart, of course, was the main attraction. With his top hat and Continental manners. When he kissed Maud Stunnel's fingertips as they left, he sent her into peals of wheezy laughter.

In the coach, Stuart only got the side of Emma's face for the first five minutes of their ride—their wrapped parcels of pies and whatever else she'd wanted to eat that had arrived went untouched. She only glared out the window, unwilling to say anything. The usually talkative woman—he loved all her blather—had so much over which to be angry with him, he didn't try to examine which part might be keeping her from throwing a coherent remark in his direction.

Oddly—undeservingly, he knew—he wished he could have one.

He remembered fondly her nice I-might-have-been-mistaken comment, when she'd realized the true depth of his financial plight. He wanted again the sweetness of her understanding. Her cooperation. As the Stunnels had received. He'd been a little jealous over that, the way she'd immediately dropped what she'd come for, even him, to figure out how to accomplish their amusing, slightly absurd commission. A fresh Christmas tree in January as a hospitality gesture. Ah, well.

Only finally did Emma deign to look at him. Yes, definitely angry, when she said, "I don't appreciate that you told my neighbor's sister that I was your—"

"Paramour?"

"I was thinking of an uglier word."

"Thief?"

The coach jostled, which gave her the excuse to slam her hand flat on the seat beside her to steady herself. He'd given instructions that the driver was to hold the speed down as much as he could, since it made Emma so uncomfortable—not that she thanked him for it. They stared, eye to eye across the coach. "You're good at fixing sentences, aren't you? Or filling in words?"

He didn't know what she was getting at at first, then realized, ah, she'd found his stutter. Which made him smile and stretch, laying his arms out along the back of the coach seat. He liked being known. And that, even angry, she could use the word *good* in reference to a speech impediment. "Very," he said. He added, "And I've done you a favor. If it's simply a matter of your reputation, you can kiss that good-bye now. It's no longer a worry."

"You take my reputation lightly."

"I think the Stunnels are nice people. I don't think it's in serious trouble."

"Perhaps we should announce we're lovers in the House of Lords."

"Fine with me." He smiled. It was. He'd be happy to tell every man there how he did it. He was damned amazed that he'd managed it on a chair. He half wanted to grab strangers by their shirtfronts on the street and tell them, *You wouldn't believe what happened to me*. And with such a fine woman, too.

The fine woman puckered her mouth. For a moment, it seemed Emma was going to say something ugly, something crude: that he could kiss her arse perhaps. Then she seemed to think better of it. For fear he might—and he certainly would love to, which left him smiling more still, a strange feeling. He couldn't remember when he'd smiled so much in one day—in one year, in fact.

Instead, though, she only screwed up her mouth a notch further, then jerked her eyes away again to look back out the window.

Ah, what faces she could made. His favorite so far was how her pretty, round doll's cheeks could pull into sarcasm that could nip a chunk out of his ego—an ego he was fully aware could lose a few chunks and not have lost anything important. After a moment, she murmured to the open window, "You had no right."

Oh, yes, he did. He suggested, "Why don't you write that down. Put it in my handwriting. Perhaps I'll chance to read it, think I wrote it: Maybe then I'll believe you."

He wasn't sure how long he could use her misdeeds to run roughshod over her, but the privilege hadn't expired yet. She threw him a glance, a look of exasperation that quickly turned to dismay. Point taken.

Still, he felt a twinge of guilt. Only a twinge, until he caught sight of her rubber, mud-colored boots, the ugliest shoes he'd ever seen on a woman. He bent, swaying a little with the coach as he picked one up, her foot in it. She had to grab for the hand strap with one hand, the back of the seat with the other to keep her balance.

"These are awful," he said, holding on to the boot—she tried to take it back. "Can we get you new shoes somewhere?"

"The shoemaker would have to make them. It would take a week."

He rolled his eyes. "Not to make a pair of shoes, it doesn't. Not if he dropped what he was doing and just made them. We'll stop and have him take the measurements."

She slid down in the seat, bracing her other foot on his seat bench, crossed her arms, and yanked her foot back. Or tried to—he had a good solid grip of gum rubber. She came away with only her bare foot in its stocking, the tips of two toes sticking out. "He has the measurements," she said. "I have a pair shoes."

"Can we get them then? I hate these."

Stuart bent to reach for the other boot. This time it was a little trickier getting her foot, since she knew what was coming, but he caught it and yanked—with her scrambling again to hold on to the opposite seat or be pulled on top of him. He yanked the boot off and, in the same motion, pitched it and its mate out the window of the moving carriage.

"Hey!" She raised up, all but coming at him, then settled onto the edge of her seat, hanging there, gripping the cushion, her back rigid. "Those were Zach's."

"I'll buy you better ones." He tilted his head. "The dead husband's?" he asked.

She wasn't going to answer at first, then bluntly said, "Yes."

"How long is he dead?"

She frowned briefly. "Ten months."

He nodded. "Time to let go then. You don't need his boots."

"I liked them."

"You don't need a man's boots, Em."

He was rewarded with a little jolt of recognition across her face. *Em.* People called her this. People she liked. It made his chest warm inside, for here was exactly where he was going, a right step. Notwithstanding, she told him, "They were warm and practical."

"What you need is warm, practical women's shoes. Pretty ones. Ones that suit you."

With great intensity, leaning forward, she told him, "*Those* suited me. You are presumptuous."

Fine. Perhaps she was right; perhaps he simply didn't like another man's shoes on her, though he truly thought it bizarre that she should be marching around in her dead husband's boots, boots that didn't even fit. Nonetheless, he wouldn't argue. In fact, he rather liked seeing yet again how little confusion there was between them as to who he was. Presumptuous. Arrogant. Certainly. Not his most sterling qualities, but not ones he would deny either. Nor even ones she was necessarily against. He suspected, in fact, she rather liked these qualities on occasion.

At which point, he felt a smile trying to break through again and had to turn to stare out the window himself for fear of offending her with it: amazed by how pleasant their sitting here together was, all things considered.

He would rather she'd have been overwhelmed by him—how nice her awe had been at the bank—but since she wasn't, he'd just have a good time at her expense. As good-naturedly as possible and to good purpose: Best she understood their relationship from the start. He wasn't taking a hard time off her—and she was a woman who could give it in trump. He'd allow no leeway; he didn't dare, God help him. And, while he counted on her help with his uncle, he also fully intended to make the worst gossip her friends could manufacture about her and himself the absolute truth.

She'd caused him all manner of grief, tricked him, stolen from him, and she wasn't even sorry, not really. She was only angry she hadn't gotten away with it. No, turnabout was fair play. She could just get used to losing for a while, the crafty little wench.

Then he glanced at her and thought, crafty little wench indeed. There was nothing conniving or manufactured about her sweet, small mouth. It had tasted better than anything he could remember in recent history. It simply was. *She* simply was. Butterscotch sweet. Sweet-lipped, warm-mouthed, round-hipped, soft-thighed. Emma. *Em.* "M" for mine. He was feeling *so* possessive, which he knew was all wrong, that she would never tolerate it, that he had to fix himself, figure the feeling out, do better with it. Because, Em-Emma-M was like something from another planet. Venus. A place better than here. Better than any latitude and longitude he'd yet to know.

And he felt he'd begun the adventure of a lifetime by more or less capturing her, taking her prisoner, taking her back as a specimen to examine more carefully. Here, gentleman, I give you the most luscious, inventive female I have yet to come across. . . .

The carriage clattered through the countryside, straining toward its usual pace. The interesting sheep farmer—with her surprising knowledge of London, confidence games, and double entry bookkeeping—sat glumly back, its passenger, as far away from him as she could get. While Stuart dozed off and on quite contentedly, slitting his eyes open only enough to steal sleepy glimpses of his prize: his new reluctant partner temporarily in her stocking feet, two toes sticking out of one stocking, the tips of three from the other. Cherub toes. So pink and precious he wanted to lick them, eat them, then use the tattered threads of her stockings afterward to clean his teeth.

Left to his own devices, he would have devoured her on the spot.

Oh, gentlemen, will you *look* at her! How symmetrically round. How beautiful. How smart. How fearless and strong. And with such a good heart, such a stalwart sense of justice!

How could any man possibly resist her? Why wasn't there a line a mile long of men trailing after her? He didn't know. He only knew he was positively thrilled with his own perspicacity. Mine. You are mine for two weeks, Emma Hotchkiss. As reluctant as you may be, it is thus by agreement between us. Mine. And these two weeks, for a dozen reasons, are the best thing I've negotiated for myself in England, since I explained, insisted, and fought my way back into my viscountcy itself.

"Pork pie?" he ventured, holding one of the parcels out.

She shook her head.

He hated to see it. He relished every curve of her, every soft nook and cranny of her body. "I wish you'd eat," he said, then realized he should have stated the opposite.

She refused the food, he was certain, just to do the reverse of his will.

Chapter 9

Patriotism . . . the last refuge of a scoundrel.

—Credited to Samuel Johnson
in Boswell's *Life of Johnson,* 1775

IT was dark by the time the carriage turned down the long front lane to Castle Dunord, entering between its long lines of poplars at either side. Dunord. Emma opened her eyes on the sight of its lit turrets in the distance, its attic windows of servants' quarters lighting the night, awaiting the master of the house.

She had never entered the hallowed grounds at night. The woods on either side were hushed, the carriage tack—mostly its single bell—ringing clearly over the quiet sweep of snow. With the castle hardly more than a distant shadow on the horizon, the coach veered from the main drive onto the side lane that ran along the lake of the parklands. They were swinging around to approach the grand old house from the rear. By moonlight, she saw for the first time the estate's rear fountains set into formal gardens full of shadowy hedges—the new viscount's gardeners had pruned the overgrowth into much as she might have imagined its former glory. Over the tops of the gardens, a small, distant building sat by the lake, a hazy full moon and a cloudy sky reflecting in the clean glass, every panel in place, of its roof—presumably the famous orangery that in past generations, so the myth went, provided citrus for the entire village at Christmas, a time when *noblesse oblige* was the castle's relationship to its tenants and economic dependents. The vehicle circled, then slowed, as it came through a small fruit orchard of some sort, rows of small symmetrical trees that stood bare and leafless, asleep for the winter, awaiting spring.

When the carriage pulled to a stop, the horses halted without a complaint, seeming at last tired enough to stop racing. Their harness bell gave one last *clink*, and all was quiet but for the slight creak of springs as footmen and driver dismounted and the easy sweep of wind beyond the window glass. Emma lay sideways on the coach seat, cozy, warm, and a little fuddled—unsure how long she'd been asleep. In the dark on the seat opposite her there was some small, indistinguishable movement, then the coach door opened and the chill of a winter night blew gently in.

Before Emma could properly explain that she was awake, strong arms were moving her around, scooting toward the open doorway.

She muttered, "Um—I'm awake. I, ah, can walk."

"I threw your shoes away, and it's snowing." Stuart, his voice low and as soft as the winter night, spoke near her ear.

Her boots. Right. She nodded, too fuzzy to work up her annoyance again. She let him pull her arm up and around his shoulder. "What time is it?" she asked.

"Just after nine." He was backlit by his house, bent halfway into the vehicle, half-out, one knee up where his foot was on the step. Behind him, more and more lights lit up the ground floor of the massive house—people inside taking note of their arrival.

The sureness of his grasp on her was a little startling as he drew her across the carriage seat, then another surprise: She'd been lying beneath his fur-lined coat. The reason she was so snug was that she was cocooned in light, silky-soft chinchilla. The viscount's dark figure bent over her, tucking the coat around her an instant longer, then his arms came fully under her, and he lifted her up.

She felt herself hauled against his warm chest, as if she were nothing, then lifted as he backed from the carriage, taking them both out into the night air. It was cold, much colder than the day, and indeed lightly snowing again. In this rather undignified manner, carried like a child, Emma bumped up the rear walk of Dunord, in time to the soft rhythm of the long stride of the lord of the manor himself. The house hulked between trees, an angular mountain of architecture so towering she couldn't see its skyline, so vast its walls didn't stop as much as were swallowed up by forest lands at either end.

Quickly, servants joined them. Maids in little ruffled hats paraded out into the cold behind a housekeeper, underbutlers in tailcoats followed the butler of the house down the walk. Some took over bags from gloved footmen. Others waited in the lit doorway—the place was crawling with servants—shielding their eyes, squinting out toward the dark. There was a faint but noticeable tension as the entourage greeted its arriving employer: a willingness to please coupled with an uncertainty in people's voices, postures, in their offers and solicitousness. The staff knew there were too many of them, while each wanted to seem necessary.

A canopy appeared over Emma's and Stuart's heads, protecting them from wind and snow as they went up the walk. Polite inquiries fluttered about them as profuse as the downy flakes in the air.

Were they hungry? Were there others coming? Did his lordship's business go well? Would his lordship care to handle the visiting cards left while he was gone, two from gentlemen of London? The cards and the post were on the tray in the library. One of the undergardeners broke his leg. . . . There were other household matters. *Did his lordship wish to review them tonight or should they wait till morning?* Then awkwardly, or awkward for Emma at least, *Should someone open up a fresh apartment for the lady?*

Stuart ignored all but the last, at which he laughed drily, then answered, "Alas, yes," with the tone of a rebuffed swain. Emma was relieved to hear the answer and—she sighed deeply to herself—reluctantly flattered.

Up the last step into the portico, just as the trip inside might have ended with her still clinging to some bit of dignity, a loud screech from the trees off to one side—like the scream of a child being murdered—pierced the night. Stuart was setting her down across his threshold, and she jerked, grabbed his neck, and all but hung there. He held on to her, fully up against him this time, as they entered his house and the door closed, but she didn't care.

"*What* was that?" she asked, her blood chilled. She had never heard such a sound.

"Peacocks. We have about fifty that live on the grounds, mostly in the trees."

Peacocks? She let out a breath of relief, frowning. Pcacocks of all things. Though, come to think of it, how appropriate. The man who dressed like a Russian tsar kept a flock of ostentatious birds. She couldn't remember if peacocks had ever been a part of the castle's history or if they qualified as one of the new viscount's "improvements."

In his bright hall, the light, warm weight of his coat lifted from her shoulders. A servant folded it over his arm. She followed along in the little entourage, her bare feet on soft carpet—silky-soft under her toes. She walked across an intricate pattern of vivid colors—a rounded tree that rose to a point, at its base two birds, all in shades of greens and blues, salmons and navy, tans, beige, beautifully woven. The colors had a sheen as she walked, changing color, the same place going from pastel to deep, rich tones, depending on the angle.

Servants went ahead, lights throughout the house glowing. Emma glanced at Stuart's face as they paraded down the length of a modest receiving hall. The planes of his face grew less sharp in the surrounding gaslight. She couldn't help but smile a little to herself, though, at the expression on his face, at his almost familiar stoicism: resignation as he attended to the matters of his complex household, made more complex still by her presence.

He directed someone to get down to her house, line up care for her sheep, cat, chickens, any creature or duty in need of attention. Questions came at him. How long had he been gone? she couldn't help but wonder. In any event, he answered the list of queries with rattles of lists back, the last of which was, "Yes, dinner. The apartments opposite mine. Yes, Mrs. Hotchkiss will be staying several days. Bring dinner to my sitting room, something to eat that is English. And baths for two."

A housemaid became confused, thinking for a moment that the master of the house was saying to bring both baths to his sitting room.

Stuart laughed again, then glanced at Emma over his shoulder, tilting his head at her, almost playfully. She realized, in the pause, that by withholding his answer for a second he was teasing her. Stuart teased without smiling.

Which, for some reason, made her smile back—she was getting used to his curiously dry humor. Plus his answer, the second on the subject, said they understood each other.

"Alas, no," he said.

Emma breathed out relief. Even if she had begun by making a fairly miserable mess of the man-woman portion of their relationship, he was apparently willing to pick up where she dictated, with little more than a bit of torment over the fact that, having known him hardly half an hour, she'd somehow managed to—

No, better not to dwell on it.

The peacock outside screamed again, a distant, haunting call that was much more charming when heard, and understood for what it was, from the warmth and security of a house full of light, convenience, and safety.

Safe. She felt safe. Somewhere down the hill, her sheep would be attended to—by strangers, but by strangers who appeared to be accountable and motivated to please. Her sheep would receive hay or sugarbeets on the days when snow covered the grass. Weakening animals would be taken into the barn. The cat would find milk in its bowl. Perhaps her bread, her sewing, the small things she did for the village would indeed even continue. Her life, as she knew it, would be put in limbo for two weeks, but Stuart clearly intended that it would be there for her to go back to.

Good. Two weeks, then he and she would be done with each other. Though the details of their arrangement didn't suit her precisely, the whole would work. In fact, despite herself, she found Stuart's home, his life, him, all rather engagingly . . . new: interesting to witness. The fortnight to come was certainly going to be a holiday from her usual existence.

The peacock-master of the household continued to lead the way, while Emma followed barefoot on carpet after carpet of such softness and beautiful colors, she found herself mesmerized by what was under her feet. As they began up a curving staircase as wide as the main street in the village, she was aware that Stuart dropped things—his gloves, his scarf, his hat, a carriage blanket (he'd given his coat over to her, it seemed, taking the blanket for himself, wearing it all to way into the house), while his man, a maid, and a butler caught or picked up the items.

When at the top of the stairs his frock coat dropped, she jerked her head up. He was unbuttoning his vest as he went down a walkway—closed doors to one side, a momentous drop down into his reception hall over a banister to the other. As they moved along this upper floor, a smell, distinctively sweet and warm, seemed to come out and greet them. As if candles or oils, exotically spiced, burned somewhere.

Stuart himself lifted his nose in acknowledgment, then gave a snort of laughter. "Hiyam is here?" he asked someone.

"Yes, sir. Sorry not to mention. She and Aminah arrived two days ago."

Emma watched the first look of genuine pleasure, homecoming, pass across Stuart's face. "Good." He glanced at her as he sniffed the air again. "I can always smell Hiyam's arrival. Tonight, oranges, I think," he said, then paused, as if trying to distinguish. "And cinnamon and cardamom, if I'm not mistaken." He glanced at Emma. "Hiyam is my self-appointed minister of candles and incense when she visits. She's never happy till my house smells like a mosque."

"Relatives?"

"No." He blinked, at a loss for a split second, then handed his vest over, beginning at the knot of his cravat. He wasn't going to explain.

"Who are they?"

"They have become my wards. They live in London, where I'm supposed to be. They have apparently taken it upon themselves to hurry me up."

"Unusual names."

"Turkish." He stopped at a door, opened it, then turned to her. "My apartments," he said and indicated inside the rooms with a nod. With his long, white-sleeved arm, he pointed toward a door across, catercorner along the walkway. "Your rooms are there."

Emma glanced behind her. The corridor bent; their doors more or less faced each other.

Stuart stood just inside his own doorway, his cravat falling loose in his fingers as he continued—in a tone not unlike that he used with his housemaids. "A bath will be up shortly. May I count on seeing you in an hour?" He wrestled the button of his collar, while again making a backward nod of his head, toward inside where he stood. "Here. I'd like to begin tonight, if you have no objection. After you've freshened up, we'll discuss what we'll be doing and what we'll need over dinner, if that is all right."

His manner said he wasn't asking her leave for anything. He was telling her to be there. In his sitting room. Just outside his bedroom. She could see a large bed through a far doorway, a bed draped and hung in unexpectedly bright colors: orange, saffron, cinnamon, ruby, as light as saree silks, contrasting with velvet pillows, many, and the sparkle of beaded fringe. Hardly a typical English gentleman's bedroom. Not that she was curious about it.

"In an hour then?" He was asking only for acknowledgment.

"Um, no. Do you mind if we have our meal downstairs."

"Yes, I do. It's inconvenient."

She bit her lip, nonplussed. Don't quibble, she told herself. He was being nice enough. And a bath. Oh, a bath sounded divine right now. With hot water, she would be willing to bet. She could scarcely bend her mind beyond the idea of clean, warm water, once it occurred to her. A bath, food, then an hour to give him the gist of the game, and she'd be ready for sleep. She was ready already; exhausted. Agree, she told herself.

While she shook her head no.

He startled. "Why, for godssake?" He lifted his chin as his collar came loose in his hand. He undid one more button, then stopped, standing straight and tall in his doorway, staring at her.

The servants, she realized, had faded away. As he and she stood alone, something changed between them. Downstairs, she could hear thunks of wood, a stove being stoked; warm water indeed on its way. Behind her the door to what would be her apartments clicked open. Someone, a woman, an upstairs maid perhaps, went in, moving about, even humming lightly.

His staff attacked the tasks they were given with energy. He was used to people who didn't flout him, who didn't wait to please.

The maid hummed faintly, tunelessly off-key, while Emma

hesitated, wondering if she resisted too fiercely, at every inch, if she were simply being difficult herself. "I don't want to be near your bedroom," she murmured to him.

He said nothing, only pulling his cravat out of his loose collar, an audible slide of silk against starched fabric—a sound that made the hair on Emma's arms stand on end. He stood there holding his dark silk cravat in one hand, rubbing his thumb absently on the fabric.

As Emma stared at his long fingers where they played with the neckcloth, her mouth went dry. Her eyes grew hot. Oh, no, she thought, I am not quibbling, not at all. The good Viscount Mount Villiars here was not being nice or even reasonable. He was biding his time. He held all the cards. Why shouldn't he be generous? What did he have to lose? She wanted to laugh at herself for being so naive as to think otherwise.

She asked, "Do you have a library?"

"Yes." He let out a snort of disbelief. "You are telling me to meet you in my library? To send our dinner there?"

"I am, I'm afraid."

His eyes widened on her, but then one of his ambiguous, faint smiles took shape on his mouth.

Neither of them moved. He let his shoulder drop against the doorjamb, while he took her in; he was measuring what her insistence meant. A man standing at the door to his bedroom, his vest hanging open on a snowy white shirt. His shirt had tiny knife pleats down the front, dozens of them in perfect little lines that tucked right down into his trousers; she could glimpse one button of the tab to white trouser braces.

He pushed that front piece of his hair back, the piece that liked to flop onto his forehead, and this brought her gaze—a little embarrassingly—from his trousers back up. To his dark, overlong, unruly hair. At the back of his shirt, it overran his collar in thick, hooking curls that lay independently, this way and that, in stark contrast to starchy white.

She wet her lips, trying to wait out their little stalemate as coolly as possible.

And he laughed at her. He was interested in nothing cool, nothing even polite: He let his gaze run over her—covering her neck, shoulders, breasts, belly, then dropping lower—till she felt it and knew what he was doing, and couldn't meet his regard at all. The stupid man. He stood there half-undressed, at ease in his own house, laughing at the fact that he held all the power.

Emma took a step back. "Well. In an hour then? In the library?"

His interest lingered up her body, unwillingly finding her face. "What a fine idea," he murmured. "Why didn't I think of that? I mean, terrible things could happen in my sitting room, which couldn't possibly happen in my library. Excellent choice." He laughed again drily, then added in a murmur, "Whatever you like."

The liar. As if he were serving her wishes. Still, when their gazes found each other's again, Emma's belly contracted. A wave of pure heat washed through her.

Then worse, he gave all her reservations tangible force by smiling faintly as he owned up to the truth. "You have it right," he said. "One of the things I had wanted to discuss over dinner, under more intimate circumstances, was the option of your sleeping in my bed tonight."

She blinked, let out a nervous laugh, bowed her head, and stared down at her cold toes.

"I could insist," he murmured.

"Na—um—you—ah—" A fine lot of sense that made. *No* was the answer, though his boldness rattled her; she couldn't seem to get a straight *no* out.

He let out a soft, voiceless laugh. "Talk slowly. It will help."

Making fun of himself again. Yet not a word would come out Emma's mouth. She felt far too confused: intimidated, flustered, indignant, while being foolishly flattered, hopelessly attracted.

His hand reached out, and his warm fingertips were suddenly against her chin, tipping her face back to him. He said into her eyes, "I won't insist, of course. Your decision. I'd just like it. I thought I'd be crystal clear on the subject—I had hoped to do so suavely over a bottle of wine by the fire." He heaved a huge sigh of his own. "I'd like you to know I can do a bit better than thirty seconds on a chair." Then he glanced down with another self-rebuking smile. "I think. I'd try." When he brought his eyes back up, his expression was earnest—in a face that was so strikingly handsome, it made her throat clutch. "I'm quite struck by you." He immediately took that back with a breath and a frown, as if he hadn't phrased it right. "By something about you." He let out a snort, still dissatisfied, then settled for, "I believe it would be a more interesting two weeks if we were lovers."

"I—uh"—she pressed her lips inward—"don't."

"Too bad." He half turned, reaching behind him for the doorknob. "Dinner in the library then."

Emma held back more nervous laughter, nodding vigorously. The end. She'd won another round. Or would have, were she not blushing so profusely her cheeks felt on fire.

Struck indeed, she thought. By a short woman in a plain skirt, tromping around in stockings with holes, her hair a mess from having been smashed by a wig. While the man's fifty-six pounds still rested in the pockets of a coat she'd watched his housemaid haul down the corridor.

She wanted to say, You'd be better off struck by an adder.

Yet she absorbed his compliment, their whole silly exchange, with enough vanity to wish she were clean, her hair combed, and that her clothes fit better. Whatever he saw in her, it wasn't anything coiffed or feigned, that much was certain.

He moved back, retreating into his sitting room a step, his hand still holding the knob. He stood there looking at her a moment, as if she might change her mind, follow him in. Damn him, he'd caught every nuance of her flattered, abashed refusal.

"Till dinner then," she said belatedly. Her tongue felt thick. When she finally padded away in her bare feet, it was with the absolute certainty that he'd tallied her hemming and hawing accurately. He understood her mixed feelings and would play on them.

As she entered her new rooms, she closed her eyes and thought, What is wrong with you, Emma? With the blasted man standing there, still holding his damned cravat? Do you want more of that insanity in the hotel room?

God help her, the question shot a thrill through her.

You are your own worst enemy, Emma Hotchkiss. You like wicked men. If you don't keep yourself out of his reach, you deserve what you get, you idiot.

Then on her bed, on the blue counterpane, she saw a white pool of heavy, silky fabric. Picking it up, she let out a sharp laugh of pure release. It was a man's nightshirt. Stuart's. Its slippery satin poured through her fingers, more like water than fabric, yards and yards of the stuff. She was supposed to sleep in it. Or freeze to death.

A fine lot of choices she had lately, it seemed. They were sublime; they were the devil incarnate.

Ten minutes later, his "ward," Aminah, brought a pair of soft, embroidered slippers for Emma to wear. They fit nicely. Though Aminah herself did not: She was a pleasant, very pretty, dark-eyed woman whose age appeared to be somewhere near thirty: far too old to be in anyone's charge but her own. And though she wore English clothes and her hair in the English style, her accent said immediately that, like her name, she was not native to England.

Chapter 10

Her breath is like honey spiced with cloves,
Her mouth delicious as a ripened mango.

—*Srngarakarika,* Kumaradadatta, 12th century

STUART was already in the library when Emma found the room. It had to be he, yet the man standing over the large desk, reading papers that lay on it, looked so different that she stepped back momentarily. His hair was damp and combed away from his face, his profile stark. His angular jaw and cheeks had the damp, faintly vulnerable look of a fresh shave. Even more unfamiliar were his clothes: a heavy, knit jersey the color of wheat, roomy and athletic, as if he might dash off at any moment for a quick game of polo. His hands were tucked casually into the pockets of dark, loose trousers—till he absently licked his thumb and turned a page on the desk. So absorbed was he in his reading, he didn't hear Emma enter.

The room was cold, though a crackling fire promised it would warm up. Dinner sat, absolutely fragrant, on a library table, its reading lamp pushed to the side to make room for two place settings of little hens of some sort.

Stuart startled when she cleared her throat. "Oh, there you are," he said. "They just brought dinner." He pointed to a table set for two. "Take a seat. Please. Start without me. I'll be right there." He waved his hand in cursory offer, then returned to whatever was so interesting on his desktop.

Even in her own clothes that fit (and borrowed slippers), Emma felt disheveled and out of place as she sat in a large, tufted leather chair. The table linens were damask, the plates china, the service silver, and the glasses cut crystal. Not her usual fare.

Dinner, though, was a fine distraction from self-consciousness: After waiting a minute or two, she did as suggested, beginning on the leg of the most delicious little Cornish hen, peppers and squash swimming in its roasting juices, onions, spices. The more she tasted, the more the liked it, though it was nothing she'd ever had before—she spotted caraway and tasted honey, this laced with a strange and wonderful combination of . . . what? Ginger, spicy-hot cayenne, cinnamon . . . and mint? Was there mint? It was an "English" combination she'd have never put together, yet so tasty; it all but sang in her mouth. She was half-finished when the chair opposite hers scooted back and her host sat.

"I'm sorry. I still haven't finished half my reading for a vote coming up in four days. God, but my fellow members of the house can go on." He lifted the silver lid of a compote—there was crème anglaise with sliced, baked apples she'd missed. "Mmm," he said, approving, then raised his eyebrow toward her. "English enough for you?"

She laughed. "It's not very English, but it's lovely, thank you."

He stared at her a moment, then nodded. "Good."

Stuart was continually surprised by the ways Emma arrested him. She had possibly the most beautiful laughter he had ever heard. Like chimes. Wind chimes. Light, tinkling tuneless melodies on a breezy summer day. No pattern, no rhythm, only the randomness of wind: of a happiness he couldn't grasp in any context of what he knew as reality.

He looked at a dinner that was as English as he ate—they were Cornish hens, after all. Well, never mind, he'd made her laugh at least—any man who could make a woman laugh, whom he'd more or less kidnaped, well, he had to hold some sort of special favor, didn't he? Even if she wouldn't admit it?

They said nothing further for several minutes. At first it seemed they were both simply hungry, which was at least partly true. Silver tapped and clinked on china, glass on crystal—Stuart poured wine Emma hadn't seen either. Still, though she could eat with gusto, she couldn't look at her dinner companion with the same directness.

As the silence stretched out, it seemed, he, too, was having to find his bearings. She could only be glad they weren't eating just outside his bedroom, for despite her best efforts to make their dinner as unromantic as possible, they were still dining alone together. It felt strange. She hadn't eaten a meal with a man alone in a long while, not across the table from a healthy man at least.

In a library, she reminded herself. Which was large and varied enough to absorb anyone's interest. Huge, in fact. She looked about her.

Even by the standards of England's grandest of houses, Stuart's library was vast. Its length was the most unusual—so long that at night the fireplace and desk light at one end didn't illuminate the far end. The walls of books simply grew dim and disappeared; she couldn't calculate how long the library might be for not clearly seeing its farthest reaches.

Beyond its gallery-like length, however, Stuart's library was wonderfully predictable: walls of dark wood bookcases lined with colorful spine after spine. Books and books and books. They ran from wall to wall, from floor to the high, coffered ceiling. Tall, wheeled ladders, at least four of them, hung on runners to guarantee access to the very high shelves. Reading tables with lamps . . . well-padded chairs . . . a settee in leather with nailhead trim. Just off to her right, the carved mantel sat huge over a stone fireplace. She liked the reassurance of the room: its pure, almost stereotypical Britishness, right down to a bust of a man's head by a dark window and half a dozen dim, old paintings in nooks between the shelving—portraits of well-dressed gentry at leisure.

Paintings of none other than the Viscounts Mount Villiars, she was fairly certain; them, their wives, dogs, horses, families. "Are you related to all these people in the paintings?" she asked as, with a thick crust of bread, she sopped up sauce from her plate. If dinner was an example of his chefs' talents, she wouldn't want to dismiss any of them either.

"So they tell me. I don't pay much attention." He cut apart the thigh of a bird, his fork down, his knife efficient, like any Englishman. The Arabs and Russians ate with their fingers, she'd heard. She'd half waited to see if he'd do something savage with his food. He didn't, a mild disappointment.

They went another minute in silence. "You don't volunteer much about yourself," she said finally. Then added, smiling, "It takes a long spoon to eat supper with you."

"Pardon?"

"A Yorkshire expression. Or perhaps Scottish—my mother used to say it. It means, you're hard to get to know."

"What is it you'd like to know that's so difficult to discover?"

She shrugged. "I don't know. All right, the portraits. Why aren't you interested in them?"

"I prefer landscapes. Or photographs of people I know, places I've been."

"To your own family?"

"My family was no prize. I've sold off a good number of their pictures and intend to sell every last one, if anyone will have them."

"And your parents? Are you selling them, too?"

He paused, looked over the top of his wineglass at her. "No." He left a space, as if he'd say nothing more, then tilted his head and offered, "My mother wouldn't allow a picture of herself to be painted; she considered herself too unsightly. My father had one done just before their marriage, which, oddly enough, my mother kept. It was the first I took down: I burned it."

"Ah." She felt suddenly awkward. The rumors of his father should have kept her quiet about family. Still, if his mother had kept the portrait, how bad could the fellow have been? "Oddly enough," she repeated. Had his mother loved his father? How? Why would a woman look daily upon the picture of a man who had publicly, disgracefully abandoned her?

As if reading her mind, Stuart said, "My father was handsome. My mother enjoyed that. Though his handsomeness, the contradiction of it, also drove her crazy." He set his napkin on the table, sat back, and smiled not unkindly. "Literally: My mother was a loon, and my father was a criminal whom no one could catch. What a heritage, hmm? It's enough to make you stutter."

Emma blinked. He was making a joke on himself again. She hardly noticed his stutter anymore, truth be known. "A criminal? I didn't realize. I'm sorry your father was as bad as rumor said. I had hoped not."

"Oh, he was much worse," he said casually. "And good at keeping secrets, while the family abetted him by not wanting to know."

She waited, morbidly curious.

Stuart watched her, seemed to hesitate, then offered, "My father hurt women. He had a sexual proclivity toward it."

Emma dropped her knife. It clinked on her plate, all but taking a chip from the china. When she picked the utensil up and cut something on her plate, she couldn't focus on whatever it was; she was carving up her napkin for all she knew.

"You had no idea?" he asked.

She shook her head, unable to avoid a grimace.

"It's true. He hurt my mother."

At first she couldn't grasp it. His father had hurt his mother's feelings, deeply, she thought. A rift had separated them.

Perhaps her mild reaction cued him; whatever it was, Stuart knew instantly what she was thinking. "Not her feelings," he said. "Everyone hurt her feelings; she was so inured to it, it didn't matter. No." He broke off a second, then stammered, really, truly stammered, "He found her r-re-repulsive." He closed his eyes a moment, slowed himself down. "He loathed her."

Loathed. The word came out long and slow and with emphasis. The pace of it calmed Stuart. He continued, though something like air had risen into his chest, his throat, like a bubble of horror.

"To conceive me," he said to the woman across from him, "the only way he could was to—" He broke off again. Then almost belligerently—since a woman of the unforgiving, uncompassionate village down the hill wanted to know—he said, "My father hurt women." He leaned back. "Sadder still, my mother was so lonely—and wanted a child so badly—she endured him."

He'd told this story exactly once before, when he was eleven, to the headmaster of his school. Happily, adulthood madc a difference. He could get it out without sobbing. Stoically, he recited facts from his life. Amazing that all this had somehow passed into a place in his memory, where it was nothing more than that. An old tale, as grim as ogres and trolls, but nothing more. "The rumor that my father left her, it isn't true. The servants drove him away. Then they tended to her. I don't know what he did exactly that finally sent them over the edge, except she had a place on her cheek that nothing and no one could hide: teeth marks; he bit her.

"She wouldn't say, because she was ashamed. But others did eventually. He was being charged in five different cases when he died, a free man, but not for long. I've tried to help the women and families involved, done what I could. Selfishly, I suspect. To assuage the guilt of leaving behind a father I knew would wreak havoc on the innocent."

Emma's blue eyes were wide. She said nothing for long seconds, staring at him. What could one say, after all? But then she did find voice. She murmured, "Was he horrible to you?"

He shrugged and leaned forward to pour them both more wine. It gurgled into one glass, then the other, sparkling in the firelight as he said, "When I was six, he broke my nose, though more or less by accident." He sat back and drank some wine, before he finished. "It turned out to be a blessing: Broken noses bleed, which frightened him. I was the heir, you see. He considered the blood his. After that, he was careful with me, even kind." He looked down into the wineglass. "To be quite honest, though, the privilege of being his favorite person was hard to absorb, especially when I was young. For a long time, it made me feel"—he paused—"awful."

"There was no love—"

"None. Never. Not even as a child did I enjoy the idea of my father. I knew the stories. The servants and townspeople spared me nothing; people hated him. I'd never even met him till that afternoon he broke my nose. When he showed up, come to 'claim' me, they said, I fully thought I'd go downstairs and have to face a monster. But the horror of it was, the man I went down to face didn't look like a monster at all: He looked like me."

Emma shuddered once; she couldn't help it. Then she furrowed her brow, shaking her head in wonder. "How horrible for you," she murmured. Instinctively, she reached out. "What a lonely, frightening childhood." She touched his hand, where his fingers lay relaxed around the stem of the wineglass, resting on the table.

He jerked slightly, looked at her outstretched hand, frowned. Then, very gently, he extricated his own. He withdrew physically from her sympathy and put his hand down to lean back in his chair. He shrugged. "It's fine. I'm quite used to it. *I'm* sorry if the facts of my parentage startle you." He set his wineglass down, pushing away entirely. "Would you like coffee, tea, sherry? I can ring for anything you'd prefer."

She looked at him, puzzled. "No, thank you." He didn't want sympathy. Where the next came from, she didn't know, but she knew she said it, meaning well, trying to cheer him perhaps with a little confession of her own. "I, ah—" She laughed at herself. "I used to see you sometimes when I was a little girl. The boy on the hill. There was an area where you played in your kitchen garden, I think. I could see it from our north pasture." She rambled on, not getting any response at all from him; his face looked stony. "I used to pretend you were the prince in the castle, and that one day—" She bit her lip. She was only embarrassing herself. This was of no use to him. "Oh, never mind. It was silly." That was graceful, Emma. A pathetic, little fairy-tale story that was supposed to counteract his recounted nightmare. More silly still: "I assumed your life was perfect."

If he thought her silly, he didn't show it. His dark, heavy-lidded eyes only stared in their unblinking way, unreadable.

Then he ignored the whole business. "May I?" he asked. Hands braced on the chair arms, he leaned forward. He was requesting permission to rise. "I'd prefer to sit by the fire." Then he didn't wait for permission and simply stood. "Feel free to join me."

He turned his back and went the other direction—to a cabinet by the window, a dark, brass-fitted kind of chest on which the stone bust sat. Its drawers were tricks, doors carved to look like drawers. Inside were glasses and a decanter.

"Brandy?" he asked without looking at her.

"No, thank you."

At the window, white flakes whirled out of the dark to settle softly against the mullions in crescents. Heavy snow blew toward Stuart's reflection in the glass. His face was stiff as he poured himself three fingers of brandy and returned, walking past her to the fire. There, he tossed pillows about, creating an expert pile that said he'd stacked these same pillows before just to his liking, then bent down onto one knee before he completely stretched out. He laid himself onto his pillows a few feet away from her, between her and the fireplace, indeed looking warm and comfortable.

Emma rotated her chair to face him, a chair that rocked and turned on pivots. She rested back, her wrists curving over the edge of padded armrests, and stretched her feet toward the fire. She envied him his full, reclining warmth, yet remained upright, necessarily distant.

"So tell me," he said from his pile of pillows, "how are we going to get my statue back? I can't tell you how thrilled I am with the idea of orchestrating its return without my uncle's usual bad faith and grumbling."

"Oh, your uncle's bad faith will be a very necessary part of it. We'll count on it, in fact."

He raised his brow. "All right. What else?" He propped another pillow under his shoulder, one under his neck, then settled back to drink his brandy, while facing her. A long man in a loose jersey. He was wearing leather slippers, not boots. Soft ones that moved with his feet.

She asked, "Is he clever, this uncle?"

"As clever as I am."

She pulled a face. "He's bloody brilliant then."

Stuart laughed, startled, but didn't deny it.

She gave him the general outline. "I think we have to run a little Weasel Ranch on him."

"Weasel Ranch," he repeated, smiling. Intrigued. Pleased.

"Something for nothing. A 'Weasel Ranch' because: you tell them, essentially, that you'll feed rats to weasels, skin the weasels, then feed their carcasses to the rats, thereby getting the weasel skins for free. It's the sort of cleverness that appeals to smart fellows. It's the damnedest thing, but it's the *smart* dishonest ones who are the easiest to take. You'd think it would be the other way around, but the stupid ones never catch on fast enough."

Which left a pregnant hole in the conversation. Since they had just discussed how clever Stuart was.

"You wouldn't swindle me, would you?" he asked.

Yes, he was fairly quick. "Oh, no," she promised. Some of the old patter ran through her mind, all the things you told someone to reassure them, but Stuart really *was* too smart for that, so she told him, "You have too much on me. I'd end up in prison."

He made a small lift of his head, a nod of thoughtful, contemplative agreement.

Dear Heaven, did she ever wish she were dealing with a man just a tiny bit stupider or less observant. Or more plain-spoken.

He kept his own counsel, staring at her, his face blank but for his brow that drew down slightly, his large, sepia-black eyes leveled on her.

"Tell me more about the statue," she said. "How big is it? What does it look like?"

"Ah. It's about this tall." He leveled one hand over the brandy glass, indicated a height of about ten inches. "And it's green."

She waited for more specifics.

But instead, he asked conversationally, "How many confidence games have you run?"

"Run? Dozens, I suppose, but only the small ones. I participated in bigger ones—every week something new. Though a long time ago, you must remember."

"What kinds of swindles?" He added wryly, "Besides cooking the books."

"I never did that before." She looked down at her fingers at the end of one chair arm, wondering if he believed her. "Though I used to forge signatures. That's what gave me the idea." No, less worry about his believing her and more about being as vague as possible, since she was confessing to a member of the House of Lords. "I kept real books for a bishop once."

Emma smiled, remembering suddenly, "There were ruses that were fun, though, funny. Most weren't illegal, or not precisely. There was one"—she laughed—"where we'd put an ad in the paper for an elixir that cost eleven shillings by post. We called it 'Man Medicine for the male of the house.' The ad promised the medicine would give the man who took it 'a return to the gusto and satisfaction, the pulse and throb of physical pleasure, the keen sense of man sensation.' " She laughed again, a little embarrassed to remember the whole spiel so well. "It was a laxative.

"Or Zach would stand up on a corner near Piccadilly and start in. He had a big, deep voice. He'd call out, 'Here, my friends, is medicine for men. I do not know how it works. I only know I was blind, and now I see. It's like Jesus. I believe. I took it and got well; others took it and got well. All I can tell you is, thanks to this'—he'd hold up the bottle and pat it—'I am a man again.' "

She glanced down at the man on the cushions, the English polo player who could stretch himself out like a sultan. She was momentarily dazed to find his attention rapt upon her, no longer blank. He'd even smiled a bit over her man medicine story. Buoyed somehow, she said, "That one truly used to make me hoot"—she laughed, shaking her head—"because he so needed something of that nature himself that, if it had worked, he would have drunk it by the gallon." She stopped, frowned.

Stuart, from his pile of cushions, watched Emma's expression change, her mirth deteriorate into self-criticism. She bit her lip again, glanced off, then sighed. "I'm sorry. How uncouth of me. I can't seem to stop talking about that." Her wide eyes settled on him. "Honestly. I never thought about it as much when he was alive. We got on. We did all right. It's just since—" She broke off.

He finished for her. "It's just, since this morning, neither one of us can quite get that subject out of our minds."

Emma. Funny, self-sufficient Emma. Had it only been

twelve hours ago that she'd sat, tied to a chair not unlike the one she inhabited now, letting him kiss her passionately. Talking to her at present—or this morning, come to think of it—one would never guess, never imagine she'd allow him to kiss her, not like that, not even once, let alone all the rest.

Once. Oh, no. He wanted more; he wasn't finished.

There was a tap at the door, and two white-gloved footmen entered to gather the remains of dinner onto silver trays. At the doorway, balancing a tray, one asked, "Will there be anything else, sir?" The man had to ask again, before Stuart heard the question.

He blinked at him. "No, Miller. Thank you. Good night."

The door clicked shut softly, just the crackle of the fire. While Emma Hotchkiss sat in her chair like a queen on a throne. Strange little woman.

What a lonely, frightening childhood. It had been, though he had never thought of it in those terms. He'd thought how inadequate he'd been at six to cope with what was asked of him. How brattish he'd been, the bane—the worry—of everyone within knowledge of what his existence entailed. A sham. A disappointment. How far short he fell of being the son his father wanted or of being the son his mother thought he was.

Emma's prince. There was a laugh. When his life had been so far from that. The little prince of Hell. Grown up now. Lying at her feet, trying not to let her see he was somewhat less interested in statues, more interested in looking up her skirt to where her ankles showed between her hem and slippers. Her legs were short, but quite shapely—and he had a rather good angle.

To his dismay, a moment later, she cleared her throat, shifted, and drew her legs up under her onto the chair. She pulled her skirts over herself, leaning to one side on the armrest. "So your statue is small and green?"

"I think so."

"You *think* so. You don't know what it looks like?"

"I've seen it a hundred times. A thousand." He laughed. "All before I was six."

She pursed her small mouth. "With familiarity like that, how in heaven's name are we to know if he even gives us the right one?"

"I'll know it when I see it." He gave her a raise of his eyebrow to shut off any further complaint. "I have the provenance." He snorted. "He has the art, though he refuses to admit it, the idiot. It isn't worth as much, though, without its bills of receipt that prove its line of authenticity. From what I remember and the descriptions in the old bills of sale, I can piece together a fairly good description for you. It's a religious icon. Byzantine. Very rare, very valuable. Its provenance goes back almost a hundred and eighty years, but the statue is much, much older—that was when it was discovered. I have the academic papers on its discovery as well. As I recall, it's a little chimera sort of character. A kind of dragon-goddess, dancing." He paused, then asked, "So how do we do it?"

Emma chewed her cheek, then seemed to finalize whatever she'd been considering. "We set me up as an art expert, I think, who works for an insurance company, one who runs a little humbug on the side. I've done that one before, though we always sent the fellow for money. I think we can send him for the statue though, if we work it right.

"Essentially, we get you and your uncle involved in making money with me, then lead him into distrusting your end. While he is busy worrying how he and I are to hoodwink you, he won't notice I am hoodwinking him." She frowned, pushing a plump lip out. "To work it right, I'll have to find one or two of my old contacts in London. Though mostly, it will be just the two of us, you and I, running the game on—what was his name?"

"Leonard. Leonard Aysgarth. Good old Uncle Leo. And

am I hearing your correctly in that you intend to cozy up to him?" He pulled a distasteful face.

"It's a job. If I do it well, he will be quite enchanted with me, very trusting. Confident of me. It's not for nothing that it's called a 'confidence' game. He'll hand the statue right over, if we do it right. Your job will be, at midgame, to become a pain in the neck, a risk. You're the distraction. Your bad faith allies Leonard and me more closely, closing ranks to protect ourselves—"

"A pain in the neck," Stuart repeated and took a long drink of brandy. So part of this would be that a woman he wanted would get chummy with a man he detested. He tried to make light of that information. Yes, becoming a pain in the backside would be quite natural at that point. But he didn't like it. "This is complicated," he said.

Emma's angelic face gazed back at him. "You're right," she said soberly. "Let's not do it. There are dozens of places for us to make a box-up of it."

"Can't it be simpler?"

"You want to take something of great value from someone you know, someone smart enough to be dangerous. You want him off your back by the end, while getting exactly what you want from him, and all without being caught. *That* is the complexity of it, not what I've outlined. What we'll run is the most elegant confidence game that exists, a variation on the payoff played half-against the wall with a poke, then a cackle-bladder at the end."

He watched her, trying to calculate the extent of his risk. And there it was: The field of power between them was going to level out. In fact, at certain points, she'd have complete control.

"You don't trust me," she said and twisted in her chair. She swung her legs over the edge of it again, leaning to sit forward, elbows on her knees, her hands clasped. Her posture, her sweet face in the firelight looked all but pious—a woman who'd made, he didn't doubt, sturdier men than he believe what they shouldn't. "Distrust between confidence partners is a horrible thing," she told him. "Because once in the midst of it, we'd have to depend on each other the way the blood in our bodies depends on our veins. Once begun, there is no turning back." She made a little, ladylike click of her tongue, which he took to mean she thought the next all but impossible: "You'd have to give up trying to run everything, including and especially me."

"All right," he said.

"Good!" She sat back. "We let it go. A wise decision. It was a stupid idea."

"No. All right, let's do it. You win." She was right. He tried to control too much. He studied her—if ever there was a woman to trust, at least up to a point, here she was: Emma was brave and unflinching, with a kind of intransigent intelligence. He liked her. Plus the idea of seeing what she'd do when she had the power to do it was interesting. He decided he could take anything she could dish out. So be it. "Once we're in London, we'll do things your way."

She blinked at him. "You still want to do it?"

"Yes. My uncle deserves it, wait till you meet him. I have seamstresses coming tomorrow. I have enough money to begin, with other accounts sure to open up soon. It can be done—"

"It's more than just the right clothes, some money, and a tricky plan." She wasn't finished trying to dissuade him—the more she tried, the more resolve he felt. It was perverse, but there it was.

She told him, "A confidence game is an illusion, like a play on the stage, where one of the players, the mark, thinks it's real. If that illusion is breached, for even a second, the whole thing crumbles." Her sweet bright eyes looked for all the world sincerely concerned for him, for them. "Once we start, you can *never* break from role. Not even when you think no one's looking. You hold to it the whole time, play it out to the end. Do you think you can?"

"I suppose. Why couldn't I?"

"Because it won't feel good to watch your uncle's trust slide toward me. It won't be nice when we both start treating you as if you had the plague. How will you feel when you watch what you know is your uncle and myself setting up a double cross of you?"

"So long as it's not true, I'll be fine."

"It won't be true, but I'll have to behave as if it is." She let that sink in. "Do you see the difficulty? And neither of us can break out and ask. We have to trust."

"Confidence," he repeated.

"Exactly."

He nodded. He was not the one who didn't trust. He could let go. It was Emma who had trouble with surrender, he decided.

She looked at him as if he were mad. "Do you understand how wrong it can go?"

"Life can go wrong at any moment, Emma. So can this."

She shook her head, no, no. Then she sighed and tilted her head back to look at the ceiling. "It was because Zach broke from role twelve years ago that our mark opened fire. Zach was smug for an instant: He smiled at me." She glanced at Stuart, then let out a disconsolate little sigh. "It was the briefest grin."

Remembering, Emma felt suddenly talkative. She wanted to spill every last reason for her own fear, then perhaps Stuart would understand, feel her dread, rethink what he considered an adventure, a lark. She sat up straight again, leveled her eyes, and told him, "But we were supposed to be at odds, you see, angry with each other. And there Zach was, throwing me this chummy, triumphant look. The mark saw it one second, and the delicate reality we'd built evaporated: He was shooting the next.

"Shooting," she said, "is clear police territory—gunfire

brings them faster than anything else. Bobbies came through an alley. They were in a back door within the minute. Zach and I had the good luck to head toward the front—I don't know why; it was the closest, I suppose. He was half carrying me by the street, the bleeding at my temple was so heavy I couldn't see. It blinded me."

She let out a little snort. "Zach used to say that the bullet ricocheted off my hard head. You've never seen so much blood though. It soaked my hair, ran into my face, my eye, down my neck into my dress. You wouldn't believe how messily ears bleed. That was what made Joanna panic, I think, the sight of me.

"Zach and I ran, with everyone else either on the floor or going the wrong direction. She was right with us, then just suddenly stopped. She started screaming. She stood there, just on the other side of the front doors, the same ones that Zach and I had fled through, fully capable of leaving, only she wouldn't; she didn't. Down the street, we could hear her crying. It was shocking. The police just waltzed in and took her away.

"When we heard of Joanna's death—they called it consumption—I couldn't stop crying for a week. Zach got drunk." So far as she knew, he was never sober again.

She added, "His sister had been sentenced to ten years hard labor." She made a feeble laugh. "Joanna, of all people. Who'd never lifted anything heavier than a stranger's wallet."

Enough. She felt wrung out. Emma rose to her feet, clapping her legs with the palms of her hands. "Well. The rest can wait till morning. I'm tired." Let him chase after her, if he wanted anything more out of her.

He apparently did and would. "A poke," he asked as he rose. "You didn't explain that part." He moved leisurely, but he kept his eyes fixed on her; she wasn't going anywhere he wouldn't follow.

She'd forgotten how tall he was. He moved past eye level

as he rose, till she found herself staring up at a man a head taller than she was.

"A lady's purse in this instance," she said. "We'll fill it with things designed to convince your uncle I'm authentic." She began toward the door, wondering if they were going to break out into a dead race for it. He stayed right beside her. "We'll talk tomorrow about how it works. It's standard, but nothing's a set plan. We'll have to discuss various aspects, and then play it as it comes. Every game involves a certain amount of invention on the spot. So tomorrow—"

She stopped. At the doorway, or just before it, her escorting host put his arm across her path, resting his palm on the doorjamb. A grandfather clock by the door cornered her further. He blocked her way. She could back up into the room or lean against the tall clock.

She chose the latter, anything but retreat. She looked up at him, at a shadowed face that hadn't the faintest interest in purses, uncles, or pokes—or at least not the sort she was talking about.

He took up the doorway completely. Though not with any particular aggressiveness. He simply did. He was tall and broad through the chest and shoulders, a man who didn't go anywhere without somehow taking up more space than one could account for.

He leaned on his arm at the doorjamb.

"Don't start again." She let out a breath.

"Don't start what?"

"Oh, for godssake." She rolled her eyes and looked away.

Stuart collapsed a little, sideways, his shoulder striking the wood doorframe. He leaned there, holding her intentionally trapped between him and the grandfather clock. Her posture said she wasn't going to fight him, but neither would she cooperate. "What am I doing wrong?"

"Nothing. There's nothing you can do to manipulate me."

"Manipulation? That's what it is to you?" When she

didn't answer, he asked, "What did that drunken husband of yours do?"

She let out a burst of breathy, dry humor, the white-gold curls on top of her head jiggling. When she bent her neck, the distant firelight lit the darker, silvery blond at her nape, making it shine like pewter. "Nothing particularly different. I'm just harder to convince these days. Older and wise, I suppose."

"Or more frightened."

"Whatever you want to call it."

He frowned as he tucked his hand into his trouser pocket. "Romance? You want romance?"

"I want love. We don't love each other." She laughed at the idea. "We can barely tolerate each other, in fact. Hate." She laughed again wanly, shaking her head, looking down between them. "There it is, the real explanation: We hate each other."

"I don't hate you. I rather like you, in fact."

She blinked. "Oh." She reconnoitered. "Well, I hate you. I hate this." She held out her hand. "I want to go home."

"That doesn't seem fair. I mean, *this*, as you call it, is simply how we met. You robbed me. I stopped you. Now you have to pay for it. I can't see why you won't be gracious about it."

"Where is the part about your killing my lamb?"

"We aren't even certain I did. Besides, you have the fifty-six pounds."

His logic seemed to stymie her for a second. She stood there blinking before she could say, "That doesn't entitle you to sleep with me."

Brave girl. She'd gone directly for the crux.

She said nothing, just her restrained, slightly indignant, feminine watching, wide blue eyes shadowed by a tall clock, looking up at him, daring him, ever so faintly pleading.

He didn't know what to do for several seconds.

He knew her to be affected by him, truly affected, though for the life of him couldn't figure out how to get around all her equally strong resistance. In a murmur, more breath than voice, he confided, "I hope this doesn't ruin your wild opinion of me, but this morning was the most exciting, most erotic thing that's ever arrived in my life. Please don't ask me to pretend it didn't happen."

When she didn't respond, he added, "You want to bury what happened. I want to award us medals for it. Emma, it was amazing. But neither of us did it on our own. It was a combined, cooperative will, which took us by surprise once, so don't pretend it couldn't happen again."

Medals? He was insane. Emma could feel the clock's *tick*, then *tock* at her buttocks, at her palms, her shoulders, her head, at every place she pressed against the wood behind her. The soft movement of the clock vibrated, as if the brass pendulum were swinging, hitting something inside her. The man before her didn't move. Her own chest rose and fell, the largest movement between them, and she realized. He was in every breath of air she took, his body, his clothes, his hair like the scented candles of his house: warm, expensive, subtle, aromatic, rising up in waves of heat, filling her nostrils, her eyes, settling into her skin, into her clothes.

She swam in a heady attraction that had nothing to do with good judgment.

Happened. This morning hadn't "happened." He'd done it. He'd tied her up and— She stammered, "It—it—I—I won't let—"

He shook his head, laughing. "You wouldn't have 'let it' the first time. But your heart beats out a military drumroll every time you think about it."

Milli-tree drumroll. Emma heard the words, and they added to her fluster. Where was his damn stutter now in this perfect, public-school accent? Nothing seemed to slow him down. No pausing. He could say some of the most surprising, ghastly things, and do so with perfect, beautiful enunciation.

Milli-tree drumroll indeed. Her heart was certainly beating one at the moment. Resentfully, she said, "I thought it was my decision. Upstairs, you said—"

"And so it is. Though, if you remember, I like to influence your decisions, when I don't agree with them."

She jumped when he touched her hair at her temple.

"Where?" he asked in a murmur. His fingers separated her hair at her hairline, looking for a bullet wound. "Ah," he said, the sound of surprise, sympathy. In a murmur, he exclaimed, "You had stitches!" His light touch slid into her hair as he leaned to examine.

Then apparently he wanted to smell the bullet wound, too, because a moment later his nose pressed to the same spot. She heard the intake of breath, felt the mass of his body as he drew as close as a man could get without laying his full weight against her. Their clothes brushed. His foot stepped between hers. Sandalwood, cloves, citrus. He was steeped in these oddly mystical smells. His soap, she decided. His hair smelled clean and good.

In fact, that was fairly much how he affected her senses: clean, good, potent, rising in waving heat all around her. Her heart began that stupid rhythm it did whenever he was this close.

He invited her into collusion against herself. "Pretend you'll go to jail if you don't," he suggested.

"You wouldn't send me to jail, because I wouldn't sleep with you."

He backed up inches, slouching till their eyes were almost at an equal level. "All right, probably not." He smiled faintly. "If you were tactful about refusing."

She pressed her lips together, resentful a moment, then said, "No, thank you."

"Mm-m." He frowned. "No," he said, shaking his head. His face came toward her again. "Not quite tactful enough, I don't think."

Emma did the only thing she had room to do; she turned

her head. His mouth found her cheek. He put the side of his thumb to her face and turned her toward him again. For a moment, there he was in all directions, his mouth one way, waiting, his palm settling against her in the other, holding her there. The sensation was fearsome—addling, blast him—her face caught between his hand and mouth, her body wedged into the corner.

At which point, having her face where he wanted it, he kissed her with a kind of precision, his mouth squarely over hers.

She jerked back, her head clonking on the carved wood just as the clock struck. *Bong Bong*. He kissed her at—*bong*—3 A.M. of what had to be the longest day of her life. And the awful part was, a part of her wanted to be trapped just as she was, no other choice.

She let herself kiss him back. He groaned, shifted. She kissed the same mouth from this morning's insane two minutes. Two minutes. She put her hands to his chest—happily free, this time—and pushed against the warm knit jersey, against the very solid man beneath, all the while her lips lingering at his, absorbing the warmth. So much ambivalence. Indeed, a part of her wanted not just to be trapped but to be thrown over his shoulder, carried upstairs, for him to make love to her so fiercely and so long, she couldn't stand to feet. Oh, yes. Take the choice away. Don't make me think about it.

While Stuart could feel physically exactly where he stood: So long as he held her face, kept her pinned there, she'd let him kiss her. She didn't even try to hide that she enjoyed it. So he restrained her, very much enjoying it himself—she opened her mouth to him, let his tongue dip into her, deep, warm, wet, delicious. Lord. The second he removed his arm, though, she moved. Or tried to. He caught her back, pushed her against the clock again.

She said quickly in a murmur, "This is going to work against you in London. Once your uncle is present, you can't behave this way."

She was trembling. He couldn't decide if this was good or bad. Good, he hoped. He could feel her heart pounding in the veins of the arm he held. "We're not in London yet," he said. He slowly released her arm, putting his on either side, by her shoulders, one on the doorframe, one on the side of the clock. He asked, "So what am I supposed to do? Tie you down?" He laughed dryly. "I've imagined wilder things."

Her eyes widened. One thing he understood: Emma loved her autonomy. She loved it the way most women craved security. She resented already his weight upon her, holding her here to their agreement. If he released the pressure, she'd fly. If he increased it, she'd fight, he was fairly certain. Which left him trying to find his balance, quiet, patient, though this didn't yield him what he wanted either.

Moreover, he wasn't even sure what he wanted. More sexual congress, yes, for certain. But more than that. He could have that, take it; there wasn't much she could have done about it. He wanted willingness. More than willingness. Eagerness. This morning. Her blind, unthinking panic to let him in.

She accused him, "You're calculating. You've done this before. You seduce women. Into awful things. Dark things."

He laughed. "The devil himself." Then he looked down. Emma realized he was amused, making fun—though whether of himself again or her, she couldn't tell. He said more seriously, "Not as much as you'd think. But, yes, I understand it: First, I figure out what you want. I seduce you with that. Then, there is the harder job of figuring out what you need—and the two are almost never the same thing. The need goes much further. And here is the challenge: to give you what you don't know to want, Emma, yet what you need so badly that, when presented with it, no matter how embarrassing or naughty, you can do nothing but surrender to it. The burning need. What is it? What do you need, Emma Hotchkiss, from a man such as I?"

She took him in, openmouthed at such a declaration. Then

asked, "W-why would you even—" She couldn't form a complete sentence. "Ah, what do you get—"

"Aah." He smiled. "I affect you. We already know that. I look at you, and you blush. One might conclude from there that, if I did things considerably more intimate, I could make your knees drop out from under you. And, if I could, well, what a feeling. It would make me so high—no, so hard, well—" He let out a little breath, an embarrassed laugh. He'd actually gone over the top, said something that made him color.

Good. He deserved a little taste of it. Emma stared, then said, "Sexual. It's all sexual."

"No. The trust involved is deeply intimate. Confidence." He laughed again at the irony of using the word. "There is a large play of emotion in what I'm discussing. We're already connected in a way that feels rare, a confiding, murmuring intimacy between us that, frankly, leaves me a little surprised and circumspect—I don't understand it."

Love. The word sprang to Stuart's mind. Is that what they were discussing? And, for no more reason than this, the Stunnels suddenly leaped to mind. Remembering the old couple, it occurred to him that perhaps the intimacy he described wasn't so dark and dirty as it sounded. That was just his own fear and embarrassment overlaying it, coloring it.

Private love. Private feelings. These were by nature so individual, they could not be understood en masse, only one to one. To accept—enjoy—filling the particular needs of another human being, was this love? Was this the union, the exchange, that became too full, too sweet, too tender to abandon? Two people touching each other in this way, simultaneously . . . rickety, bent hands, reaching toward each other . . . glaucous gazes, winking, sparkling in rheumy connection . . . embracing each other flaws and all.

What do you need, Emma? And can I fill it or at least a part of it? What is your burning need?

He came up close enough to murmur in her ear. "Let me kiss you and slide your skirts up your legs right now, till I can touch your skin . . . curve my hand under your buttocks." He let out a soft breath, desire, and closed his eyes. "Just that. While I kiss you." Oh, she was so delicate, would be so delicious to touch. He remembered. He remembered too well at the moment. She was more powerful than a shot of whiskey—he touched her waist, encircled it, and was drunk on her in half a second.

Behind her, he lifted a handful of her skirts, taking them up a foot, just as far as the small of her back, nothing crazy, just to see how she'd handle it. His fist, full of fabric, settled onto the top of her warm buttocks, such round female flesh.

Emma jumped as his hand came to rest on her bum. She reached, too, around, just as he brought himself forward to kiss her again. She tried to grab at her skirts, stop their movement upward. But just as she reached, he leaned, and her arms caught.

As his mouth touched hers, she struggled this time. Stuart didn't understand. She twisted in his embrace, a squirm of panic.

The next seconds were insane. Emma let loose of fears, huge ones that roiled up out of nowhere. She flailed, swung, thrashed. To keep from being bashed, Stuart caught hold of this unexpected amount of female energy—all focused on the idea of striking him, wounding him. He dodged her leg that would have kneed him if possible.

"Easy," he said. To save himself, he had to tighten his grip on her—which made her resist like a madwoman for a full minute. God, she was strong for someone so tiny. "Easy," he kept saying, trying to calm her, make her rational again.

Finally, panting, she grew still, a kind of wiry awareness in his arms that measured his own actions.

"I'm not moving. I'm not doing anything," he told her. Then, "Look at me."

Her eyes rose to his. Her face was pale, eyes wide.

She was terrified, he realized. Of him. What the hell? Then her direct regard grew watery, and with a little burst, a kind of mew, she let out a whimper. She began to cry. Good God.

One of her arms was caught behind her, he realized. No, both of them were; he'd pinned her to the clock. He let go, stepping back. The second a space opened in the doorway, she bolted past him, a churn of soft skirts on a dead run.

"Emma." He caught her by her faded dress and pulled.

She was brought up short as he pivoted in the doorway. He thought, if he didn't move farther but rather stood to speak now calmly, rationally, he could cut through this—though to do so, he had to hold her there by the skirt—

Emma jerked on her dress, whirling this way, then that, like a rabbit caught in a trap—she'd gnaw her leg off any second. She yanked on her skirts so hard that they ripped before he could let go. What had got into her? Finally, he held his hands up to show her: bare hands, surrender.

"*What* is wrong?' he asked.

She stared at him accusingly, then backed up all the way to the far wall of the corridor, a full five feet. She was breathing like a steam engine.

"I'm not moving. I'm staying right here," he told her. "I won't even approach you. What's wrong? Me? You're frightened of me. Why?" He let his shoulder fall into the doorframe, more than a little upset himself.

The degree of her alarm was startling. Then he understood partway at least.

"You thought I was going to—" He broke off with laughter. "What?" he said. "Say it."

She wouldn't. He watched her roll her lips inward, wet them.

"Look, I pushed you very hard. I was using every ounce of power I have over you, and you don't appreciate it, but, Lord—" It didn't matter what he said.

Oh, sweet, delicious woman. Her sexual interest was palpable. He could smell it, taste it; it vibrated in his bones whenever they were near each other. It was as real and solid as the bookcases behind him.

And she was afraid of it. It made her believe things that weren't true.

He tried to tease her back into reality. He said, smiling, "You thought I was going to force a little game of—what do you call it? Pickle-me-tickle-me? The old bellybump? The matrimonial polka? What's your name for it, Emma?"

She blushed. She sniffed.

"Make love to you?" he said softer. "Without your consent? You have rather a bizarre imagination yourself, don't you, Mrs. Hotchkiss?" Kindly, "No. I wouldn't do that. I didn't realize *that* was in your head. If I pushed you too hard, I'm sorry. Don't cry over my mistake."

She blinked, not accepting his apology. "You're the sort of man who can tie a woman's legs—"

"To keep her from kicking me."

"Back there, at the hotel— You—you said you could do anything—"

"And I could have. You took a horrible risk. By the time you kissed me back, though, I thought you understood my limits: that you were safe in that regard. My God, I'd never force you." He had to amend, "Well, not beyond a kiss. I *like* your consent."

She was shaking her head. "You thought about it; you wanted to. I think you might—"

He became incensed.

He made a face, then once more, he reined himself in. "Emma, you need a man, and you're looking at one you want."

"I'm not." She closed her eyes and turned her head; now she wasn't for sure.

"I can take care of you in that way. I long to. Let me. Let me touch you the way you want to be touched. Let me show you what I want to do."

She shook her head, then sniffled again.

He let out a frustrated snort. "You're insane. But it's your call entirely. In any event, don't cry over my misjudgment. I pushed too hard." He shook his head, still not certain what had happened, where he went wrong. "It's just, you seem so strong—"

"I *am* strong."

"Yes. All right." He nodded. "But no one's invincible." He folded his arms across his chest, his fingers into his armpits, and looked down. "I'm going to bed," he said. "I wish you'd join me. But, no, for your information, I don't force women. I like power, and I'm good at controlling people with it; but even I, son of a madman, have my limits."

He glanced up, adding, "For your information, it's the other game I like. The chair game, where I theoretically hold control, but you are willing as the devil." He narrowed his eyes in contemplation. "So watch yourself. I'd like to hold you to the bed and do things to you, kiss you, bite you ever so gently, leaving little marks where my mouth has been, before I take you while you're helpless. I love that, the power in it, the pretense of being a god. And I like other games, some I daresay I haven't even invented yet. When it comes to sexuality, I'm perfectly adolescent about it. No," he recanted, "more like an eight-year-old. I play. I have no shame. Only imagination." He laughed again, a cynical staccato this time.

"You're demented," Emma accused him, though her own tears—and his relative self-possession—seemed to undercut her judgment.

He raised a wry eyebrow. "Perhaps." Then shrugged. "Though I think it's more that you're prudish. Why does it matter what category my sexual interests, or yours for that matter, fall into? It's private, no one's business but the people involved."

Then he took a breath and let out the longest, most rapid flow of words she'd ever heard from his mouth:

He said, "I've never encountered a woman with such fortitude and resourcefulness, whose trust and respect, both, I want—I don't know why—to test, know, have, spend? I'm not sure. I only know I have never found such remarkably attractive, single-minded, self-sufficient integrity as I see in you. Which makes me think, fool that I am, that if your damned letting-go is half so magnificent in scope as your holding-on—a full, resounding canyon echo of your will—then your surrender would be a spinning drop into mindless, limitless bliss, and I want to be there to drop with you." He kept going, building steam as he spoke. "Odd, weird, wrong, bizarre. Yes. Perfect. Drop all those judgments in the face of passion, the uncontrolled moment. I stand here, wide open to anything you might like, to receive it, give it. Surrender to me, trust me in this large way—" He broke off, taking a huge gulp of air from having spoken at length without drawing breath.

Trapped. Emma felt trapped, first literally, then by the man's upside-down logic, now by his impassioned plea the like of which she'd never heard.

She searched for words, answers. But after all this, all she had to say for herself was, "I'm not prudish."

And even that, she said to his back, because at the same moment she opened her mouth, he muttered, "Good night," and turned.

He disappeared around the bend in the hallway, by the music room of his vast house.

Emma was left befuddled, not sure whether to be angry or not. Irritated, robbed. She had seemed to have a great big, perfectly good reason to hate him, yet the substance of it had evaporated. He wasn't going to force her? He hadn't been? The imminent sense of her doom had seemed so real for a moment, so frightening.

From nowhere, the idea came: She was not in favor of passion. She did not aspire to love. Either, both, were too painful.

Chapter 11

Read the police reports . . . nineteen out of twenty times they commence, "A young man dressed in the highest style of fashion . . ." Hence, the tailor is indispensable to the swindler.

—*The Handbook of Swindling,* 1839

EMMA lay tossing and turning that night in a huge, gentleman's nightshirt, the heavy fabric slipping and sliding against her as she tried to find sleep. Alas, the nightshirt was too lovely, plain and simple: warm as butter when she lay in a spot a few minutes, cool as a winter lake wherever she found a new position. Under her head, the plump, downy pillows were no less affecting. First one cheek, then the other lay on the fresh pillowcase, her nose pushed against fabric made steamy-smooth with lilac-scented linen water. Luxuries. Particular to Stuart. While, equally daunting, they seemed like mileposts back into an old and dangerous life. Seductions.

Ultimately, she sat up in the bed amidst a heap of pillows and covers—higher than she was in some places, piles of encased down and eiderdown, soft and warm and light as air. It was hopeless.

Quietly, carefully, she slipped from bed. The clock on the mantel of her sitting room said it was just after four in the morning. Wrapped in a blanket, wearing Aminah's slippers, she wandered downstairs, looking for God knew what. A place that felt safe perhaps, more like home.

She found herself aimlessly peering into rooms, opening door after door, room after room, not sure what she was hoping to see in the dark. Most smelled of construction, their shadows monuments to halfway-ness: half-cleaned, half-reorganized, half-finished in renovation. She ended up back in the only room that felt familiar, Stuart's library, his walls of books, where for amusement and curiosity, she lit the lamp, then went through his desk drawers.

He didn't keep anything of interest in them: plain white paper, a basket of ink, a blotter, a box of calling cards—clean, embossed with his name, plus a collection of cards from others carelessly tossed into the back of a half-empty box—bookplates, a ledger (on paper his estates yielded a handsome income, what would tally into five figures, though bank account after account had "hold" or "limited" with probable release dates noted at the side, some within days). Nothing revealing at all, which was a disappointment. She wanted some juicy bit.

The best she got, though, in the way of entertainment was, in a bottom side drawer, a dozen decks of cards. They lay with scoring pads, card trays—refugees from his game room under major reconstruction. She took out a deck, pulled up Stuart's desk chair, and cleared off a little space for a quick game of solitaire.

The cards felt good, slick and new, as she cut them, then mixed them. Comforting somehow. And, ah, the old fingers. After only a shuffle or two, the cards fluttered through her hands effortlessly. She laid a game of solitaire out, slapping cards down, and played for ten minutes.

As she played her mind wandered. What might the wickedest man she'd ever known—or at least the wickedest for whom she'd ever felt any attraction—do, if she'd let him continue this past night? What was Stuart like, naked and set loose on a woman? With more than two minutes to spare?

What happened inside her, when he was around, was so bizarre, so extreme. As if the man could dislocate gravity, negate what she'd experienced thus far in life as fact. No rules. She half wished she could have a do-over of this evening, like a child's game—a secret, private do-over that wouldn't count, where she'd surrender just to see what happened next. Whatever you want to do to me, Stuart. I'm yours.

The king of hearts. If the king of hearts had been two cards sooner, she'd have won. She stared at the last nine cards in her hand, knowing the order well enough she could have called it out.

She compressed her mouth, frowning at the cards, then passed her palm over the king, and, voilà, it wasn't the next card, then not the next either. Then, lo, there it was. She played it on a queen, and all the rest of what remained of the deck fell into place. Her hands were empty of cards.

She stared at the desk, at the neat stacks, yet felt unconsoled somewhere.

Once, she had taken comfort in her own dexterity and resourcefulness: so much more dependable than luck. She'd thought, once, that being able to take care of oneself was always better than depending on fate. Or, God forbid, another human being. Tonight, though, she didn't take much comfort in her manipulations.

"Congratulations," she told herself sarcastically. Then she got up and went back to the lilac sheets slipping against silky nightclothes.

Where she slept for minutes, or it seemed so. Dawn brought the house alive again with the will of Mount Villiars, the viscount of the district in residence. The sound of steps outside her rooms woke her, then wouldn't let her go back to sleep: people jumping to please his lordship, vying to do more, quicker, cheaper, make him happier, court his favor.

Shortly thereafter, there was a knock on her door, and a kitchen maid entered, carting a breakfast tray, then humming as she opened window curtains.

Emma put her pillow over her head, hearing through the layer of down: "The seamstresses have arrived from Leeds, ma'am. The' be downstairs with bolts and bolts a' be-yoo-tiful stuff. Looks like ye'll be gittin' new dresses, t'day. Aren'cha a lucky lass now?"

Emma could only groan.

The next three days were busy ones—and ones wherein Stuart found himself sent on a great many errands. All of them appeared to be necessary, yet he was also fairly certain Emma had devised her list of what had to be done in a way that kept him out of the house and out of the way. And in a manner that left her inaccessible. When he spoke to her, it was usually over the heads of seamstresses, with Emma's arms outstretched.

They remained cautious of each other after that evening in the library. Cautious and artificially polite. He hated it.

He took solace in the company of Aminah and Hiyam, who stayed for a day and a night more, then returned to London. They checked on him, he realized, and was amused. Two women, who had been so dependent on him at one time, had adjusted well to England, better than he perhaps. Both had friends, a developing life that suited them; Hiyam had a gentleman who called on her. Both women, like relatives who had a stake in any new arrival who might become permanent, were curious about Emma, but accepted when he said that she'd be gone again in two weeks.

Two weeks. Less than that now. He had to say, the time seemed well spent: the most interesting project he'd found in England to date. He rather liked watching Emma's becoming an elegant London "art expert." His neighboring sheep farmer was more and more a surprise. As she picked fabrics and put colors together for a small, efficient wardrobe his help, other than paying (or promising to), proved completely unnecessary. She listened to the seamstresses as to what was up-to-date, then made her own decisions; she knew the ins and outs of society style. In fact, she seemed to have a rather lovely feminine flare, uniquely hers, from dresses to gloves and hats and handkerchiefs. Moreover, she knew the etiquette and protocols. If he had ever doubted her ability to pass herself off in the upper class, his doubt relaxed. He began to feel even a little pleased with himself as tangible proof mounted—Emma could fulfill or exceed what he'd hoped for.

There was a matter-of-fact quality to her competence, an ease, as she manufactured the details of Leonard's undoing, and this made the whole enterprise take on an edge of anticipation. The game itself, quite aside from the lovely Mrs. Hotchkiss, was going to be fun.

None of this hit home so directly as on the third afternoon, when he arrived home early from a trip to the telegraph office. As he entered the house, he could hear Emma and two of the seamstresses working in the direction of his front parlor. When he came into the doorway, there the three of them were: A Mrs. Hobbly at the sewing machine set up by the front window, her daughter Louise in front of Emma, pinning something at her shoulder.

The room was a lovely, feminine mess: bolts of fabric partially unrolled across the sofa, buttons laid out on the writing table next to a tin. The floor had seemingly miles of lace and ruffled trim stretched out on it; the women appeared to be sorting and choosing next to a blue wool. The seat of his favorite parlor chair was taken up by measuring tapes, pincushions, and spindles of threads of various colors. All this to the snip of scissors, the clapping of sewing machine foot pedals pumping up and down, its wheels clacketing faster, then slower as blue wool rolled out from beneath its needle. And the sounds of the women themselves murmuring, two of them with pins in their mouths, as Emma's wardrobe came together: On a rack by the fireplace hung three dresses very near completion.

"How are things coming?" he asked from the doorway.

The nearest seamstress turned and pulled a pin from her

mouth—and opened up a clear line of vision to Emma herself, and Stuart felt something in his chest lurch.

Often, now, he had daydreamed what she might look like naked. Round, female, curving, inviting to touch. But never dressed, God help him. And there she was: far lovelier than he would have dared presume in his imagination. In a striped silk blouse and tailored, tiered skirt, she looked like a kind of cross between Bo Peep and the biblical Delilah just before she'd leveled Samson. A soft, small woman with a latent cleverness that somehow showed in the cut of her clothes.

Stuart found himself removing his hat, combing his fingers through his cold hair—his ears, his face, his fingers were nearly numb. The weather outside was windy and frigid; all that was missing was sleet to make it as ghastly as Yorkshire ever knew. He stood there unbuttoning his coat, unwrapping his scarf, and marveling: Emma Hotchkiss was a sweet, petite vision.

What had he expected? He hoped his surprise didn't show on his face: He'd thought her pretty, if a little short, a bit stocky. Raw-edged perhaps. A woman who cared more for smelly sheep than a long lady's toilette. Indeed, though, in a skirt that fit, she looked more a little doll with her tiny waist and full curves. Her blond hair was neat and swept back in shining ringlets, as demure as a princess royal. And her eyes . . . her face . . . good God. He was simply speechless for several seconds.

If the season had been in full swing, she would have set the gossips of London going. She could not go unnoticed, and her present clothes said she didn't intend to.

"Ah," she said, when she saw him, and smiled shyly. "Not bad, hmm?" She even made a kind of sly flutter of her lashes, the vamp.

"Beautiful." He laughed. "You look like—" He broke off. "Well, like a lady, as elegant a lady as I've ever seen," then he added, because it was true, "only prettier: a lady I would like to know better."

Which brought her mixed reaction again. His attention pleased her; it made her uncertain. She let her smile expand a little, deciding to have the compliment as it was meant. Then shook her head, pursed her lips, and looked down. He could never tell how much of her reaction was honest, how much was part of the charade. Sometimes her actions so lined up with an innocence, a sweetness of spirit, he couldn't help but believe in it. Yet the next moment, she would be so cynical and knowing, he would end berating himself for having ever been taken in.

He stood in the doorway for several long minutes, trying to invent a further purpose for remaining, simply to stare at her. From behind him, his butler took his coat, then cleared his throat.

"Your lordship," the man said. In a murmur, Stuart heard vaguely that his mail was on the mantel, that there was a problem in the stable with a horse, that one of the underbutlers was ill and needed a leave of absence. The landscape architect's plans required his signature. One of the beams for the game room had arrived split down the center. These matters and more awaited his attention. Distractedly, he turned and went about his business.

But the sight of this Emma Hotchkiss, emerging as from a cocoon of old, ill-fitting clothes, affected him enough that he dreamed about her that night: himself escorting her to various gatherings, the fun of fooling his most pompous friends as he introduced her—his and her private joke. "This is my Yorkshire neighbor, a landowner with a fine sheep enterprise." It wasn't a lie, but the rich look of her belied the truth.

Or the other way around, he thought when he awoke. A sheep farmer, a landowner in Yorkshire, was perhaps a finer thing to be than he'd first considered.

Her fourth day at Dunord began for Emma fairly much as the last several: She was up by dawn, sipping coffee with one hand while she held the other out, so two women could alter a seam from her waist to her armpit. She ate a meat pie for lunch with half a dress pinned to her, then stood most of the afternoon and into the evening in various pieces of clothing that formed around her. By supper, the last stitch was in, the last ribbon tacked down. She had five dresses, with the promise of two nightgowns to be sent on to London, a lady's wool coat, and—having arrived the evening before under Stuart's arm—a pair of pretty blue kid lace-up boots along with a rather gorgeous pair of evening slippers. Hair ribbons, jewelry—fake but still lovely to her eye—more of Stuart's doing. Scarves, kid gloves, a hat.

And a beaded silk purse. She'd given her new confidence partner a list of what it should contain. He'd disappeared till after dark, till after dinner in fact—he was quite late.

From her bedroom, she heard the front door open—when there was nothing to unload, the coachman deposited the master of the house at the front door, then took the carriage around to the carriage house. She came out onto the landing and looked over the balcony.

"Were you able to get it all?" she asked.

He strode, all but about to pass under the balcony of his wide staircase, handing off his hat, coat, gloves in the offhand way he had of continuing to walk as his servants vied to catch items as he dropped them. She bent over the railing, looking down.

Her words stopped him. "I made a dent in the list. It was the best I could do."

"The ladies left after dinner. And your uncle?"

"He telegrammed. He expects to see me in London, though not till Sunday. He's in Hampshire till then."

Four days, she thought. They'd start in four days.

Then the heart-stopping words. Stuart said, "I think we've done as much as possible here. We're ready. Let's head toward London tomorrow. We'll pack in the morning."

She bit her lip, absorbing the idea. London.

It would still take the rest of the week to organize what

remained, but he was right: London was the best place to do it, the city of opportunity. She made a jerk of her head, agreement.

"Good night then," she said, looking down on a handsome man she couldn't understand, who attracted her in ways that unsettled her.

He stared up at her a moment longer. "Good night," he said, then walked forward, under the balcony.

Emma found herself bending over its railing, trying to follow him with her eyes, but she saw only the top of his head and wide back disappear into shadows.

The words were from a bit of poetry about God, Stuart thought, since that was fairly much all that the Sufi poets wrote about. And sugar. God and sugar, as he recalled. A poem by Rumi, though a few lines applied to Stuart, to the present, right now. He lay in bed trying to remember them, a little obsession—or rather something to do with himself, since sleep seemed elusive. His arms under his head, he lay a long time, staring up at the ceiling, trying to summon the full meaning, the full text from memory. Finally, he got up, put on a long, roomy robe, an old, favorite bisht, and slippers, then padded down the corridor and stairs, off to search the matter further in his library. He knew just where the book would be.

He was surprised to find his desk lamp burning already. He must have forgotten to turn it off, with his butler having already gone to bed. He shrugged at the lamp burning in the empty room. Then frowned to see the fire in the hearth wasn't out either. Well, good, he reasoned, and threw another log onto the embers, imagining he might read, even doze here, once he'd located the book. As he stood, he considered taking the lamp up the ladder with him, then didn't. He'd come back for it if need be.

At the top of the ladder, though, he had to roll the contraption down the runner by hand a few feet, further into the dark than he'd planned. The volume wasn't where he'd first thought, though by author and within a few shelves. He ran his finger along spines, pulling himself and the ladder along as he checked in Arabic and English, thinking to find a good translation, then decided, no, he wasn't going to be able to read the spine without better light. He was just looking down to find his footing, about to fetch the lamp, when a sound made him jump, then look across the room toward the doorway.

And, lo, Emma Hotchkiss, wearing his own nightshirt with a blanket wrapped round her shoulders, walked in on the soles of Turkish slippers, her hair tumbling down over the blanket at her back, loose, and over one of her shoulders: three feet of silvery gold ringlets as curly as swaying, jiggling springs.

Stuart was brought up short for an instant, then wanted to laugh. She did a kind of double take with regard to the fire, as if it had started itself. She looked around—she seemed to look right at him for a moment—then her eyes passed him over. She didn't see him. He was apparently too far into the dim rear of the room and higher, at the top of a ladder, than her usual line of vision.

Assured she was alone, she walked over to the fire and tossed several more logs onto it, emptying his basket. Well, he laughed to himself, she was planning on staying a while and readily made herself at home in his house.

He liked that she did. He watched as she bent, chucking logs a bit heavy for her, then closing the fire screen, then pushing her hair back from where it had slid to the front. She shook her head as she stood, an unconscious gesture—she had the prettiest hair he'd ever seen on a woman. Thick and healthy and of such a delicate color. Such a pretty woman, he thought.

Who then walked over to his desk as if she owned it, and reached into a bottom drawer. She took out a deck of cards, then, pushing his parliamentary papers aside, dealt out a line of playing cards as if for solitaire. He liked that they both seemed to have the same problem, he, combating sleeplessness with poetry, she, with cards.

He leaned on his elbow, raising his foot one rung, and settled himself comfortably to await discovery.

She slapped cards down with a vengeance. *Flap, flap, flap*, they went, as quickly as he'd ever seen a person put them down. She looked like a dealer at one of the gambling houses in Monte Carlo. She certainly would have been the sort of distraction welcomed there, with her hair down and her blanket sliding off one shoulder.

After a minute or so, she frowned at the lay of the cards, raised one hand a moment, wiggled her fingers in the air—then let out a snort of disgust and threw the whole mess down. Cards slid, several *pat-pat-patting* off the desktop entirely onto the floor on the other side.

With a sigh, she stood and came around, picking some up haphazardly. Then she didn't put them immediately together with the rest. What was she doing? Stuart squinted, leaning a little to see as she walked toward a dark window, then turned her back. When she stepped away, he almost lost his balance: She'd perched a card on the bust of old Uncle Theo, between his deep brow and upward-turned nose—making him look like a circus seal. She had no respect at all for the Mount Villiars heritage, which made Stuart smile and smile, because it gave them yet something more in common.

"Oh, yes," she said, chuckling gleefully over her trick. Her voice carried very well down the length of the library gallery. "That suits you. If only the master of the house was here, why, I'd tuck one right there." She flipped a card at the stone bust's ear.

Stuart watched her arrange three more playing cards, like a fan, balancing them carefully where the old fellow held his fist against his carved throat: Uncle Theo became a performing-seal cardsharp, balancing one card with his nose while holding the rest close to his chest.

She tried to fit a card into the statue's pinched mouth, but the card would only stay briefly. As she fiddled with it, replacing it several times, her blanket slid down, off one arm entirely, hair running down her back in the lamplight, a kind of pale, liquid, rippling gold. In profile, while chuckling to herself, she played, then caught her blanket, swooping at the knees to yank on it, jostling it up into place again. An elf, he thought.

Neobychny. Incomparable. The Russian word had sprung to mind before with regard to Emma. She certainly was unique.

As the blanket slid again—she had its weight and volume unbalanced, too much to one side—his nightshirt moved against her body. One moment, the fabric rounded at her buttocks, the next, it sloped at the sway of her hip. In front, the pleats that usually ran straight down his chest shuddered over the jiggle of breasts, while Emma laughed lightly—so beautiful, this woman's laughter—amusing herself.

Stuart felt the lift and change in his body and dropped his head. He stared down at the rungs, at his feet in the dark for a few moments. Watching her felt suddenly less than innocent. She was in her nightclothes. Or in his, technically. He should clear his throat, let her know the master of the house was here—he smiled—should she want to tuck anything anywhere.

Then she pivoted, and he drew back against the ladder. She walked directly toward him—surely she saw him. For a moment, she appeared to stare up, directly where he stood at the top of the bookshelves. Or at the ladder itself. She walked toward him for the thirty or so feet, yet her attention kept glancing sideways, at books against the wall. She reached out, her fingertips touching their spines. As she walked along, the pads of her fingers made a light little patter, *poppa-pappa-pap-pap, poppa-pappa-pap-pap*. At his ladder, she didn't even hesitate. She walked right under him—he smiled down as she passed between his feet and the wall—then she stopped just beyond to lean close to a photograph, trying to decipher its content in near darkness. She gave up.

Emma did a full turn of the library's circumference. It had become her favorite room of the house. Her eyes lingered over the shelves and shelves of books. Oh, so many. It would take a lifetime to read them all. The books were in several languages beside English, several alphabets for that matter, Cyrillic, Arabic, Latin letters, everything but Sanskrit, it seemed. Little volumes, thin ones, tomes, colorful, drab, they encircled the room. As she emerged from the far end, the dark end, photographs on both sides of the room took over in the niches of the shelves. Once portraits had hung in the spots, discolored places on the walls indicating they had been a long time before being recently removed. By the fireplace, she gravitated toward a well-lit collection of photos, their sepia tones reflecting the layers of silver in the firelight and the light from the desk.

The subject of these was otherworldly—pictures with surprising clarity, of a surprising reality: the desert, a low palm, camels, foreign people in loose clothes, their heads covered, their robes flowing. A caravan. In one photograph, a group of Arab men stood before a long line of caparisoned camels with saddles tasseled and ornamented. Of the three men, one looked familiar, a dark, thin face with dark, intense eyes and a gleaming black beard. She thought she knew him from a book or the newspaper, a famous Arab—a prince from the House of Saud, a caliph from Persia.

She'd studied these pictures and others over the last several evenings. Stuart was slowly replacing his family's portraits with modern photographs of foreign places. The photos never failed to draw her, like riddles, though they never yielded an answer. Tonight, she dismissed them as always, padding off to collect her playing cards from the floor, then from the bust by the window.

What silliness. At the desk, she carefully ordered the cards this time, watching as she shuffled, then picking at them with a few quick flips of her fingers, after which she smacked them down in under two minutes, *thwack, thwack,*

thwack. "Ta-da," she said listlessly. "You win again, Emma."

"You cheat," said a deep voice. It laughed at her, welling out of the darkness, making her leap: low, the devil's own mirth.

She jumped so high, her buttocks thumped upon its return to the chair seat. She lost her breath: Better the devil, for out of the dark from the back of the room, like a phantom she'd summoned up, came Stuart Aysgarth, looking a little bit like a caliph himself in a loose robe of dark purple. She put her hand to her throat, her heart *thump-thumping* like a parade drum.

"Y-you frightened me," she choked out. "H-how—"

He pointed up and behind him. "I was looking for a book." When she still didn't understand, he smiled. "I was at the top of the ladder back there, when you came in." He laughed. "You walked right under me." He explained, "I couldn't help it. You looked so sneaky"—he paused—"and, well, lovely in my nightshirt, I couldn't resist watching what you'd get up to." He laughed more openly still. "Clever card trick there"—he indicated the bust by the window—"Very creative." Smiling, he teased her. "Do you always cheat at solitaire?"

"No," she began and rolled her eyes. "God—" She broke off, then admitted, "Sometimes." Then came totally clean. "Yes, lately."

He came fully into the light. His loose robe was of doubled fabric, an inky purple on one side, a bluer tone on the other. It looked warm. Under it, he wore a nightshirt not unlike the one on her own body, though hers dragged about her ankles. His—white, pleated, and plentiful—stopped just below his shins.

"What is the point of playing alone," she asked, "if you can't win?" She made a yawn. Self-consciously, she stacked the cards together, tapped them into place, then slid them into their box: in preparation to go. More for politeness, a nicety on which to leave, she asked, "What are you doing here? Why are you up?"

He answered by raising his hand, a small, red leather-bound book in it. When neither of them could think of anything further to say, he added,

"Rumi. A poet. A Sufi."

"What's *Sufi?*"

Instead of explaining, he paged through the book, then said, "Here. Listen," as he put his finger on a page and read:

" 'Dissolver of sugar, dissolve me.
If it is time, do it softly
With a graze of the hand or a look.
I anticipate with each dawn.
That's when it happened before.
Or do it in a flash like an execution.' "

He paused to look up at her. He had a lovely reading voice, his pauses lending the poetry an idiosyncratic, unduplicatable lilt. He finished quietly without looking at the book:

" 'You keep me at arm's length,
But the keeping me away is pulling me in.' "

She wet her lips, blinked. "It's you." She glanced to the wall by the fire.

"What?"

"The man in the photo, the one with the beard who looks familiar. He's you." She realized, with a full beard and in the right clothes, Stuart could perfectly well pass for an Arab. "You fit right in, didn't you?"

He looked toward the wall, then wandered toward the photos she pointed to. "I tried to, that much was certain. For a time at least." He set his book on a reading table.

"Where was it taken?" Emma followed him over.

"Near Cairo."

Emma stood next to him to examine again these particular images. Indeed, a young version of Stuart Winston Aysgarth gazed at the camera, his somber eyes unmistakable. How could she have missed them? Only the top of his face, though, was truly visible. He looked thin, sinewy, beneath the flowing robes and a headcloth tied with a twisting band. His amorphous clothing emphasized the clean line of his high forehead, the leanness at his cheekbones; the beard disguised the rest. He was tanned by the sun, dark-skinned, looking directly at the lens: seeming for all the world a native of Arabia or Persia or Turkey.

"Were you there long?"

"No. I made my home in Istanbul at the time, though I traveled quite a bit. I lived in Istanbul for three years."

"And after that?"

"Russia. Apartments in Petersburg, a house in Tzarskoe Selo, and a small country estate outside Odessa. Mostly, I moved between the three, though I liked Peters best, the place I chose when I could."

"Peters?"

"Saint Petersburg."

"Russia," she said to confirm her poor geography. She knew enough, though, to understand that, culturally, he had put as much distance between himself and England as possible. Curiosity for other places made her ask, "Did you ever meet the tzar?"

"Several times a week. I was something of an English novelty at court whenever I wished."

With wonder, she asked, "What's the tzar like?"

He shrugged. "Kind, well-meaning. Unsure. The head of a despotic government tempered by assassination. The court is splendid. The country itself is turbulent, its poverty so widespread and extreme, you can't begin to imagine from this side of the Baltic Sea."

"You speak all these languages? Russian, Arabic?"

He snorted. "Yes, besides English, I can stutter my way into Russian, Turkish, Arabic, French, with some Farsi, Urdu, Punjabi, and a bit of Kurdish." He laughed at himself.

What he liked best about the next was that she didn't deny it, yet spoke immediately. "I like the rhythm of your speech. It's interesting." She blinked, looking sheepishly sincere, then added, "I, um, have to be careful sometimes or I'd find myself imitating it, answering back in the same rhythm, or some facsimile of it." She shook her head. "I couldn't do it as well. But sometimes I know just how you'll say a sentence, before it's out, and I want to say it, too, like wanting to dance with you."

He folded his arms and stared down at her over the top of his own arm, waiting for a disjunction, a qualification, anything that tagged the compliment as something less. Then he had to close his mouth. It had dropped open slightly. She meant it, which left him speechless.

How incredibly good her words struck him: that she should admire a flaw that not everyone even kindly tolerated. He smiled for a second, then looked down at his folded arms, not sure he wished for her to see how foolishly pleased he was by such a small matter.

"You've traveled a lot."

"Indeed." He looked back at the photos. He had walls of them. His photographs of the East and Near East drew him still. He pointed to another photo, part of the next set down the wall, at a picture of white trees and a long line of white bench tops sitting quietly before wide, neoclassic columns: the Kazan Cathedral, glittery white fresh from a snowstorm. "In Russia," he recalled pleasantly, "high society went to Moscow for the cold months. Not myself. I loved Petersburg best when the tzar and court emptied out of it." He smiled at the thought. "I loved the bright cold days. Nothing so serene, I say, as kicking up knee-high snow as you walk through the city, so alone it all but belongs to you."

She threw him a tentative look of agreement. "Petersburg?" Then a dismayed click, tongue to teeth, an apology for not being sure: "The Russian capital, yes? Is it very far north? Colder than here?"

"Yes to all. It's on the Gulf of Finland—Denmark is southerly by comparison." He said, "The only thing farther north in Russia is tundra, sections of which I've also crossed."

"Tundra," she repeated. Her face had no idea what he was talking about.

He smiled faintly, then looked away, sure he'd lost her completely. "I'm boring you."

"No," she said quickly, "not at all." She arched, then twisted, reaching back to hike her blanket back up about her shoulders, all the while staring at his photographs, one to the other. As she settled, she said, "I can't imagine living somewhere else. I like hearing about it."

"A glutton for punishment," he told her, laughing. But he was delighted by her interest. "The tundra is a kind of ice plain, arctic. The ground would be a morass from rainfall and river flow, except the cold keeps it frozen to a depth of no-one-knows how many feet. Ice as solid as land. White in all directions, as far as the eye can see."

She was contemplating him, he realized, not the tundra. "Why?" she asked. "Why did—do?—these places appeal to you?"

He said immediately, "They're not English." He snorted, "They aren't even Continental, though Petersburg was a nice compromise. Other. I'm sure it had to do with their being as far from my English father and responsibilities as I could remove myself." He snorted, self-deprecating. "Too far, as it turned out. I was hunting bear near Caucasia, a long trek even from my home in Petersburg, when the news of my father's death found me. The old devil had only been fifty-seven. I would have thought that a man as mean as Donovan Aysgarth would live to a hundred—too vile even for Death to approach, except cautiously.

"Leave it to my father to take matters into his own hands and have even Death on his own terms."

Her face looked blank. She wasn't conversant with this detail, either, with regard to his father.

He clarified. "He shot himself."

"Ah." She nodded. "Yes, I think I remember reading in the newspaper. I'm sorry."

"Don't be. He did us all a favor."

She frowned: a look of concern for a man who loathed his own father.

Though, if she had only understood, such a look would have been reserved for the man who didn't. "He was a horrible person."

Horrible didn't sum up Donovan Aysgarth, either. Too mild. While Stuart was afraid of another round of explicitness for fear of putting her off—his father's blood flowed in his own veins.

"Well," he said, pivoting. He headed for the desk again. "That shortens your spoon more than necessary." He referenced her Scottish expression from the first night here.

She didn't comprehend, then did, giving him more of her lovely, light laughter.

The sound always caught him aback. And the sight of her tonight. Did she grow prettier by the day? Was that possible? Lord, she was a vision tonight: looser, more relaxed.

"Well," she said. "Thank you for the brief world tour. I like your photographs."

He was reluctant to part company from her, when the atmosphere between them was so unusually pleasant, yet that was where she was headed.

The clock in the corner arrested them both as it struck the half hour. It was three-thirty. The long, low *bong* reminded him, sourly, of her rebuff that first night, of her fear and her tears and his part in it. One of the most resilient women he'd ever met, he hadn't allowed for her to have a tender place, a vulnerability—a mistake he would make less quickly at least, given a second chance.

He picked up the deck of cards, then—a brainstorm—offered them out. "A game of cards," he suggested, "since neither one of us can sleep?"

He raised a challenging eyebrow toward a woman who could deal—and cheat—with the sangfroid of a croupier.

"Poker?" he asked. "Three card draw, nothing wild. We can bet these"—he reached into his desk drawer, then dropped a box of roulette tiles on the desktop—"with a prize for the winner, just to make the game interesting."

She was slightly taken aback, but the cards, the tiles held her. As she looked at them, he caught a twinkle in her eye: She thought she could beat him.

"What would you want for a prize?" she asked.

He teased. "Oh, if I win, I get to tie you to a chair." He widened his eyes, mock anticipation.

"Oh, please."

"No. Really. I do."

She laughed.

Still smiling at her, he wiggled his eyebrows, feeling triumphant. "Oh, wait, you *like* the idea. All right, I've changed my mind. If *you* win, I get to tie you to a chair." He laughed outright.

"Stop." She shook her head, though her smile hadn't completely evaporated. Traces of it remained around the corners of her mouth.

"For five minutes," he said, as if truly naming terms. "During which time I get to do whatever I wish."

She settled a look of forbearance on him—though her expression hinted at required indignity, the prescribed, in the face of such childishness. "You know I won't allow that. What would you truly want?"

Emma felt warm and comfortable, able to discuss their odd first hour together somehow now in the middle of the night, tease about it, which was a release of sorts. For the first time, it didn't feel embarrassing. It struck her as funny, in fact. Who could imagine such a thing? If she tried to explain to someone those two minutes on the chair in Hayward-on-Ames, not a soul wouldn't buy it. It didn't seem possible. Yet the two of them knew, understood; they were baffled by it together. And their togetherness suddenly seemed to breed an odd rapport.

"I just told you what I'd *truly* want," he insisted.

She sniffed. "You are so bizarre."

"So you keep saying." Behind his desk, he stretched, unfazed by names and judgments. "Perhaps I am, perhaps not," he said as he arched, raising his shoulders as he spread his arms, making a kind of far-reaching shrug.

She watched, more attentive than she liked: Her gaze covered him—his wide chest, his shoulders, the full reach of his outstretched arm—as he released tension from his muscles. For her benefit, she suspected. Yet still she couldn't look away. She stood there by the fire, fiddling with the ends of the blanket, holding it up, while watching a man—bizarre, power-hungry, manipulative, perfectly open about it—who attracted her despite herself.

He reversed his stretching and wrapped his arms about his chest, loosening his back. In this position, he tilted his head, a faint smile on his lips. "I enjoy tormenting you with the idca that you're at the mercy of a lunatic, I promise you that." He relaxed and pulled out his desk chair. "Though not to the point of making you cry. I've felt quite sorry for that." As he sat, he resumed his teasing with his not entirely nice laugh as he shook his head. "If you ask me, though, it's you: You are *so* constrained, Emma, all the while congratulating yourself that you aren't. *That* is bizarre."

He leaned back in the chair and raised his eyebrow, a trademark at this point, then asked, "Don't you ever do *anything* Mama and Papa might not approve of?"

Why, yes, she did. Every day. "I ran away to *London* when I was only thirteen." Then immediately the "daftest" adventure of her life was tame for having told it to a man who *lived* in London, who'd run away to Russia. She looked at the cards on the desktop. "If we played and I won, what I'd like is my freedom. I'd like to walk out of here, without worry that a sheriff would be at my door tomorrow."

"Ah. Well." He snorted. "Since we're both asking for the impossible."

For a moment, she felt angry. He'd won too much already. And now he believed he'd simply sidle up; they'd be friends. When they weren't. She looked for a harsh thing, a mean name, anything that would be indicative of her absolute authority over herself. "I'm not here for your entertainment," she told him. "I'm here to get myself out of trouble. I certainly don't intend to compound my problems by playing kissing games with you in the night." A phrase she remembered from London rose into her mouth: "If you don't like that"—she folded her arms—"you can saw it off."

Stuart jerked, blinked.

Yes, precisely, she thought. Exactly the reaction she wanted. He should jolly well be taken aback. Don't fool with Emma Hotchkiss.

He was annoyed one moment, then he tilted his head, frowning as if somehow skeptical. He narrowed his eyes, though not with the undiluted anger for which she had hoped. In fact, he almost seemed to smile. What was happening? What was changing? Why was she losing his sense of outrage before she'd even claimed it again? She'd insulted him, hadn't she? She's just said the most disparaging thing she knew.

" 'Sod off,' do you mean?" he asked.

"Sawed off?" she repeated. Was that it? She furrowed her brow, compressing her lips till she held them between her teeth. Yes, she was missing something. *Saw it off* wasn't quite right, was it? Though how could she be sure? She'd only heard the expression once, and that was outside a men's club years ago. "Yes, sawed off," she corrected. That sounded a fraction more like it, though it made less sense.

He snorted, smiling now. "It has nothing to do with sawing." He eyed her as if looking for confirmation, a hint that she understood.

"Not 'sawed off'?" She blinked. Was there a trick in here somewhere? Then it occurred to her. "Sod?" she asked, her eyes going wide all on their own, cool to the air. "Like sodomy?" She was suddenly breathless.

"Yes."

She opened her mouth, couldn't close it. She'd horrified herself.

By then, though, Stuart had burst out laughing, uncontrollable. "Though 'saw it off' sounds fairly dreadful.' "

"I thought so." Still, sodomy was much worse. She blushed. She bowed her head. Her cheeks heated till they seemed as hot as the glowing logs of the fire. She didn't know where to look.

While Stuart truly got going, laughing so hard he held his palm to his abdomen. He nearly fell out of his chair.

Always, he was eye-popping handsome, but when Stuart Aysgarth smiled—God, when he laughed—he became approachable, human, lavishly appealing. The most attractive human male she had ever encountered. His eyes crinkled. His mouth widened into creases and a flashy display of teeth. And the sound was carried in that smooth, deep voice of his: If a smooth-bowed cello could laugh on its lowest strings, Stuart's laughter was what it would sound like.

After a moment, her mistake was simply too good. She found herself laughing also. Oh, Emma. Oh. "Saw it off," she repeated.

The two of them sat there laughing for five minutes, till embarrassment mixed with mirth to such high degree that tears were streaming down Emma's face.

He said then, "You are the best, do you know that? You are the best woman I've ever met."

"Daft," she said, gleeful, yet wanting to temper his praise with reality. Praised for getting something wrong. Wrong and obscene. How like Stuart to enjoy her for that.

"Exciting," he said. "Daft like a fox. Adventurous. Fearless. Unpretentious. You are something, Emma."

I am something. She lifted her chin and beamed.

Their laughter slowly calmed till they stared, eye to eye, and still they did not break eye contact. The air seemed dense with affection, palpable, buoyant with it. She floated upon it, as if there were not a harsh surface anywhere, as if she were a feather aloft on the sweetest, warmest breeze.

"You wild thing, you," he told her. "I could teach you dirty expressions, if that's where your curiosity leads you. In five different languages." He clicked his tongue, a mock risqué sound, then said, "How about, if you win, you can flip cards at my ear. How's that?"

She shook her head at herself, reddening a little. Oh, Stuart. She hated him; he entertained her. He made her laugh. He frightened her, outraged her. He made her dissolve into tears of mirth.

"For myself," he told her, "I'll take a kiss. That's all I want, if I win. Though a long one. So is card-flipping sufficient for you? Is it commensurate with a 'kissing game,' as you call it? Name your price, Mrs. Hotchkiss, and deal the cards."

She frowned at him. "How long in 'a long kiss'?"

"Five minutes."

She shook her head, almost laughed, but held it at bay. "Too long," she said seriously.

"Three."

"One."

He harrumphed. "Whatever you want better be small. A minute of kissing you is hardly worth anything. What'll it be?"

She began, not knowing where she was going. "If I win—" She paused, then settled on, "If I win, you stop this. You forget awarding anyone medals for—well, for deeds better off not done. You let this whole"—she had to consciously allow herself to pronounce the word, "*sexual* business go. You stop entirely." She leaned onto her side of the desk, leveling a serious gaze down on him. "We can't afford it, not in any sense, and it's making me crazy."

"All right," he said. "If you win."

Which seemed to give him carte blanche if she lost. "And your coat," she added. "Since you already should be leaving me alone."

"My coat?" He laughed, startled. "Against kissing you for a minute? I don't think so. Ten minutes."

"Five."

"All right. And a coat *like* mine; mine wouldn't fit you anyway. I'll have yours lined with fur, any you name. If you win."

"Fine."

They looked at each other. Then Emma grabbed a chair on her way over, plonked it down on the opposite side of the desk, sat her bottom on it, then held out her hand. "I'll deal."

"You will not. We'll cut for the deal."

The game was laid. More or less. They counted out fifteen tiles apiece, which Emma complained was too few for much of a game. She was right. When he bet all his remaining tile on the second hand, she didn't have enough to call.

"And you're bluffing," she said. "You think you can outpower me because you have more tiles than I do after only one hand. That's unfair. Let me call with what I have."

"You only have four tiles. I just put in eight."

"Take back four."

"No. I have a good hand. I want to win a lot with it."

"You're bluffing," she said again.

"All right. I'll allow you to call with your four and my nightshirt. The one you're wearing. I won't even make you ante it up—you can keep it on till you actually lose."

Emma twisted her mouth, her tongue to a side tooth. He didn't have a good hand. She did—she had two pair, queens and jacks. "Agreed," she said quickly, and pushed her last four tiles to the center of the desk.

He laid down a full house, kings high. She pursed her lips, frowning at his cards.

"More tiles," she said.

"Thc nightshirt first."

She raised her eyes to his. "We've only played two hands. I told you we needed more tiles to make it fun."

"I'm having fun," he insisted. Smiling, he pointed at the nightshirt she wore, which she had been so blithe with.

She balked, smiled, cajoled. "Don't be mean."

He twisted his mouth. "I fully will, when the time comes, but, all right, if you're going to be a poor sport about it." He lectured with a finger as he dealt out a dozen more tiles complaining, "I would bet money that, if *I* had lost in two hands, I'd have to pay up with a rather expensive coat. Now, I have to win twice—"

She stacked her tiles, then offered four out. "And I want to buy the nightshirt back."

"No." He smiled. "You can win it back. We leave it in the pot. Bet, if you want it back."

Cocky blighter, she thought. She could beat him; she was a more experienced player than he. Then the next hand, even after drawing three extra cards, all she possessed was a pair of nines, jack high. Was he cheating? Was he stacking the deck somehow?

She smiled at him as if she held a flush.

And watched him put all his damn tiles into the center again.

She threw her cards down and stood. "Oh, for godssake, what kind of a game is this? You're cheating."

He reached swiftly across the desk and pulled all the cards, hers included, into a pile in the center of the desk, then said, "Take it off."

"What?" She watched him tap the cards into a neat pile, both amazed and irritated. "Wait one minute. Gathering the cards that fast is the lamest old ploy in the business: for a player whose hand was bust."

"The nightshirt. I won."

"No, you didn't. You took my cards. I intended to call you. What did you have?"

He laughed. "It doesn't matter. You folded."

"I did not. You grabbed the cards up before I could call. I had a pair of kings," she lied. "On your honor, what did you have?"

"A royal flush," he said and laughed heartily. "Nice try. Take off the nightshirt." With his thumbs, he aligned the edges of the deck neatly, then almost absently shuffled. The cards fluttered in his hands, obedient. "I lived in Monte Carlo for a year. Did I mention that? I did nothing but gamble there, mostly cards. I won, Emma." He looked up, cackled in that wicked way he had, then said, "The only thing better than a woman standing across from you in your own nightshirt is a woman standing without it: because you bluffed her with a pair of threes. Take it off."

"You cheated!"

"I bluffed. You threw your hand down because you believed my hand was much better than it was. Em, I tend to follow the rules—I'm a member of Parliament, remember? We make them. You're the cheater."

"That's not fair!"

"Bluffing?" He laughed. "Bluffing is the way the game is played. It's the heart of the game."

She hated the schoolgirl sound of herself in her own ears, yet what she felt was nothing mature. "You wouldn't. You're a gentleman!"

"No, actually, I'm not: That's also a bluff. Come on, Emma. You already know that."

"Monte Carlo," she muttered. He'd conned her.

She was furious, yet something deep down was laughing. It was funny. She was funny. And the conning of cons wasn't over yet. She still held an ace he wasn't acknowledging.

She stood up and backed away in her blanket. She let out a dramatic sigh, a woman resigned. "If you think you're having the nightshirt before the kissing part, think again. First, the kiss. Then the nightshirt."

He blinked, stood up partly, looking a little flummoxed that any of this was coming his way at all. He hadn't believed she'd pay up.

Oh, she'd pay up all right. She'd kiss him voluptuously, strip naked, and walk out. It would serve him right.

Things started out all right. Stuart came around the desk cautiously, watching her. Then he drew her into his arms by her hand. He snugged the blanket up around her, then reached one arm inside, under it, and pulled her against him.

He wasn't wearing anything at all under his nightshirt. Of course. She'd known that. No man did. Yet it came as a kind of surprise to her own body, also naked beneath her nightshirt: nothing but two heavy silk nightshirts between them. Then his mouth on hers.

She couldn't remember how long, what the point was, how they'd come to this, not much of anything, as he kissed her: only that her own intent had been to kiss him back and enjoy it, even entice him. Yes, that was the plan. A perfectly good plan. Tongues, teeth . . . warm, gentle lips . . . strong arms around her . . . a firm, long, muscular body against hers. A body that grew interested in the way a man's did almost immediately. That part of a man's body that could be so light grew thick and heavy; it began to prod against her belly.

Her head felt light as Stuart let her go. She staggered a little, but found her balance. "Th-there," she said.

He wasn't smiling any longer, his face serious, his breathing audible with the rise and fall of his chest.

Emma stepped back. She shook her head. "We're being foolish," she murmured. "We were inventing a way to do this and—" She pressed her mouth into a line. "And we shouldn't. It's going to make it too difficult in London. And after that—oh, after that, I'll still live down the hill from you. Let's say good night. Let's stop right here."

He shook his head. "Take off the nightshirt," he whispered.

She frowned deeply. "It won't do you any good. I've figured myself out. I won't—" She broke off. He didn't believe her or else he didn't care. "Fine," she said. "Be an idiot: I'm going to take it off, then walk out on you."

All he answered was, "Move toward the fire. You're going to be cold." He was absolutely in earnest.

She undid the first button slowly, trying to gather herself. Her hands shook.

He wet his lips and took a step back, allowing enough room between them to see up the full length of her.

Sarcastically, meanly, she asked, "So do you want it over my head or down my shoulders?"

He looked surprised that she even had a voice. "What?" As if he no longer spoke English.

"The nightshirt. Do you want it off going up or coming down?"

"Oh, here, let me." He came forward.

"Oh, no." She walked backward, away from him. "You won your nightshirt. I'll give it to you. If you take it, though, well, I'd consider such action in the same league as, well, pickle-me-tickle-me without my consent." She felt the faintest smile, as if it lived in her belly, warmed her there.

He looked alarmed for a second, then made a low and soft laugh. Playing. It was a serious game they were playing, but involving. Deeply involving. And she was taking part in it. There was nothing dangerous here so much as a line they pushed back and forth. It was a game where neither of them exactly knew the outcome, because neither controlled it completely.

"All right, I won't touch you," he said. But next thing she knew, he was right beside her, pulling her blanket away. He tossed it, then his finger touched the neckline of her nightshirt.

"Stop," she said immediately, even a little angrily. "You can't touch me."

"Of course not," he said. "I was touching my nightshirt, which I won fair and square." He began at the buttons himself, opening the placket, very businesslike. She watched as he slid his finger into it and helped himself to a glimpse of the inside curve of her breast. "How very"—he let out a breath—"wonderfully rounded you are."

She felt another little jolt of arousal, a fearsome strength to it. The sensation settled in a knot at her belly while she looked at him, making a line of her mouth, part put out, part riveted, engaged in what they made up as they went along.

She held her arms out. "Fine. If you can take the nightshirt off without touching me—" She didn't even get the sentence completely out. Immediately, his hands clasped her waist, lifting her, nightshirt and all. "Wh-what are you doing? You-you're touching me!"

"No, I'm not. I'm carrying my nightshirt over to the pillows by the fire. You just happen to be in it. You should thank me, in fact. You're going to be damn cold without it."

On the pillows, where he unceremoniously plopped her, he ran his hand straight down the nightshirt, from her collarbone, down over a breast, to her belly, curving his hand to go lower—

Emma started wiggling and sputtering, "My God, my God, my God, let me get this dratted thing off!"

A slightly bizarre struggle ensued: She, of all people, struggled wildly to get out of the nightshirt, while Stuart tried to keep it on her, touching her through it in the most unholy ways, unspeakable—

Until, with a lift of her arms and a blast of cool air up the front of her, she won at last, panting from her efforts: naked on a stack of pillow by his fire, all but for a pair of slippers, with him on his knees, panting over her. Staring down.

Won? Goose bumps of cold chilled her skin, even next to the fire.

"So get up and go now," he murmured, a contradiction to the fact that he straddled her on his shins. Then he did something so unfair, unconscionable. He slowly dragged his eyes up the length of her till his gaze had risen to her face, then, shaking his head, he said ever so softly, earnestly, "I am wild for you, Emma Hotchkiss. Over the moon. In heaven when I'm near you, happiest when I'm touching you."

Then he lowered himself over her completely, hands at either sides of her shoulders as he took his weight down onto his forearms. His body came to rest on hers, the feel of his both heavy and lithe. And warm, so warm.

He added, "And if you think you're getting up and going anywhere anytime soon, you are very much mistaken."

His double-lined robe was soft and light and warm as he pulled it over both of them—he brought it up over them as if it were Count Dracula's cape, covering them both with it. Even the first thing he did was to put his mouth to her neck and gently bite. Aah. She turned her head to give him better access and felt something in her shoot forward, as if she'd realigned herself, was suddenly swimming with a current she hadn't known was there; she felt a momentum that had been waiting for her: where turning herself over to him was as easy as rushing along in a swift, strong stream.

Beneath the sheltering robe, he stripped away his own nightshirt, shouldering out of sleeves and pulling a wad of it from between them. Emma found herself helping him. Then skin. When his skin settled against her, the humid heat of Stuart's flesh, the weight of his bones, her head reeled. She felt the thickness of him trapped between them a moment, then he pushed himself up onto his arms, shifted his weight.

Looking down at her, his dark eyes dilated to black, he said, "Say it."

"What?"

"Tell me you want me inside you."

Her body quivered. She wanted him inside her so badly, she lifted partway up, reaching for him. "Yes." Alas. "I want you, yes."

He entered her, a swift, deep thrust, and her hips rose to meet his. He remained straight-armed, above her, his shoulders and chest flexed, their bodies joined at their sexes, and they both held, staring.

Their gazes locked.

Perhaps it was nothing more than feeling at the same moment the shock of crystal-perfect pleasure, these tender places of their bodies so delicately and substantially united. A connection passed between them, bewildering, surprising, something beyond the physical union. Whatever the feeling, it was sweet and faintly painful, prohibited . . . an unexpected, inchoate connection too stunningly strong to name.

He shifted his weight, adjusted the angle, and Emma's head grew light. It was sublime. His fingers brushed her face. She reached for him, his hair, his wide shoulders, and he sank downward onto her. She clutched him, letting out a small breath of satisfaction as she arched her back, pushing her body more tightly onto him. She closed her eyes, and her head dropped back. He bent her backward over a pillow.

Oh, the pleasure of Stuart inside her. It was vividly similar to their insane morning in Hayward-on-Ames, yet distinctly more. Slow. Watchful. She would open her eyes to slits and find his own penetrating gaze right there, on her. He smiled faintly at one point, moving his hips into her with a rhythm that had taken them both. He clenched his jaw, groaned softly, trying to hold back.

No use. As they watched each other in the firelight, face-to-face, body to body, sensation washed over both of them like a tide coming in in a rush.

Emma jerked, panted . . . that feeling, that perfect, spasming satisfaction peaked inside her, then—shocking—mounted again, peaked higher. Then again. Stuart let out a muffled cry, his body shuddering. Hers answered again. He drove himself into her, muttering pleas, prayers, invocations, lowering on bent arms to kiss her neck, the insides of her arms, both about his neck. Her body contracted in more small shocks of pleasure, uncontrollable, one following after another, again and again and again.

He finished, groaning softly as he ground his hips against her; he licked her collarbone. And again she shuddered, hard, vibrating from it. She half feared she'd never stop.

But at last the sensation became echoes. Stuart backed onto his knees and kissed her belly, then the backs of her knees. His hair tickled at her waist, then at her cheek as he moved to suckle her breasts, one, then the other. Only to return to take her mouth over and over, wet passionate kisses, deep and strong.

He was beginning again. He didn't even lose entry, but rather slowly brought them both back around again. Her own body was so responsive, she felt electric, a touch sending her off.

This time, he'd rock himself deeply into her, pausing at the end of each stroke with a swift pulse of pleasure at full penetration. Then he'd draw himself out slowly, maddeningly to the very edge, pausing before he'd swiftly take her again.

He made love to her for what seemed an endless rise toward release, then withheld release till she was squirming, till the blood of her body throbbed at the surface of her skin, welling up from the hot pounding that roiled in her belly. His hands began to explore her more freely. He rolled, took her with him, moved pillows. His broad chest, hard and muscular, flattened her soft bosom one moment, then pressed against her shoulder blades a minute later. Their skin slid, warmed by the fire, warmed by contact, gliding against each other, wrapped together, hips undulating, their legs entwined. Oh, nothing left undone, left unattended. She had him at a new angle in each passing minute; she wanted him with the sharpness that seemed to bend her in half. She wanted to take him in, swallow him, hold him inside, tighten around him.

"Now," she whispered urgently. "Now." She became the aggressor.

He let out a startled groan and was lost. As he turned himself loose on her a second time, it was close to violent. Then they plummeted into the dark release together, an abyss . . . a loss of conscious self . . . nothing but pleasure, clean, clear, pure, blissful pleasure . . . an explosion of it, followed by throb after throb after throb. . . .

They lay there panting, Stuart's weight on her, both of them damply hot on a cold night. Emma closed her eyes and languished in the feel of him, heavy, limb on limb; she couldn't move.

If she could find any remorse at all, it was distant: intellectual, rhetorical. She felt in fact relaxed, relieved in a way that made her legs ache, her belly liquid. Some part of her said, *Finally* and *Thank God*. While another part said, *Oh, no. This complicates everything.*

Did it?

"Are you all right?" he asked.

All right enough. They didn't sleep till dawn had drifted into the room, faint beams of sunlight through tall, sheer draperies between rows of dark books. Only then did they finally collapse into a haphazard tangle of limbs, their bodies beneath the outspread robe and her retrieved blanket, buried in piles of pillows. They slept curled together, Emma in the crook of Stuart's arm, half-draped across his bare chest, which proved to be a marvelous place to sleep. She lay nearly unconscious for hours, as did he. A sound, sated sleep as she hadn't known in months.

No, not in years.

It was servants who finally, somewhat delicately, woke them. "Excuse me, your lordship," said Stuart's butler from the doorway, pointedly looking over their heads. "You have tickets for the train, I think, in an hour." For a train half an hour away in Harrogate. "Shall we send someone to change them?"

It took some scurrying even to make the last train for London. Their tickets were for separate compartments: They began separating their lives, preparing to be strangers. If she closed her eyes, though, they weren't separate in her imagination; she could conjure him up in a moment. That look on his face as he stared down, moving over her . . . the feeling as his eyes met hers, held . . . the pleasure of their bodies that linked them . . . the cold beyond them of the room, the warmth between them.

It was a heady note on which to part company. Handsome Stuart, so powerfully built, so memorably beautiful when naked . . . while his eyes seemed so in love with what he looked down upon. Or at least so in love, engaged completely, in what was going on between them at that moment.

Chapter 12

There was a small incident on the way to the train station. Almost to Harrogate, with the coach going pell mell, a fox darted across the road. Stuart's driver reined the team sharply to avoid the fox's getting slaughtered under the hooves, not for the fox's sake but for the sakes of the horses' vulnerable galloping legs. The maneuver should not have been worth noting, so matter-of-fact that the passengers of the vehicle would have been all but unaware of it. Instead, though, mayhem followed for a full two or three minutes after the driver first called out, "Whoa," and shortened the reins. Rocking, the coach zigged, then zagged across the country road. It wobbled drunkenly on its springs as first one of the horses, then the rest went wild, the passengers inside battling to hold their balance as if a cyclone had hold of them.

When all at last settled and Stuart could be heard, he rapped for the coachman to pull to a stop. At the side of the road, he descended his carriage, inordinately irate. "What the hell was that?" he shouted.

"The left lead," his driver called—the same horse the man had pronounced was trouble just before their trip to the Stunnel Farm. "When I pull the reins taut, he heads for anything that moves."

"Cut the team," Stuart yelled. "We'll run a team of six in London." They were shipping the carriage and horses by train, an expensive but fashionable convenience. "There's a trainer there who is supposed to know what he's doing. I'll hire the fellow to work the damned animal, see if we can sort him out."

When Stuart climbed back into the carriage, he shoved through the doorway like a man who was more than merely frustrated by a wayward horse. He was angry. He sat back heavily into his seat, then glanced at Emma. "Happy?" he asked, as if she'd had something to do with it. "No more wild, whirling rides once we get to Harrogate."

Mystified, she told him, "It's a good decision."

But he didn't like it. Reducing the team to six, removing perhaps the fastest, strongest animal and its harness mate, seemed to mean more to him than giving up "wild, whirling rides." He saw it as giving up something else, something she didn't grasp, though nothing he would speak about.

Then, when they arrived at the train station, he slid across the space between the seat, took hold of her, drawing her near, and kissed her on the mouth. It was a feverish kiss, passionate, warm where their mouths met over their winter-bundled bodies, slightly awkward for his angling his head so their hats didn't collide. Yet, for all this, there was a clear, sharp edge of desperation to the kiss.

After a moment, still holding her, eyeing her, his dark eyes beneath his hat brim narrowed, and he asked, "You *will* be there, won't you?"

"I will, or I'll end up in jail. That's my understanding."

He drew in air, a long inhalation, then nodded and let her go. He reached across, opening the carriage door from the inside. As she passed in front of him, lifting her skirts, bending, he called from behind her, "Emma?"

She looked over her shoulder, one foot on the step.

"I can't even explain why, but it's important to me, and I wish—" He broke off. He looked down. She couldn't see his eyes at all for the shadows of his hat. "I wish," he repeated, "you were doing it because"—another pause—"because you knew my uncle or knew more about me and the statue than even I do"—again he bowed his head, then snorted, laughing at himself. "Or just because," he said, "I've made it affordable for you to do and because"—he hesitated, then laughed again—"because you like the rhythm of my speech."

After a moment, she answered, "I do like it." Then she turned and stepped down.

The door closed. And Stuart's huge black carriage, with its troika bell clanging, pulled off under the power of his eight, glorious stallions. What a sight. She didn't blame him for not wanting to give it up.

He would see it loaded onto the train as well, then take up his first-class compartment down the train from hers.

London. Even in the dark of evening, the smell of it, the *clop* of the carriage, the streetlights, the bends and turns of the avenues. Oh, how little the city had changed.

From the train station, Emma took a hansom to the Hotel Carlyle just off Belgrave Square, where she stepped out into a mild winter evening—that is to say, it was rainy, windy, and forty degrees. From beneath her umbrella, she glimpsed the front of a hotel she'd lived in on three other occasions—if one pretended to immeasurable wealth, only a handful of hotels in London would do, and the Carlyle was indisputably one of them. Gas lamps lit its pale brick and stucco facade; it looked not a whit different from a dozen years ago. Its architecture was not its hallmark, however. Its fame lay in its interior, its service, its appointments, and, most of all, its clients: the rich and famous who came to stay.

Inside, except that frock coats had gotten longer and women's dresses a bit more natural—as if a deflating pin had at last been put to all their bustles—the Hotel Carlyle's elegant front foyer and reading room could have been a window into a decade ago. Its guests flowed like the cream they were through its chandeliered rooms. As she signed the register (discovering that Stuart had put her into one of the expensive suites on the top floor, a floor she had never laid eyes on), as she directed her trunks, enjoyed the service of a concierge, two bellmen, a maid, and another uniformed fellow who followed along, his only duty to lay, then start the fires in the rooms' hearths, Emma was assailed by the steadfast English tradition of the place—nothing ersatz about it even if the woman partaking wasn't exactly authentic.

One took a carpeted staircase to the first floor, the famous restaurant where the well-to-do writers and artists of London ate beside its peers and cabinet members and financiers. From the first floor, one took the modern lift to get to the suite level, her rooms. Her trunks were already within, new, bright, and shiny on a thick carpet of mossy greens and blues. The largest trunks she'd ever owned looked small in a room with a high gilt-and-aqua ceiling, a large canopied bed, a bay window wide enough to hold a small dining table and two cushioned chairs—one could dine overlooking the square below.

Which is what she did that night. She sent for a light supper, that turned out to be faintly amusing: A "small meal" consisted of a roasted breast of quail with capers and greens, a white bean cassoulet, and poached pears and cherries with cheese. As she picked at her food, Emma told herself the lonely feeling she felt was due to missing her sheep, her cat, her neighbors. Yet that all felt distant.

Stuart. Here was what she couldn't move away from—the idea of a man who was no doubt having supper somewhere only a few blocks away.

Emma held to her room the entire evening, no stomach for mixing with people, for pretending when she didn't have to. When she went to bed early, she dreamed so vividly of a tall Englishman, that in the morning she startled an instant upon finding the white sheets beside her rumpled but empty, absent his dark limbs, his dark, mussy hair. Stuart.

Oh, Emma, she thought and sighed. You are wholly infatuated. What to do about it?

Nothing. There was nothing to do. Except meet him at

nine o'clock as planned at the art gallery. And begin the game he so richly paid for, that was so "important" to him.

The Henley Gallery of Classic Art was a large though relatively new exhibition hall connected to the Sir Arthur Henley Art Institute, a small, endowed art school in a rather unfashionable part of the city. Emma was not originally in favor of Stuart meeting her there, but he'd insisted. He wanted to meet the people he'd be depending upon, know what was happening, how she was setting everything up. Her main objection was that he and she should not be seen together. She'd relented fairly quickly, however. The gallery was a long way from Belgravia and Mayfair. London itself was hardly populated for the season. And, too, Stuart's presence, just the look of him, would add the credibility of money behind her plan. If she could find some of her old cohorts, they would know immediately they could trust the profitability of the venture.

Thus, early the next morning, she entered the gallery to find Stuart already standing next to the main staircase, tapping his trouser leg impatiently with the brim of his hat.

"You're late," he said.

"You're cranky."

He made a face, frowning, and looked away.

At the Rembrandt collection, where she'd hoped to find an old fellow who had once specialized in copying the old master, there was no one about. A little disappointing, but not completely unexpected.

The great collections attracted budding artists all through the day, setting their own hours. They'd come, set up easels and paints before a masterwork of their choosing, proceeding to copy it, brushstroke for brushstroke. Some, in fact, would actually be quite good—Bailey's, the man she looked for, were on the mark so identical to the originals that his work had fooled art experts upon close examination—once even fooling the artist himself. It had been much the joke once that Alphonse Pietre, a minor French painter of some popularity, had acknowledged one of Bailey's paintings, a "new" pose of a model Pietre had often used, giving the painting a genuine provenance.

"Many artists, these days," Emma told Stuart, "learn to paint by imitating the masters. So long as the replicas are sufficiently larger or smaller than the original, it is perfectly legal."

Not so with sculpture, though. The "master" whom a sculptor was taught to imitate was the one who'd designed the human body—students modeled their work off live models. Or some did. Sure enough, in the first room of small statuary, an elderly man sat slouched, doing sketches of small Greek statuary—something of an unusual practice.

Emma walked around so he could see her and asked, "Charlie?" She smiled. It was indeed Charlie Vandercamp. "How are you?"

"Emma?" His voice was faint, half the strength it once had. "Emma!"

She felt her smile stretch her face. "Indeed." She held her hands out, saying and meaning every word. "I can't believe how wonderful it is to see you!"

He stood up, a little more bent than he'd been a dozen years ago, then asked immediately, "How's Zach?"

She shook her head. "He passed on almost a year ago now."

"Aw, girlie, I'm sorry."

"It's all right. Still doing it, I see," she said, indicating his sketch.

"It's all I know how to do. Doesn't net much money these days."

"Are you still as good?"

A little smile played across his wrinkled mouth. "Would you like to see?" His eyes, all but blank the moment before, suddenly danced.

In Charlie Vandercamp's very humble East End flat, the

statue he was sketching was all but finished. He was filling in details.

"Can we use this for a few days?" Emma asked, holding up a small *Psyche*. "And is Bailey or Ted around? We were hoping for one of the small Rembrandts, two or three copies of something like *Christ at the Column.*"

Charlie's eyes opened wide and a grin stole over his face. "Art insurance!" he said and laughed. He threw a glance at Stuart—Emma hadn't introduced them, letting the two men look each other over and come to their own conclusions.

"Against the wall," she told Charlie. "Though I might be able to use a hotel maid in full uniform, dressed for the Carlyle."

"Ah, boy, Emma. You never did flinch at the tough ones."

"You have any faith in me?" she asked.

"Always did."

"You in then?"

"I am."

"Know anyone else still around?"

"Not Bailey. Dead. But Teddy lives in the back. And Mary Beth knows the maid role, plus she might know where Mark is."

"Good. I'll need her, Ted or Mark, plus your delicate expertise. Any chance either one of them have some paintings already done? Something going to waste in a cupboard somewhere?"

He shrugged his hunched shoulders. "It's possible." He smiled fondly at her. "We could all use the work."

"You have it. Get in touch with me at the Carlyle."

He smiled. "The old Carlyle. Good for you, Em."

She shook her head, refusing his admiration. "Just for a few days, then back to my sheep."

Still, the pleasure she felt in that moment was an unexpected bonus. Not only would she help Stuart stiff his thieving uncle, but she was also going to help people she'd loved as a young girl, people who had not been as lucky as she. Charlie, Ted, Bailey, and Mark had all gone to jail, and Charlie limped because of the bullet she'd watched go into him.

Just as they were leaving the flat, Charlie took hold of her arm, eyeing Stuart over her head. Her old friend pulled her toward him, then said loud enough that Stuart could hear, "If he's your roper, he needs a better English tailor. Good-looking fellow, Em, but don't let prettiness blind you: He'll never pass for a nob."

She laughed. "No?" Then smiled. "Not even a foreign one?"

He pursed his mouth, looking Stuart over. "Can he do accents?"

"I don't know. He really *is* a nob, Charlie."

But her friend disapproved; he frowned.

"He'll do," she told him.

He waggled his head. "Maybe. If you say so." As she passed through his doorway, having to step over a bucket in the hall that spoke of a leak in the roof, he added solicitously again, "Sorry about Zach, Em. Right sorry."

"Thank you," she acknowledged. "He didn't linger. It was quick."

"Glad to hear it. Sorry though, you know? Right sorry. He was a good bloke. The best."

She stared at him for half a second, before she was able to smile. "Right."

In the carriage—pulled by six horses that made Stuart sigh every time he saw them—her English viscount asked her, "What you're setting up for my uncle you did before with your husband?"

She nodded. "Something similar. The art insurance swindle was one of Zach's best. He invented it, though it's a variation on an American confidence game that Charlie taught him." She rested back into her seat, then pulled the carriage blanket up—the temperature had dropped again below freezing, snow expected tomorrow.

"What was he like?"

"Who?" she asked, then owned up with a shrug. "Zach."

Stuart took his hat off. The carriage rolled away from the curb. "What made you marry him?"

"I don't know." She looked out the window; she was going to leave it at that. Then she said to a passing flower cart, "When I first met him I didn't believe he was a vicar. I thought vicars had to be stuffy. You know"—she laughed—"*good*." She laid her head back onto the seat cushion. "I met him over a poker game. Charlie had taken me under his wing only the week before. So my first night I watched Charlie, Ted, and Bailey mostly work a three-card monte in a public house on Chaney Street, and in comes this clergyman, complete with white collar and Bible. They ran a quick crooked poker game on him, cold-decked him on his own deal.

"The thing was, though, Zach had amazingly deep pockets—he could collect money from strangers. He had an uncanny patter. It turned out, to get by, he gambled with church money, returning the principal and keeping the 'interest.' Except of course that night they took it all. But he only raised more and came back. That's when they told him the truth—no point in wasting a fellow as talented as Zachary Hotchkiss, Charlie said.

"For Zach, it was a kind of revelation: 'Separating the greedy and dishonest from their money,' he called it. He enjoyed the retribution, saw the whole thing in somewhat righteous terms, I think, though at the time I didn't realize. He seemed to be having a good time with it, was clever, and I admired his cheek. He ended up organizing much larger shenanigans than any of the small-timers had gotten up to. For a while, he made us rich."

She sighed into a turn of the carriage, jostling, then repeated Stuart's question almost to herself. "Why did I marry him?" She answered, "Because I was young. Because I thought he was daring." She sighed. "But he was a walking shell game. He knew only one trick: Move the shells faster."

She didn't say anymore. Enough.

Then Stuart interjected, "He was charming."

Taken aback, Emma blinked and looked at him. His dark coloring and clothes were set off against the shadowy red carriage seat. She laughed—a little pathetically. She said, "Zach could smile at you like you were the sun of his universe. Except, of course, his universe had a new sun every ten minutes." And his favorite by far was a bottle of gin.

"So was the vicariate just another scam?" asked the man across from her sarcastically.

"You mean Zach's? In Malzaard where we lived?"

He nodded, his attention fixed. It wasn't casual information he sought, though she wasn't certain exactly what the point was of his asking.

"No, not really," she said. "He had a year at Cambridge in theology, two years in an Anglican seminary. As a young man, he wanted to be a vicar. Then, as he put it: He decided he'd rather fool people some other way." She laughed. "He came to think of religion as a kind of confidence game. Until things went very wrong finally. The night I was shot, he prayed. I'd never heard him pray like that. He wanted me alive and his sister free." She made a wry laugh. "God gave him one out of two, I suppose."

"The ambivalent, agnostic vicar. How interesting."

"Oh, no, he believed. He just wouldn't admit it. Deep down, all along, he believed absolutely in Heaven—and the fact that he himself was going to Hell. He was already there by the end."

Stuart's face was stone. He stared at her.

At first, she felt sick inside, as if she'd said something wrong—offended him with regard to his ideas of God or by consigning her husband to Hell.

She didn't dare tell him the rest: that shot, ill, trundling along toward a place she didn't want to go, home, she'd felt a victim of a kind of fraud herself. Her wild, lawless husband muttered over her all the way back on the train, the full litany; he knew the entire Book of Prayer. Her sense of betrayal was complicated. It wasn't that she minded that Zach turned out to be a real clergyman, or nearly one. Only that she minded his sloppy slide into religion when the chips were down. Zach played hypocrisy from the other end. He took the classic offense of bad vicars—a pretense to more godliness than one had—and turned it inside out, pretending to less, the worldly sophisticate. What was the opposite of sanctimonious? That was Zach. A boy who thumbed his nose at God, misbehaving—when she'd thought she'd married a man with difficult, but considered convictions.

For Stuart's part, any enjoyment he might have had from the story of Hotchkiss's downfall was muted by the fact that, even dead, the antics of her wayward husband could make Emma laugh.

She glanced at him again. He lifted his head enough that his eyes from under his hat met hers. He forced a quick smile at her. An offered consolation.

And Emma's sick feeling lifted a little; it turned to something else. A possibility dawned, like some great, fond hope: Stuart was jealous of Zachary. He didn't like him. Could it be that the Viscount Mount Villiars resented a fondness, mixed though it was, she'd had for a man to whom she'd been married, for a husband now dead?

Emma looked away, out the window, trying to hide the smallest, inappropriate smile; it wouldn't stop asserting itself. While in her belly she felt a lightness, a sensation akin to giddiness, pleasure.

As to Stuart, jealous? Dislike? He out and out loathed Hotchkiss. If the man weren't already dead, he would have wished him so.

Noon and finished. There was nothing more they could do until they heard from Emma's friend Vandercamp. And it frustrated Stuart no end that this left him watching her round, rather stylishly dressed bottom climb into a hansom cab alone, on her way back to her hotel, while he had to return to his house, a mere three and a half blocks away from the Carlyle. He would like to have claimed her for the afternoon. For tea at his house. For a walk. An afternoon's talk. All right, for more, if possible, though he loved simply looking at her.

It also occurred to him that he was putting her in danger. For the first time, this struck him with certainty, and he vacillated as to whether the statue and a bit of jewelry were worth what he was doing.

Up till now, any doubt was overshadowed by the memory of Leonard's smug face. The obnoxious relative had no right to precious items that had graced Stuart's childhood, some of the few pleasant and interesting associations Stuart could conjure up from Dunord.

Then a new emotion: He felt grateful. He believed in Emma absolutely and loved her help. Her competence, as she breezily proceeded, amazed him; it worried him a little: She could, he realized, just as easily cut him out and abscond with a valuable statue herself, not to mention all the money that would float through her fingers. Not that he thought she would. She wanted to live down the hill from him on her sheep farm. Plus knowing her intentions, reading her mind, didn't matter. He'd once invited her to trust him, like a free fall, simply drop into it. And that was what he did in return.

Do with me as you will, Emma. I trust you.

A week and a day remained of their reason for staying together. He suddenly realized it wasn't enough. Down the hill? Why not live up the hill with him? Or in a house of her own he would pay for? She should live better. He would keep her; he would offer. She should wear lady's blue kid ankle boots every day. Her ankles and small feet looked neat as a pin in them.

A note later that afternoon brought Emma to Stuart. She arrived, tucked back into the dark of a cab, at his very own front curb and sent her driver to the door.

"The miss in my cab says ye'll be wanting to come right away, sir." The man handed Stuart a note.

Charlie Vandercamp. What a fine fellow, Stuart thought as he shouldered on his coat. The note read:

Ted's hands aren't steady enough, we've decided. It's been too long. No one can find Mark. But we've located Bailey's son. Two copies are even finished. If you want more, say. He's quick, very happy to continue the tradition, and needs money. Find him at the Henley this afternoon. He's short, thin, with very red hair. He'll have an art case with him so you can see what he does.

The note didn't give more information, which Emma took in stride. "He probably doesn't know when or where he'll be exactly. We have to look for him and wait."

If she was happy to deal with the fellow, so was Stuart.

"We couldn't do better," she told him. "He'll know that we need oil on canvas, something small, and he'll be excellent if he has even half the talent of his father."

Stuart was content knowing he had the afternoon with Emma after all. He hoped the fellow didn't show up till evening.

Emma was impatient at first, then began to enjoy strolling among a new collection of art at the rear of the main building. "Would you like to know my favorite painter?" she asked of Stuart whimsically as they walked through a room of French paintings.

"All right, who?"

"Manet."

"Why?"

She smiled. "Because I like the look of his canvases, nothing more. They don't require anything beyond looking at them. They're clever on their own."

"I like the *Bar at the Folies-Bergère*."

"I do too! My favorite!" she exclaimed. "I like that the viewer isn't in the mirror and the man in the top hat at the side."

"And the daydreaming barmaid. What *is* in her mind?"

She smiled at their agreement, looking down as they walked. There was hardly anyone about. They had the place to themselves. "To paraphrase Zola," she told him: "To enjoy Manet one must forget everything one knows about art."

Stuart laughed at her. "Ah, there's the reason you like him. A breaker of rules." Then he felt his brow furrow, even as his lips remained in a smile. "And when do you read the French newspaper?"

"Pardon?"

"Zola."

Then she didn't have to say. Stuart took one look at her face, groaned, and said for her, "The omnipresent Reverend Zachary Hotchkiss. Have you any idea how much I am coming to detest that man?"

In a kind of apology, she explained, "He was full of irrelevant facts like that, an encyclopedia of them." Then she laughed. "Which he knew so flat-out he could recite even foxed. In fact, foxed was when he usually spewed them best, his vicar's collar standing askew, straight up by his ear with indignity, as if to say, How could a man so intelligent and educated be such a horrible mess?" She stopped herself. Here was the closest she'd come to speaking aloud how much she resented Zach's drinking, to admitting to herself how truly enormous the problem was. It was ghastly. A pathetic, sad truth that underlined everything else. She sighed deeply and long, then said, "He was so useless sometimes. I would go to him when I was sad or angry or feeling muddled, and he'd just wave his hand and say, 'Oh, you'll figure it, Em. You always do.' Then I would, of course; what choice did I have?"

"He couldn't get it up. Ever. He was worthless that way."

Emma turned her head sharply around to look at him,

partly from the surprise at the statement, partly for the surprisingly base euphemism she would not have put with Stuart. Was he being condescending, saying it that way for her benefit? "Excuse me?"

"You know what I mean. You mentioned before, though not in much detail. Could he ever take care of you that way? How am I supposed to phrase it?"

"You said it all right," she decided. Should she answer honestly? Oh, why not? "No," she said. "Or not after his sister died, at least." In fact, by then, Zach drank too much to do anything that required much concentration.

Stuart smiled his slow, sly smile. "I can," he said. "And I take care of you emotionally also: I should spend the night with you at the hotel. Or you with me at my house. We have one more day till Leonard actually arrives. And afterward, if you would allow it, you could live with me here. Or I'd find you your own house here in—"

"Stop—"

"No. I'm good for you. Recognize it. You look better for your few days with me. I'd wager you feel better, too."

Did she? She supposed he was right. It was good to have someone to complain to, an understanding ear. Then she made a face, though. "Well, I'll let you listen to my problems, if you're determined to. But we stay in role in London, then I go back to my sheep. I won't be your mistress—you can whistle 'Dixie' on that score. Do you know that expression?"

"No."

"It's from the American South." Many confidence artists in London were American. "Their anthem: the anthem of the losing side," she said and laughed. "Your anthem with regard to the way you badger me on the subject."

"You know a lot."

"I learned a lot—" From Zach. No, to give herself credit, "I read a lot of Zach's books." She snorted. "Till he sold them. I talked endlessly into the night with his friends in London, many of whom had bits or whole chunks of education—confidence gaming is the cream, you see." She laughed. "The *smart* thieves."

"You have a hunger for knowledge."

Did she? "I suppose."

"You should go to university."

This truly made her laugh out loud. What a hilarious idea! "Oh, fine, Stuart. Right after we're finished, I'll shut down my farm, all my village duties, my sheep, then saddle up Hannah and ride her down to Girton," the girl's college at Cambridge. "I'm sure they'd admit me. At nearly thirty. Without a penny to my name." Her laughter grew ironic. "And where they would be happy to let me sit for the Tripos examination, but unwilling to admit me fully to degrees and university membership. What would be the point? At Cambridge, we may as well enroll Hannah, both of us being girls." She frowned, giving him a look of mock-seriousness. "Why don't we do that: apply on behalf of Hannah T. Mule."

Then she felt relatively as smart as Hannah The Mule for allowing her resentment to reveal too much: her excessive knowledge of Cambridge, its colleges and policies toward women, especially poor ones.

When she and Zach had first come home, she'd talked to him about her possible admission there, since he was a one-term fellow of Trinity. She'd thought, bumpkin that she was, he might be able to pull strings. Instead, all she'd done, because a one-term student couldn't do anything, was point out that he was inadequate again. She'd actually made him quite angry for considering, wanting, her own education. She'd let the matter drop. University. Honest to goodness. A poor Yorkshire lass, daughter of the local shearer, now the local vicar's wife, wanting a formal education. How hilarious was that?

"You could go," Stuart said. He studied her. "Though I'd suggest one of the new, more open-minded universities. The girls' colleges at Cambridge fritter away more than a little time on things like domestic organization, dancing, art, which

I don't think are your inclination. I think mathematics would be good for you. I think you'd be a prize at it."

Emma stared at him, then let her . . . what? Surprise? Fear? Agitation? Challenge? Whatever emotion, she let it break through on peals of laughter, pure giddiness. "Oh, Stuart. You think you can do anything. It's one of your great charms, but it's also one of your most aggravating qualities when you think you can move unmovable mountains. I have a farm to run. I love my sheep."

He asked, just as a matter of fantasy, "So what might you envision yourself reading at university? What would you like to learn?"

"Not mathematics," she said quickly. She thought a moment, though it didn't take more than that to know her mind on the subject. "I'd like to learn to write, to express myself better. I might like to write a book someday."

"About what?"

"I don't know. Something I know about." Like a sudden bright idea, she said, "Yorkshire," then looked down, laughing at herself. "Sheep and swindling. That's what I suppose I know about." She shook her head, dismissing the whole notion.

Only later did she realize he didn't much care for London and cared even less for his house here. The place where he offered to let her live, while she went to school, had been in the city, in the very house, of his despised father. She shuddered to think of living in *that* place. (Would the cellar have torture contraptions? Or skulls wobbling on their spikes. Ugh.) Yet Stuart was apparently willing. To please her. She was touched. Deeply. Though she couldn't think how to say it without starting the whole educating-Emma conversation again. So she said nothing.

But she made a point of being nice to him all the rest of the afternoon. Stuart responded politely, then even enthusiastically. They ended up having a peaceable, very enjoyable time at the museum, where they met their young artist and paid for the art case he gave them. Before, though, they just wandered together, going from room to room to look at the paintings. Emma loved the idea of art museums: so many beautiful pictures all in one place, till one was overwhelmed by it all. She and Stuart settled simultaneously on one particular bench, staring up together in long, mutual silence at a painting of Christ by El Greco, struck dumb by it together. Not unlike a moment half an hour later, wherein they were both, at the one and the same time, struck by a fit of mirth over a fellow in a bowler who carried a long, neatly folded and wrapped black "walking" umbrella, the long, thin sort that was becoming a fashionable accoutrement of the understated gentleman in London.

They grinned at each other as he went by. *"Umbraculum,"* said Stuart, the happily sartorially overstated. Latin.

Which made Emma blush because she liked it so well that he knew the Latin or Russian or French for nearly everything.

When he saw her pleasure in his word, he added, "*Cuniculus*."

She asked eagerly, "What does *that* mean?"

"Underground passage," he said with a kind of secretive, smug smile, then gave her that once-over he could do, from head to toe.

Sexual, she knew immediately, and glanced away.

Though she was so, so curious. What was he thinking? *Cunicu*-what? Like the song, "Funiculi-funicula." Say it again. He wouldn't. Nor explain, not even when she worked up the courage to prod bluntly a few minutes later. It had to be not only sexual, but raw, she decided. Stuart, with his silk top hat and silk manners, could say the craziest things.

But he was the nicest lunatic she knew. Her sort of lunatic. They enjoyed the paintings of the museum together as much as they enjoyed laughing at the occasional pompous Englishman around them—goodness, but she and Stuart were of a piece. In an understated country, they both overstated themselves regularly and loved doing so.

Renegade and misfits. Outlaws in their hearts somewhere, even if one of them sat in the House of Lords, both of them chose to push the limits, abiding only by their own.

And so it went, as they had a photograph taken of Emma, as a friend of hers superimposed this in his darkroom over a photograph of a real Rubens that truly had been stolen, then found several months before, as the result printed on newsprint, as they withdrew two thousand pounds from an account of Stuart's that opened up, became fully functional—as they tidied the final details: They got along so well, with such care and interest in the other, it seemed impossible they could argue as fiercely as they could, as they had on paper for the first four months of their acquaintance.

"Emma, don't disappear down to the bottom of the hill, when this is over," Stuart murmured to her in the dark of his carriage. They were stopped in the street, about to transfer her to a hansom again, send her back to the Carlyle alone. "We're lovers. Admit it. Let's play pickle-me-tickle-me until—" He paused, teased. "You never did say what you call it."

The nicer things were between them, though, the more they seemed to exchange places; as Stuart became happier, more at ease, Emma was given to bouts of all-but-sullen quiet.

"Coitus," she said. "Sexual congress. I use adult names for it." She scooted forward, a woman preparing to leave the carriage.

He leaned near her, touching her arm, and whispered, "Oh, my apologies. We're grown-ups, how nice." He enjoyed tormenting her too much; it was impossible not to. "Of course, your names are a little clinical, aren't they? 'Adult' in a rather intellectual, constrained way." He laughed.

"It's not funny. It results in children."

"Ah. Well," more soberly, "if you're— Well, if it turns

out—" He frowned at her shadow in the dark. The clop of her arriving hansom stopped beside them. He whispered, as she leaned forward to go, "You couldn't know if you were pregnant yet, could you?"

"No." The silhouette of her hat shook in negation. "I doubt I am."

"Good. No point in worrying in advance—and I'm a responsible man. I wouldn't leave you to cope alone. Just let me know, if— Well, you know."

She snorted. "There's some solace. If I'm pregnant, you'll own up. I'll be sure to remember how responsible you are when mean people cross the street so they don't have to walk near me and my bastard."

"Why are you angry? There's no bastard yet. As to mean people, yes, I know there are a lot down in Malzaard, enough to keep an ugly, frightened woman in her house."

Emma sat back a little again, trying to see him. She could discern his knees and the upper part of his body, but the streetlight left his face and shoulders in shadows. She could see no expression.

He referred to his mother. There had indeed been those in the village who had been horrid to her, called her names, made fun. Emma herself had known the woman by the name "Ugly Ana" long before she'd known her true name, title, or history—acquainted with the woman's vulnerability before she'd been aware of her mysteriously untapped power: a viscountess so reclusive that she rarely came out, so skittish that, when she did, she usually ran away quickly, taunted for her fey, outmoded ways and unattractive appearance.

He said, "I can't protect you from mean people, because they're everywhere, but *I* would be nice. That much, I can promise."

"Fine," she said. "If I'm pregnant, you can marry me."

He folded his arms and contemplated her motionlessly from the darkness. Then said, "Not that nice."

Because he was a snob, she thought. An arrogant, upper-class *yah*, who thought it was his perfect right to play pickle-me-tickle-me with the local women, so long as he was "responsible"—never mind that his idea of responsibility made whores of the women themselves.

How Stuart's mind actually worked, though, was a long way from how Emma imagined: He himself sighed as he looked toward her, as he watched her step out into the light of a streetlamp.

Stuart despaired of his own romantic nature. He wanted to marry a woman because he was in love with her, completely, enraptured in love, no other reason. He wanted a marriage like—

Like what? Whose? Certainly, his own parents' marriage had been a horror.

The Stunnels suddenly came to mind again. The funny old couple with the delayed Christmas tree—smiling, bumping up against each other, so content in their joint purpose, their joint lives. He marveled at them. How had they begun? What had connected them so indivisibly for sixty-seven years?

It didn't matter. Stuart would not have married a princess royal simply because he'd impregnated her. No one could make him. No one. Not the queen of England herself. The fact that his own parents were married had not improved his childhood, quite the contrary.

Was he in love with Emma? He didn't know. He only knew that nothing short of loving her was enough, not for him, and neither did she deserve anything less.

By the gaslight of the overhead streetlamp, Stuart watched the cab driver open the half door, then Emma stepped inside and leaned back out of sight.

Chapter 13

There is nothing harder to shear than a big, wrinkly old ram.

—Mrs. Emma Hotchkiss
Yorkshire Ways and Recipes

LEONARD Aysgarth, Stuart's father's younger brother by fifteen months, could be said at age fifty-six to be, at least from certain angles, a handsome man. He was tall, had a thick head of hair, graying in a pattern that was often called *distinguished*, and the angular build—long-fingered, long-limbed, a deep brow with a wide jaw and cleft chin—that characterized the men of his family. His dark hair and dark eyes had not missed an Aysgarth in generations, the family joke: Even the Aysgarth genes were dominant.

Here, though, was fairly much where any similarity to his nephew ended. His long, lanky body had developed enough of a sagging paunch that, when his frock coat was open, a strip of shirtfront showed between his waistcoat and trousers—alas, he saw the need to button his trousers under his belly rather than admit their waist needed five inches more to fit his middle.

While the waist of his trousers was too small, everything else about him was designed to aggrandize. His house, to Stuart at least, had become downright amusing: a shrine to Leonard Aysgarth. Any award, since he was twelve, a ribbon for jumping, a mention in the social columns, a note from a peer, anything was worthy of hanging on a wall. If a knight's wife wrote him a thank-you letter for attending a funeral, he framed it. As if his esteem in the world would be weighed, pound for pound, at the end in written certificates, as if he needed visual proof of his worth.

Stuart greeted him with, "Good evening."

Leonard sat at a window table in the early evening at the Carlyle's first-floor restaurant, La Tosca. "To you perhaps," his uncle answered. "By my standards, the weather is wanting, and you are three minutes late."

Ah, the joy of Uncle Leonard. It was never an issue to measure up: No one could.

Stuart sat, determined to enjoy what would be an excellent meal despite the company. All he had to do was think of what the evening held in store.

The waiter came and took their orders, Leonard ordering roast beef, Stuart, a breast of quail. A bottle of champagne arrived with a starter of Russian caviar, crème fraiche, and toast points.

"Are you still eating fish eggs?" Leonard asked with distaste as he poured the champagne. When he lifted his head to look at Stuart, his chin did something similar to his belly: a battle between his newly acquired beard and his collar left a new flap of flesh showing above his cravat.

"Yes."

"So why are we dining together tonight, Stuart? We don't like each other."

"The statue. Have you sold it yet?"

"I don't have your damn statue, I keep telling you."

"I found its provenance."

"Its what?"

"Its bills of sale over the last two centuries, that sort of thing, that proves it's authentic. It makes it much more valuable."

Leonard shrugged. Though he eyed Stuart now over his soup as it was set before him.

He'd tried to sell it, Stuart concluded, and was having trouble, something Stuart and Emma had been counting on. The collectors able to spend the large money were more sophisticated buyers than Leonard was a thief.

Stuart pushed his own soup aside to finish the caviar. "I was going to suggest we come to an agreement and both profit from its sale."

Leonard gave a haughty guffaw. "Last I heard, you didn't want to sell the thing for some sort of sentimental reason involving the troll."

"Excuse me."

"Your mother."

Stuart looked down, smothering a zing of rage by digging the edge of a small toast directly into the thick cream. To his knowledge, his uncle never had the temerity to say anything mean to Ana Aysgarth's face. And there was no point in being wounded on her behalf now. His expression must have given him away, though.

"You're miffed, old man," Leonard said.

"Insult someone else's mother."

Irritably, as if he was being censored unfairly, "You aren't going to tell me she wasn't the most hideous thing on two legs."

Stuart stared up at him, rigid. "She was a lot of things. *Hideous* is not one, though, that comes to my mind. She was gentle. She never faulted anyone, outside his or her hearing, or within it, for that matter. She never did a mean thing to a soul." Which made him look down at the pearly gray caviar, mounding it. Her lack of willingness to assert herself, to hurt someone when necessary, had been his mother's downfall.

Leonard frowned a moment, looking perplexed, as if Stuart had just posed a difficult riddle. Then he laughed suddenly, awkwardly, and reached across to give Stuart a good-natured gouge on the shoulder. "You'd never guess you were related to her," he said like a mate offering consolation.

"Actually, it's my mother I'd prefer to favor," Stuart murmured, but Leonard didn't hear him. He was already signaling the waiter for something.

Stuart shifted in his chair, then said, "Sorry. Was that your foot I was on?"

"No." Leonard followed Stuart's suit and lifted the white table linen on his side, both men looking under the table.

It was Leonard who brought forth the lady's blue, beaded silk drawstring purse.

"What do we have here?" Stuart asked and reached for it.

Leonard pulled it back. "A lady's bag, it seems." He didn't even hesitate, but opened it immediately.

Stuart had to hide his amusement at the bottom of a champagne glass.

While onto the table, Leonard laid out a lady's satin change purse—it contained four shillings and eight fifty-pound notes—and a silver card case with a dozen cards in it: Lady Emma Hartley, Appraiser of Fine Art, Representative to the Insurance Consortium, Valuable Collections, New York, Paris, Lloyds of London. In addition, there was an unopened telegram, also to E. Hartley, and a newspaper clipping from a French newspaper, with a captioned picture of a woman using her arm, trying to avoid her photo being taken. The caption read, "Lady Hartley, la veuve du chevalier anglais, Sir Arthur Hartley."

Leonard handed the article over for translation. Reading it, Stuart said, "She's a widow to an English knight. The article goes on to say that the lady is the leading sleuth these days in finding stolen art and seeing it returned, the very large and valuable Rubens on the wall at the Louvre behind her being only one of four such paintings in the last year." He looked up at his uncle. "So do you imagine this Lady Hartley is staying here?"

"I would think. Or only had dinner here and left her purse behind." He kept digging in the bag, though, bless him.

"Ah!" he said, triumphant. "Here is a key!" He held it up. "It's to one of the suites. Number 3 at the very top. Egad, posh."

Stuart wiggled his eyebrows. "Shall we let ourselves in? I've never seen one of the suites."

Leonard pursed his smug mouth. "We should return the purse to the lady immediately. She must be damned worried."

"What about dinner?"

"Finish up quickly." A rich, pretty woman with a lost purse turned out to be a lot more interesting than an irritated nephew.

Leonard raced through his beef, motioning with his fork for Stuart to hurry along. He could speak of nothing else the rest of the meal, but speculation as to this Lady Hartley and exactly how grateful to them she might be.

Leonard did not stand on the formality that a gentleman did not approach a woman's door uninvited either. "She's going to be thrilled to see us," he assured Stuart as he took the lift up.

The lovely Mrs. Hotchkiss-cum-Lady-Hartley, his dear Emma, surprised Stuart, however, by being decidedly *not* thrilled. Not in the least.

She cracked the door. "What do you want?" she said as if annoyed.

Leonard cleared his throat. "We, um—"

"If you're from the newspaper, I have nothing to say. Now get out."

"We're not," Stuart said quickly. "We found your purse."

The door cracked a bit more. "You what? My purse? You're joking."

Leonard held it up. "We most certainly are not. Is this yours?"

Emma's door came all the way open, as her beautiful blue eyes went wide. Stuart saw past her into her suite himself for the first time. "Please, come in," she said.

She'd made herself rather graciously at home. A shawl they'd bought her the day before lay draped over the back of a stuffed chair by a bay window. Her bags were tucked away somewhere, the whole place perfectly neat. One of her nightgowns lay out on the pillow of her bed, her slippers on the floor, as she'd been getting ready to sleep.

On the writing table—ah, on the writing table, were three rolled canvases. Stuart could hardly wait.

Leonard didn't notice. He drew himself up, then asked, "You can identify the purse as yours, of course."

Quite politely, Emma recounted, "Yes. It has my business cards in it: Emma Hartley. I'm an art insurance agent and appraiser. My coin purse has some loose change in it and cash: about three or four hundred pounds in large bills." She frowned. "And a telegram I didn't read." Then she made a face. "Oh, and there's a newspaper clipping in the bag as well. Those newspapermen have barely left me alone since I tracked that Rubens to a janitor's closet."

"It absolutely is yours." Leonard offered the purse to her.

Very casually, she turned her back on it, and instead went to a cabinet, opening it. "Would you gentlemen care for some brandy? Let me pour you some while I read that telegram. I didn't have a chance to before I lost the blasted thing. You have no idea what trouble you've saved me." All the while, she was getting out glasses and brandy—the expensive French cognac they'd bought that morning. "I am so in your debt. Here." She brought a tray of three brandies, set it down on a side table, then took up the purse. Opening it, she said, "Let me pay you." She looked from one man to the other. "Fifty pounds each?"

Stuart quickly waved his hand. "Certainly not. Our pleasure."

Leonard sputtered for a moment, but then contented himself with picking up a glass, looking through the perfect, amber liquid. "A bit of brandy would be nice."

She lifted her glass then and smiled so radiantly even Stuart was taken aback. "To gallantry," she said. "So long as you gentlemen exist, it shall live."

Leonard blushed, cleared his throat. Stuart couldn't keep his eyes affixed on her. He glanced at the rolled canvases again. He was frankly flabbergasted—she was so good at this it was frightening.

"I can't tell you how indebted I am," Emma continued. "I was in some considerable distress over my loss. Now, if you'll excuse me a moment, while I read my telegram." Quietly, as they watched, she opened it, followed the lines with her eyes, then smiled broadly. She looked at them. "Three," she emphasized, "*three* buyers. My, this *is* a good night. Please." She smiled again that brilliant smile that simply bowled Stuart over—he couldn't imagine how his uncle was dealing with her, when he himself knew what was going on and still was having a hard time. "If you won't take my money, let me show you my gratitude another way then."

That got Leonard's attention.

She paused, rubbing her earlobe, a delicate gesture of thoughtfulness, as if debating how far to trust them. All the way, her forthright voice said as she told them, "You see, I have a little business that is highly profitable. Suppose I could make you a good deal more money than fifty pounds in twenty-four hours that would cost none of us anything and did no harm anywhere?"

"I'm all ears," Leonard said, staring over his glass.

"Well." Emma held out her hand, gracefully indicating her writing table. "Over there. No, here, let me show you." She went over and unrolled a canvas. "You see?"

She looked over the edge, while Stuart and Leonard stared directly at the young redheaded artist's facsimile of Rembrandt's *Christ at the Column*.

"It's fake," she said cheerfully. Then invited, "Come closer. Look." She reached behind her and opened the writing table's one drawer. "And here are their provenances."

Leonard jerked, scowled at the word, then watched her remove from the drawer a thick stack of pages as she said, "They're bills of sale, letters, some exhibit contracts and brochures, some newer, some aged, anything having to do with the painting's history that proves it—them"—she laughed—"authentic: These were also forged."

Leonard frowned for a moment. "I thought you were a legitimate art expert of some sort."

"I am. I work for Lloyd's among others. I'm quite respectable. A few of my smaller companies and I, though, have a bit of business on the side that leaves everyone happy. You see, here is how it works.

"An insurance company is the key. First, as a matter of course, the company can't help but end up with lists of art collectors who buy heavily, fanatics. I get to know some of these people, take them to dinner. It is simply part of my job, in general, to foster good business relations. In the course of my association with these clients it comes out who might and might not be covetous for great art that is impossible to obtain legally. Second, the guards at the museums are often hired by the insurance companies. When one of my associate companies finds, shall we say, a guard who is willing to put a painting in an out-of-the-way spot for a day or two in exchange for some extra cash, well—that's where I come in.

"I wine and dine the people who might long for a masterwork owned by a museum, finding out how sincere they are until I get the one with fire in his eyes, who wants his heart's desire. At the museum, thanks to the guard, the artwork disappears for sometimes no longer than an hour or two—enough to make the newspapers, often as a kind of chuckle. But the client now knows that 'the switch' has taken place. A 'fake' has been substituted for the 'real thing,' which is now on its way to him. Because I'm so 'clever,' I find the work, oh, like the last one, in a mail room or such, packed up, just about to be mailed out to a post office box that is a dead end.

"The art is returned. The insurance company not only doesn't have to pay, they look like heroes for finding an irreplaceable piece of art. I tell the buyer that no one will check the museum piece's authenticity because they found what they were expecting to find—or if someone does insist on verifying it, I do it or arrange for it. Meanwhile, an insurance company appraiser quietly assures the client that his new art and provenance are genuine, and he privately pays a fortune for it: I can usually make three or four copies and sell one 'stolen' work a number of times. Like these little paintings. As you can see, the enterprise is risk-free, since the people in charge of arresting anyone are essentially the people who have taken the art. It's absolutely foolproof; everyone wins."

"It sounds illegal," Stuart said.

"Well, it is," she admitted readily, then smiled again, full-blown. "But it shouldn't be," she said charmingly. Then added, "My point is, I have a third buyer I didn't expect for these." She indicated the three fake Rembrandts as she set the third back on the writing desk. "My fellow happened to do three, while I only had two provenances done; I only had two buyers. But now another source has wired me that he's changed his mind. Let me take the money I offered you, the two fifty-pound notes—and have another set of bills of sale made. Then we'll sell the third, and you two get the profit. On me. My pleasure."

Leonard's eyes grew wide. "What kind of profit are we talking about?"

"Two thousand—a thousand pounds for each of you." She apologized with a shrug. "These little things are nothing. Tiny. You should have seen that one." She pointed, then shook an irritable finger at the newspaper clipping on the liquor cabinet, the one showing her trying to shield herself from a camera, while a very large Rubens stood behind—the one her photographer friend had taken, then superimposed over another he had, putting Emma in Paris via his darkroom. Stuart and Emma had had a grainy newspaper photo made of it as part of their setup.

She shook her head. "I must say, these newspaper fellows are ruining my business. I have to lie low, do small paintings now that don't make the news, till they ease up." Then she smiled and sloughed the matter off. "Hardly a problem, though. I still get my insurance commissions." Her smile grew sly. "And the side commissions off the small things."

Leonard looked at Stuart as if to say, *Small things. Her small "side commissions" netted two thousand pounds a pop, six thousand for all three pictures.*

"Actually, when you look at it correctly," she said, pouring them all a second brandy, "it's harmless. The museum loses no work of art. The insurance company loses no money, in fact they look smart, competent at their job. Meanwhile, art collectors get the secret joy of owning an original. Never mind it isn't; their joy is authentic. And we make a tidy bundle. It's a sure deal, where everyone has a stake, and everyone wins.

"So how's that?" she asked, blinking, fluttering her long eyelashes. "May I use what you won't take to make this third buyer happy? Get a good set of provenances done quickly, then hand you the profit? It costs me nothing more than what I'd have cheerfully given you anyway, while I get to extend my gratitude more substantially: A thousand pounds should cover a nice stay in London for you fellows, first-class all the way. What do you say? Let's do it. It would make me happy."

Lord, not a man in England would want anything more at that moment than to make Emma Hotchkiss happy.

At which point, she held up her hands and said, "No. Say nothing." She went to the door and in a very friendly manner, opened it, lifting her hand outward. "Just go, then tomorrow morning check at the front desk. If you take the envelopes waiting for you, I'll know I've pleased you. If you don't, no hard feelings. I understand, and thank you again."

And, like that, Emma had both out the door, their hats in their hands.

Stuart was left breathless. His dear, sweet Em was a first-rate hustler, if he'd ever met one—far better than he'd ever realized.

* * *

The next morning, uncle and nephew met for breakfast. Stuart had never seen his damned relative so much, yet more was to come if all went well.

The concierge in his morning suit, striped tie, dove gray coat, smiled at them from the front desk on their way to their table upstairs. He called to them before they even asked. "Gentlemen, these were left for you." Envelopes. They each contained ten hundred-pound notes. A thousand pounds.

"How did she do it so quickly?" Leonard asked.

Stuart—for this was his job now—relieved his concerns. "Her buyers must be in London, all of them waiting. I suppose there is an advantage in doing something like this fast and in person."

Leonard nodded and examined the inside of his envelope again, counting, amazed. "I think she's crazy," he said.

Stuart laughed. "Without doubt. The smartest crazy woman I have ever met."

Both men nodded.

Leonard added, "I like her." He couldn't quit looking in his envelope. He sat down for breakfast, then counted the money again.

Stuart waited till their tea came, then said, "Are you thinking what I'm thinking?'

Leonard glanced up.

Stuart continued. "The statue. I don't know if she can do sculpture or artifacts, but we can ask. She has a lot of art world contacts. So I supply the provenance, you, the statue itself. All you wanted was to sell it for the money, so we get three copies made, complete with three forged sets of provenances. We sell the copies. I get the real statue and the money from one fake, you get twice that—the money from the other two. We can cut her in in some way, if she likes."

Leonard rolled his lips together, reluctant to make his admission. Then, "Y-y-y-yes," Leonard said, dragging the word out with dawning understanding. "It could be done."

Their first inch of success: Leonard had admitted possession of the statue.

Stuart smiled. "Shall we go see her?"

Leonard blinked, then nodded. "Let's."

They put their napkins down, abandoning the idea of breakfast altogether.

Uncle Leonard had bit, as Emma called it. He was in, hook, line, and sinker.

While Stuart was beside himself with pleasure and anticipation.

It was with joy that Stuart watched Emma repossess his two thousand pounds. She took both envelopes back, then put the money into the center drawer of her writing table. As she said, "You fellows certainly catch on." She smiled with approval, turning to face them fully as she leaned back on the safely returned money. "You have indeed struck on the way to turn this found money into a fortune."

"Do you need all of it?" Leonard asked. He looked anxiously at the desk behind her.

"How many duplicates do you want?"

"Three."

"With the proper papers to get full value for the work" —she narrowed her eyes, a woman whose mind worked like an abacus, counting up costs—"two thousand pounds might do it." Then she asked the appalling question, "If it takes a bit more, can you raise it on short notice?"

Leonard and Stuart looked at one another.

While Emma expounded: First, Leonard as the owner would have to "insure" his statue with one of her companies. "The insurance is absolutely legitimate," she assured him. "If anything should happen to your statue, the company would have to compensate you. What a clever man," she said and tapped Leonard on the chest once as she walked by. "You use money you didn't have a day ago to protect your only risk, your statue"—she nodded at Stuart—"and provenance. I must hand it to you. You certainly know how to make the most of circumstances. If all you tell me holds true, I could see the statue's selling for upward from a hundred thousand."

Leonard's eyes grew round as crumpets. Besides the insurance, she explained, there would be costs for the forger who did the provenances, the sculptor who made the imitation statues, and the services of a jeweler who'd do the statue's jewels in paste. "You can trust each buyer to be very careful of his rare old object, so as long as we get the look, substance, and weight of it right, I see no reason to use expensive materials." Part of the statue was in jade as well as precious and semi-precious stones.

"This, you realize," she said, swishing around today in a lavender gown—it fit so well and so encouraged a man to look at her shape, Stuart could hardly follow along with what she was saying: a good thing his main function just then in their little game was to ogle her. "This, you realize, is ideal in that there is no guard to pay off, and it is so private the newspapers won't pick it up."

"Look," Leonard offered, "if you think you should have a cut of the profit—"

"I absolutely will hear of no such thing. I'll set you up with the right people, but you'll be doing most of the legwork. And I get a commission off the insurance, remember. That is already enough. My pleasure, gentlemen. When my purse went missing yesterday, I thought I'd go mad. You saved me. It is my pleasure to throw a few names at you today. My pleasure," she repeated.

"And now if you'll excuse me," said the bustling Emma, "I have my own business to attend to. Here." She scribbled a name and address on a blank piece of hotel stationery. "Go to this man. Tell him I sent you. He'll do a brilliant job on your statue, I promise."

Stuart reached for the paper. Emma looked up at him, frowned, and jerked back. He'd been expecting something exactly like this, though he hadn't known in what form it would come: Emma beginning the process of distrust in him. Even knowing it was feigned, the pit of his stomach clenched as he watched Leonard accept the slip of paper, with Emma smiling warmly at him.

She continued, "You should get the real statue as soon as possible. I'll tell him to expect it and pay him his first installment." She nodded toward the drawer with the money, then glanced at Stuart. "Get me the real provenance also," she said coolly. Then to Leonard, with another smile as warm as sunlight, "We'll take care of the rest."

Leonard was watching all this, but not entirely taken in. He balked. "I'm not simply going to hand over a hundred-thousand-pound statue to a stranger."

Emma lifted her hands—but of course—unfazed, still smiling. "You're in charge, sir. Tell him where you want him to do the work. The simpler you make it, the quicker it will all happen, but by all means make yourself comfortable. All I can tell you is I've dealt with him, oh, eight times—" Almost absently, she went over to her breakfast table on which sat a tray containing several telegrams. She picked up one, sliding her nail, then her finger, under the flap, and continued, "He has been entirely reliable. Plus I believe he'd like to work with me again. Your statue will be perfectly safe." Indulgently, she smiled again before she unfolded the telegram. "Plus it's insured, dear heart. I'll write the policy up as of today, though I'll need to see the statue as soon as possible so as to get all the particulars right." She looked down at her telegram, then muttered, "You know the way out, gentlemen. I'll meet with you as soon as you have the statue and provenance."

On their way down in the lift, Stuart murmured over the sound of chains' and cables' clanking, "The provenance is in Yorkshire." It wasn't; he'd brought it with him. "It'll take me a day there and a day back. Is the statue far?"

The elevator operator lowered them slowly on the swinging cable as Leonard whispered, "Here in London."

Oh, the joy of hearing the whereabouts after all the denial! Stuart kissed Emma on her imaginary cheek. "Will you take it to this fellow?"

Leonard nodded, though he spoke with some doubt. "I thought I'd go have a look at him first. I don't know whether to trust her or not."

"I know what you mean," Stuart said seriously. "It all seems too easy. I myself don't trust her."

The lure of large profit and a history of opposing his nephew combined to make Leonard throw Stuart a worried glance. "You won't get the provenance then?"

Stuart let the elevator noisily ratchet down another floor before he murmured, "No, no, I'm going to get it. I just think we should proceed cautiously."

He and his uncle watched through the lift's grate as the lobby slowly rose into view. Then Leonard said, "Of course, as she says, it's all insured, even if her fellow suddenly took the statue."

Stuart let a few more thoughtful moments tick by before he said, "Get the policy from her, then tell me who the company is. I'll see if I can mention the company casually at my club, see if anyone knows—"

"God"—Leonard grabbed his arm—"don't talk to your House of Lords cronies about this, you idiot."

Stuart raised his brow, staring at where his uncle had hold of his coat sleeve.

Leonard continued, "I say we move carefully, but speak to no one about it. That's the safest thing."

"All right," Stuart agreed happily.

The lift's door accordioned back. "The lobby," said the operator.

As they exited, Leonard asserted in a whisper, "You don't trust her because she likes me."

"Does she?" Stuart glanced over his shoulder as they walked. "I hadn't noticed."

"And she doesn't like you."

He stopped and turned to look at his relative, raising a disputing eyebrow.

They stood at the side of the lobby, beside a huge pot of palms, his uncle smirking at him. "While you can't take your eyes off her. The Lady Hartley. Dear Emma. You fancy her."

Stuart played it evenly. "And your point is?"

Leonard chuckled. "She's a bit bottom heavy, don't you think? A little thick?"

"Emma?" Stuart scowled. For a second, he wanted to wrap a lift cable around his uncle's neck, shift the gear knob, then drop the fellow down the shaft. "Emma's waist"—he made a small circle of his thumbs spread away from his hands—"is like this."

Leonard was amused by the diameter, then intrigued. "And how would you know?"

Stuart raised his eyebrow higher: at himself. He cleared his throat, trying to clear his mind. "I came back last night," he said. Which did not sound half-bad—not as a lie nor as a future idea. "I told her I'd lost a glove and asked if I could look for it."

"And?"

"The glove wasn't there."

His uncle made a sarcastic face. "How did it go?"

Stuart shrugged and let out air noisily through his lips, looking down. "Not well." He shook his head, then smiled up slyly. "But I can tell you her waist is small. She's as firm as a little gazelle." As pretty as a doe. As soft as a dove. To touch her hair was to run one's fingers through manifest moonlight.

"I know," Leonard said. "She's something. A lush little thing." He glanced at his nephew, an agreement at last. "I was having a little fun with you." He laughed. "By jove, but I'd have a go at her myself if we didn't need her so badly."

Stuart felt heat rise up behind his eyes. "Go get the statue, will you? And mind your own business. My personal life is my own."

"Not if you make a ballocks of it, it isn't. Leave her alone. She was clearly taking pains this morning to keep her distance from you. Your stupidity last night explains that."

Stuart pressed his mouth tight, holding back a retort. That Emma should pretend a partiality for Leonard was part of the plan, yet it was more difficult to bear—and far too easy to play the fool—than he'd imagined.

His uncle continued, "Let her do her job without annoying her, will you? We are dependent on her good graces." He eyed Stuart, earnest.

Which meant the man was taking the hoax all very seriously.

Stuart nodded curtly, which was the best he could do for a second. Then he got out, "You're right," all but choking on the words—they came out through his teeth.

All the better. It confirmed the status quo. Leonard chuckled at him, making a rare avuncular shake of his head. He was still grinning over the business all the way through the foyer and out onto the street.

And, thus, Stuart's uncle was successfully put "on the send" for the most valuable of the desired items. Neither Stuart nor Emma was sure how to approach the lost earrings, though Emma, if all went well, would get closer to Leonard while Stuart was "gone." An unsettling prospect. Yet the one most likely to yield information on the subject.

PART THREE

The Send

Yorkshire Rarebit

In the oven, toast four thick slices of farmer's bread. When lightly brown, remove the toast from oven and spread with lots of fresh Yorkshire butter. Meanwhile, in a pot on the stove, melt together, stirring regularly: two ounces of good Yorkshire ale, six ounces of sharp Yorkshire cheese, a dash of prepared mustard, and a pinch of butter. When all has combined, pour cheese mixture over buttered toast, covering the bread in the thick mixture. Let sit a minute, then eat it up. Serves two people a hearty meal.

—EMMA DARLINGTON HOTCHKISS
Yorkshire Ways and Recipes

Chapter 14

To press kisses on her skin is to taste the lotus,
The deep cave of her navel hides a store of spices
What pleasure lies beyond, the tongue knows,
But cannot speak of it.

—*Srngarakarika*, Kumaradadatta, 12th century

STUART circled the block in his carriage, thinking to be sure Leonard was gone before returning to the Carlyle. He was in the mood to celebrate a little with Emma. Plus he had in his carriage two different packets of papers, one of which made him rather pleased with himself. A kind of present, he hoped. Never mind that she wouldn't approve of seeing him turn up at the hotel. Leonard had things to do; it was perfectly safe.

Moreover, Stuart was getting to the point where he didn't care if it was safe. If Leonard caught him returning to Emma, he'd only think his nephew more the fool.

A fool. There it was. He was becoming a fool over Emma Hotchkiss, with or without his uncle knowing it. *He* knew it. Stuart felt half in love with the woman.

No. He was completely in love with her. That must be what the feeling was, though it worried him. And buoyed. He'd thought love, if it ever came to him, would be a cleaner, purer emotion, that the object of his affection would be more . . . angelic. He smiled to himself. Emma only looked like an angel. Thank goodness. Nothing felt so fine as standing beside the devilish woman, looking at her, talking to her, touching her.

Ah, yes, touching Emma. Wouldn't that be lovely after days of hardly doing more than bumping against her, if he were lucky, if he connived right.

How to tell her what he felt? He wasn't even clear himself, so words suitable for her hearing were scarce. He had to think about it, word it to himself for a while. God help him, if he tried right now to get it all out to her, he would be nothing but a stuttering mess. Then he smiled to himself and patted the papers beside him. They were a beginning.

At Eaton Square, he watched Leonard's carriage, ahead of him by several vehicles turn. Good riddance. Stuart signaled his own driver to take King's Road, circling through the square, and return to the Carlyle. Thus, he was happily jostling along, enjoying the cool of early midday in what he considered his own neighborhood, the very civilized Belgravia, watching the gardens and boulevards pass, the usual traffic, only half what it was on a weekday—it being Sunday—all to the sound of his familiar troika bell jangling faintly against the clop of hooves on an English boulevard.

By the time he had the Carlyle in view again, however, he was cursing under his breath. His damned uncle had done the same thing in the other direction. Stuart gave the ceiling of his coach a quick rap. His footman's face appeared in the rear service window. "Have the driver turn quickly. Circle wide, around the Palace Gardens, then let me off. I'll take to foot." His own carriage was too conspicuous to wait in it. "Wait on Halkin Street."

Emma opened her door, then had to hide a mild start. It was a little soon for Leonard Aysgarth to seek her out, yet there he stood in the corridor outside her suite at the Carlyle. He didn't have any genuine grievance against his nephew—yet.

So why was he here? She was never comfortable with winning a mark's confidence too quickly; it meant it could be lost just as easily, a fragile thing.

"Why, Mr. Aysgarth," she said in a tone of pleasant surprise. "What brings you back this morning?"

He stood there a moment, a well-tailored, nonplussed Englishman, turning his hat, running its brim through his gloved fingers. Then he said, "I know how busy you are." He made a short nervous laugh. "But even such a very busy lady as yourself surely has time for a bit of refreshment." He made what she was sure was supposed to be a suave smile, then asked, "Elevenses?" The traditional hour of English morning tea, if one had the leisure to enjoy it.

She glanced behind her, at the "mounds" of work such a "busy lady" as herself must surely have. She closed the door a little, so he couldn't see there was nothing anywhere for her to "work" on. She smiled back hesitantly. "Is it business—"

"No, no, no," he said immediately.

How curious.

"We are set there. No, I simply would like your company while I had a sweet with a pot of good tea. The Carlyle is known for their morning and afternoon tea services, the best in the city. Won't you join me?"

She blinked, hesitated another moment, then said, "Oh, why not? I'm hungry. Let me get my shawl."

The tea parlor was on the ground floor overlooking a small courtyard garden. Leonard pulled out her chair, then stood, removing his overcoat, gloves, and hat.

"A fine day," he said, indicating the window by the table where the maître d' had seated them. It was the first day since she'd arrived in London that she'd seen the sun. It was a nice day, in fact.

She nodded, smiled some more, then touched her throat, tracing her collarbone with her finger, and fluttered her lashes, touched her curls, then accepted the vellum page that outlined their choices for tea. Why had Leonard brought her here? she kept wondering.

Ah, to slander Stuart: "My nephew has been a handful since the day he was born. I know what he got up to last night with you, and I want you to know I am here for you, should you need any assistance. His father—" Leonard shook his head, implying great similarity between the two men.

The waiter came, and they ordered two cream teas. With Emma wondering what exactly Stuart had "got up to" last night. He was improvising somewhere, and she didn't know why.

Leonard dropped his voice as the man withdrew. "His father, and I suspect the son, could not be trusted around women. I simply wish to put you on your guard. A bad nut, that one. Which falls close to the tree, if you get my drift."

Emma lifted her head, half a nod. The other half of her wanted to laugh. Was he serious? "I thank you for your concern," she said.

He waved his hand. Then expanded his slander to include Stuart's mother as well. "My brother didn't want the marriage, you know. And Stuart himself was a great surprise. Donovan wrote to me the night before his wedding. He said, and I quote, 'I beseech you, use any influence you have with our mother and father. I do not want to marry this woman. She is quite the homeliest creature I have ever set eyes upon and bland and timid as a mouse. How I might be civil to her for an entire wedding day, let alone a lifetime, is beyond me. Please help me, Leo. Don't let our family ruin my life, sacrificing me on the altar of their greed.' "

Tea arrived, a white china pot of steaming darjeeling, along with three tiers of pastries, scones included, and bowls of clotted cream and raspberry jam.

He continued, "I don't know how Stuart was conceived at all. Oh, those many years ago now, I took one look at my brother's wealthy bride-to-be and was sure I would be the next Viscount Mount Villiars, that my brother would live richly but without heirs. Then, lo, almost immediately, the little toad was pregnant."

Emma drank a sip of tea, having to swallow to keep an unpleasant expression on her face. *Toad.* The poor woman.

Onward Leo went, regaling her with the unfairness of Stuart's having been born, the wretchedness of all concerned in his family, the suffering he himself had gone through, feeling superior to it all at every moment, while remaining annoyed—thirty years after the fact—that he was unable to claim what he thought more his due than anyone else's.

Emma left him to the pastries, while she fiddled with her earlobe, trying to figure out what his ramble was supposed to gain him.

Then he smiled across at her, conspiratorially, and she realized that Uncle Leonard was making a play for her. How . . . nice? Absurd? Was any woman ever flattered by the attention of a man so nauseatingly blind and self-serving?

Emma smiled at him nonetheless, and made a play for him right back, of sorts. Her knuckle grazed her very nice faux pearl at her left earlobe, as large as a small marble. As she fiddled with her earlob, she dug her thumbnail between the pearl and its mount, to see if it could be popped off. Then, "Oh, dear," she said with a jerk and looked down into her palm.

Yes, it could be. Her pinkish mock-pearl sat in the cup of her hand. She made a tsk of dismay. "Oh, my. Another trip to my jeweler." She smiled across the table at Leonard. "I so love beautiful earrings. What a shame."

"Pearls?" he inquired, glancing into her hand.

"Oh, it doesn't matter," she said. She clenched her fist before he could inspect too closely; she didn't know if he'd recognize a genuine pearl from a fake. She laid the pearl in her skirt, then, turning her head to remove the back and mount, said, "Pretty ones. Lately, I've been eyeing some dangling ones at Garrard's." She laughed coyly as she dropped the parts of her earring into her drawstring bag, then flashed him a smile. "The gypsy in me, I suppose."

He looked at her absolutely blankly. Earrings, Leonard. Where are Stuart's mother's earrings that you stole? And why? What would you do with them?

But then the conniving fellow reached across and patted Emma's hand. He smiled a knowing look. "Earrings," he stated.

She nodded, mildly ill at her stomach to understand that he thought she was bartering God-knew-what, some intimacy, for a pair of earrings.

He lifted an eyebrow—a gesture so like his nephew's without having a whit of the same elan—and said, "I shall have money enough soon to buy a great many pretty things for a lady I like." Then he sighed and held out his hands. "But now is . . ." He let the thought trail off.

Yes, Leonard. That's the idea. Can you think of a pair of earrings you already own? What use could you possibly put them to? What could they possibly matter? Do you wear lady's earrings when you are dancing about alone?

A blank wall. All he said was, "So, you see, Stuart is less the English gentleman than he might first seem. I just wanted you to know that. Of course"—he cleared his throat, a harrumph—"he hasn't lived here very much. He couldn't stand to live in the same town, same country—not on the same continent—as his father." He made a philosophical, world-weary shake of his head. "Though a son can't truly flee a father, can he? I mean, the man is swimming in his veins."

An idea, she suspected, that some days frightened Stuart out of his wits.

"In any regard, he went to Turkey and lived among the barbarians for a time." He gave a self-righteous grunt. "I'm not sure whether to call him immoral or"—assuming a grim mouth of self-righteousness—"merely adolescent: He went there so he could have a harem."

Emma blinked, leaned forward. She couldn't have heard correctly.

Leonard laughed heartily at the surprise on her face. "A

harem," he repeated. "My nephew had a harem in Istanbul for several years. Upwards of half a dozen women, I think. How rich is that?" He chuckled some more. "Hardly the civilized sort of thing a gentleman might want to do."

Emma wasn't too sure of that. Half the gentlemen with whom she'd been acquainted seemed to think a harem of sorts was exactly what they needed. It was more than a little disappointing, however, to realize that Stuart was one of these gentlemen.

His uncle continued smugly, "Quite the barbarian himself." He leaned toward her, adding all but covertly, "I worry about him, truth be known. I'm sure he's a clear-thinking man, but then—" He paused, she was sure, for dramatic effect. "He's decidedly odd, isn't he?"

Yes, he was. In a decidedly interesting way. Emma suffered another ten minutes of tea with the most bombastic, obliviously narcissistic blowhard she'd ever had the misfortune to need for the time being. She said, rising at last, "Well, thank you, Leonard"—smiling across to him as he stood as well—"I may call you Leonard, yes?"

"Leo."

"Leo, then. Lovely." She drew her shawl up. "I must get back to work."

"Oh, yes. Work, work, work. You are a busy little woman. I admire that," he said sincerely. "I admire you most heartily, Lady Hart-i-ley." He added the extra syllable, a bad pun.

Emma managed a half smile.

"My dear," he told her, "I take my responsibility toward you very seriously. I worry"—he drew himself—"that Stuart could get cold feet or say the wrong thing to the wrong people. He even suggested briefly he might discuss our business with other MPs at his club." As if it were headline news, he said, "You know, he actually goes to the House of Lords? Regularly. He cultivates associations there. For political reasons." Oh, the mess and dirt of that game, he implied. "Why, placing his confidence in the wrong person could damage us irreparably."

Indeed. Confidence was not the problem that morning; Emma had almost more of confidence than she wanted. Forbearance was her problem. Besides being as slimy as a worm, Leonard Aysgarth was a crashing bore.

A morning that Emma had expected to be fairly uneventful, even restful, was full of surprises. In her room, when she returned, a silver tray sat on the table by the bay window. There, on the tray, lay a small envelope, hand-delivered while she was out. She didn't recognize the handwriting, which made her laugh when she opened it. It was unfamiliar and unsigned, but there was little doubt whom it was from. It read:

I am in my carriage on Halkin Street, waiting. You know what the carriage looks like. Come down or I'm coming up. I'll be punching Leonard in the nose, if I have to, to get by the asinine pisspot.

She took the lift down as far as the restaurant, borrowed a long cloak with a hood from the cloakroom there—a good enough disguise that she should have returned to its hook in less than ten minutes—then bundled herself up. She cursed Stuart for the entire walk to Halkin Street, telling herself she should ignore him.

As she turned the corner of Belgrave Place, though, she could not deny the small lift in her chest at the sight: His carriage faced her, pulled to the side behind six shining horses. The vehicle waited restlessly, all its privacy shades down, shrouded. The footman startled as she came up to him, but he was quick enough to get her inside the coach.

The door closed on the daylight. The inside of the vehicle was as dark as a cave.

"Would you like me to light a lamp?" said the low, even

voice she easily recognized. Did Stuart plan this sort of melodrama or did it come naturally? A bat's cave, she thought. Count Dracula.

"Yes, please."

A spark, a flicker, then long fingers holding a match, a dark, graceful hand shielding it. These cupped hands came toward her, lighting an angular face in gutters, the Prince of Darkness's own. Stuart lit the small gas lamp beside her, above and to her right, hovering near. His fur-lined coat was open, the warmth of him seeming to come at her from within it. Then the wick caught. The crystal clinked down into place as light sparkled out into the little interior. Stuart's face, well lit now, was close for a moment, then he sat back onto a seat bench that pooled with chinchilla, crossing one booted leg to his knee.

His hat sat upside down beside him on the seat, his gloves draped into it. He raised his neatly tailored arm in his Russian coat and relaxed back onto the bench seat.

"What do you want?" she asked. "Emma Hartley would not meet Mount Villiars in his coach. This is dangerous. I've already explained why." Sitting here, outside her pose—this was what made her heart thud so hard in her chest. Indeed, memory was with her of the last time her partner hadn't paid better heed to the rules of the game.

Then, to her surprise, with a jerk the coach rolled out into traffic.

She swiveled her head. Uselessly, since all the windows were blocked. "Where are we going? What the hell are you doing?" she asked, frowning, her voice rising.

"I'm taking you to my house."

"Oh, fine, Stuart." She crossed her legs under her skirts with a brisk churn of taffeta and soft wool. "Why not simply take me to Leonard's? Announce our association, tell him what chums we are, see if he'd like to get a pint at the pub with us?"

"Before you get too much further up on your high horse, would you like to know why I want to talk to you privately?"

She said nothing, folding her arms.

"I was trying to bring you some things, to ask you a question, then I discovered Leonard had beat me to you." He let out a grumbling sort of snort. "I don't much like the part I play in this."

"I explained what it would be like—"

"Yes, but hearing it and living it are different."

"I told you that as well. We can stop anytime you'd like."

Another snort from him, then he tossed some papers, clipped together, toward her. They landed in her lap, a light puffing *plop* of paper on silk.

"The provenance. You told me to short it one page. Which page? Does it make a difference?" He left a pause, then let out a long sigh and looked at his boot. "And, all right, I wanted to look at you. Without worrying if I was behaving properly or what some arsehole might think or do if I stared at you. Having to worry about what Leonard thinks—something I have never done in my life—is trying, to say the least. I'm not good at it." He took in a breath, needing air after his long speech.

She felt a moment's sympathy, even a warm little ping of flattered femininity. Emma frowned at his lordship, the Viscount Mount Villiars, in his beautiful coat, in his extravagant carriage, at his broad-shouldered, long-armed reach; massive, masculine. The man from the bank. Then the word *harem* came to her, and she scowled at the thought.

Harem. She wanted to believe it to be a vicious lie by the uncle, but it fit. That's what the mysterious Aminah and What's-her-name were about. The residual of half a dozen or so women he'd enjoyed in Turkey. A bloody harem. And why not? Here sat a man who was handsome enough, rich enough. What should stop him from "staring" at as many women as he wanted? She wondered if he still slept with his "wards."

She picked up the papers in her lap, thinking to be rid of

him as quickly as possible. She eyed bills of sale, art exhibit booklets, a lot of mismatched papers of various sizes, held together with a metal clip. She thumbed through the documents, looking for, say, the most recent, his own claim to the statue. That would be a good one to leave out. She found it, then frowned, blinked, and focused for a second look. Emma peered at the documents again, their order, their substance, then examined the bill of sale closely. Goose bumps rose along her arms.

She looked up at Stuart, then let out a laugh. "You won't believe this," she said. "These aren't authentic. I know these pages or pages like them. I knew the man who used to forge these."

Stuart's mouth opened. He said nothing, his brow drawing down, then murmured, "What do you meant they aren't authentic?" He understood the next second. "Oh, wait—" He smiled faintly. He blinked. Then he burst out with a low chuckle. "One of your friends? You think one of them sold my father a bogus statue with a bogus line of history?" He slapped his boot, shook his head, then reached across the coach, his hand open. He was asking for the papers.

She handed them to him.

He paged through them, smiling. Far from being disappointed, he said, "How delightful! Let's take it from Leonard anyway."

She gaped. "Why?"

For a second, he didn't know. He looked up. "I can't explain it, but it's a feeling, a very personal . . . feeling. I remember vaguely that as a child—" He squinted, as if trying to force better recall. He seemed disappointed only to produce, "The statue frightened me, I think. And fascinated me, too. It sparkled, was riveting, but also grotesque somehow. I detested it. Yet anything that I attach that much feeling to, my uncle has no business stealing, fake or not." He shrugged as if to dismiss what he'd just admitted. "I want to *see* the unsettling thing again. It feels important somehow." He added, "And the earrings, don't forget. My uncle has no right to them either. They're mine, connected to my childhood. I want to hold them in my hand again."

"I don't know if I can get the earrings. I took a little stab at it this morning, and he seemed utterly nonplussed, absolutely uncomprehending. Are you sure your uncle took them? Perhaps a maid or footman stole them, with your uncle simply happening to be about at the time?"

"No. When he knew I was on my way, he ransacked the place for anything portable, then fled. He took all my mother's jewelry. I don't care about the rest. But these I remember somehow. A pleasant connection; I'll be damned if my despicable uncle is going to possess the only pleasant association I have." He raised that eyebrow, then pulled his mouth up into a rare wide smile. "Plus," he said, "now I can look forward to seeing a statue that got the better of Donovan Aysgarth. Do you suppose my mother knew? She's the one who kept it. I remember it from Dunord. Oh, Emma," he said and shook his head, laughing. "You are wonderful." He picked up the provenance again. "So you know the man who did these?"

"Knew."

"Who? That Bailey fellow?" His face asked for the information with childlike relish.

Information which, now that she thought of it, would not light up his heart. She hesitated.

Stuart waited, then narrowed his eyes again. There was a moment wherein he wanted it to be someone else, then the next wherein he couldn't avoid who it was.

He threw the papers at her. They went everywhere, fluttering about the moving carriage like a mass of large butterflies suddenly taken to flight. One tickled her nose, then landed in her lap. Others settled onto the seats, the floor.

Her companion didn't speak for a few seconds, then said,

unreasonably angry, "He was a mess, you know." He said vehemently, "You were married to a clown."

She lifted her chin, loyal to the last. "Clowns make you laugh, and he did sometimes."

Stuart focused on her, wanting to shove her. My God, he thought, what he'd give to inspire such constancy. What did he have to do? Become a vicar? Grow a halo and wings? Then the whole past twenty-four hours struck him like a slap across the face. His resentment of his uncle mingled for a moment, adding to the resentment he felt for old, dead Hotchkiss. Zach. God, but he hated that man. A dead man, no less. There was productive animosity.

Stuart, old boy, you are losing your mind.

More annoying still, Emma suddenly said—a clear accusation: "Leo"—*Leo*, no less—"said you had a harem in Turkey."

"And you believed him." He twisted his mouth, consternation.

"You either did or you didn't."

He grew defensive. "When I was nineteen. It was a terrible idea. It lasted eleven months—"

"You actually had one? How many wives did you have?"

"None. A harem in the Near East is where the women of a household live. They were all of lower status than wives."

"And what would that be?"

"Concubines. It is perfectly respectable there, Emma."

"Not here, it isn't."

"I don't have them here." He said, "It was a lot of youthful idiocy. The whole idea was a mess. The women were angry with me most of the time. I had no idea what my role in it was—and it is structured, things are expected of a man who takes on that kind of responsibility there." He sighed. "It took me three years to untangle it all, to see that all the women were situated where they wished to be. Hiyam and Aminah chose to come with me as part of my household, as my wards, as I said. They are rather like sisters to me."

"You slept with them."

He looked down. "Things change. I don't now. I haven't for years."

She leaned forward, rocking to get her cloak out from under her where it had slipped.

Stuart slid to the edge of his seat and bent forward—she was meant to think he was helping her.

He didn't fool either of them. She grew rigid, eyeing him. He didn't let that stop him, but rather eased his arm further around her, taking her about the waist. He had to brace himself with his other hand on the coach side as they hit a pothole in the cobbles, but all the same he managed to pull her forward.

He kissed her, because he purely needed the touch of her mouth and could have it. And perhaps to say whom he wished to sleep with now. Only one woman, Emma. He looked for gestures, afraid of words.

He felt her warm lips respond. He smelled the powdery clean scent of her smooth cheek, heard the softest sigh in her throat. A part of her lit up like a sky full of fireworks every time he touched her. While a part of her resented his mastery so much, he could do little but let go. Which he did.

He slouched back, then had to shift to be comfortable, already partially erect in trousers not constructed for a lot of frustration. He winced as he found a position, then put his hand to his mouth, automatic, covering where her face had been the instant before, not wasting the faintest taste of her, holding it in.

She watched him with the widest, bluest eyes he'd ever known. Her full breasts rose and fell in mesmerizing unison. Then she closed her eyes rather than meet his.

Ah, Emma. What you want and what you need . . . there is too large a disparity. Until she understood herself better, he would always appear a worse villain than he was. A man in cahoots with a woman's sexual instinct was the devil himself, for he had the united power over her—himself and her own longing—greater than a mere man.

He murmured, "Englishwomen are so strange."

"Speaking as a man who has made the acquaintance of the strangest, I'm sure."

The carriage jostled around a corner. He'd had plans of wooing her with the other papers sitting beside him—not the mess he'd strewn about his coach now. Wooing her, taking her in the back entrance to his London house, showing her around in the dark. No lights anywhere to indicate anyone was home. No servants, all on two days' holiday, since he was supposed to be in Yorkshire. Taking her upstairs . . . relieving all his jealousy and insecurity. . . .

Then she asked, "Have you ever hurt anyone?"

He was taken aback.

Before he could say anything, she murmured, "I never want you to hurt me," she murmured.

"Then I never shall." After what seemed an eternity, he offered nonetheless, "But don't limit yourself, Emma. Anything. If you are shy or can't speak or think of something interesting, may I also mention, I have a very rich imagination myself. You need only put yourself into my hands."

She frowned, frightened. "You are—"

He interrupted. "You keep saying I'm unhealthy, and I may be, but not here. Not on this. In this regard, I am open and adventurous—absolutely healthy in my tolerance and appreciation of the diversity of life. Emma—"

She looked at him.

"You're brave. You're good. Why would you hesitate to explore yourself? Your dark nooks and crannies? With someone who is fascinated by the whole of you? You aren't a bad woman, merely a human one, which entails a certain amount of"—he cocked his head—" 'awfulness,' as you call it. Think about it. What could possibly happen that would be bad, so long as we communicate and honor the other's needs and wants?"

She felt the coach pull to a halt, heard the driver get down. Their destination. It was a short ride.

"I'm not going inside with you," she said. "We agreed I'd make the decisions in London. I explained how unpredictably this sort of thing can end. I'm getting out and walking back. Don't stop me. Don't come after me. Don't do this again. I can't help you get what you want if you won't play it my way. You have to listen to me."

"I'm not good at that," he admitted and shifted his jaw. He said it humbly, but a jaw muscle twitched.

Despondent, Stuart happened to glance at the seat beside him. There lay his small gift. He'd hoped for better circumstances to give it.

But he took a deep breath and launched into his best intentions. "Here," he said. He held up the five sheets of paper he'd obtained. "These go into considerable detail: They're descriptions of university courses you do by mail."

She laughed, disbelieving. "You've brought me a mail fraud, Stuart."

"No, no. It's real. I know the university. It's a new one in London, absolutely on the up-and-up. Though the correspondence courses are not for degree. If you'd like to try one" —the papers he'd brought her were a list of "remote courses"—"then you find that you like the study, the reading, and want to pursue a degree, any of it, I can make the arrangements. We could stay in London. I could open my house year-round till you were finished."

Oh, fine. He'd have an *educated* concubine. A geisha. How like the Viscount Mount Villiars to want his paramour to have a university degree.

She handed them back. "No, thank you. I'm fine as I am."

He frowned, as if misunderstood, possibly hurt. "I didn't mean to imply you weren't."

"Find yourself another protégé, dear. I had my fill with Zach and the University of Confidence Art."

He looked puzzled. "Don't let other people define you," he said, thinking of her little speech about Hannah The Mule, her belief that she was unqualified for enrollment or to sit for university exams.

She pulled a face. "Fine. I'm Queen of the May."

"No. I don't mean you get to say who you are. But you do get to *be* who you are. And you get to figure out who that is, no one else: You're the only one with all the information."

She stared at him, those large blue eyes in her fair face, as if he were certifiably deranged. Then repeated, "I don't want a university course."

He tapped his boot once, then nodded. He held up his palms, surrender. Then when he let his hands drop onto the seat again he inadvertently fluttered the university papers onto the carriage floor.

Emma leaned forward, at first merely to clean up the mess. The floor was strewn with things they needed, though not these. As she gathered them, she had to fight the urge to glance over what she took from under her toe. The classics? Is that what it said upside down? Latin? Something about Virgil? Greek? And a new-minded course on Russian literature. Pushkin. Though she had to be reading wrong upside down as she tapped them into a pile on her lap. The instructor for the course could not possibly be the Right Honorable the Viscount Mount Villiars.

She offered these, the collected provenance beneath them, in a relatively neat pile again, back across the space of the carriage. "Here."

A lot of rubbish for a sheep farmer, she thought, gathered together as they should be, among the pages of a forged provenance that Zach himself had penned.

She pulled the cloak up, tucked her hair securely under the hood, then wrapped the whole thing tightly to her shoulder around her dress, in front of her face, to hide as much of her as possible. She held this with one hand and reached to open the carriage door herself. Stuart let her step out without another word of remonstrance.

It was brisk but sunny. His house was set far enough back she didn't have to look at it. As she marched forward, though, she noted that tall, old trees overhung his property's walk. A high hedge, an evergreen of some sort, climbed black spear-points of iron, a fence that ran along the front for more than half a city block.

Chapter 15

It well may be that in a difficult hour,
pinned down by need and moaning for release
or nagged by want past resolution's power,
I might be driven to sell you love for peace,
Or trade the memory of this night for food.
It may well be. I do not think I would.

—Edna St. Vincent Millay
"*What Love Isn't,*" lines 9—14

The restaurant floor had a snug—a small secluded room for private dinner parties rather like those found at public houses, only ever so much more elegant. It said a great deal about what sort of business the room saw in that it contained a long blue velvet, button-tufted chaise and paintings of Bacchus and nymphs. It was also furnished with high draperies, drawn closed for the evening, a private liquor cabinet, and a large dining table with plump-cushioned, high-backed chairs. Just the place for a rendezvous. Though in this case, it was a rendezvous of three. Emma was to have dinner with Stuart, just "returned" from Yorkshire, and his uncle, who would—she hoped—either have the statue in his possession or have delivered it himself to Charlie, who'd send it directly to Stuart's house, if such was the case. So far, no word though.

Emma was dressed in evening attire, feathers and low décolletage, a midnight blue gown that swished as she walked, evening slippers, and sapphire earrings, paste but beautiful to her. She stared at herself in the mirror before she went down and thought, The only reason she'd ever looked this nice was to seduce someone into giving up something they would otherwise not. Deception. And she stood there wishing she were in a pair of rubber muck boots instead.

Never mind. She picked up her fan, her beaded drawstring, and a lined evening cloak and went downstairs.

Leonard had arrived early. He waited alone in tailcoat and white tie, his belly protruding from beneath a white vest. Thankfully, not two minutes later, Stuart walked into the room. He was quite the handsomest she'd ever seen him. Black evening attire, his hair slicked back—she recognized the way he combed his hair just after a bath—a white silk scarf and top hat that he removed along with his coat—always the same coat, even in the evening apparently, a favorite item, despite an inkstain somewhere near its billowing hem.

"Do you have the statue?" were the first words out his mouth, directed to his uncle.

"No. I'll take it to Mr. Vandercamp, thank you. You needn't worry. I visited him yesterday." He smiled from one to the other, knowingly. "A very capable artist."

Which meant they still didn't have the statue. But would apparently. Charlie Vandercamp could put on an impressive show.

Emma chimed in. "There's plenty of time. Did you bring the provenance?"

As Stuart laid his coat over the chaise, he reached into an inside pocket. He withdrew his pile of bills of sales and catalogs, handing them to Emma.

She set them down for the moment, taking a seat at the table. Champagne sat in a bucket by the table. "I can't stay for dinner," she said, "though thank you for inviting me." Leonard had arranged this private gathering. "I will delight in toasting your success, though, gentlemen."

Leonard looked disappointed for a moment, then popped the cork on his champagne. Its neck smoked as he tilted it to pour.

A moment later, they all three lifted their glasses. "Here's to sudden wealth, gentlemen," Emma said. "And chivalry." She drank a sip, then picked up the provenance, glancing at it.

She furrowed her brow and set her glass down. She removed the clip that held it together and glanced through it, page at a time. Once more, she marveled at the trouble Zach would go to for some things, his thoroughness. There was a French scholar's paper on finding the statue, in French, translated into English. Academic documents. Notes on the expedition that turned it up. Two different appraisals, eighty years apart, showing the statue increasing in value tenfold. Plus all the usual exhibition documents and transfers of ownership. She shook her head, frowning, about to begin: to chastize Stuart for not having the page they had intentionally, privately held back, all part of the game to make him look bad and woo Leonard to her.

"Is something wrong?" Leonard asked.

"It only goes up to 1873." She looked across the cozy table to Stuart. "It's missing the bill of sale that would make it belong to your father."

Stuart raised his eyebrows as he casually drank some wine. "Is that important?"

"The final bill of sale would make it complete. It gives you the legal right to sell it."

"Well, it's mine. No one will contest it." He threw a pull of his mouth at his uncle. "Except my uncle, and he's selling it with me."

Emma frowned, confused. "To whom does it belong?"

In unison, Leonard said, "Me," as Stuart said, "Myself."

Emma blinked at them, from one to the other. "Well, whoever you decide, you need a bill of sale that says so to offer it to a buyer—or buyers, in this case."

"You're looking at everything I have," Stuart told them. "That's all that was there or ever has been, so far as I know."

"It's incomplete."

Anxiously, Leonard asked, "Does this mean we can't go through with it?"

"Well, you can," Emma explained, "but you'll have to pay someone to, um, rather fix it."

"Pay?" Leonard was crestfallen. "Much money?"

"No," Emma said, then announced, "a few hundred pounds."

Stuart was the one to explain. "Actually, ah, Leonard and I have had a small disagreement. It went to court. Neither one of us can lay hands on much money very quickly."

Her eyebrows went up. "How are you managing then?"

"On credit," Stuart said. Which wasn't exactly true anymore on his part. All his accounts, save one, were now free-flowing—a development too recent for Leonard to know about it. It was a great burden off Stuart's shoulders and well worth the legal costs. Leonard, however, he was fairly certain, was not enjoying such good fortune. Mounting debts, overspending, and Stuart's own lawyers had seen to it.

"Goodness." Lady Emma Hartley looked from one to the other, giving them a wide-eyed, tight-mouthed look worthy of a reprimanding parent: designed to make Leonard feel ashamed, even vulnerable, for such childish mismanagement. "Well," she said, "you *are* in a bind." She pressed her lips, then shook her head, frowning.

"I *have* the statue," Leonard said, making it perfectly clear that their problem was due entirely to Stuart. "I can have it at Mr. Vandercamp's tomorrow." His expression, though, was genuinely worried. "Is the two thousand already paid out?"

She nodded. "I had to send in the policy. The money's gone. In fact, I brought you your copy." She went over to the pile of coats and scarves and produced a folder of papers, pages and pages of fine print, the top page reading in scrolling script, "Cambrick's of London." She continued, "It's a small company, but reputable and very cooperative, shall we say. Then I had to pay the fellows—Mr. Vandercamp and the jeweler and the man doing the provenances—a portion of their money in advance so they would do their jobs quickly, so they'd know what was coming and be able to expedite it. They're waiting. I have it all set up to happen as quickly as possible. I'm lining up buyers for you."

"Well, I did my part," Leonard said staunchly, even daring a sarcastic twist to his mouth that said he was always besting his nephew.

Stuart looked down into his champagne glass. He hated this, she knew, but he did it seamlessly. He quietly took the blame.

"Never mind, I'll help you," Emma said. With a disapproving click of her tongue, she asked Stuart, "Do you remember whom your father bought it from?"

"A fellow in France."

"There are a lot of fellows in France." She shook her head, then looked at Leonard: Your nephew is hopeless, which was a favorite refrain—a now uniting theme. "Never mind," she told them. "If we can't trace it, no one else can either. What was your father's name? I'll have the last bill of sale duplicated."

"Duplicated?"

As if laying it out for a child, Leonard explained, "Forged, Stuart. She's going to have her man invent that last bill of sale that you lost."

Stuart frowned, "I didn't lose it. It wasn't there." He looked at Emma. "And I don't have the money to pay for anything extra."

"I do," Emma said, jotting something down in a little book from her purse. "Don't tell anyone, but I have an account here. My company wouldn't like it. But I'll pay for it, and you can pay me back from the monies you receive. Just a little loan until this plays out. It won't be long."

"Really?" Leonard exclaimed. "My God, this is first-rate of you!" His eyes fixed on her: Here was a woman a man could count on.

"I can't just leave you fellows in this mess. What else can I do?" She shot Stuart a reprimanding look, then settled a pleasant smile on Leonard. "I won't have given you anything, if I abandon you here." She sat down, opened her purse, and took out a blank bank draft and fountain pen. On the spot, she began to write them money.

Leonard was transfixed.

As she wrote, she said, "I must say, I'd hoped my gratitude would come at less bother." She offered the wet-ink draft to Stuart—on a bogus account, of course—shaking her head. "I should have known you fellows would get yourselves into trouble. Now take this to the address here." She tore a slip of paper from the book she'd written in. "Give this fellow what you have of the provenance. Explain the problem as I've outlined it. For the extra money, he'll make it work. Tell him, if it isn't enough, to see me."

She stood, swilling the last of the champagne in her glass. "Now I must go," she said. "I'm meeting clients for dinner. I'm so sorry to rush." She smiled brightly. "But you understand." She picked up her things.

Leonard stopped her at the door, taking her hand. "My dear Lady Hartley. If there is ever anything I can do." He drew his brow down in such earnest gratitude. He put his card into her gloved hand. "Ever," he said.

Yes, as a matter of fact, there will be, Leo, she told herself. She smiled gratefully, though. "No, no, you and your nephew did me a huge favor already several days ago. I only hope that my favor in return now runs smoothly from here."

Once she'd gone, Stuart continued to play the part assigned.

"I don't trust her," Stuart told his uncle. "The money's

gone. I want to ask one of my friends in the House—Motmarche knows something about art, insurance—"

"God, no, that's all we need!" Leonard insisted. "I tell you, I saw the statue her fellow is making for someone else. It's brilliant. And I trust her completely."

Over dessert he mentioned, "I wish I knew this insurance company. I'd been hoping for Lloyd's of London."

"Oh, I know of them," Stuart told him. "They're smaller, but they have offices on Bond Street."

And so it went. If Leonard voiced doubts, Stuart assuaged them. While he attacked Emma herself, letting Leonard buoy his own trust by having to buoy up Stuart's. All the while, threatening to tell someone, the police, a Member of Parliament, a friend.

Stuart was fairly certain, though, as he picked up his coat—having suffered the longest dinner he'd ever endured—that Leonard had the picture. The nephew he didn't like was vacillating dangerously, though still expecting half the earnings of a project he had done nothing but bollix up, while the woman he was coming to adore, the dear, clever Lady Hartley deserved something more for all her generous bother.

Emma was reading in bed when movement, what appeared to be a shadow, leaped from the balcony of the suite next door onto hers. Silently, her bedroom's French doors opened, her light curtains billowing up into the room like caravan scarves, and the shadow entered. Wide-eyed, she drew back, taking the covers with her up to her chin. She fell back, one elbow onto the pillow. "W—who the—"

"Easy." The voice was familiar, even reassuring. Stuart. He came fully into definition at the foot of her bed, in the glow of her bedside lamp.

"What are you doing here?" she whispered.

"I've had enough," he said.

"Enough of what?" Then she realized he might not know:

"Stuart, Leonard was waiting for me in the reading room when I came in." She let out a soft giggle. "You did a very good job at dinner. Too good: He took the suite across the hall."

"What?"

"He doesn't trust you." She let out another breath of laughter. She told him, "You have to go. Now. I'll suggest the double cross in the morning. He's ready. I'll push him. By afternoon, if all goes well, it will be over. Your being here is dangerous."

His silhouette against the curtains absorbed what she said, then only shrugged loosely. He didn't answer for a few seconds. Or didn't in words. *He* was dangerous. His eyes dropped from hers to her mouth to her breasts, then slowly crawled back up to meet her gaze. And Emma felt like a vampire had entered the room, a bat flapping in, materializing in the form of a man, a man of supernatural beauty.

And darkness.

"I'm ti-ired"—he took his time saying it, breathing it, prolonging the syllables more for pleasure, she suspected, than any impediment—"of waiting. I wander my house alone. I can't sleep. While all I think of is you. Emma, I'm jealous of every man who comes near you. I hate the concierge for handing you your key when you come in. I envy the doorman for watching you pass each time you come or you go. And Leonard. If he so much as looks at you, I want to kill him. Then there's the dead husband, especially your dead husband, whom oddly enough I'd like to exhume from his grave so as to grind his corpse into dust."

He finished, "Who cares where Leonard is? I'm frustrated from a dozen directions, and I'm here to do something about it."

"Um"—she shook head, trying to think of an answer to this long list of complaints, while having to work at keeping her voice down—"Stuart, I've told you the danger of breaking from character—"

He let out a quiet rasp of laughter. "Does this strike you as my breaking from character?"

"You know what I mean. We're supposed to be angry with each other."

"I can work up some anger. I'll force myself on you. You can complain to him in the morning. Say yes once, then say no all you'd like and I'll know it's part of the game. I'm good at games."

Yes, she was coming to believe he was. She shook her head firmly. This was absolutely not part of the plan.

"It will work fine," he told her. "So long as he doesn't march in here and shoot me. So keep your voice down. If he asks, in the morning you can tell him I was a rascal, a cad. Which I am. That I had you against your will. Which you want. Say it. Tell me." He held out his hands, as if he'd explained everything.

"Stuart—"

"You're repeating yourself. Besides—" He lowered his voice to a whisper again. "If he's across the hall, you'll wake him. Shut up or he'll be in here—and armed." He whiffed out the lamp as he rounded the bed, nothing but moonlight and his approaching shadow that said, "In the dark"—a low chuckle—"he might miss and shoot you instead, my dear collaborator. Now collaborate a little bit here. How would you like your ravishment to begin?"

"I—I wouldn't!" She was going to add, *Don't!*

But, by then, when she opened her mouth, he was close enough to lay his finger over it and say very quietly, "*Shhhhhhh.*"

Why should this have been soothing? No reason, but it was. The sound and his smell. Oh, the smell of him, as rich as a Persian bath. And *shhhhhhh*—like a rush of steam over cardamom and orange peel and rose petals. Why did Stuart smell so blasted good?

He leaned over her, brushing his lips at her neck. He'd

been outside, his mouth, his skin cool. She found herself breathing in the warm odor of him, a sunny, spice market brought into her dark English bedroom . . . straw baskets of colorful powders . . . umber, ocher, saffron . . . cinnamon, russet, red, orange . . . fire, heat, eye-blaring waves of it that rippled the air.

He spoke softly into her ear. "I hope you don't mind, but—" A pause. Mind what? It was the pauses in his imagination that gave her, well, pause. He continued, fulfilling the gasping promise. "But I can't, *aa-ach*," he made a little vocalized sigh, "I just can't get the sight of you on that chair out of my mind. It drives me wild. So I'm going to tie you to another and have you the first time like that."

She was already shaking her head so vigorously, it was hard to shake it more. "No, I—"

"All right. Then to the bed. Turn over."

This was her choice? A chair or on her stomach on the bed? His shadow yanked at something at his neck. His damned cravat. The man was insane. "Stuart—" she started. "I'll make room." She scooted over.

"Oh, that would be nice." He was immediately pacified—then let out a little snort that said just possibly he'd been aiming more or less in that direction all along. He joined her. "Now open your legs a little. I think that would be fairly consoling."

She let out a breath, anxiety and, God help her, excitement. She wet her lips.

"Can you open your legs a little wider?" he asked, as she rise onto her elbows, moving.

"Give me a minute, will you?"

He laughed, shoving back covers, and took her ankle, pulling it all the way out to the bedpost. She had to scramble back toward him to accommodate how tight to the bedpost he wanted her foot.

She couldn't help it. "Stuart, I—I—I don't like losing control. It frightens me."

"I know. That's why I'm going to help you." He pushed her back flat, her elbows going out from under her. "Relax." He bent one of her knees so as to get her legs as far apart as he wished.

He immediately pushed her nightgown up. All the way. Till moonlight poured over her, privately bare.

Oh, God, the feeling of it. She rose onto her elbows again, lifting at her belly, watching. While Stuart knelt over her, coming up onto the bed, where he loosely tied her foot to the bedpost with his cravat. Then he looked over at her, gazed down. And gazed and gazed, as if he could indeed perceive in the dark like a bat. In the moonlight. She felt exposed, that was certain, though it wasn't enough. He reached out and cupped her pubis in his palm, then pressed.

And she arched, her head back. She let out a kind of gulp. Pleasure. He brushed his warm palm up, then down, rubbing, feeling his admittance, announcing his arrival at the door to what he wanted. Stuart, beautiful, dark Stuart, spreading her flesh with his hot fingers.

She heard his low laughter. "Clearly too tame," he murmured, "since you've given in already, you strumpet."

Oh, she had! When he slipped his finger into her, she didn't even consider stopping him, protecting herself. She opened her legs wider on her own, kicking her ankle free of the cravat—he hadn't been very businesslike about it. She held her arms up to him. "Come to me," she said in a whisper that had turned so husky she barely recognized her own voice.

"In my own time, my own way."

He slowly unbuttoned his shirt, watching her. He was bare-chested when he bent and undid the ties of her nightgown. He pushed it off all the way, up over her arms, up and up. "Lift," he said softly and took it over her head. He drew back to stare again at her nakedness. Then he settled his weight on her. His trousers were open already. It was happening so quickly. Her mind rushed. Privacy gone . . . intimacy present . . . Stuart's body, bare where it touched her.

He was thick and hard, hot, when he entered her. He made love to her, holding them both back briefly, but they were each too eager. In minutes, she was near screaming . . . coming . . . climaxing. . . . He kept covering her mouth with his, taking the sounds, his own as well, into his throat. When they finished, they were both shaking. He was laughing silently.

Then he murmured at her ear again, "Too tame. Roll over. Put your hands over your head." He drew his hands firmly down her bare back, kneading her ribs, then her waist, then her buttocks . . . dark Stuart with no rules, save one: if it sent her into rapturous shivering pleasure, he'd do it . . . his own damp body, hot, aroused, glistening in the pale light with sweat . . . in her ear, the quick, emphatic pant of breath, of exertion . . .

She was going to make sounds again . . . the urge to call out. She kept biting her lip, tightening her throat, but it was no use. The realization made her eyes wide with fear. Anyone nearby would know what she was doing. Anyone awake . . . everyone. . . .

Stuart whispered, "You're going to have the whole place, Leonard included, in here, Emma. We have to go up on the roof."

"The roof?"

"Yes. We'll walk naked there. There's a set of fire stairs at the end of the hall just down half a dozen doors. Go out, turn left. The fire stairs are over a dead-end alley. The alley is dark and a little smelly, because it's over the kitchen, but the kitchen is closed. No one will see. I looked it all over. You can count on it. It's safe."

"You *planned* that we'd walk naked to the roof?"

"Yes. I like to play. I thought it would be fun."

"Fun?" She was bewildered. "No," she whispered, "I won't walk naked down any hall to any fire stairs." She laughed at the absurdity. Safe. Oh, yes. "People would see us, Stuart. Plus, it's the dead of winter. We'd freeze to death." My goodness, the man needed a warden. Preferably someone with experience from Bedlam.

"No one will see us. It's the middle of the night. Plus there's a steam vent from the heating system or the laundry, I don't know which. But it's a pipe with a little tin hat on it. Steamy-hot air blows straight down all around it. I took one look at it and thought of you." He made his breathy, dirty laugh. "Naked," he said. "Under it. It's toasty warm—"

"Fine. Feel free. You go. I'm staying here. I'm happy here. Stuart, look at me. I'm short and, um, a little pudgy. You aren't. I understand. If people see you naked, they might secretly admire you"—she laughed again, light-headed from the insanity he continually came up with—"once they got over the shock, that is, of a naked viscount. Me, though, they'd laugh at my belly—"

The blessed man interrupted immediately. "No, they wouldn't." He added with what seemed perfect sincerity, perhaps even surprise, "Your belly is beautiful, Emma."

"Reubenesque." She snorted.

"Exactly."

"Which means *fat*, Stuart. In a nice way, of course." Didn't he see her? She was plump: fat in a nice way. Not that she didn't like herself; she did. She simply had no delusions that every human on the planet might enjoy the sight of her round and generous naked body, though she trusted that Stuart did, believed it for a fact. She told her lover, "My sweet man, I don't pretend it's entirely propriety that stops me—it's partly vanity—but I wouldn't walk naked anywhere in public, let alone down the hall of a posh hotel."

It turned out, though, she would *run* naked down one. Because in the next moment he picked her up in one arm, the bulky duvet in the other, and carted them both through her front sitting room, then out the door, with the room key in his teeth. In the hallway, he pulled the door to, thus locking them out, with her squirming and pounding and trying to crawl over him to get back inside, all in a kind of wild, silent pantomime, since God help them if anyone heard them, let alone their neighbor across the hall.

He set her down and simultaneously reached overhead to lay the room key above, on the doorjamb of the mammoth double doors to her suite. Emma stared upward for one flummoxed instant. Which was how she learned she was willing to tear down a public hallway, barefoot, starkers, and giggling, as Stuart chased after her.

On the roof, on the duvet under the steam vent, with the planets overhead, he let her scream all she wished. She screamed into the night. To the stars. At one point, with his lying atop her, he said, "Look over my left shoulder. Venus is visible tonight." Then he pulled the covers away from her, wrestling her for the duvet, as he called, "Here she is, all you Venusians"—he lifted out his arm, using it to span the celestial horizon—"and the rest of you planets out there: the most beautiful woman on Earth, spread-eagled for your pleasure!" He laughed. "At my disposal, *mm-m-m*." He bent down, nibbling, kissing her neck with his teeth, his lips, his mouth.

What a night they had. Normal? Had she actually ever thought the word to apply to herself? If so, she took it back; Emma was no longer a fan of *normal*. It seemed synonymous with *commonplace, ready-made*. When she wanted a custom life, bespoke, not bound by others' measurements. Hers were good enough. Anything else would be a sloppy fit. Thus, she entered new sexual territory, one full of imagination and dark, serious, enormously fun play. Intensely involving. As when a child, pretending scenarios of adventure. Only this was an adventure of the senses, an adventure of her own body.

While Stuart loved giving Emma more than she bargained for, then withholding what she demanded. Power. It was a wonderful game to him. In a world that was hard to affect, Emma wasn't.

He had no illusions as to who was truly in charge though:

Emma. In this game, it would always and forever be sweet Emma at the helm—and denying it, taking no responsibility for it: the perfect seat of power. She could go merrily along her way, while he, the "bully," struggled to know her, please her in ways even she didn't grasp. How to please the deep, dark Emma at the back of Emma's mind. That's who was truly in command here. He served Emma's desire. Her libido. He and this Emma were in cahoots against the vicar's widow who raised sheep—and could shuffle cards so fast they were a blur or bend and unbend the corner of the queen so quickly you never saw the movement of her agile little finger.

Stuart let his fingers glide up the inside of her thigh, such a delightful thigh—generous and substantial with muscle. He stroked the strong thigh of an active woman, thick, sturdy, shapely, its resistance against his drifting fingertips a beautiful contrast to skin softer than silk, flawless. Every inch of skin on her whole body was like that.

Emma's waist was surprisingly narrow. She had a small rib cage. Not so surprisingly, though, her belly was round: a soft, curvy little pot. She was in fact very shapely—just small and short-waisted with lovely melon-sized bosoms, so that on first glance, especially if she didn't wear a frock that cinched at the waist, she appeared pudgy. She wasn't. Or not exactly. Everything on her was firm, youthful, nicely contoured muscle rounded out with delicious, soft feminine flesh.

Her cheeks were apple-round. Her friendly blue eyes danced over them. Her nose was small and turned up. A pixie. An elf. With little cherub toes as pink and clean as a baby's.

Afterward, the two of them lay bundled up together. The vent grew less warm—perhaps the sheets were clean for the next day or the steam had been turned down inside. He huddled, extending their time as long as they could, two silly people enjoying themselves when they shouldn't be, against all the odds.

"A harem," she murmured into his neck and laughed at

last at the notion. "I can't believe you had a harem. You are hilarious, Stuart."

He laughed. At himself. "I hated men. I loved women. I wanted them all. It seemed logical to start to accumulate them."

"What an amazing life you have had." Her own seemed so prosaic beside his.

"What an amazing life we both have had," he answered. "And for neither of us is it over. How amazing life itself is." He smiled at the stars. "And here we are. You're going to let me buy you a house in London, aren't you? Your own? Or are you going to come live in mine? Whatever you wish."

"Marriage," she said, "is what I wish." Lying curled up against him made her bold. She couldn't believe she'd said it. A sheep farmer telling a viscount, if he wanted her, he had to marry her. Yet this was what she'd been raised to want, and she wasn't going to fight it. Not even after having it work out so badly once—there was nothing wrong with the concept, just the partner she'd chosen for it. "I believe in marriage," she told him. "I believe in husbands. In fidelity, loyalty. A wedding, friends, a respectful place in the village, a union before one's peers."

Which was, of course, the problem. Stuart was a peer. Her peers weren't his.

His face, lit only by moon and stars, faintly frowned as he contemplated her. He said nothing.

She recalled his telling the Stunnels matter-of-factly, "Since we can't marry of course." She recalled his saying that if a child came along, it could live as his bastard. He'd been blunt: *not that nice*, she remembered. No, they would never live as husband and wife.

She was not the answer he was looking for. He was not hers.

He nodded, a silent understanding. Then said, "I will attempt to respect your wishes. I'm trying. I'm not very good at it." He laughed, looked down into her face, stroking her hair, his palm curved to her skull. "A natural-born tyrant rehearsed from birth to rule the world." He smiled and changed the subject. "You are remarkable," he said.

"Not so much." She laughed ruefully.

He contradicted. "You told me once, 'Clowns make you laugh.' But you make yourself laugh, Emma. You see the humor and fun in life. What man could possibly not be laughing beside you?"

And something deep inside her sighed, pleased to hear him speak thus, to know he meant it. Stuart, who laughed so seldom, laughed a lot with her, she realized.

Did she make herself laugh? she wondered. Had she learned to do for herself what Zach used to, since he had given it up? Stroking Stuart's bare chest under the blanket, she wondered, Had she moved on to other needs and desires?

It seemed possible. Stuart would have intimidated her at seventeen. She could have swindled him back then, but her heart would have been beating in her throat, frantic to get away as soon as possible, because she also would have been intimidated by his power and confidence. She would never have let him near her.

"So, was he any good at anything besides swindling people?" Stuart asked out of the blue. "He must have been for you to love him? A good vicar perhaps?"

"He was middling. Good enough."

People had liked Zach. They came to him. He discharged his duties to the best of his abilities, limited though they were. He was a charming man, especially when he bordered on sober. He no doubt charmed a good many people into a better life, a better way of thinking and behaving: charmed them right into Heaven, Emma used to like to think. That Zach: turning his talents at the end to the use of God.

Did it count, she wondered, if it was not out of charity or goodness but out of sheer guilt that he did so?

Yes. She liked to think it did, that God didn't care what drove a person into goodness, that He only judged one's intentions, and Zach's intentions were flawless. No, God didn't take off points from a good deed for being, while you were at it, self-abusive. In fact, maybe it counted more, if a man had to struggle so hard for it. Zach had died with a short list of good works to his credit that took a lot of effort on his part, considering he did most of them blind drunk or between binges while enduring sweating, shivering hangovers and always, always under the pall of believing he'd let everyone down who loved him, which, most of the time, he had: a good man, if an imperfect one.

"How old was he?" The sun was beginning to show on the horizon, but Stuart lay as wakeful as she. They were both either too happy or else both a little anxious about tomorrow. In harmony, in any event.

"Fifty-one when he died," she answered.

"Fifty-one! I thought he was young!"

"He was. In the head. The most immature man I ever knew, but that could be fun, let me tell you. He was thirty-five when I met him, and more fun than a twelve-year-old with a pocketful of firecrackers. Mischief, oh, the mischief that man could get up to!"

"And he drank. You've mentioned he drank. How much? A lot."

She sighed. "He was a lush, a drunkard." There, she'd said it, betrayed her dead husband down to the last. His secret, which she'd conspired with him to cover, was out in the open, spoken.

And wasn't Stuart thrilled to hear it! "Zachary Hotchkiss was an impotent, old lush!" He laughed triumphantly, a man discharging demons, belly-laughing, cackling over Zach's many weaknesses.

Emma did indeed feel a little bit faithless for putting Zachary up for ridicule. Yet why be faithful to a man who was gone, who probably didn't deserve all this loyalty to begin with. Let him go.

Stuart needed no such encouragement. If he was letting Zach go, it was with flags and parades and confetti, a celebration. He added up more against the man: "And you were young when you met him. Then you matured, and he didn't. And he wasn't your first choice anyway. You said so."

"No, my *first* choice"—*would be an English peer I know*, which left an awkward pause she quickly bridged with—"when I first came to London as a young girl there was a sixteen-year-old boy of the world who took to signing my name to his bills. I couldn't get him to stop doing it. So I went for Zach instead."

"Zach," Stuart said, and the name sounded odd for so seldom coming out his mouth. "Oh, if you only knew how I've been *hating* him. The husband. This vicar. This paragon who tippled perhaps. When all the time he was an old drunk." He laughed, beside himself, delighted. "With nothing but a flaccid little—"

"Hey! It wasn't so easy to live with. Don't be so glad."

"I'm not glad." He shook his head, becoming serious. "It was terrible, I'm sure." Then he burst out laughing again. "Yes, I am glad. I'm thrilled. I thought you loved him."

"I did. Rather. To the extent you can love someone who just keeps raking you over the coals, over and over and over. I was always covering for him. He was never where he said he'd be. Sheep would get sick because he'd forget to feed them but tell me he had, because he didn't want me to know he'd fallen over drunk and been out cold all day—he could do things like that for days, sometimes weeks, before I'd realize. The only reason he himself didn't die from being passed out all day in the barn in dead winter was because, I think, the alcohol content of his blood was so high, he didn't freeze like a normal human being." Emma laughed. It was dry laughter, not pure humor, but it was amazing enough to hear herself laugh over the matter at all. Her sheep. She loved her sheep. *Their* sheep. And Zach could have died in the bargain. Still, remembering made her laugh now for how stupid it was, though it had been a long way from funny or merely stupid at the time. Die from the cold? By jings, she'd been ready to kill him some days herself.

"How did he carry on—write his sermons for one thing—if he was always on a bender?"

"Oh, he was very good at covering. With a lifetime of practice. Plus I wrote most of the sermons."

"You did?" Stuart's incredulity gave way to a little knowing snort. "Come to think of it, I can imagine."

She twisted in his arms to give him a look, a pull of her mouth. He was calling her sanctimonious again.

"So you wrote his sermons, and he gave them, taking credit?" he continued.

"Oh, no, it wasn't like that." She shook her head. "He'd be too drunk to write anything, but come Sunday morning, if I could shove a speech into his hand, he was willing to get up there. Cold, sight unseen, he'd read what I wrote the night before, usually in a monotone—about God and fairness or whatever moral binge I happened to be on." She laughed at herself. "Sometimes it was about the anger a woman or family could feel when one of them was drunk all the time." She grew quiet. "Anyway, he inevitably would get to some part that touched him and start to cry, then he'd take off. It was magic. He'd leave my words behind, the orator, the confidence man winning the confidence of every soul in the church. By the end, there was never a dry eye in the place. Very moving sermons, the Reverend Hotchkiss gave. Half-mine, half his own on the fly. And all, one hundred percent, full of repentance and prayers for redemption."

He looked at her. "Except your eyes. They were dry, weren't they?"

"My eyes?"

"You didn't cry over his sermons."

"Of course not." Emma blinked. Why *of course not*? And how did Stuart know? And why did he ask? "Well, I wrote the speeches. I knew what they said. And I knew Zach. I usually knew where he'd go with them."

"No one's mark," was all Stuart said. "Not even your own."

She paused, frowning into his chest. "I'd cried already over most of my complaints. I cried; I moved on. No point in prolonging the agony."

"Unless you were Zach."

"Right." She nodded and grew quiet, very still. Zach. He was in love with it. No woman could compete with his passion for pain.

Lying there, suddenly Emma was struck by a bolt of honesty. She needed it, went for it like a nun marching into the confessional. "Stuart?"

"Mm?"

"I was leaving him. I wouldn't have stayed." Here was something no living soul knew, that the vicar's wife, as much as she loved the title, the job, and the village it embraced, had been giving it up. "Just as we'd decided I couldn't stay with him, he grew ill. Very ill. I stayed to take care of him, knowing he was dying. A few days before he went, he said, 'At least I had the good grace not to survive this too long, Em. Sad that it's probably the kindest thing I have ever done for you: to die quickly.' "

Then—such a surprise!—a sob did break out. It was like a hiccup, rising up from inside, from nowhere, and bursting out without the first warning or ability to stop it. And it brought another and then another, and suddenly Emma was crying, turned into Stuart's arms, where she sobbed for ten minutes at least, maybe more, such sorrow unleashed: like a child's whose Christmas was canceled.

Where did this come from? The hurt and anger and pure unadulterated grief—though less for the man who died than for the man she'd thought Zach was at one time, the man he might have been, who saw what he did, what he was, the ambiguities, so smart, so educated, or who could pretend to be so at least—oh, Lord, and for herself. For her duping herself with regard to him. Not her own mark? Think again, dear heart. *I am my own mark. I was.* She muttered words like these against Stuart's chest as she made such a wet mess of the silky hair there, making his skin slick with her tears and the ensuing, highly unattractive runny nose that went with them.

He didn't seem to notice. He only petted her head and held her bare shuddering shoulders, two naked people. Nothing more vulnerable, she thought, than two naked bodies without the power of sexuality to make them into angels, into gods and goddesses on the Mount Olympus of desire.

"Ah, us," he said after the torrent had died down, holding her in the crook of his bare biceps and chest. "Orphans." He meant they were different—misfits, renegades—that it was harder for people like them to find a place to belong. And he was right.

Us. Orphans. All of us are orphans, Zach used to preach to the masses; these were his words, not Emma's. Orphans looking for a home. Come home, he'd preach.

Not Emma. She'd left home to find Zach. She'd left Zach, emotionally at least, because it hurt too much to stay with him. And she was leaving Stuart, though he didn't know. *Us.* What a dear word. Enough to make her melt with tenderness for her misfit viscount.

Why was she leaving him? At that particular moment, she couldn't say. It didn't feel all that wrong to stay with him anymore. Who cared what people said? Who cared that she was a little ewe in his big tup's barnyard? That he'd leave her backside with paint on it, raddled, and be on to the next? Let it happen. Let it be. Could she stand it? Could she stay till he was finished with her, wait to move on herself till then, so as to get every last little moment of happiness out of him? Sell her pride for every last precious second?

Maybe. They were damn fine seconds lately, each one as they came. So fine that maybe he wouldn't—

She caught herself. Her own mark. She was doing it again, tricking herself. No, she wouldn't do it twice. She knew who Stuart Winston Aysgarth was and where his affair with a local sheep farmer was going. No point in prolonging the agony, as she'd said. She didn't need to get there to know what was coming. Better to continue on her own way, as planned, and save them both all the explaining and sighing and maybe even crying.

Since Zach—maybe even before Zach, maybe she'd always been, maybe she was born this way—Emma was a big proponent of sparing everyone, especially herself, any unnecessary pain.

The next morning, Emma was lying in her hotel bed, half-awake beside a lightly snoring, naked viscount, when the fact of the matter dawned: She loved him. No, all those tears last night, all that crying into Stuart's shoulder? It hadn't been for Zach, or what he'd been or could have been, or even for herself and all she'd wanted and not received.

Her tears, her sobbing were for the man in her bed, the long, handsome, slightly rangy fellow, the *living* man lying beside her. She couldn't have him, and she'd cried like a child for the fact.

She ran her eyes up and down him, lingering over his sleeping penis where it snoozed, nose down, in the hollow where his leg met his groin. Her gaze traveled downward along his sinewy thigh, the sheet a tangle around it, down his bony shin to his high instep, his long, graceful toes. Stuart was on the thin side. It was why clothes looked so fine on him. He could wear layers of them and look elegant—unlike herself. And he could have been thinner still and yet handsome, because his bones themselves were beautiful.

And, like that, she recognized the depth of her affection for him. Marrow-deep. Once acknowledged, it seemed everywhere in her, welling up till her breastbone ached from it. As if her heart could literally swell too big, putting pressure against her sternum. Indeed, her tears the previous night were for this fine-looking, slightly odd nobleman whose criminal father had married for money and who would undoubtedly be courted by real titles himself, honest titles, while she, a farmer and former thief, wore nothing but pretense and clothes he'd bought her himself.

And he didn't understand that yet. He would. But he was too wrapped up in his fear that his own heart wasn't good enough, a man who truly searched himself on the matter, never satisfied with a good act alone, wanting the motives that drove it to be pure. Oh, what a creature. What a man. How she loved him.

Alas, she'd cried for having nothing better than this—love—to offer as a reason for him to stay with her forever, to keep her, to court her, to marry her: and for having learned and learned and relearned with Zach that nothing was more poignantly inadequate.

Chapter 16

During shearing, there are pressure points to keep a sheep still. Press a palm to the flank, for instance, and he will stretch out his leg.

—Emma Darlington Hotchkiss
Yorkshire Ways and Recipes

EMMA sent Leonard a note to join her for breakfast, then took a back corner table, ordered tea, and told the waiter not to bother them until she or her friend signaled they were ready.

As Leonard came up to his chair, before he even sat down, she began. "Oh, I'm so glad to get you alone for a moment. Last night—" She broke off and looked away, bringing her fist to her mouth. "Oh." She looked back briefly as if embarrassed, then down and murmured, "Last night," as if correcting herself, unwilling to say more, "last night," repeating it though to give it significance, "I—well, I thought about all you said, how Stuart truly isn't a part of us. He hasn't put in as much money. He's fearful, worried about his position in Parliament, his friends there. I'm anxious that he'll say something to someone." She sighed with a huge heave of breasts. "We must cut him out."

"Really?" Leonard's eyes all but popped out of his head with glee and greed and, alas, possibly lust. "Why?" He sat, mesmerized.

Quickly, "Because of everything you outlined last night."

"Something happened," he said insightfully, the goose—he didn't even wait for act two. Emma had been all ready to have the story pulled from her in bits and pieces. But, no, Leonard leaped to it immediately. She might as well spit it out. Looking down, reluctant in every syllable, she told him, "Last night he pushed his way into my room. He—"

"Why didn't you call out? I was right across the hall!"

She whispered across the table, "I didn't want to cause a scene. I thought I could handle him."

"But you couldn't!" he asserted. "Did he violate you?"

Lord, Leonard, let a girl get it out, will you? "Almost," she said, just to frustrate him. A near seduction was better anyway. "I was so frightened. I didn't want to make a scandal, you see? With his being your nephew." She winced sympathetically for his having such a horrible relative. "Plus, with all we have going, we don't need public attention. At any rate, I prevailed finally, after, oh—" She looked away, a woman unable to tell him all the indignities.

"After *what*!" He leaned on his palms, even rising a little over the table, on tenterhooks to know the lurid details.

She shook her head. Far too discreet to say. "Never mind. The point is, we must cut him out completely."

"You are absolutely right. You couldn't be righter. He's a menace, just like my brother, his father. We must . . ."

He blathered on. She let him rant till he was finished. Conclusion: Leonard's confidence was hers completely. He'd been converted to the game, as they said. In up to his eyeballs, his complete faith in her won. He trusted fully that he was about to become filthy rich, get back his own statue, possibly have Emma in the bargain, and betray, for good measure, the nephew, for whom he bore incredible, competitive ill will.

He made only one digression. "I'm simply aghast," he said with gentlemanly affront, "so very upset, my dearest

Emma, that Stuart would be such a cad. How did you possibly stand it? What exactly did he do—no, no, don't say. It must be painful to remember. Thank God, though, he didn't fulfill his intent. Still, I wouldn't have thought Stuart had the nerve to force his way into a lady's bedroom, no, not the ballocks for it, if you'll pardon my French."

Ballocks? What a lovely euphemism! Oh, he had them; she'd seen them. "You have no idea," she said dramatically to Leonard. "We must move immediately, because he has—well, there is no predicting him."

"Immediately?"

"Yes. You must get the statue today. Now."

"Now!" He was startled. "But the forged provenances aren't ready, and Stuart thinks—" Leonard then made the longest dawning moment of recognition—in fact, reveled in it—in Emma's history of hoodwinking men by means of their own greed and dishonor. *"A-a-a-ah,"* he said, lifting his head in wonder and appreciation. It took almost a full minute for him to get the full *a-a-awe*-someness of his esteem for her thinking out and expressed.

"Right." You clever bugger, she thought. "We flee, take everything with us, then run the game from, say, New York without him."

She had trouble getting him moving. He wanted to celebrate their good notion, their "brilliant idea," "the best effing scam ever invented by man or woman." Eventually, she had to claim her "ordeal" last night had left her too overwrought, in need of a rest—which was not entirely false, since she had been at Stuart's beck and call all night long. They'd moved to her bed, with him rousing twice more in the night. The man was amazing—they'd made love more often, more ways in one night than she had in the last ten years of her marriage. And it was divine—if a little wearing on a body unused to such things. That either one of them could walk today was little short of a miracle.

Emma didn't have to exaggerate when she rose carefully. "I'll go lie down," she said with the valor of someone holding great distress from her voice.

"You do that," Leonard told her, though his sympathy seemed a little preoccupied: He was so happy to be knifing his nephew in the back.

Leonard left to get the statue in such high spirits, she was worried he would wander into traffic and get killed before he could deliver it.

Stuart was late. Emma spent the time, till she heard his boot strides, trying unsatisfactorily to manufacture summonses for him to appear in Yorkshire, thinking to hire someone to deliver it to him, so as to send him on his way quickly once he and she were finished in London.

She'd decided, once she had done what he'd asked of her and he had his statue, she should leave as quickly as possible, and she didn't want any battles or pleas or arguments. She debated about the two thousand pounds still in her drawer. If she took it all, she could make a fresh start anywhere. It was his, but it was there. She'd decide later if her conscience would let her take it. Getting rid of Stuart long enough to go truly where he couldn't come after her seemed the main problem. That and her sheep. Her sheep and farm and cat and friends.

Yet she couldn't think how she'd ever live beneath the shadow of Castle Dunord again and be happy.

Then Stuart himself relieved her of writing her dismal, poor facsimile of a court order by arriving with a reason of his own that would take him away almost immediately after Leonard was disposed of.

Breathless, he whisked into her room and said, "They took my horse this morning. I argued for half an hour, then raced here. I'm sorry I'm late."

"It's all right. Leonard won't be back for a good forty

minutes yet, if he hurries." Of course, there was always the chance he'd never come back. Or come back with the police and arrest them both.

"Why did they take your horse?"

"The trainer's assistant pulled on its lead, apparently a bit hard, and the damned horse went for him. He tried to kill the fellow. I was able to have the judgment delayed, but the horse was taken away, impounded. I have to go argue with them as soon as we're finished. The trainer's assistant is saying he wants it put down, and the trainer isn't helping."

"I'm so sorry. If Leonard actually arrives and actually brings the statue, we'll get you out straightaway. How long can you afford to wait?"

He took out his watch. "If he doesn't come within the hour, can you delay him?"

She nodded.

Leonard came within forty minutes on the dot, huffing and puffing because he'd used the stairs. The lift was busy, and he didn't want anyone seeing him carrying a hatbox—the container into which he'd bundled his precious statue. He, of course, found Emma alone.

"Here it is," he said as he brought it in and set it on her table by the window.

A lady's pink hatbox. Almost surely Stuart's mother's. Emma couldn't resist. She opened the lid and peeked inside. There was a lot of old newspaper, which she pushed aside, then frowned down at what she saw.

It was disappointing. Small, green, and gaudy. Full of jewels. A beastly face peered up at her, inhuman, wearing a sly grin of merriment. She pulled the little thing out a moment, turned it in her hands. It was no particular animal but several, a mishmash pastiche. Indeed, it looked like an ancient deity of some sort. Powerful in its ugliness, like a Foo Dog. She laid it back in its paper, in its box, more puzzled than before she'd seen it as to why anyone would want it.

That Zach, he'd been a better confidence man than she'd known, if he'd sold this to the old viscount.

"So are we ready?" Leonard asked, his eyes alight.

Her bags sat packed by the door. She went for her coat. Stuart had to have heard his uncle come up the stairs. He and two of Charlie's people were in the room next door, waiting. From here, timing was crucial.

Indeed, as she came from the bedroom, carrying her coat, her suite doors burst back on their hinges, and Stuart pushed his way in.

He looked livid, his face red with rage—a look he'd been working on next door under Mark's and Mary's tutelage, holding his breath, patting his cheeks. The look was important, because talking had to be minimal: Anything he said had to come off his resistant tongue around a bladder of turkey blood held against his cheek. "I—I thought as much!" he proclaimed. He pointed at his uncle, then at Emma. "You—you—you—"

Leonard's face went white with shock upon seeing him. "How the blazes—"

Stuart continued, puffing his cheeks, spitting the words. "You—you take my lands,"—a grunt—"my title,"—pause—"the woman I want,"—a deep, very threatening scowl that quite frightened Emma, and she knew it wasn't real, making her back up—"then double-cross me—"

Leonard said quickly, "I-It wasn't a double-cross exactly—" He stepped backward.

Ha. Stuart went toward him. The idea was to get Stuart's body between Leonard and the statue, which worked fairly well. As Stuart bore down on his uncle, the man moved away backward, then, glancing at Emma, even sidestepped from her to the door. Good, good, Leonard.

"I'll wring your bloody—" Stuart said. He was doing brilliantly with that thing in his mouth.

"Stop right where you are," Emma said. She'd produced the small pepper-box pistol from her purse—or actually she pretended to, since she'd had it in her hand since the bedroom, because she hadn't wanted to fumble.

Leonard's eyes all but bulged from his face at the sight of the gun. His complexion grew ashen. He took a step sideways along the wall, inching toward the exit. Perfect.

"Stay where you are," Emma said.

Stuart halted. His hands raised slightly. Behind him and to his right, Leonard grew motionless, transfixed.

"We're leaving," Emma told Stuart. "Move over there." She motioned with the gun.

He laughed and let out a most believable derisive snort, then managed a whole flow of words, "You wouldn't use that little toy on me." He took a step toward her.

She fired, hoping she missed him entirely; blanks could still do some damage at close range. He bit the bladder as he grabbed his white shirt front—there was another bladder in his hand. Blood spurted from his mouth. It leaked between his fingers. A very nice job, if she'd ever seen one. Stuart stumbled, looked shocked, then keeled over, rolling at the end to get the full effect: on his back, his chest red, his head lolled to the side, blood trickling from his mouth.

Emma dropped the gun as if it were a snake and put her hand to her mouth, her heart genuinely pounding. It was far too similar to another time, another place, while the sight of Stuart on the floor was horribly disturbing.

She looked up at Leonard, a kind of true grief in her throat. "Let's get out of here."

"What?" Leonard glanced at the statue.

A hotel maid, Mary Beth in uniform, exactly six counts after the gun shot, came to the open door on cue with fresh sheets in her hands. "Ah!" she let out, pulling the white sheets to her white apron. "You've killed him!" she said: looking from Emma momentarily to fix her eyes upon Leonard.

"I—I—I—" Leonard was so speechless he couldn't get the denial out.

Emma began her most crucial minute. Mark theoretically, when Stuart left the room next door, summoned the elevator to this top floor. There were only two suites on it, hers and Leonard's. Mark should be inside the elevator, keeping the operator and elevator itself busy. Anyone who wished to respond to a commotion that was going to get louder would have to come up six flights of stairs.

She rushed Leonard, grabbing him by the arm, drawing him toward the little desk with the drawer as Mary began screaming. "Listen," she said with professional sang-froid over the noise, "It has gotten out of hand. Here." She handed him a packet, then explained what was absolute fact: "It's your ticket to New York—the ship leaves Southampton tonight. Get on the liner, whether you see me or not. I may take a different one. We can survive this. Get to New York, then make your way to a place called Wyoming. It's very remote, unpopulated, a fine place though, trust me. No one will know you. Get whatever money together you can immediately and take it to Wyoming. I'll meet you, when the coast is clear."

"But—but—" Leonard was not only terrified, he was inconsolable. "If he's dead"—he jerked a hand toward Stuart—"*I'm* the heir. I'd inherit everything, even the statue." He looked at the box containing the statue, a last, longing gaze. For he knew as well as Emma.

She said, "Murderers don't inherit. Get going."

Mary punctuated this with a loud, moaning plea for help.

Leonard gave the statue and the deadly still Stuart one last glance, then asked, "Where in Wyoming? That's an entire state."

Was it? Oh. "The capital," she said, rolling her eyes as if he should have known.

Leonard nodded. "Cheyenne."

Criminy, his geography was good. She loved university men. It was the rule, not the exception that smart men made the best marks; they usually out-thought themselves. "Right," she said. Perfect.

"I should take the statue," he said and was going to step over Stuart's body.

Mary, bless her, stopped him with a truly shrill scream.

Emma latched hold of Leonard's arm again, leaning up toward his ear to hiss vehemently, "Do you want to hang by the neck till you're dead?"

He turned, like a child in her arms, shocked recognition spreading over him visibly. Everything. Everything lost. Nothing to do but run.

She explained rapidly with infallible logic, "Everyone knows that the two of you have been arguing horribly, especially about that statue. All the bills of sale make it his. So he ends up dead, and you have it? They'll think you killed him for it or conspired at least." She put the liner ticket into his fingers, then curled them over the paper with her own hands as affectionately as she could, and sealed his fate, she hoped, with a quick kiss on his cheek. "We're both leaving it," she said. "There are other works of art, but we each have only one life. Let's go!"

She gathered up her own coat and bag—Leonard was too dazed to help. She pulled him along by his arm toward the fire escape. Sure enough, in the hall she could hear people stomping up the stairs.

Outside, at the base of the fire escape, Leonard repeated as if to make sure, "Cheyenne, Wyoming."

"Yes," Emma said and smiled radiantly. "I'll see you there, dearest." You toad of a human being.

Leonard took off in one direction, she in the other. Emma, however, only circled around to the side entrance of the hotel and went in the lobby and through the foyer-reading room, quite calm.

Cheyenne, Wyoming. May you live long and prosperously there, Leonard. And never, ever return.

Stuart, meanwhile, with Mary the maid's help, wiped off his face, yanked off his shirt, and put on a fresh one. When the hoards of curious from downstairs finally appeared, he explained that Mary had seen a mouse, but that he had dispatched it. Disappointed, people dwindled away. It took less than ten minutes.

Where after, he went calmly downstairs and out the front door of the hotel. There, he proceeded to have an argument with his coach driver—all the while, in the back of his mind, feeling he had left Emma alone to cope with a madman.

What if Leonard suddenly wanted better proof? What if he turned on her? What if he saw her go back for the statue? Stuart worried he shouldn't be running off for his own purposes. He should be helping.

And his driver agreed to an extent. "The horse, my lord, if you'll forgive my saying, ain't worth the trouble."

"I want to argue for him. I'll tell them I'll pasture him. He won't be put on the road or near people again."

"He should be put down."

"That's nonsense. We don't run him with the team anymore. I'll hire another trainer, a new one."

"You have no idea what you're talking about," the driver insisted, then realizing what he'd said, added, "with all due respect, m'lord."

Stuart blinked. The man had spoken out to him, defied him.

The coachman himself backed up, aware of what he'd done. "I'm sorry, I didn't mean—"

"It's all right." He was having a dispute with a coachman. New territory. He had to take a breath and remember it could be good. He might learn something. "Why do you think the horse should be put down?"

Encouraged, the man said, "He bit me, then tried to kick me. He veered toward the lamb, sir."

"He what?"

"He goes after small things in the road. This horse is insane."

"He was beaten," Stuart said, thinking to defend the animal to his own coachman. Why was this horse so important?

Even as he fought for the stupid animal, some part of him thought the whole thing was out of proportion.

"The others were beaten, too, with all due respect. This one is crazy."

Was it true? Was the horse past redemption? Honesty. He wanted Emma's brand of integrity, the way she faced reality. It was what he wanted for himself, though it felt faintly nauseating at the moment: to embrace the idea that his horse, a favorite prize, was exactly as he most feared—irredeemable.

No, he reminded himself. Seven horses were doing fairly well. Only one was a menace. One. Perhaps his father hadn't even made the animal thus, only contributed to it. What was reasonable to do with such an animal? What was right?

With a kind of release, he realized, he hated to lose the horse, but if the law stepped in, so be it. The horse wasn't helping. He couldn't save the damned creature without the creature's cooperation, though he'd certainly been trying.

And it didn't matter anyway in light of the fact that Emma was handling alone what they had intended to handle together. He had to go back, see if she was all right, if Leonard got off as planned. What had he been thinking? He didn't have time for a horse that wouldn't stop hurting things. Not when Emma might need him.

"All right, fine," he told his driver. "You go. Tell them I don't want him put down, that I'll pasture him, if they turn him over to me. I can't think what more to do. Tell them, then let things run their course. I've lifted the last finger to help that animal. He's on his own."

When Emma returned, thinking to collect her bags and possibly the money, she was shocked to discover Stuart, in hat, coat, and gloves, standing perfectly healthy in her front sitting room.

"Oh, you're all right," he said with genuine relief. "Did he leave? Did he take the ticket?"

"Like a baby to a bottle. So far as I know, he won't consider any other possibility but the reality we made for him till he hits New York." She shrugged, smiled. "Maybe all the way to Cheyenne."

What to do about Stuart though?

At that particular moment, there was a knock on the door. "Ah," said a constable, standing at her door. "I have a report of a commotion, screaming, someone thought perhaps even a shot. Is everything all right?" The law officer walked into the room.

Emma took one look at Stuart, waiting for her, the dear man, then a look at the law enforcement officer, and she said, "Actually, it's not. If you look in the rubbish there, you'll find a summons for this fellow here, sir, to Yorkshire. The man who served it was just here, but Lord Mount Villiars refused to go. He clubbed the man till he fled. If you look in the wastebin in the bedroom, you should find a shirt with blood on it."

Stuart stood up straight, his mouth opening a little, but his shoulders slumped. Oh, she hated this. She wanted to tell him, I have to, dear heart. I have to go, and you can't follow me.

The constable came back with the shirt and the rather poor summons she'd tossed in the bin for lack of liking her own work. It was good enough, apparently, for a London policeman. "It certainly looks legal." To Stuart, he asked, "This true, sir—I mean, your lordship? Did you refuse to answer a summons?" He looked down at it. "For contempt of court in a matter involving killing a sheep?"

Stuart blinked, then said, "No, it isn't true." Contempt of court was one of the few exceptions to the no-arrest rule.

"It sure looks incriminating," the constable said, making a suspicious, hard roll of his mouth, while eyeing Stuart.

Stuart lifted his eyes to Emma and stared steadfastly.

She grew slightly fearful. If this didn't work, God knew what he'd do. She recognized in his quiet a kind of alertness that was worrisome.

She said. "The other fellow's mistake was, Mount Villiars here said he'd go in quietly, and then he didn't."

She and the small constable both turned toward a man over six feet tall who looked larger still in a thick, wide-shouldered coat.

Emma added, "He's dangerous and tricky. You won't keep hold of him if you don't restrain him."

Stuart gawked. "Pardon me?"

She walked up beside the constable and murmured, "He knows no limits. He's strong as blazes. You'd best contain him, or be prepared to face the worst for your incaution."

"I am a gentleman," Stuart said. Then to the constable as he picked up his hat, he said, "We'll settle the matter at the station, if that's what you'd prefer." To Emma, "I'll take care of *you* later."

"You should take him in handcuffs at the very least," Emma said directly to the police officer.

Stuart's head rotated around, his mouth open, disbelief. If she had been within distance, she thought, he might truly have swatted her.

When he did lean a little, trying to make eye contact with her around the police officer, she ducked behind the constable, and the lawman thought the worst.

He took Stuart by the arm brusquely. "Sorry, sir," he said, following the words with a satisfying rattle of steel.

With a firm snap and latch of metal, Stuart's hands were cuffed behind him in a new and shiny piece of police equipment. Stuart was startled. She saw the first flick of anger in the twitch of one eye, in the rising color of his cheeks.

Whether out of fear—goodness, did his temper rise fast, his expression quickly livid—or from amusement at the turned tables, Emma would never knew. But a drop of meanness in her, she supposed, made her brush against the constable and light-finger his pockets till she came up with the key to the cuffs. Behind him, she showed it to Stuart.

Who sputtered, "She took the key."

"Who took the key?" asked the man in uniform. "The key to what?"

"The handcuffs, would be my guess. And Mrs. Hotchkiss took it. Look." Stuart nodded his head toward her, his eyes never leaving her face.

The constable patted his pocket. "Don't be foolish, sir. I have it right here."

"Check. You don't."

Emma delicately dropped it back into the pocket the second before the constable fished down into it. He brought the key out, holding it before Stuart's face. "Shame," he said. He pocketed the key again. Or thought he did, for Emma lightly held the pocket closed and let the key drop directly into her own palm.

"She took it again," Stuart said, this time resigned. He didn't show much hope of the man's believing him, only shaking his head at her, staring.

Emma stepped back toward the forced-air fireplace. She cleared her throat as she dropped the key into its wall grate, then coughed to cover its fall down somewhere into the mortared masonry, gone forever unless they wanted to tear the fireplace out.

"Good-bye, Stuart," she said as he was unceremoniously hauled out of her rooms. Good-bye, dear.

All easier than she'd thought. From here, resigned, she knew what she would do. Or thought she did. She took the envelope containing the two thousand pounds and picked up the hatbox with the statue.

So many options suddenly opened out to her. Yet only one truly appealed. At the curb outside, her bags loaded into a hansom, she gave the driver Stuart's house address. "Then wait for me, please. From there, King's Cross." The train station. She had her fifty-six pounds he'd let her keep. That was enough of a start, and it was hers.

Once inside Stuart's house, however, still empty of staff, she found things she never expected.

She discovered his library. It wasn't as large as the one in the country, but it was very like him. A large desk sat by a window. She opened the hatbox, took out the statue, and unwrapped it. Like a present, she set it squarely in the middle of the desk. Then she took from her drawstring the envelope containing two thousand pounds and stood it up against the statue. It looked quite suitable there.

That was when she noticed the wads of crumpled paper on the floor. Some, she realized, were strewn even across the far corner of the desk.

They were a lot of wadded-up notes: none good enough apparently.

She couldn't help but see what one of them said. "Emma"—the next crossed out—~~"will you do me,"~~ then, "would you please do me the honor," then a long slash that ran off the page.

Another said, "My dearest Miss Muffin, you are the only woman I have ever" then said nothing more.

While yet another said, "I love you, be my ~~life~~"—the slash ran to the bottom where he'd scribbled—"damn it anyway, wife, Miss Muffet, share my tuffet, oh, strumpet whom I love."

Your nervy bum, she thought and smiled.

There was a box by a crumpled paper behind where she'd put the statue. In it was a ring, a diamond ring. He'd picked a pretty one, but then Stuart would, wouldn't he? She let the box close with a snap.

But the notes—ah, he'd made eleven attempts. These, she gathered up, every one, taking them into her skirts, then turning toward the light by the window. She read them and read them and read them, till there was no more light, till it was dark. Then she folded them up and took them with her as she left.

The cab was gone. The driver had unloaded her bags, setting them just inside Stuart's gate. She walked away from them too. All the things he'd bought her. Good-bye.

She only got down the street, though, as far as the first streetlamp. There, she found herself sitting on the curb, where, one by one, by streetlight, moonlight, she unwrinkled her unfinished love notes, spreading them over her knees, her skirts. One after another, she pressed each out into full light, pushing at the crumples as if she could smooth out her own actions, as if she could take out the creases. She smoothed them all, one by one, till each was soft, all but limp from rubbing, then she organized them into a stack, righting the edges till they were neat—a tidy pile of misunderstood, stuttering emotion: hers, every last inchoate, only partially realized emotion, her own, only fully realized too late.

Trust. It was the one thing you always had to do in the game. Trust your partner. Never doubt him.

It had never occurred to her to trust Stuart to do this: to make her happy. To flout everything else, even his own desire for the statue, and think of her. Why not? Where had her faith in others, in a special other, gone? Had she ever had it? Had she ever believed a worthy man would find her, want her, seek her out in favor of all others, against all objections, even her own, and ask to have her for his own for life?

If she ever had, she'd given it up somewhere. She'd lost it, lost him. Locked him out and, literally, thrown away the key.

She hiccuped once as she stared down at her would-be love letters, then folded herself over them, pulling them to her belly as she put her arms between her knees. She buckled over into this lapful of skirts and papers and arms and despair for herself. She cried like that, rocking, her face in her knees, hugging her own shoulders, bawling for half an hour, perhaps more. She wasn't sure.

She only knew that somehow, sometime after, she made her way back to the hotel. The doorman helped her get another cab. Then she slumped back in her seat and jostled along toward the train station. She didn't know when she bought the ticket or how she got on the train. She only knew it was a slow one that stopped at every blessed town along the way. All in the dark. Daylight seemed to take a lifetime in coming, and, when the sun finally did glint under the blind of her second-class compartment, it found her dazed and empty.

And alone. Perfectly, absolutely, forever alone. By her own doing.

A man's character is his fate. Touché. So was a woman's. She would never want any man less than Stuart. And he had been a miracle. A miracle she'd missed for lack of trust. What cruel shortcoming in herself had made her forget to have confidence in the most trustworthy man she'd ever known?

Stuart's lawyers did not have him free till five the next morning. Of course, he raced to the hotel, but was not surprised to discover that Mrs. Hartley had checked out. He was in less of a hurry to go home. He thought he knew what to expect: nothing. He expected the place possibly ravaged, a search for more money or other valuables. Perhaps the larcenous Mrs. Hotchkiss would even take the statue, since it looked fairly authentic and had its papers of authenticity.

What a surprise to recognize it, even before he'd lit the lamp, in the faint light of dawn where the figurine sat on his desk.

He lit the gas lamp and picked up the small statue, holding it toward the window, the morning's rising light.

La Truie qui danse. The Dancing Beast. He touched a grinning female chimera: head of a pig, tail of a dragon, with an undulant skirt of snakes that swirled to reveal dragon shanks poised with unaccountable grace on emerald cloven feet. It was an odd little piece, encrusted rather convincingly with a small fortune of gemstones. The dragon tail was an imbrication of emerald scales, so many, overlaid one on the other, each cut in multiple facets till it became a shimmer of every imaginable shade of green, from pale leafy green to deepest, darkest moss. This came up from the front of the animal till the pig breast became a deep swell of dark jade.

Green. A little, green, grotesque statue. Its snake skirts were beads of many crystalline green stones, wired together in a spine of green gold. Green gold filigree elsewhere.

Then the startling discovery: Amidst all this sparkle, in tiny holes in the pig's ears, there they were: the earrings. An intricate, coherent piece of the whole. The pig-dragon wore Stuart's mother's dangling, gypsyish earrings of emerald and peridot and green tourmaline. When he picked the odd little creature up, its earrings made the little *clack* he remembered: his mother's only vanity.

Ana Aysgarth's favorite earrings. To wear them, she'd borrowed them from the gay Dancing Beast, the creature that pranced on its hooves, enjoying itself, despite its mythic, fire-breathing ugliness.

Staring at them, it was not the heartbreaking self-awareness that pierced Stuart first. Rather it was the joy in the pig's expression, its posture that seemed to toss its pig head in simple insouciance: I don't give a damn what I look like; I'm dancing.

He had never thought that, for even a second, his mother had known this variety of happiness. Or could even dream of borrowing such power or autonomy as might be had by a fire-breathing chimera. So restrained, so obedient, so relentlessly dutiful, biddable, proper, she was. Yet now a pure, devil-may-care joy seemed plausible, at least somewhere in his mother's imagination. And a stab of relief, such relief, cut through him. Along with something else. Something dearer, sweeter.

Because his earliest memory of his dotty, lonely mother was of her wearing these earrings while building castles from matchsticks on the floor of his nursery with him.

Fine, he had the statue. He was glad. But at what cost, he didn't know. It all depended on how difficult it was to find Emma again.

Chapter 17

You can't cheat an honest man.

—A saying among confidence men, circa 1900

SHE arrived home, her farm, in the afternoon, to find the place not too bad off. Her neighbors and Stuart's people had done a good enough job. And John's ram had been brilliant: Marigold looked to be pregnant, a cherished and unforeseeable blessing since the ewe was old—her raddling hadn't taken last time. All five of Emma's other ewes were also showing signs. She went about that afternoon looking under sheep like a pervert, happy with all the dark, purple-pink tissue at their hindquarters.

New lambs in the spring.

Ah, what hope, she thought, as she settled in that very first night. Yet she didn't sleep. She lay awake all night thinking, You have done the right thing. All the way around. Congratulations. You are hereby an adult. A full-grown woman.

Living alone. Because you're in love with the wrong man. Whom you betrayed.

Her first morning back was cool, but lovely. Emma rose with the sun, knowing all she had to do: her old chores. In fingerless wool gloves, she made her tea, then warmed her whole front room by baking scones in the oven, with old flour but new sultanas that she bought in the village. Then she put on her plaid shawl and walked out her back door to eat and drink her breakfast in the sun.

And there was that damned castle, up on its hill. Empty. The turrets of Castle Dunord peered between treetops from above, its distant arching windows looking ominous, eternal: like blind eyes that did not see her, so far above a little village, looking down blankly on all that could not be. Emma sighed. Could she live under Dunord? In its shadow?

She was going to try.

Did she miss its owner?

She closed her eyes. Oh, only with every breath she took.

It would get better. Like having a stitch in one's side after a long, hard run, she decided. One simply kept moving till the pain eased up. When she opened her eyes again, though, her gaze connected to the skyline of Stuart's turrets, and the pain of his absence all but doubled her over. She jerked her gaze down, purposefully staring across the dale, seeing nothing. Why look up? When had she started doing that? Looking up? Putting on airs? Pretending she was other than what she was, a thirty-year-old quasi-sheep farmer, so distrustful of life she'd betrayed one of its rarest gifts: love.

Her dissatisfaction with herself didn't get better. Over the next several days, it grew so bad she could hardly move, hardly function. Finally, in the middle of the night, she decided what was required was action on her part. She had to make amends somehow, do something for Stuart, something tangible that expressed her distress over hurting a man who had a history of those closest to him treating him miserably. Yet what did one do for a rich, powerful viscount?

A horse. His horse team was so important to him, while his eighth animal was unusable. If she could find him a replacement, he could run his team of eight again. Oh, if only she could find one that came close to matching.

Quite surprisingly, in relative short order, the local trader who specialized in fine animals, indeed was offering one that sounded good. When Emma went to she it, she was elated. It was a coaching stallion with beautiful white socks up its legs, the perfect creature! The only thing was, it cost more than she could ever have dreamed a person could pay for a horse.

She laughed to John Tucker over the price. "A person could ride my entire farm for that kind of money."

Which was how the idea came to her. The next day, she sold John Tucker her farm. He couldn't pay cash, but he, herself, and the horse trader in Ripon came to an agreement. John arranged that Emma would stay with his sister, helping her and her aging husband out for a modest wage, while John made land payments to her—payments that would go straight to the horse trader in exchange for the animal, the land as collateral. The amazing horse became hers. Or Stuart's. She wrote a polite letter, saying merely that she hoped the creature suited him and would fill out his team again. Please accept it and ask no questions.

She made arrangements for the animal to be delivered to him in London the following week and indeed felt much better for her efforts.

Maud and Pete Stunnel. She took up residence at their house, where on clear days she could still see the castle, but only distantly. On the very day that the horse and letter were to be delivered to Stuart in London, Emma was outside, helping Maud sort sheep into lambing groups according to when lambs were expected. The ewes were near lambing. First, the older crossbred ewes would give birth, then the younger fell ewes, then the shearling ewes. Spring in Yorkshire, on its way, was a time of renewal, new generations, new hope.

She and Maud looked up at the noise. The racket brought them into the house, then Emma picked up her step till she was running. What was that din? That familiar, horrible clatter? She reached the front drop, opened it, stepped through it.

And there, from the stoop, she saw a team of six shiny

black horses, heads bobbing in unison, galloping shoulder to shoulder, quite nearly at the exact same breakneck speed as last August, pulling behind them a large, dark, barreling, recognizable coach. It trundled toward her for all it was worth. Then as it neared the front gate—astounding—the noise grew worse: a lot of annoyed, resisting, complaining animals, clopping, cobbling hooves, many *whoa*s and *hey*s with much lurching, creaking of springs, a lot of jangling tack. The coach came to a complete stop right there at the end of the Stunnels' winter-dead vegetable patch, a big, fancy, crested vehicle with six shiny, black coaching stallions, all of them stomping and neighing out warm blasts of visible breath into the Yorkshire February air.

Emma was transfixed. Behind her, Maud murmured, "I have something in the kitchen that needs tending." While before her, a footman dropped down from the back of the vehicle, came around, and opened the carriage door. Stuart stepped out, no coat on a sunny brisk day, though he took his hat off. Emma could hardly grasp it.

She feared the worst as she greeted him by calling, "Have you come for revenge then?"

Without answering, he sailed up the Stunnels' garden path, between dormant rosebushes pruned to nothing and rows of empty bean trellises, he himself looking strikingly alive, his frock coat flapping against his striding legs. Vigorous, teeming with good health and purpose. He took the two steps up to the front stoop in a single leap, bouncing on his feet.

"I've given revenge up. I've come with a future in mind, not a past," he said and pulled flowers from—yes, one rubber muck boot. He held another, a mate, under his arm. Red roses protruded from the one he offered. Her favorite, even though they were trite, the sort of predictable flowers everyone bought to express a whole range of predictable sentiments.

She stared at them, then braced her fists on her waist,

blocking the doorway. "They didn't hold you in jail too long, I take it?"

"No," he said, smiling.

"How did you know where I was?"

"I threw my weight around. Brute power. I'm very fond of it. Did you honestly think you could keep me away very long?"

"I sold my farm."

"I know." He nodded, frowning. "But you didn't go very far away. I'm glad."

She shrugged. "Not enough money to do much."

"You could have had it. You held two thousand pounds in your hand." He pressed his mouth, then twisted it sideways into contemplation.

Why was he here? she wondered again. "Are you angry about being arrested?"

He seemed to think about the question, as if truly mulling it, then said, "No."

"Why?'

"I killed your lamb. I'm fairly sure. I'm sorry. I didn't know. I didn't mean to. I wasn't driving the coach." He added, "Please accept my apology and these flowers and new boots." He held his offerings out again.

She didn't take them. "You should sack your driver, you know. He drives too fast." Then she realized, "You're not in London. I sent you something. You're supposed to be there to receive it."

"What?"

"A horse, so you can have eight sane ones."

"Well, I'm here instead, because I want you," he said.

"Yes, you and the British government. For fraud. None of you will ever have me though."

Still, to see Stuart Aysgarth standing there at her own front door. Just to set her eyes on him again—it really was he! Not a dream. The sight made her eyes want to water. He was such a handsome fellow. Tall. The sun gleaming in his dark hair. His large, beautiful-sad eyes with the darkest, most dramatic circles she had ever seen under them, as if they said, *I can't sleep without you. I'm up all night. Please.*

Rubbish. She told him, "I always take up with outlandish men. I'm not having another one."

"Ouch." He winced. Then laughed where he stood in the shade of the meager three-foot-wide portico. "All right. I'm a little outlandish," he admitted and held out his hands, his bootful of red, leafy flowers in one of them: as if helplessness against his own nature was a form of pleading his case. "Only a *little*!" he insisted. "And in an excellent way much of the time."

She pressed her lips together, feeling flummoxed, confused; she didn't dare hope.

He said, "Perhaps it simply hasn't been the *right* outlandish man. Do we men all have to be perfect?" He pointed his finger—"What if we were?"—then wagged his finger at her, a stuttering finger trying to make a cogent point. "Then what would you do? You aren't so perfect yourself, you know, Miss Muffin. How would you keep up with us then, hmm? Tell me that."

She eyed him, raising one eyebrow, while she lowered the other one—a trick she'd learned from him. What did he mean, *she* wasn't perfect?

He immediately saw his mistake. "I take it back. You are perfection personified, my dearest. A princess. A jewel. An example of everything exquisite known to comprise female form and grace." Then he laughed.

He didn't mean it! He wasn't serious! "Outlandish," she muttered.

"In love with you," he said. "In love. Insane, upside-down-on-my-head in love. With the most splendidly imperfect woman on the planet. I wouldn't have you any other way. Your imperfections are juicy, delicious, wonderful bits to you." He laughed again, a smart aleck if ever she heard one: "Some of them are your best points."

Did she like this? Well. No. All right, yes. Or at least the "in love" part.

He was in love with her?

"You aren't," she said bluntly.

"What?"

"In love with me."

"Did I bring you flowers?" He added, smiling, "*And* muck boots?"

He had.

Then the indictment: "Did I not even consider rescuing my horse in London, when I was more worried about you, which by the way, they shot. I lost my horse." His voice broke. He looked down.

"Oh, Stuart. I'm so sorry." His crazy horse. His crazy horse was dead. She tried to help. "He wasn't right, that animal. He was bad, he was sick. He hurt things."

"He was beaten; *he* was hurt."

"You can't save all the things your father tried to destroy."

"M-my father," was all he could get out.

Emma's throat grew tight for him. "I—I—ah. I bought you a beautiful new horse to be delivered today. It matches so well, you won't be able to credit it. You'll have eight again!"

"No." He shook his head. "I sold my extra horse to some woman in—" His brow went up. "Oh, dear. To some woman in Yorkshire. You?"

She frowned. They both realized at the same moment, then laughed together.

After a moment, he looked at the ground and explained slowly, "My driver tells me that whenever he pulled the reins tight, the one horse went wilder than the others. He—he thinks it went for the lamb, in-in—" He couldn't get it out. She waited, patient. "In-in*tend*ing to hurt it." He compressed his lips taut, his expression sad, so sad, as he tried to explain. "It-it was a kind of mistake, you see. When the reins pulled tight, a pressure the horse hated, it mistook the lamb for the enemy somehow. He thought the horrible control he was subjected to, the rein, h-had to do wi-with the lamb."

"Yes," she said with wonder. It occurred to her: "Like your father."

His face filled with surprise, yet he nodded. Then he looked up. His head stayed like that a long minute, his eyes fixed on a cloud in the sky perhaps. Or a man balancing an overflow of tears he refused to shed.

They were quiet on the stoop for a moment. Quiet for a father who mistook whatever happened to be in his path for the enemy. The lambs of the world. No, Stuart couldn't save everything his father had gone after.

After a moment, Stuart recovered and continued. "Did I bring roses and muck boots?"

She laughed and held out her hands, receiving his gifts. "Thank you." She drew her presents to her chest.

"Did I say 'I love you'?" he asked.

She blinked. "I don't think so. Not those precise words."

"Well, I do."

Then he dumbfounded her. "Did I bring you an engagement ring so heavy that your hand will shake when you wear it?" He hesitated. "Only I'm afraid to show it to you, because now it seems excessive and I'm not even certain ya-yo-o-ou'll take it?"

Oh. Bless his heart. Her own melted. "Oh, Stuart." Did he do such a thing? Bring a ring? To a sheep farmer? Then stutter over it? A man who had worked most of his life around not stuttering—or at least learned how to make it his song? Oh, Stuart, don't let me do this to you.

But he only smiled. While her throat tried to close. He bowed his head and looked down, as he sheepishly bent his elbow. He dug his hand into his coat pocket.

In the sunlight, the ring was glorious. "Ah, coo, will ye fancy that?" she said, when he dropped it into her palm. It was heavy, with a diamond the size of a pea. The ring itself had a white ribbon tied through it, connected to a dangling little note, a slip of paper.

The note read, in Stuart's beautifully florid script:

Untie me. Let me up. Wear me. I love you. Untie my heart. I will never be right without you.

Six Tips to Planning the Perfect Wedding...

WITH A LITTLE HELP FROM AVON ROMANCE

Everyone knows that a great love story ends with "happily ever after" . . . and that means a perfect wedding. But before you get to the Big Day, you have to iron out the details . . . picking out a dress, getting the right flowers.

Oh, and there's that little matter of finding the groom.

Now, take a sneak peek at these Avon Romance Superleader heroines . . . as created by these talented authors—Cathy Maxwell, Victoria Alexander, Susan Andersen, Jennifer Greene, Judith Ivory and Meggin Cabot—go about finding that husband-to-be.

TIP #1:
IT HELPS IF YOU GET ENGAGED TO THE RIGHT PERSON TO BEGIN WITH.

When Anthony Aldercy, the Earl of Burnell, has the bad manners to fall in love with someone other than his fiancée, he does everything in his power to change his own mind! But pert, pretty Deborah Percival unexpectedly captures his heart in

The Lady Is Tempted

BY NEW YORK TIMES BESTSELLING AUTHOR

CATHY MAXWELL

July Avon Romance Superleader

He turned—and for a second, Deborah couldn't think, let alone speak.

Here was a Corinthian. Even in Ilam, they'd heard of these dashing men about Town. Every young man in the Valley with a pretense to fashion aped their casual dress. But the gentleman standing in Miss Chalmers's sitting room was the real thing.

His coat was of the finest stuff, and the cut fit his form to perfection . . . as did the doeskin riding breeches. His boots were so well polished that they reflected the flames in the fire, and the nonchalantly careless knot in his tie could only have been achieved by a man who knew what he was doing.

More incredibly, his shoulders beneath the fine marine blue cloth of his jacket appeared broader and stronger than Kevin the cooper's. And his thighs were more muscular than David's, Dame Alodia's groom's. Horseman's thighs. The kind of thighs with the strength and grace from years of riding.

He was also better-looking than both Kevin and David combined.

He wasn't handsome in a classic way. But no one—no *woman*—would not notice him. Dark lashes framed eyes so blue they appeared to be almost black. Slashing brows gave his face character, as did the long, lean line of his jaw. His lips were thin but not unattractive, no, not unattractive at all.

Then, he smiled.

A humming started in her ears. Her heart pounded against her chest . . . and she felt an *unseen* pull toward him, a *connection* the likes of which she'd never experienced before from another human being.

And he sensed the same thing.

She *knew*—without words—that he was as struck by her as she was by him. The signs were there in the arrested interest in his eyes, the sly crookedness of his smile.

Miss Chalmers was speaking, making introductions, but the sound of her voice seemed a long distance away. ". . . Mrs. Percival, a widow from Ilam. This is our other guest, a great favorite of mine, Lor—"

The gentleman interrupted her, "Aldercy. Tony Aldercy."

TIP #2:
REMEMBER, THIS IS YOUR DAY TO BE TREATED LIKE A PRINCESS . . . AND IF YOU ARE ALREADY A PRINCESS, SO MUCH THE BETTER!

Women never said no to Lord Matthew Weston, but he never met one he'd wanted to say, "I do" . . . until he impetuously married a beautiful woman named Tatiana. So imagine his shock when he discovered his marriage bed empty, his bride gone . . . and his wife was of royal blood!

Her Highness, My Wife

BY **VICTORIA ALEXANDER**

August Avon Romance Superleader

"If you are to be my wife, you are to be my wife in the fullest sense of the word."

"But surely you cannot expect me to—" Tatiana caught herself and stared. "What do you mean *fullest sense of the word*?"

"I mean my wife has to live on my income." Matthew's grin widened. "It's extremely modest."

"I see." She bit her bottom lip absently. There were benefits to being in close quarters with him. He certainly could not ignore her presence in a—she shuddered to herself—cottage.

"And I have only one horse and he is better suited to pull—"

"A carriage?" she said hopefully.

"It's really a wagon." He shook his head in a regretful manner she didn't believe for a moment. "In truth, more of a cart."

"To go along with the shack, no doubt." She would put up with his living conditions, castle or cottage scarcely mattered as long as she was with him.

"And there will be no servants," he warned.

"Of course not, given your modest income," she said brightly. "Is that it then? Your conditions?"

"Not entirely." He studied the apple in his hand absently.

"Really? Whatever is left? You do not mean—" She widened her eyes in stunned disbelief. "You cannot possibly believe—" She wrung her hands together and paced to the right. "Surely, you do not expect that I—" She swiveled and paced to the left. "That you—that we—" She stopped and turned toward him. "That you think I would— Oh Matthew, how could you?" She let out a wrenching sob, buried her face in her hands, and wept in the manner of any virtuous women presented with such an edict.

"Good Lord! Your Highness. Tatiana." Concern sounded in his voice and she heard him step closer. "I didn't mean—"

"You most certainly did." She dropped her hands and glared at him. "*This* is exactly what you wanted. Was there a moment of regret over your beastly behavior?"

"There is now." He glared down at her but held his ground.

"Ha. I doubt that. Your intentions with this and every other of your ridiculous conditions was to shock me and, furthermore, to put me in my place. These stipulations of yours, especially the last one." She shook her head. "Did you really believe for a moment I would fall to pieces at the idea of sharing your bed? I am not a blushing virgin. I have been married."

"To me." His eyes narrowed dangerously. "Or have I missed another marriage or two?"

"Not yet," she snapped. "But the day is still young."

TIP #3:
THE PROOF IS IN THE KISS!
IF THAT FIRST KISS IS AT THE ALTAR,
YOU REALLY ARE IN TROUBLE . . .

Tristan MacLaughlin is sent to protect vulnerable dancer Amanda Charles from the crazed man who is stalking her. At first Amanda thinks MacLaughlin is overbearing—and overwhelming—but she soon discovers the unleashed passion in his arms.

Shadow Dance

THE CLASSIC ROMANTIC NOVEL

BY **SUSAN ANDERSEN**

September Avon Romance Superleader

Tristan yanked her forward and kissed her. And, if before that instant Amanda had thought he stood aloofly by and observed life from the sidelines, she discovered then that she was mistaken. For there was nothing detached about his hungry mouth moving over hers, nothing aloof about the powerful grip of his arms on her back as they pressed her forward into the heat of his body, or in his blunt fingers, tangled in her hair, grasping her skull. There was nothing detached at all, and his intensity laid to waste her powers of reasoning.

He had pulled her to him so quickly, she had hardly had time to react. Automatically, she raised her hands to push him away. But, for just an instant, she was caught up in the contrast of how things as they appeared to be and as they actually were could be so devastatingly different.

For instance, MacLaughlin's mouth appeared hard and stern, but, Lord help her . . . it was soft. Strong. Hot. But not hard—not hard at all. The only remotely harsh element of his kiss was the heavy morning beard of his unshaven jaw, abrading the tender skin of her face.

Having hesitated for even that brief an instant, she forgot exactly to which it was she had been going to object. Being manhandled again, maybe? Um. Something like that. She didn't remember and she didn't care. Any objection she might have raised was swamped beneath a wave of sensation.

Tristan's mouth kept opening over Amanda's. Restlessly, he slanted his lips over the fullness of hers. When she didn't open to him immediately, he raised his head, stared into her eyes for a moment, and then came at her from another direction, using the hand in her hair to tilt her face to accommodate him. He widened his mouth around her lips and then slowly dragged it closed, tugging at her lips.

She didn't even think twice. Amanda's lips simply parted beneath his, and Tristan made a wordless sound of satisfaction deep in his throat.

His tongue was slow and thorough. It slid along her bottom lip and explored the serrated edges of her teeth. Releasing his grip on her head, Tristan pulled her closer into the heat of his body, moving his pelvis against her with suggestive need. His tongue rubbed along hers. Nerves Amanda hadn't even known she possessed flamed to acute, throbbing life. Her tongue surged up to challenge his and she arched against him, sliding her arms up to wrap tightly around the strong column of his neck, plunging her fingers into his crisp hair. She was aware of every muscle in his body as he pressed against her.

Murmuring soft sounds of excitement, she raised up on tiptoe, lifting her left leg with an agility borne of years of dancing, to hook the back of her knee behind his hard buttock.

Tristan groaned and kissed her harder, aroused nearly to a frenzy. Meaning only to lean her against a support, but misjudging the distance from where they stood, he slammed her up against the wall of the apartment and rocked against her with slow, mindless insistence. One large hand slid slowly up the leg locked around his hip, stroking from knee to thigh, pulling her closer into him before it eased beneath the high-cut leg of her leotard to grip her firm, tights-covered bottom with wide splayed fingers. "Oh, lass," he breathed into her mouth, and then, unable to bear even that slight separation, he kissed her harder, his mouth hungry and a little rough against hers.

Amanda tightened her grip around his neck and kissed him back, following his lead exactly.

He was frustrated by the tights and the one-piece leotard she wore. She looked smashing in it, but it protected her flesh from invasion like a high-security alarm system.

TIP #4:
MAKE SURE YOU AND THE GROOM SHARE COMPATIBLE HOPES AND DREAMS . . . REMEMBER, THERE'S MORE TO MARRIAGE THAN A GOOD CHINA PATTERN!

Susan Sinclair is strong, capable, and can deal with anything—after all, everyone tells her so a million times a day! Surely she can handle a man like Jon Laker . . . even if she melts into a puddle every time he comes around. After all, she "got over" Jon a long time ago—didn't she?

The Woman Most Likely To . . .

BY **JENNIFER GREENE**

October Avon Romance Superleader

When Jon realized his heart was beating like an overheated jackhammer, he stopped dead, determined to head back home and forget this nonsense. If Susan was in the area, then she was staying at her mother's. He could call her. And if she'd wanted him for something critically important, she could have—and would have—said something on the spot. It was stupid to think that he had to track her down this second . . .

He was halfway to the marina, when he spotted her. Her hands were in her pockets, her hair kicking up in the breeze; she was ambling near the docks, toward the beach, heading for nothing specific, as far as he could see.

He charged forward until he was within calling distance. "Suze!" An out-of-breath stitch knifed his side. His shop keys were still dangling from his hand. "Susan!"

She turned the moment she recognized his voice. From that angle, the sun slapped her sharply in the eyes, where he was in shadow, so he could clearly see how she braced, how she instinctively stilled. "Honestly, Jon, you didn't have to run after me."

"I figured I did. It's not like you go to the trouble of tracking me down more than once in a decade. What's wrong?"

"Nothing."

He wasn't opposed to wasting time on nonsense. But not now, and not with her. "You didn't show up at my place to discuss the weather."

"There's definitely something we need to talk about together. But it's not an easy subject to spring into. I can't just . . ."

"Okay. So. Let's sit somewhere."

"Not *your* place."

God forbid she should trust him after twenty-two years. As if he'd jump her if he caught her alone . . . well hell, come to think of it, he had. But only a few times. And only when she'd wanted to be jumped. And that hadn't happened in a blue moon because they'd both spun out of control the instant someone turned the heat up—and then they'd both been madder and edgier than fighting cats afterward.

Even the best sex in the universe wasn't worth that.

It came close, though.

TIP #5:
A FINE TROUSSEAU IS AN ABSOLUTE "MUST HAVE" FOR ANY PROSPECTIVE BRIDE. AND IF MR. RIGHT GETS A PEEK A LITTLE BIT BEFOREHAND, SO MUCH THE BETTER!

Stuart Aysgarth might be the Viscount of Mount Villiars—and he might consider himself extremely *important—but that doesn't mean he is above the law . . . and Emma Darlington Hotchkiss is determined he honor his debt to her. And nothing—not even seduction—will change her mind!*

Untie My Heart

BY **JUDITH IVORY**

November Avon Romance Superleader

There was nothing innocent in how his finger continued over the curve of her jawbone to her neck, taking the hem of her dress down her tendon all the way to her collarbone. His eyes followed his finger to the hollow of her throat, where at last he hesitated, paused, then—thank goodness—stopped. She shivered involuntary, tried to speak, but ended up only wetting her lips, dry-mouthed.

The path his finger had traveled left a tiny, traceable impression down her neck to her clavicle, a trail so warm and particular it seemed traced by the sun through a magnifying glass.

"You," he said finally, then paused in that soft, slow way he had that was mildly terrifying now under the circumstance, "are a very hard woman to frighten, do you know that?"

She blinked up at him. "I can assure you, you're doing a good job. You can stop, if that was the goal."

He laughed. A rare sound, genuine, deep, though she definitely didn't like his sense of humor, now that she heard it. For a second more—with him leaning on both arms, his shoulders bunching, pulling at his shirt where they held his weight—he hovered over her, surveying her in that very disarming way again. Then he stood up completely.

Good God, was he tall. From her angle, his head seemed to all but touch the ceiling.

He stared about them, perplexed for a moment, as if he'd lost track of what he was doing, then seemed to remember. And he backed up.

To take a gander at his handiwork, it seemed. Over her knee she watched him withdraw two feet to the window sill and sit his buttocks onto it, his back flattening the lace curtains. There, he crossed his arms over his chest, tilted his head, and viewed her incapacitation from this new angle.

He then said, "Do you know, I think I could do anything to you, absolutely anything, and there would be nothing you could do about it."

"What a cheerful piece of speculation," she said, a little annoyed.

"Save complain. Which you do very well."

She shut her mouth, advising herself to take John's advice and be humble. Or at least quiet.

Mount Villiars laughed again, entertained by his own iniquitous turns of mind. "And whatever I did, afterward, I could hand you over to the sheriff, and, even complaining, he'd just haul you away." The sarcastic jackanapes shook his head as if in earnest sympathy. "Such is our legal system and the power behind the title of viscount. I love being a viscount. Have I mentioned that? Despite all the trouble that arrived with my particular title, I find it's worth fighting for. By the way," he added, "I like those knickers."

TIP #6:
IF THE NEWSPAPERS ARE TALKING ABOUT THE "SURPRISE WEDDING OF THE YEAR," MAKE SURE IT'S YOURS!

Lou Calabrese never dreamed she would be left behind when her boyfriend ran off with a bimbo! And when she is accidentally stranded with that same bimbo's sexy, stubborn Hollywood hunk of an "ex" she learns that sometimes the surprise wedding of the year turns out to be your own!

She Went All the Way

BY **MEGGIN CABOT**

December Avon Romance Superleader

"Sorry," he said. "I don't really watch movies all that much."

For a moment, Lou forgot she was the victim of an attempted murder and a helicopter crash, and gaped at Jack—Jack, the moviestar—as if he'd just done something completely out of keeping with his manly image, such as order a champagne cocktail or burst into a rendition of "I Feel Pretty."

"You're an *actor,*" she cried, "and you're telling me you don't really watch movies all that much?"

"Hazard of the trade," Jack said lightly. "The magic of Hollywood doesn't hold much allure when you know all the secrets."

Lou shook her head. Oh, yes. They were definitely in Bizarro World now. No doubt about it.

"Maybe," Jack ventured, as if he hoped to change the subject, "we should build a fire."

"A fire?" If he'd suggested they strip naked and do the hula, Lou could not have been more surprised. "A *fire?* What do you think *that* is?" She pointed at the burning hulk of metal a dozen yards away. "What, you're worried when they start looking for us they won't be able to spot us? Townsend, I don't think they're going to have any problem."

"Actually," he said, in the politely distant tone he reserved, as Lou knew only too well, for incompetent waiters and crazy screenwriters, "I was thinking a fire might warm us up. You're shivering."

She was, of course. Shivering. But she'd hoped he wouldn't notice. Showing weakness in front of Jack Townsend was not exactly something she wanted to do. It was bad enough she'd been unconscious in front of him. The last thing she wanted was for him to think she was afraid . . . or worse, uneasy about their current situation—that she was stuck in the middle of nowhere with one of America's hottest Hollywood idols. She had had more than enough with Hollywood idols. Hadn't she lived with one for eight years? Yeah, and look how *that* had turned out.

She was certainly not going to make that mistake again. Not that she was about to do anything as foolish as fall in love with Jack Townsend. Perish the thought! So what if he seemed to be concerned about her physical comfort, and had saved her life, and oh, yes, looked better in a pair of jeans than any man Lou had ever seen in her life? *Are we having fun yet?* Right there was reason enough not to give him the time of day, let alone her sorely abused heart. Besides, hadn't he had the very bad taste to, until recently, date Greta Woolston? There had to be something wrong with a man who couldn't see through that vapid headcase, as she knew only too well.

It was as she was thinking these deep thoughts that she noticed Jack had stood up and wandered a short distance away. He was picking up sticks that had fallen to the ground, branches that, too heavily laden with snow, had fallen to the earth.

"What . . ." She started as he leaned down and hefted a particularly large branch. The back of his leather jacket came up over his butt, and she was awarded a denim-clad view of the famous Jack Townsend butt, the one women all over America gladly shelled out ten bucks to see on the big screen.

And here she was with that butt all to herself.

In the middle of Alaska.